Heartless Duke

League of Dukes Book Two

BY
SCARLETT SCOTT

Heartless Duke
League of Dukes Book Two

ISBN: 978-1-091063-21-1

Edited by Grace Bradley
Proofread by CM Wright
Cover Design by Wicked Smart Designs

For more information, contact author Scarlett Scott.
www.scarslettscottauthor.com

He's a heartless cad. A relentless rake. Dangerous to know. As cruel as can be.

He's the Duke of Carlisle, leader of a secret branch of the Home Office charged with keeping the peace amidst great peril and upheaval. By day, he hunts anarchists and murderers with savage intensity. By night, he rules over London's darkest, most depraved souls.

But he's about to meet his match in his latest prisoner.

She's a strong, independent woman. Fearless and determined. Unlike any lady he's ever known. As unfettered and plucky as can be.

She's Bridget O'Malley, a trusted member of the underground organization to gain Irish independence. By day, she is a respectable young woman of modest means, attempting to make her way in the world through honest employment. By night, she is embroiled in a world so treacherous and dangerous even she finds her own life at risk. To save herself, she will commit any sin.

When the heartless duke and the fiery rebel clash in a fierce battle of wills, unexpected passions flare to life. Threats lurk at every turn, and no one is as they seem.

Will they be each other's ruin?

Or is love enough to become their salvation?

Playlist:
open.spotify.com/playlist/0eKt6UyaSvLWsGQjCWaoNP

Dedication

Dedicated to the memory of J.S.
and to everyone who suffers from depression.
You are not alone.

Know, that I would accounted be
True brother of a company
That sang, to sweeten Ireland's wrong,
Ballad and story, rann and song;
Nor be I any less of them,
Because the red-rose-bordered hem

~ *"To Ireland in the Coming Times"*
William Butler Yeats

Chapter One

Oxfordshire, 1882

THE DUKE OF Carlisle landed at his half brother's estate in Oxfordshire with a small cadre of servants and one armed guard, dusty, travel-worn, and weary. It seemed wrong somehow to arrive at Clay's wedding after having spent the previous night surrounded by the most depraved and licentious acts imaginable.

Or at least those imaginable to Leo, and his mind was blessed with a boundless creativity for the wicked.

But here he was, prepared to do his duty.

Duty was everything to him, for it was all he bloody well had.

He was also late, the hour approaching midnight, but he had allowed himself to be distracted at a tavern blessedly in possession of a hearty store of spirits. It was possible that he was drunk as well, having consumed roughly enough ale and wine to float the Spanish Armada.

A poor decision, that. He ought to have arrived earlier like a gentleman.

He flung open his carriage door and leapt down without waiting for it to reach a complete stop. Fortunately, he was blessed with a cat's stealthy reflexes even when bosky, and he landed in the gravel on two booted feet with effortless grace.

Farleigh, one of the men standing guard over Harlton

Hall whilst his brother's wife-to-be continued to be in danger, approached him first. The political assassination of her husband had left her a target for a particularly ruthless ring of Fenians.

An unfortunate business indeed. One Leo was doing his utmost to rectify. The criminals would be brought to justice by his hand, one way or another. Death was just as swift a sentence as prison. He would choose death for the miscreants over imprisonment every time.

"Your Grace," Farleigh said, bowing. "You ought to take better care. You could have been injured."

Leo flicked a cold gaze over the man. "Yet, I was not. Is the entire household abed, sir?"

"There are some who have awaited your arrival. They will see to it that your belongings are taken to the proper chamber and you are settled."

Leo's lips thinned. Apathy, as vast as it had ever been, was a chasm inside his chest, threatening to consume him. Likely, he ought to find his chamber, order a bath, and scrub himself clean of the stink of London and the road.

But all he truly wanted was more liquor and some distraction, not necessarily—but preferably—in that order.

"Have there been any incidents since the relocation from London?" he asked sharply.

Even in his cups, he could not shake himself of the burden of his duties. He was the leader of the secretive branch of the Home Office known as the Special League. The safety and well-being of England's citizenry was in his hands. And the plague of the Fenian menace was evidenced everywhere these days: bombs exploding across England, vicious murders carried out, all in the name of Irish nationalism.

Some days, he needed to over imbibe.

He allowed such a weakness once per month, no more.

"There have been none, Your Grace," Farleigh confirmed. "The decision to leave town and come here with Her Grace was a wise one."

"Of course it was," Leo drawled. "I made it."

Aware of his rudeness and not giving a good goddamn, Leo stalked past Farleigh, his long legs taking him up the stairs leading to Harlton Hall. He did not bother himself with the details of his trunks or even which chamber had been assigned him. Instead, he went in search of his quarry.

Whisky. Brandy. Ale. *Holy hell*, even Madeira would do at the moment, and he disliked it intensely. He was in a foul mood, and he did not know why, other than that the Fenians continued to outmaneuver him.

No one outmaneuvered the Duke of Carlisle, by God.

He stalked through the entry and main hall, and was about to acknowledge defeat, when he strode into a darkened chamber and collided with something soft. Something feminine and deliciously scented.

Ah, lemon and bergamot oil.

Something—his hands discovered a well-curved waist—or rather *someone*.

"I beg your pardon," the lady said with a huff and the slightest lilt to her accent he could not place.

"You may, but perhaps I shall not grant it," he said, feeling like the devil tonight.

"Grant what, sir?"

"My pardon." He dipped his head lower, drawn to her warmth. Though he could see only faint outlines of her as his eyes adjusted to the dim light—a cloud of dark hair, a small, retroussé nose, a stubborn chin—he was nevertheless intrigued. "Have you done something requiring it?"

She made a sound of irritation. "Release me, if you please. I have neither the time nor the inclination to play games with a stranger who arrives in the midst of the night, smelling of spirits."

"Allow me to introduce myself." He stepped back, offering her an exaggerated bow. "The Duke of Carlisle, m'lady. And you are?"

She moved forward, into the soft light of the hall. With the gas lamps illuminating her fully at last, he felt as if he had received a fist to the gut. She was striking, from her almost midnight hair, to her arresting blue gaze, to the full pout of her pink lips. And she was proportioned just as he preferred: short of stature, yet shapely. Her bosom jutted forward in her plain dove-gray bodice.

Damn him if the woman wasn't giving him a cockstand here and now, at midnight in the midst of the hall with the hushed sound of servants seeing to his cases fluttering around them. They were not alone, yet they might have been the only two souls in the world.

Her eyes sparkled with intelligence, and he could not shake the feeling she was assessing him somehow. "I serve as governess to the young duke."

Governess.

That explained the godawful gray gown.

It did not, however, explain his inconvenient and thoroughly unwanted attraction to her. He did not dally with servants.

More's the pity.

Leo frowned. "What is the governess doing flitting about in the midst of the night, trading barbs with a stranger who smells of spirits?"

He could not resist goading her, it was true.

Her brows snapped together. "You waylaid me, Your Grace."

He would love to waylay her. All bloody night long.

But such mischief was decidedly not on the menu for this evening. Or ever. He had far too many matters weighing on his mind, and the last thing he needed to do was ruin a governess. He had come to celebrate his brother's nuptials, *damn it*, not to cast the last shred of his honor into the wind.

"Whilst you are being waylaid, perhaps you can direct me to the library," he said then. "I am in need of diversion. My mind does not do well with travel."

The truth was that his mind was not well in general, and it hadn't a thing to do with trains and coaches. But that was his private concern, yet another weakness he would admit to no one.

He expected the woman to inform him which chamber he sought and how he might arrive there. He did not expect her frown to deepen, or for her to turn on her heel and stride away down the hall in the opposite direction.

"Follow me, if you please," she called over her shoulder. "I shall take you there."

Leo followed, admiring the delectable sway of her hips as they went.

The governess intrigued him far too much, and he hoped to hell it wasn't going to become a problem. As it stood, he would only be at Harlton Hall for a few days' time. What could possibly go wrong?

A whole bloody lot, answered a voice inside him.

He ignored it. A faint hint of lemon taunted him. Nor could he wrest his gaze from her. She was exquisitely formed.

And a governess, he reminded himself.

When had he last been intrigued by a female?

It had been years. It had been Jane, to be precise. Her name still curdled his gut, even after all the summers and winters since she had married Ashelford, back when Leo had been a callow youth still foolish enough to believe a woman's heart could be steadfast. Good of her to rectify his ignorance. His allegiance belonged to the League now and forever, just as it always should have done. Crown and country. The safety of England.

Not the tempting swell of the governess's lower lip. So full and bewitching, that succulent pink flesh. He longed to sink his teeth into it. The spirits he had consumed were making him maudlin and randy in equal measures, he decided as they entered a long, narrow chamber with shelf-lined walls. A bloody terrible, dreadful coupling. He required more liquor at once, for nothing blunted the furious grip of lust like the obliteration to be found at the bottom of a bottle.

The gas lamps were low, bathing the room in a soft sensibility which did nothing to alleviate the inappropriate bent of his meandering thoughts. His brother had yet to fill the shelves. The books were scarce, though the carpet was new, and a banked fire crackled in the hearth.

She stopped on the periphery of the chamber, spinning toward him, hands laced together at her waist. He noted the bones of her knuckles, white through her skin. Her shoulders were stiff, neck rigid, and her entire body appeared immobile, almost as though she stood on a slippery slope and didn't wish to move lest she go tumbling down.

Leo was trained to observe. He trusted no one but his brother Clay and the woman he considered his true mother. Everyone else was suspect.

What could a pretty little governess like her have to hide? What did she fear?

He moved nearer to her, driven by suspicion. Driven by need. Driven by the darkness inside him. By desire. Today, he could not rein himself in. He stopped just short of her, crowding her with his considerable height. She scarcely reached his shoulder.

The deeper note of bergamot hit him. Her eyes widened. They were not pure blue. Flecks of gray adulterated them. Her brows were fine and dark, elegantly arched. A flush stole over her cheeks at his silent regard.

"Here we are, Your Grace," she said softly. Her voice was husky, like a plume of fine cigar smoke, unfurling to envelop him. "The library, just as you requested."

She remained so still and tense. A doe in the wood poised for flight.

Was he the hunter, his arrow nocked?

He was too intrigued to step away. Too intrigued even to search for more spirits. Surely Clay had whisky, and he would find it at his leisure. First, there was something about this blasted governess. Something he could not shake.

"Your name." He meant to ask her in the form of a question, but he was not terribly adept at polite conversation. He led his agents. He hosted depraved fêtes at his townhouse. He did not speak to governesses, pay social calls, or whirl about at balls. He was a machine. And like any machine, he was beginning to show wear.

"Palliser, Your Grace."

"Miss Palliser," he repeated, thinking the name familiar. He searched the dusty corners of his mind before lighting upon it. "Glencora, by any chance?"

It was meant to be a sally, a reference to the Anthony Trollope character—an irregularity for him, as he had not much cause for levity in his life—but the governess paled, her lips parting. "Jane Palliser, Your Grace."

Christ.

There was that hated name again. Surely, this was the Lord's idea of a cruel jest. A means of retribution for the vast catalog of sins Leo had committed in the name of serving his queen. Why else would a governess with the face of an angel and the body of a courtesan be placed before him on this day of weakness, bearing the same name as the woman who had nearly been his ruin?

His lip curled. "Jane." The name felt heavy on his tongue, acidic and bitter, the taste of disillusionment, and even though this was a different Jane before him, he could not separate the emotions from the moment. "You do not look like a Jane to me."

Her eyes widened almost imperceptibly. "And yet, that is what my mother chose to name me, Your Grace. I am so sorry to disappoint you."

He did not miss the undercurrent in her voice, a strange hint of something suggesting Miss Jane Palliser harbored secrets. Perhaps he would make it his mission to uncover them during his brief stay at Harlton Hall.

Leo raked his gaze over her in an assessing fashion, unable to resist the urge to discomfit her. "I doubt you could disappoint me, Miss Palliser."

THE DUKE OF Carlisle had come to Harlton Hall. It was almost not to be believed, far too fortuitous a circumstance to be ascribed to anything other than fate. And he was not just here, within her presence, within her reach, standing near enough to touch in the barren library, but he was *flirting*. With her, or at least with the woman he presumed her to be. Pretty London lass Jane Palliser. Nothing but a fiction.

The anxiety she had known upon his sudden proximity and odd queries—the dark, plumbing gaze of his that seemed to see far more than she wished, cutting straight to the heart of all her desperate prevarications—lifted. She was accustomed to men who thought they could have everything they wanted.

She had spent her life in their shadows.

She gritted her teeth and forced herself not to allow her hatred to show. He wanted her, and if there was one thing she had learned in her life, it was the power a woman wielded over a man. One twitch of her skirts, the revelation of an ankle, the flit of her tongue over her lips, and he would be in the palm of her hand.

Precisely where she wished him.

For she may have arrived at Harlton Hall as Miss Jane Palliser, but in truth, she was Bridget O'Malley, and she had come to fight a war.

Sármhaith. She favored him with a slow smile and lowered her gaze to his mouth, which was—she reluctantly admitted— sculpted with a perfection that defied reality. "I am certain I could prove a source of great disappointment for you, Your Grace."

One dark brow quirked. "Indeed, Miss Palliser? Do tell."

Oh, she could tell him. But that was not part of her plan. Baiting him, however, was. "My position here is new, sir, and I do not dare jeopardize it. If it is female companionship you desire, I suggest you return to the place that stinks of cigar smoke and stale ale."

His eyes were almost obsidian, his gaze probing, searing. For a moment, she fancied he could see all the bruises she hid beneath her skin, and then she shoved that nonsense into the ether where it belonged. If a trill of something unwanted went down her spine at his perusal, it was a mere natural reaction to him as a man and nothing more.

She could not deny he was handsome. Large and strong too, just as she preferred. His body radiated with an intensity she had never before seen in another man. But this man was her enemy. He was different from all the others.

This man, like the rest, she could not trust.

But this man, unlike those who had come before him and those who would come after, she was destined to defeat. She had no choice. Everything she did now was for Cullen's sake.

"And how do you know I came from a place stinking of cigar smoke and stale ale?" he asked at last into the heavy silence.

"Your jacket reeks of it," she said. "I must retire. If you will excuse me, Your Grace."

She knew this sort of man, had met him before: a powerful beast who had so much thrown at his feet, the chase intrigued him. He hungered for it. Indeed, the more brusque and dismissive she was with him, the more he emanated a raw, smoldering hunger.

Once, a man of his size and handsome virility would have shaken her. He was a duke who governed England's most elite clandestine forces with so much effortless grace, it had taken years for his identity to be uncovered. But she was not the girl she had once been, and she had only two things left to lose, neither of which she was willing to give him.

She turned on her heel without curtsying, the slight deliberate. A mock she could not resist, and it was for herself rather than for him this time.

"Miss Palliser."

Bridget almost failed to stop at the name, not recognizing it. She went a full three steps farther before halting, her skirts swishing in the suddenness of her pause. Certainly it was not the Duke of Carlisle who had caused her to forget her assumed identity. It was the newness of it, surely.

She turned about, catching her bottom lip between her teeth and studying him boldly before lowering her lashes. "Your Grace?"

Those molten eyes of his—*predator eyes, like a fox's,* she thought—dipped to her lips. And for some reason she could not comprehend, her mouth burned as if he had placed his own upon it. Awareness hummed between them. She felt it, an ache in her core, and she was not supposed to. She did not want to. She wanted to be numb as she always was. As she forced herself to be. As she had to be.

"You are awake when the rest of the house is abed. Why?" His tone was innocent enough, but the undertone, one of interrogation, chilled her.

"I do not sleep well when I am establishing myself in a new circumstance," she lied with ease. In truth, she did not sleep well at all. For with sleep came darkness, and with darkness came remembrance.

"Nor do I," he surprised her by admitting.

The Duke of Carlisle had a weakness?

She had been told he was formidable. Untouchable. As cold as ice. Heartless in his pursuit of his enemies.

How intriguing.

She studied him. "Forgive me if I find it impossible to believe that a duke should ever have difficulty finding his rest."

"You are a bold one for a governess, Miss Palliser." He moved toward her with slow, purposeful strides.

With him came his heat, the reminder of how large and menacing he was. How beautiful. It seemed a sin that the Lord should have bestowed the looks of an angel upon a man with the devil's own heart.

"I am bold when I need to be, Your Grace," she said pointedly.

Perhaps with a bit more condemnation than she should have, for he stopped.

"I have no wish to affect your position here, Miss Palliser. I merely desire likeminded company."

"I would not imagine we could ever be likeminded about

anything," she argued, in spite of herself once more. "Similarly plagued, perhaps. Moreover, my remaining here with you is highly improper, and we both know it. I must go."

He continued forward until he was near enough to touch. "Must you?"

She swallowed. It was true he wore the scent of a tavern on his coat, but it was also true beneath that, there was a deeper hint of musk and wilderness, as if it had been plucked from the deepest depth of the most verdant woodland and placed lovingly upon his skin.

Lord have mercy on her soul. What ailed her?

She was not...*attracted* to this man. To this duke, who had by definition, been given the best of everything. Who had all the power. Who had never been taught to listen to the lowly. To hear their cries and their wants and their needs. Who thought it was his right to rule an entire nation of people simply by the nature of his birth.

Nay. Nay. Nay.

She was not.

Bridget compressed her lips as she studied him. His expression was inscrutable. He smelled of spirits, but he did not act as if he were inebriated. His speech was not slurred, his eyes were not glazed. Nor did he sway on his feet. His words made sense. But while her observations suggested otherwise, her instincts told her the Duke of Carlisle was vulnerable to her. He was in his cups, and he was attracted to her. She could take advantage of that, of him. Now, in this moment.

If she waited until tomorrow...

If she waited until the next day...

It may well be too late. Here was an undeniable opportunity. He could have brought sensitive documents along with him. He could reveal information to her with the proper incentive. She had found him unawares, the illustrious Duke of Carlisle, who scarcely emerged from his London lair. Pried from his familiar surroundings, plied with drink, he could be malleable. All she needed to do was give him the proper lure.

She could allow some kisses. Perhaps even more. She had suffered unwanted attentions before, and she would do so again.

Of course, if the Duke of Carlisle kissed her, it would not precisely be suffering, and she knew it.

Curse his miserable hide and equally miserable face.

John had told her so much about the duke. He had fed her every detail of pertinence. But he had not warned her against the magnetism the man exuded.

"You have not answered me," the duke reminded her softly, and he was even nearer now, even more of a threat. More of a temptation. "Must you go? I have any number of distractions for you here if you but say the words."

"Of course I must." She pretended to hesitate, running her tongue over her upper lip once, twice. The stab of guilt she ordinarily experienced whenever she thought of Cullen eluded her now. In its place was something else. Something worse. A deeper, darker want. Some base part of her was *enjoying* this. "I must bid you good evening, Your Grace."

His eyes were on her mouth again. "No one need know."

She imagined if the devil were to appear before her, tempting her to sin, his voice would sound the same as the Duke of Carlisle's: low and smooth and laden with wicked promise. "I run the risk of losing my position."

"You ran the risk of losing your position the moment you entered this library with me, and yet, here you stand."

One more step, and he was now close enough to tip up her chin with one long finger. Just a slight touch, scarcely any pressure behind it. But the contact of his bare skin on hers was a maddening jolt to her senses. Her body did not understand this man was her enemy.

"As I said before, you waylaid me." She remained still with great effort. Part of her wanted nothing more than to move closer to him, and part of her wanted nothing more than to flee.

"Have you always been a governess, Miss Palliser?" he startled her by asking, allowing the pad of his thumb to settle upon her chin as if it was where it belonged. "Was it your choice for yourself, to live a prim spinster's life and tend to the children of others?"

"Most born into this life do not have the liberty of choice, Your Grace." But she would not expect someone like him to understand.

And here, again, he had shaken her from her path. Distracted her from the role she was meant to play. She was not meant to clash with him, but to protest. To allow him to persuade. Make him think her a conquest. Encourage his lust.

"It may surprise you to discover how little choice any of us has." He sounded grim, as if he carried a great burden. "Myself included."

More vulnerability. She could press it like a broken rib, cause him pain. Parting her lips, she allowed her eyes to search his before lowering to settle upon his mouth. "What choices were you robbed of, Your Grace? I find it difficult indeed to believe a man as powerful and wealthy as a duke would not have his complete liberty."

"As I said," he began then paused, withdrawing his hand, "the truth may surprise you."

What choice had been taken from him? She wanted to know, and it disturbed her greatly to realize that want derived from herself, from Bridget, and not from the machine of war she had been forced to become.

She searched his gaze. Within it, she found a haunting

sadness. Something inside her shifted, and for a moment, she knew a surge of empathy before she ruthlessly battled it down. "What is it you want from me, Your Grace? The more I linger here, the greater the danger of my discovery. I cannot think the duchess would approve of my presence here in the library, so late at night, alone with you, or any other gentleman for that matter."

Her employer the Duchess of Burghly cared deeply for her son, that much was apparent. She had rigorously interviewed Bridget upon her arrival, and in her prim widow's weeds, she seemed the sort who would not countenance her son's governess dallying with a gentleman, be he a duke or even a king.

"Stay with me."

Three words. Separately, they held no significance. Strung together, spoken by the Duke of Carlisle, they held untold meaning. The tone of urgency in his voice—as if her presence was not just something he desired, but a necessity—meant even more.

"It would be folly," she argued softly, stepping closer to him in such proximity, her skirts swayed against his trousers. *Play the game, Bridget. Do your duty.*

"Please." His jaw tightened after he conveyed the lone, raw plea.

He seemed a man who did not often need to ask for what he wanted. She longed to discomfit him, to sneak beyond his defenses. To probe and nudge him, to make him reveal himself to her. "Why?"

"Because there is sadness in your eyes, Miss Palliser, and I know it well," he said, surprising her again. "Because I am lonely. Because you are beautiful. Because I want very much to kiss you."

She hated this man, hated everything he stood for. And

yet, he moved her. Some part of her she had thought long banished returned. For a beat, she forgot who she was. Forgot who he was. Forgot this was war, the battle formations clear. Forgot the hatred burning inside her, the need to save Cullen and herself.

And in that brief, terrifying, ruinous moment, she became merely Bridget, whose heart thumped madly, who was staring up into the face of the most handsome man she had ever seen. A man who had just declared he wanted to kiss her. A man she could not deny she wanted to kiss in return.

Rising on her toes, she cupped the Duke of Carlisle's jaw and pressed her lips to his. If his touch on her chin had been a spark, this—his mouth on hers—was an inferno. He made a low sound of need as his hands found her waist. In an instant, he took control, his mouth opening over hers, his tongue swiping over the seam of her lips, demanding entrance. And she gave it to him. With a soft mewl of surrender, she opened.

His tongue was a warm and welcome invasion, and she ran her own against his experimentally. When his grip on her waist tightened and he drew her closer, she knew she had pleased him. She had been kissed before, but never with such hungry precision. Never with such wildness, as if she were the air he breathed, as if he needed her. She kissed him back, desperate and greedy, lips moving, tongue sliding, teeth scraping his lips. She wanted to bite him. To make him bleed. To consume him. To take part of him and never let it go.

But her mind intruded before she could lose herself completely.

Cullen.

Guilt skewered her.

What was she doing? What had she been thinking?

She was not meant to be attracted to this man. Not meant to enjoy his kisses. Her duty lay elsewhere.

She thought of her homeland then, and she released him, pushing at his shoulders. Putting some distance between them.

Frozen, she stared at him. At the Duke of Carlisle, the man who would happily see her swing from the gallows if he knew who she truly was. The voice inside her head returned, louder, more menacing. But this time it was John's voice.

Know you are a soldier, Bridget. Cullen's life depends upon you. Our independence depends upon you.

She clamped her hand over her mouth, tingling and swollen from the duke's kisses. She had betrayed herself. Had betrayed everyone depending upon her. "Forgive me," she muttered from behind her hand, hating herself.

Bridget O'Malley did not forget who she was and what she fought for. She did not enjoy kissing English dukes. Bridget O'Malley was heartless. Emotionless. She was impenetrable. Untouchable.

Or at least she had been, until the man before her had touched his lips to hers.

She spun away from him, needing space and distance. Needing time. Separation. She could not do what she needed to, not tonight. Not with him. Not after this.

"Miss Palliser!" he called.

Ignoring him, she fled as fast as her feet would carry her.

Chapter Two

$\mathcal{B}$RIDGET WOKE AT dawn as she always had. After so many years, the habit was ingrained in her, even when unnecessary. This morning, unlike so many others, she woke with the aching sting of regret. She had failed herself. She had been presented with a drunken, defenseless Duke of Carlisle, and she had not pressed her advantage. She had not slipped laudanum into his whisky. Had not accompanied him to his chamber to search his possessions whilst he passed out on the bed. The plan her quick mind had formed had deserted her.

Instead, she had fled like a coward.

She rose and lit a lamp, beginning her morning ablutions. The face staring at her in the glass was pale, hair a tangled mass of ebony. Her expression was drawn, tight, laced with worry. She had not just failed herself. She had failed Cullen.

Bridget knew she had made a grave error. She had allowed her base urges to overrule her head. Carlisle's kiss had affected her. It had not been anything like other kisses she had suffered. It had not been hard or punishing. Not even unwanted, though she was loath to admit it to herself.

She took a deep breath and forced herself to recall who she was. Forgetting was easier than remembering. All she needed to do was look around her, at the opulence wasted upon a world she was not meant to inhabit.

The chamber she had been given, adjoining the nursery

and the young duke, was larger than she was accustomed to, bearing three eastward-facing windows. It was lovely, so lovely, she could stand in the center of it and banish from her mind the bitter knowledge of why she was here and what she must do.

But like dawn, reality always returned.

With a grim air, she dressed in her simple dove-gray gown and fastened her hair into a tidy governess's bun. Her charge would not be awake for another two hours, which meant she would have some precious time to herself—so dear—before her duties of the day began.

A restorative walk was in order, she decided, donning her ankle boots. The early morning at this time of year tended to be cool, so she fetched a wrap before leaving her chamber, then hastily made her way down the corridor to the main floor. Something—foolishness, or perchance wild fancy— made her walk past the library door.

And that was when she heard it.

Gentle, rhythmic snores.

She paused in her traverse of the hall, listening. The sound was unmistakable. Undeniable. Someone was sleeping in the library. It could have been an overworked parlor maid, but the timbre suggested otherwise. Her instincts suggested otherwise.

Gooseflesh rose on her arms.

It was him.

The Duke of Carlisle.

Here, perhaps, was her second chance at gaining information from him. John would be more than happy for any gem of knowledge she could beg, borrow, or steal. She lingered outside the library, hand on the latch, wondering if she ought to enter or if she should wait.

Wait, said something inside her.

And then another voice, equally forceful said, *Press your advantage. Now.*

She opened the door and crossed over the threshold. The slow, steady sounds of a man breathing in his sleep reached her as the door closed. Her eyes adjusted to the darkness of the room, settling upon the opposite wall where a large, leonine body was draped across an oversize settee. Yet even though the piece of furniture was immense, he still managed to dominate it, his long legs protruding from the end.

It occurred to Bridget here was a glaring, unprecedented opportunity: she could seek out his chamber, search it for any insights she could pass on to John in an effort to help the cause. But instead, something else made her feet move. Across the library she traveled, boots thumping steadily against the carpet. Until she stood before him.

The ghost of a fire in the grate crackled, and the sun sent a trickle of light glinting from the eastern windows as it began to rise. He was a study in contrast: dark, yet golden; fearsome, yet beautiful.

There he was, at her mercy, stretched out like Christ on the cross, just as vulnerable to her attack. Even his arms were splayed, almost as if in a parody. She could do him harm. Pull the knife from her boot. Find his vein and cut.

Bridget swallowed, looking down at him. Even in the semi-darkness, he was beautiful. Compelling. A formidable foe. One she could end so easily. Now. Within seconds.

Yet…she could not. Removing this man as an obstacle would be a boon to the cause. She would be hailed a hero. But while Bridget wore many mantles, murderess was not among them.

Even so, how convenient of Carlisle to drink himself into a stupor and spend the evening drunk as a lord in the library. John had told her League members often secreted correspondence in hidden pockets in their waistcoats. Her quick eyes spotted a bottle of spirits on the table alongside him, half-empty. A fortuitous happenstance.

Poor Duke. He would not know what hit him. Bridget truly ought to thank him for making this so easy.

She took up the bottle and doused him with the contents, taking great care to keep the seams of his waistcoat, where it was easiest to insert documents, dry. The duke continued snoring, sleeping right through her endeavor. She laid the bottle on him gently, tipping it to its side as if he had fallen asleep while drowning himself in drink, causing the spill. With quick, quiet movements, she took a handful of steps in retreat.

And then she started forward.

"Your Grace," she called, hoping to rouse him with the volume of her voice.

It would look far more natural, more innocent to him, if he woke with her starting toward him rather than hovering over his supine form. She had but one chance to get her hands on his waistcoat, and she was determined not to squander it.

The strident call of her voice had its intended effect. With a broken snore, he suddenly moved, sitting up on the settee, eyes blinking open. For a heartbeat, he appeared defenseless and innocent. He seemed nothing more than a handsome duke who had likely earned himself a stiff neck and a handful of regrets by over-imbibing and falling asleep in the library, rather than one of the most feared spies in all England.

A man who would have no qualms about sending her to prison, she reminded herself with force, lest her unacceptable weakness for him attempted to sway her from her course. She rushed forward with that thought, feigning concern.

"Good morning, Your Grace. Pray forgive me. I did not mean to intrude, but I prefer to take my walks at dawn, and I heard someone within. I knocked, but there was no answer." Bridget pinned a false smile to her lips.

"Good morning, Miss Palliser," he growled, his expression turning thunderous. "Why, in the name of all that is holy, am I wet?"

She stopped herself just short of reaching him, relaxing her face with studious effort in an attempt to feign ignorance. "Wet, Your Grace?"

He tested his waistcoat with two fingers, grimacing. "*Bloody sodding.*"

She would have flinched at the bite in his tone, but Bridget was accustomed to mercurial men. She was prepared for anything. For anyone. She could meet the Duke of Carlisle in a match of wits any day and turn out the victor.

"You appear to have spilled upon yourself," she observed calmly, and without a trace of guilt underscoring her words. She plucked the tipped bottle from his person and held it aloft for his inspection. "This, I daresay, was the culprit."

"Christ," he muttered, sitting up and grimacing down at himself.

"How may I be of service, Your Grace?" she asked, not wishing to appear too eager to make off with his waistcoat.

"You may go away, Miss *Jane* Palliser," he said, his tone blistering.

She did not understand the emphasis he placed upon Jane, but it was noteworthy in its oddness. Bridget tucked the observation away inside her mind and proceeded with her plan. "Allow me to take your waistcoat, sir. It appears to have absorbed most of the damage. I will see it laundered and returned to you."

His brows snapped together. "You are not my valet, madam. I shall attend to the matter myself." He paused, seeming to belatedly recall the necessity for niceties. "And thank you."

"Please, sir," she persisted, making her voice small. "It would be my honor."

Carlisle's dark gaze, as sharp as a knife, homed in upon her. "How very agreeable for a lady who could not wait to be free of my presence yesterday. Tell me, Miss Palliser, what is the difference between last night and this morning?"

Responsibility. Duty. Her mind overruling her...*everything.*

She swallowed. "I am sorry, Your Grace. This position is new to me, and I cannot afford to lose it."

Something in him softened then. She could see it as well as sense it. Could it be a man who would so vociferously fight against her native land to keep it from having its own rule, possessed an inner sense of fairness?

It seemed improbable indeed.

"Forgive me, Miss Palliser." His fingers were at work on the buttons of his waistcoat, flicking them from their moorings.

She could not wrest her gaze from his long, patrician fingers nor his broad, strong shoulders shrugging. To her amazement, he divested himself of the garment and held it out to her, an olive branch of sorts.

Bridget took it, her fingers brushing his. A fresh spark of awareness jolted through her, singeing down her spine and landing between her thighs in a blossom of heat she could not deny no matter how much she tried.

If only they had not touched. If only she had never kissed him.

For all she could think now, in this moment, was the delirious luxury of his lips upon hers. That mouth—all sin, all seduction—had worked over hers with skillful precision.

"I shall see to it that your waistcoat is properly cleaned," she forced herself to say.

"I don't give a bloody damn if it is."

She stared at him, struggling to understand. "Your Grace?"

"I can purchase another hundred to take its place. The loss of one is no loss at all. But since you are so determined, take the waistcoat, Miss Palliser, and go," he ordered coolly.

And once again, everything in her attempted to overrule all the rest. She wanted to tell him what he could do with the scrap of soiled fabric in her grip. She wanted to rail against him. To remind him her nation deserved to be represented by its own people rather than drowned out by English MPs, by people who lived within its beautiful shores, who knew the struggles and the land.

Clutching his waistcoat firmly in her grasp, she curtseyed and did as he bid. Her heart hammered at the idea of uncovering his hidden correspondence. But as she turned her back on him and left the library, the scent of him, stronger and more delicious than any spirit, dogged her.

Gripping his drenched waistcoat, she hastened back to her own chamber. Her walk could wait. The promise of information proved too potent a lure. She had at least an hour before her charge, the young duke, would arise. Moreover, far too much depended upon the information she could glean. She would not disappoint those relying upon her.

John awaited her. Cullen had no one, save her.

Cullen's life, more than hers, was her motivating force. For he alone was her responsibility. He alone was where her allegiance lay, more than herself, more than Ireland, more than Home Rule.

She had been born without a choice. After all, she was but a woman in the world. A woman in a society fashioned to drown out all females, to overrule and silence them.

A woman who had never had a chance.

Bridget sat by the light of the windows, turned up an oil lamp, and examined the Duke of Carlisle's whisky-soaked waistcoat. It was of excellent construction, crafted from expensive fabric. At first glance, it looked like any other garment a wealthy gentleman would wear. But upon closer inspection, she spotted evidence of stitches that were less refined, made in a slightly different shade of black—darker, more pure.

She took up the blade she always kept sheathed in her boot and carefully attacked the seam in question. With tender precision, she sliced the stitches holding the lining of the waistcoat in place, taking care not to damage the fine fabric itself. She inserted her finger, wiggling it about until she found what she was looking for.

A folded scrap of paper.

She withdrew and cut again, creating an opening large enough for the paper to emerge. Bridget extracted it, heart fluttering wildly. Here perhaps was something of value, something she could offer John to ensure Cullen's liberation in addition to the task originally assigned her.

She unfolded the paper to find a neat, masculine scrawl blurred by the whisky it had absorbed, rendering it almost illegible. What she could discern appeared to be a series of letters and numbers.

A cipher key, she realized. Perhaps a means for him to recognize correspondence he received. She consulted the mantle clock in her chamber—half an hour until she was on duty for the day. Plenty of time to copy everything legible to a fresh sheet of paper. The more she could bring back to John, the greater the chance of Cullen obtaining his freedom.

And that, she reminded herself, was all she could afford to care about.

Even as her lips still burned with the Duke of Carlisle's kiss.

"My darling boy."

Leo had yet to make good on his escape from the library—and his ignominious stay there on the settee—when he was importuned by yet another female. He was dressed in only his shirtsleeves of the night before, he hadn't shaved, his head thumped, and his neck and back ached. Moreover, he was certain he looked as bedraggled as a man who had been drawn on his back behind a runaway carriage.

But that did not stop the next woman who intruded upon his solitude. Nor did it hamper the beaming smile on her face. Lily Ludlow was the woman his father had loved, his longtime mistress, and more of a mother to Leo than his own mother could ever hope to be. She was the one female he trusted implicitly in this life, and the only one he would happily sacrifice his for.

"Mother," he greeted her, aware the word still sounded stiff on his tongue. She was the mother of his heart, but some part of him was still the young lad he had once been, who had only known rejection and his own mother's icy resentment.

"Son." Her smile was as warm as the bright golden-yellow of her dress as she opened her arms to him. "Why has it been so long since I have last seen your handsome face?"

Guilt snaked through him, landing heavy as an anchor in his gut. Though he had written, he had not visited her as he had promised he would do. There had never been time. His days and nights were spent stalking his prey and determining the means of not only defusing their bombs, but seeing them all in gaol where they belonged.

And now he stood before her bleary-eyed, mouth tasting as if he had been drinking donkey piss the night before. He may as well have been.

What the hell had he been thinking?

A woman, that's what.

A beautiful, raven-haired governess whose lips tasted like bergamot—surely from her tea, unless all goddesses tasted like citrus. Who kissed like a courtesan. Who he had wanted so badly, he'd sported a cockstand until he had been too inebriated to recall he even possessed a cock.

Fuck.

It would seem Fate's fickle wheel had decreed he must be plagued by Janes.

But he could say none of that aloud, so he smiled at Lily, embraced her, and bussed her cheeks. "I have been otherwise occupied, and for that I am wholeheartedly sorry."

She took several, exaggerated sniffs. "Darling, why do you smell as if you have fallen into a river of whisky?"

Why indeed?

He was reasonably confident he had fallen asleep only after placing the bottle of Clay's excellent liquor atop the table. He had never previously awoke drenched in spirits. How fortunate for him that pretty, vexing Jane Palliser had been present to witness his shame.

Unless…?

Suspicion stirred within him. There was something different about the governess, and it was not just the melancholy in her eyes. She had seemed awkward this morning, and though he may be wrong, he suspected the change in her air was not because of the kisses they had shared the night before but for another reason entirely.

One he would necessarily investigate as soon as possible. Jane Palliser was an enigma. A beautiful, lush-lipped mystery. Perhaps it was that she was looking after his nephew. Perhaps it was something more. Whisky-bit as he was, he couldn't say.

"I have no notion why," he answered his mother's query

with utter honesty.

"No notion at all, Leopold?" Lily's voice, taut with concern, splintered through his thoughts. He scarcely recognized the name "Leopold" as referring to himself.

"None," he agreed, knowing he was playing the role of cad and not having anything to say for himself. She had already caught him at far too many games. "Please do say whatever it is you wish, Mother. You know I cannot abide by your looks of quiet censure."

She pursed her lips. "I am sure I have no such looks. You were drinking, Leo."

He tensed. "Yes."

"Oh, my darling. You are not over-imbibing again, are you?" She frowned.

Of course he had been. He closed his eyes for a moment, wincing. But that did not mean he was once again drowning himself in drink. There had been a dark time in his life where he had turned to spirits and opium to sate the restless devils in his soul. But altering his mind did not kill the devils—it only drowned them out temporarily. And he was of no use to anyone when he was lost inside himself or lying abed, coming down from a cloud of indulgence.

"Only last night," he admitted with great reluctance. Here again was one of Lily Ludlow's unique talents: she could make him confess almost all, lay him low, with one soft look or one sweetly crooned *my darling son*. He bit his lip before he mentioned last night had been the first he had slept in three days. Spirits were not a cure, but they were nevertheless a balm for the darkness burning inside him. An escape, albeit a fleeting one.

"Are you certain?" Her worried gaze searched his.

Brilliant. Just bloody brilliant.

"Certain, Mother. It was a long and trying day."

Her gaze narrowed. "Leopold! Did you *sleep* in the library last night?"

He grimaced. "Yes, but as I said, it was a long and trying day."

"Is this about Clay's impending nuptials?" she asked softly.

"No."

Yes.

Partially, anyway. It was about living his life beneath the thumb of the League and all his infinite duties. About realizing his brother was about to find happiness, and he would never find his own because he no longer had the capacity to feel.

"It is about Jane, is it not?"

He frowned, thinking of the perfect pink lips he had kissed, the compelling sadness in her eyes, the way her voluptuous frame had felt against him. "The governess? Of course not. Why should she concern me?"

Lily raised a brow. "I was referring to Lady Jane Reeves, now the Duchess of Ashelford."

Damn it.

"Yes, of course." He cleared his throat, aware his cheek-bones were scalding hot and likely red. *Devil take it*, he never flushed. Never showed a weakness. Except before Lily Ludlow, it would seem. "I cannot deny weddings grieve me."

As did Jane.

Jane. Beautiful, golden-haired Lady Jane Reeves, who had stolen his heart and then mashed it to bits with her defection. She had been promised to him, and yet she had thrown him over for another. When last he had seen her, she had been happy, belly swollen with Ashelford's get. Little wonder why he no longer participated in societal whims. He had no time, nor did he care for reminders of the crushing sting of betrayal.

He preferred not to think of her, but Lily's mentioning of Jane sent a crashing wave of memory over him. The sort that could only be stymied with more drink. He closed his eyes for a moment, willing himself to find the strength to abstain. He was pleased for his brother. No one deserved happiness more. No one deserved love more.

As long as the Duchess of Burghly was worthy of him.

"Your brother is marrying the woman he loves at long last," Lily said. "I know it will be difficult for you, but nothing will please him more than having you at his side."

"She makes him happy?" he asked his mother, for the question had eaten at him for his entire trip to the countryside. He knew what it was like to believe himself in love with a woman. To believe that love was returned. And then, to have it all torn away from him as if it had never been.

"Yes. She loves him, and he loves her." Lily's expression softened, a smile curving her lips. "I want more babes, Leo, and they shall give me those. You must as well, with the right woman. At the right time."

Those two things did not exist, but he didn't bother informing her of that. He had learned his lesson, and he had learned it well. Dallying was well and good. Slaking his needs. His heart had died a long time ago, and nothing remained but a blackened husk where it had once beat.

He inclined his head. "I am happy for the two of them. The duchess seems to be a good woman."

"The best," Lily agreed. "And now I must have both my sons so happily situated. I shall go into my dotage the happiest grandmother in all the world."

He frowned. "I *am* happily situated, Mother."

He had the League. He had his duties. He had two dozen men beneath him, all awaiting his orders. He had lives to protect, loyalties and oaths to uphold. That was what made him content, what made him feel at home.

Sadness lurked in her eyes, her expression sobering. "And is that why you spent last evening sleeping in the library and why you stink of spirits?"

Ah, hell.

The answer to that question was simply, hopelessly complicated: yes and no. More no than yes. Or perhaps it was more yes than no?

Damn him for drinking so bloody much swill at the tavern and then upon his arrival. His head felt as it were stuffed with jeweler's cotton.

He decided a change of subject was in order. "I have come bearing good news for Clay. The Crown is bestowing a viscountcy upon him in recognition of his service. He will become Lord Stanwyck."

"Oh, Leo!" Lily wrapped him in another impulsive hug. "I know how hard you fought for him. Thank you. You are a good brother."

The back of his neck itched, but he returned her embrace just the same. Emotions were a devilishly tricky thing for him. He did not like the unfettered showing of them. "Clay earned the right with his dedication and selfless devotion."

Lily was aware of their covert work, though not the precise nature of it, nor the details. "Of course he did, but pray, do not act as if you had no hand in this, for we both know you did."

Yes, he had, but that did not mean he wanted his praises sung. Praises, hugs, and treacly sentiments made his gut ache. "Nonsense." He extracted himself from her arms. "It was Clay and nothing more. Where is my brother this morning? I ought to impart the news."

"Still abed." Lily's dark eyes shone with tears. "I love you, my darling son."

Christ.

Crying appalled him.

He fidgeted, needing to escape. "Well. I ought to restore myself to a civilized state before greeting the groom and bride." He bowed. "Mother."

With that, he took his throbbing head and his body that smelled as if he had spent the evening on the floor of a dockside tavern, and all his regrets, and fled.

Chapter Three

THE DAY OF the wedding had come, and Bridget was a bundle of knots and worry, for she knew what it meant. She would have to steal away her charge, the young duke, as she had been ordered to do. The commotion of the celebrations, combined with the new addition of guests, and the couple's wedding night would facilitate her actions.

She sat at the wedding breakfast, surrounded by merriment, guilt rendering her stomach an acidic churn of bile. The bride, the Duchess of Burghly, was radiant. The groom, Mr. Ludlow, looked upon her with such naked love, Bridget could not help but feel as if she were intruding whenever she glanced in their direction. Their love was obvious, and it glowed like a lighthouse beacon from the shores at night, guiding ships safely into harbor.

Envy mixed with her shame.

What would it be like to be loved with such undisguised devotion? And how could she bear to torment these two people who had only shown her kindness and compassion by taking the young duke from them? Moreover, how could she bear to lead the lad she'd grown rather fond of to an uncertain fate with John?

You must do it, she told herself. *For Cullen's sake. John vowed he would not harm the boy.*

But did she dare trust John? Did she dare do as she had

promised she would before leaving London on this devil's mission?

She gripped her wine goblet, raised it to her lips, drank. The sweet yet bitter liquid slid over her tongue like an elixir. Perhaps it would numb her. Relieve some of the tension threatening to choke her alive. Two more hasty gulps were all she would allow herself before she decided any more would draw curious stares. Strange enough that a governess would be present at the wedding breakfast alongside her charge. But that she was surrounded by dukes and certain enemies, alone in a chamber filled with people she was deceiving—people she would hurt—only served to heighten her tension.

"Perhaps you need not look so grim-faced, brother." The Duke of Carlisle raised his glass in a salute then, stealing her attention. "I received word not long ago of arrests having been made in Dublin."

Arrests. Dublin.

Those two words, along with Carlisle's relaxed, almost self-congratulatory manner, could mean only one thing: some of the men responsible for the Duke of Burghly's murder had been captured. They had been men like John. Like Cullen.

Dead men did not talk, but imprisoned men did, which meant everyone in the organization was vulnerable to implication.

Including Bridget.

She went numb, but not numb in the manner she had hoped. Her fingers ceased to function, and instead of placing her goblet calmly upon the table linen, she dropped it. With a dull thud, the goblet upended, and a dark stain spread all over the white cloth. She watched it grow, thinking it oddly reminiscent of a pool of blood from a body.

Was this how it had looked when the Duke of Burghly was slashed to death with surgical knives in Phoenix Park in

Dublin?

When would the bloodshed end?

And why, *oh why*, had she become complicit in this madness?

The cause was right. The actions being taken were wrong. Too extreme. Too dangerous and deadly.

What if the dropped glass, the spilled wine, were an omen meant for her? A sign she too would be claimed as a victim in this war they waged against the English menace?

All sets of eyes were upon her, curious, concerned, startled. The Duke of Carlisle's were dark and narrowed. Calculating. She looked away, lest he read something in the depths of her eyes, and reached for her napkin. The man was dangerous. Her enemy in every way. She could not allow him to see her, the real her. According to John, observing people and judging their weaknesses was one of the duke's gifts. One she could not afford for him to use against her.

"I do beg your pardon," she muttered softly to the table at large, attempting to dab at the offending spill. "I am not ordinarily so clumsy."

"You must not concern yourself with such trifles, Miss Palliser," offered the Duchess of Burghly sweetly. "Today is a day of joy, and not even a thousand spilled glasses could spoil it."

Bridget swallowed, wishing herself anywhere else. Wishing they had not insisted upon her presence here, where she did not belong, amongst all the people she would shortly betray. She knew she was not meant to think of them as people. That they were in fact her enemies. Obstacles standing between Cullen and his life, between herself and her freedom, between Ireland and the right to be governed by her own people.

But yet, despite all that, Bridget felt her cheeks go hot with shame. She did not deserve this woman's compassion.

Not when she would soon abscond with her son.

She would have responded, but her tongue refused to move, singularly frozen by guilt, shame, and self-loathing. Bridget felt the Duke of Carlisle's gaze like a touch before she even scanned the assemblage to find him watching her.

"All the men responsible for the outrage against the Duke of Burghly have now been captured," Carlisle said, his gaze remaining pinned to her. "Just yesterday. A treasure trove of information has been discovered along with them, and my Dublin sources assure me that more arrests will inevitably follow." He paused, shifting his attention to Mr. Ludlow. "This nightmare is at its end. I was saving the good news for after the nuptials."

Bridget felt the air expel from her lungs as if she had been issued a blow. Around her, the other wedding guests gave their reactions. There were sounds of joy, disbelief. Relief. Her gaze traveled to the bride, who was ethereal in her gown, her vivid red hair swept into a simple Grecian braid and knot.

The Duchess of Burghly raised a hand to her mouth, stifling a sob as she turned to her husband, her heart in her eyes, hope evident in her expression. "Oh, Clay, does this mean we are free at last?"

"It is my greatest hope," said her husband, tugging her to him, and pressing a reverent kiss to her forehead, before the entire assemblage.

Nausea churned inside Bridget. Partially because she feared the release of the treasure trove of information the Duke of Carlisle promised, along with the additional arrests. She had friends and acquaintances caught up within this web. Too many to count. But also because she was witness to the sheer joy and relief of the duchess and her husband, on their wedding day, of all days, while she knew herself to be the evil in their midst. She knew she would—must—rob them of their happiness. Time was running out for her. If arrests had been made, her identity could already have been revealed.

She would have to act now, or never.

"This is wonderful news indeed," said Mr. Ludlow's mother. She was one of the kindest ladies Bridget had ever met, possessing a boundless heart and an infinite desire to get to know those around her. She had already coaxed Bridget into revealing more about herself than she would have comfortably dared. It was a gift the woman had. "I could not be more pleased. I only wish your father could be here now. How proud he would be of his two sons. How happy he would be to welcome Ara and Edward into our family."

"My mama says that everyone in heaven is still with you in your heart," the young duke offered solemnly, his earnest words tugging at Bridget's heart in a way she wished they did not. "They will always be there, and no one can remove them or their love."

Bridget bit her lip at the boy's speech. Such a young child, without a father. How she hated that it had all been because of the cause she believed in, the cause she fought for even now. She felt too much for this young man. For his family. These were not faceless, unfamiliar enemies, but people she had come to know. People she respected. Cared for even.

"How right your mama is," Mr. Ludlow said with a gentleness that belied his large, hulking form and the vicious scar cutting down his cheek. "No matter how great the distance, or how long the time apart, the ones you love will always be there in your heart."

"I love you so," the duchess whispered to her new husband, but it was loud enough for everyone to hear.

Even so, the entire table was smiling. It was a time of celebration. Of great relief. Of love and looking to the future. Bridget hated herself for what she would soon do. For being the one who would destroy this moment of perfect, absolute peace.

"That is certainly true," added another one of the wedding guests, offering her husband a look that shone with unabashed adoration "Would you not say so, my husband?"

The look her husband gave her in return was every bit as lovestruck. "I would most certainly concur."

"Forgive me," drawled the Duke of Carlisle then, with the icy hauteur only he could affect. "Excessive sentiment makes me bilious. Let us carry on with the breakfast before I lose my appetite, shall we?"

"You do not appear to have lost your appetite, Your Grace," Bridget's charge observed out of turn.

Bridget had been watching Carlisle surreptitiously over the course of the breakfast, and she could not deny the lad's truthfulness. The Duke of Carlisle had, unquestionably, cleared his plate of this course and all those that had come before it.

But she supposed it would require an immense appetite to satisfy a frame as large and as strong as the duke's. He towered over everyone, save Mr. Ludlow, his height and his strength both formidable. Everything about him suggested he was dangerous.

"You may call me Uncle Leo, scamp," Carlisle admonished Bridget's charge without a trace of heat, his harsh exterior softening with an almost boyish quality. "And I will thank you kindly to mind your own plate. I do not suppose you can finish yours and watch mine at the same time, can you?"

The young duke smiled, undeterred. "No, Uncle Leo."

"Just so." Carlisle's attention abruptly returned to Bridget, his dark eyes boring into hers with an intensity that stole her breath anew. "Perhaps your governess ought to teach you about manners if she has not yet done so."

It was churlish of him to make such a remark. She pressed her lips together firmly, staving off a response. How dare he accost her and importune her in the library, make advances— flirt blatantly—beg her to stay, and then question her ability in her post?

She was about to speak, defending herself, when her employer saved her the task.

"Miss Palliser has only just joined us recently," the Duchess of Burghly spoke up, flashing Bridget a reassuring smile.

"Plenty of time then," Carlisle said mildly, his stare lingering upon Bridget with a noted intensity. "Plenty of time."

Her cheeks went hot beneath his scrutiny from a combination of fear and embarrassment. She could not be certain if he had already received damning information concerning her true identity and was merely prodding at her like a wounded animal he would kill when he had grown bored of the game, or whether he simply enjoyed flustering her.

The moment was severed when Mr. Ludlow motioned discreetly for the next course to be served. "If you were hungry, brother, you would have only had to speak for yourself. No one knows better than I what a bear you become when deprived of nourishment, and we cannot have that on a day of such unmitigated celebration."

Blessedly, Carlisle turned his attention back to Mr. Ludlow, grinning. "Today is not about me, brother dear. It is about you and your lovely bride. I wish you happy, today and every day that follows."

"Thank you, Your Grace," said the Duchess of Burghly.

"Yes," her new husband agreed. "Thank you, brother."

Only Bridget knew that their gratitude would be short-lived. That the joy and love surrounding them was transient. That nothing good was ever meant to last. Of course it wasn't.

Not for the quality any more than it was for those who toiled in their service. For people like Bridget. Lord knew she had never known joy a day in her life. It was the coin of the wealthy, reserved for those with the time and leisure to pursue life beyond the ugly necessities of survival.

Bridget had been born the bastard child of a hideously wealthy American and her Irish mother, a tavern wench who got lucky—or unlucky, depending upon whom one asked— and tupped a rich man one evening. The unlucky part had been that the wealthy American didn't give a goddamn about the babe he left in a tavern whore's belly in Ireland. He had returned home to New York, to his life of wealth and privilege, and forgot all about Bridget. She had lived her entire life scrabbling for everything—every scrap of fabric she wore, every bit of meat and bread in her belly.

A servant delivered her a fresh goblet and poured another generous portion of wine into its waiting maw. Bridget reached for the stem, fingers clamping on it in a tight, painful grip. She raised the glass to her lips and drank. Then drank some more. For the remainder of the meal, she studiously avoided the probing, searing gaze of the Duke of Carlisle.

THE EVENING WAS dark, which suited Leo's mood as he stalked through Harlton Hall's gardens alone, holding the neck of a fresh whisky bottle. He had fled the company, the merrymaking, unable to stomach another moment of felicitations, smiles, and lovelorn glances between not only Clay and his bride but the other couples in attendance as well.

His brother was married. Married and in love. In hideous, soul-draining fashion. So in love, he could not speak without grinning. Could not go half a minute without gazing adoringly at his bride or surreptitiously touching her when he thought no one else was watching.

Leo had been watching. He watched everyone. More than he ought to, likely, but being observant was one of his many curses, along with possessing a bedeviled mind which betrayed him when he could least afford it.

Instances such as these, when he was in charge of more covert agents than ever before, when his Special League had just absorbed an entire branch of the Home Office dedicated specially to the Fenian menace. When two public figures had been slashed to death only months before in a Dublin park. When shadows lurked at every corner, and men threatened the lives of innocent women and children.

He pressed his thumb and forefinger to the bridge of his nose, pinching to stave off the headache threatening to claim him. Now was not the time to allow the inner beasts of his nature to roam free. The moon was full overhead, drowning out hundreds of stars glittering from the midnight depths of the sky. Most nights, even though sleep eluded him, he forgot to look, or they were blotted out by the pernicious London fog, forgotten as the dead.

Tonight, he saw them, fighting against the silver-white moon, struggling to be seen, and they reminded him of the fragility of life. Of how cruel and fleeting it was.

Do not drink the poison, said a voice inside him. *One night was enough. Sleep another day.*

Caution and the voice could both go to hell and dwell there with the devil until Leo was ready to join them. He opened the bottle, held it to his lips for a long, steady pull. It burned a path to his gut.

In the otherworldly sheen of the moon, Harlton Hall's gardens appeared manicured enough. He walked a gravel path until he came upon an obelisk rising imperiously from the center, then lowered himself to the dirt like the animal he was and began to drink in truth.

He drank away the day. Drank away his worries and cares. Memories. Guilt. Darkness. Shame. Fear. Responsibility. The whisky was a benediction, anointing his gullet with its velvet promise of momentary amnesia.

The nuptials nonsense had been more difficult to endure than he had imagined it would be, and not because he was bitter about the wedding day he had been denied—that was old, unwanted news. But because he was an observer. He prided himself on his ability to watch others, to study them and make inferences from what he saw, to predict and dissect and understand.

And yet no part of him could comprehend a man falling so helplessly in love with a woman he would bind himself to her eternally. Irrevocably. It was loathsome. Horrid. Terrifying. Everything he stood against. Everything he had learned was impossible.

Thank you, Jane, for the schooling.

He would never forget.

Even so, Leo had done his duty. He had been coherent and present, happy for his brother, happy for his new wife, thrilled to have a nephew—in truth, he adored the lad. It was something new for him, he had to admit, enjoying the presence of a child. But the young duke—Clay's son, though he had not been aware of his true parentage until recently—affected Leo. He slipped past his wizened, cynical skin, straight to his tender marrow.

Yes, the lad was intelligent and kind, brave and funny, quick-witted and unafraid to challenge Leo as he had done at the wedding breakfast. He could only silently applaud him. The dark-haired scamp, with his awkward body and his shy mannerisms, had instantly won Leo's heart. He resembled

Clay so much, it was uncanny, and Leo could not look upon him without recalling all the scrapes he and his brother had managed to get into during their youths.

Though Clay was his half brother by nature, the only son between Leo's father and his mistress Lily Ludlow, Leo had never been closer to another. Not even to Jane, and he supposed it was just as well, for he had not been close to Jane after all, had he? No indeed.

Oh, Christ. Stop thinking of bloody Lady Jane Reeves.

Leo lifted the bottle of his brother's whisky to his lips. He was well on his way to becoming soused once more. This made two nights in a row. This meant...

Well, fuck.

The quiet night laden with its brilliant moon and shy stars seemed to mock him, for they reminded him of a different Jane entirely.

A dark-haired beauty who neither looked nor sounded anything like the flaxen-haired Lady Jane. Strangely, when he thought of the lady who had once owned his heart, all he could see was blue eyes flecked with gray, fringed by long, ebony lashes.

Why did he keep thinking about the haunting eyes of the governess? Why did he keep recalling she tasted so sweetly of bergamot, that she made a delicious, breathy sound when he kissed her? That her body had been so pliant and curved against his, so soft in all the ways a woman was meant to be? That her mouth was not only kissable, but fuckable, the kind of mouth he wanted to slide his cock inside?

"Hell," Leo bit into the oddly illuminated darkness. "Bloody hell. Bloody, bloody hell. Bloody fucking, goddamn hell."

He could not seem to utter enough epithets to rectify the burning, forbidden need inside him. He could not swallow enough whisky to make thoughts of her disperse, though he aimed to try. He could not will away the stiffness of his cock, even now, knowing how wrong it was. The woman was his nephew's governess. She was a glorified domestic. Untouchable.

Why was he so drawn to her?

The unexpected crunch of shoes on the gravel path reached him then, jolting him from his maudlin reveries. Tensing, he abandoned the whisky and reached for the small pistol he had worn for the day's festivities on the chance it was required. He rose to his full height, prepared to attack any interloper if necessary. He had felt comfortable in the knowledge that more than a dozen armed men prowled the grounds, ensuring that nothing and no one would intrude upon Clay and Ara's idyll.

But his instincts had him on edge despite the skills of the trained assassins he had scattered throughout Harlton Hall. Until the mysterious interloper emerged from behind a hedge.

And there she was.

The governess.

He could not stay the smile that curved his lips as he carefully replaced his pistol in its hiding place. "Miss Palliser."

She stopped in her tracks, skirts swaying in the moonlight.

"Your Grace!" She dipped into a passable curtsy, and villain that he was, he imagined her dropping to her knees entirely. Staying there. Asking him to come to her, opening her sweet pink lips to accept his cock. "You gave me a fright. I did not expect anyone else to be in the gardens this evening."

He swallowed to banish the unworthy thoughts adulterating his mind. "Miss Palliser. What are you doing out here all alone, in the darkness? Has no one ever told you nothing good can come of ladies wandering at night?"

"I could ask the same of you," she said with her signature brand of boldness. "I was given to understand you were taking your leave this evening after dinner."

It was true that had been his plan. But then his head had begun to feel as if it were laden with Fenian dynamite, and the darkness had threatened to claim him, and for the first time in quite a long time, he had not wished to be alone. But he would admit none of those weaknesses aloud to anyone, and certainly not to this lovely, yet strange creature, who had chosen to tempt fate by walking nearer to him instead of turning and fleeing in the opposite direction as fast as her feet could fly.

Leo allowed his gaze to travel over her fine figure, noting the way the gray color of her gown took on an almost otherworldly sheen beneath the bright moon, that she wore no hat, and the lunar glow turned her raven hair to an enchanted silver. "Yes. That was to have been the plan. But I have decided to alter my travels. I will be remaining for the next day at least."

"I see," she said, and he could not miss the note of disappointment in her voice.

Had she wished him gone then?

He recalled her passionate response, followed by her hasty retreat, the evening before.

Did she fear for her position?

If so, he could allay her concerns. Though his baser nature longed to take her in his arms and claim her lips once more, he had not come to Harlton Hall to dally with the governess. Nor had he suspended his return to London to do so.

"Miss Palliser," he began coolly, "you need not be concerned I shall relay what happened in the library to the Duchess of Burghly. Your secret is safe with me."

"Secret, Your Grace?" Her tone was hushed, equally

frosty. "I confess, nothing about my time in the library was particularly memorable for me, and I cannot recall whatever it could be you refer to."

Her goad made him grit his teeth. He ought not to remind her, but he had already downed far too much whisky to make rational decisions where she was concerned. Something about the governess vexed him. Lured him. Intrigued him. "Delude yourself all you like, Miss Palliser. I am certain we both recall the manner in which you clung to me and offered me your lips. The way you kissed me back as if you wanted to devour me."

He had not meant to say the last, but it was true. She had kissed him with a tumultuous frenzy, and he had never in his years experienced as searing a joining as the kisses he had shared with Miss Palliser. A buttoned-up governess he could not touch. His nephew's governess, he reminded himself. And if there existed any governess he ought not want to fuck, surely it was his nephew's.

"*You* kissed *me*, Your Grace," she returned, chin tipping up in defiance.

Her bravery knew no bounds. Nor, it seemed, did her capacity for deception.

He moved closer to her, the moonlight and the whisky rendering him reckless and foolish. "You seem to be confused, my dear, for it was undeniably *you* who kissed *me*."

"You are wrong, sir," she contended, holding her ground.

One more step. Then another. And another. Until she was near enough to touch. To take in his arms should he wish it—*strike that*—should he deem it wise. For everything inside him wished it. Screamed it, in fact.

Something about this woman called to him. Something made him want to haul her in his arms, slam his mouth over hers, and consume her. To make her his. To peel back the prim layers of her governess weeds and reveal the wildcat he knew lay hidden beneath her careful exterior.

"I have it on good authority that I am never wrong," he argued, his lips quirking into a smile he could not quell. This woman invigorated him as well. Intrigued him. Who was she? Where had she come from?

To Leo, it was painfully obvious she was no ordinary governess.

"Indeed?" Her voice had taken on a breathless quality, betraying her susceptibility to him. "And on whose authority would that be, Your Grace? Your own, perhaps?"

What was it about this governess which made matching wits with her so bloody enjoyable?

Christ knew, for Leo did not.

"My authority would be the very best. *Good* authority is that of my mother, who trusts me implicitly in all matters." He could not resist the taunt.

"The Duchess of Carlisle believes you are never wrong?" the governess persisted, her words finding his softness like a blade sliding between his ribs.

One swift jab, and he was bleeding, damn near incapacitated.

He did not speak of the woman who had birthed him to anyone.

His smirk died. "The Duchess of Carlisle is not my mother. Lily Ludlow is the only mother I have ever known. She is, in fact, the embodiment of what a mother ought to be."

And he had said far, far too much. Likely, it was because of the whisky he had consumed. Perhaps too because he was on the brink of the darkness. He could feel it, the heavy weight of the angry cloud spinning, churning like a storm about to unleash its rage upon the land below.

But he could battle it back. If he was busy enough, inebriated enough, distracted enough, strong enough, he could fight off the coming tempest. He damn well knew he could. He had done it before, and he would do so again.

"Forgive me, Your Grace," the governess said quietly into the awkward silence which had descended in the wake of his pronouncement.

"You need not offer apology," he bit, cursing the whisky for rendering him too honest. Cursing his weakness for the governess who made him too vulnerable. "I stated fact. That is all."

"My own mother was not a mother a'tall," she said softly. For a brief moment, her words had carried the sweet lilt of a brogue.

What in the name of all that was holy?

Could it be possible that Miss Pallister hailed from Ireland?

His spine stiffened, blood running cold. Whispers abounded over the last few months about a woman in the most dangerous of all the Fenian circles.

"Where do you hail from, Miss Palliser?" he queried with deceptive calm.

Surely this woman, who was so diminutive in stature, so flawless of face and form—surely the woman he found himself attracted to in a way he had never felt for another before her—could not be his enemy.

He was being overly cautious. Lack of sleep, coupled with over-imbibing and the added weight of his brother's wedding, had rendered him far too susceptible to suspicion and maudlin sentiment both.

She stilled at his question, like a wild animal who knew a hunter watched, one who was poised for flight and certain safety. Despite himself, his suspicions continued to rise.

"I hail from London, Your Grace. I was born there, raised

there, and it is where I call my home."

How quickly and neatly she had answered him. Even dulled by whisky, Leo's senses began to hum. "Indeed, Miss Palliser?" He moved nearer to her still, crowding her with his body without touching her. "What street?"

"Street?" The breathless quality of her voice had only heightened. Her hands fluttered in the air like butterflies, as if part of her wanted to lay them flat upon his chest and push him away, and yet, part of her did not dare to risk a gesture so foolhardy.

"Yes, Miss Palliser." Despite himself, despite his better intentions and the need to question this mysterious creature rising within him, he lowered his head. His lips wanted hers. Had to have them beneath his, against his. He hungered for her, for another taste, another exquisite glimpse into paradise. "What street were you born on? Where did you live?"

By the time he had finished his clipped enunciations, his lips were perilously near to hers. Instead of waiting for her response, he moved. And then, suddenly, he had her in his arms, and her mouth was on his, open, warm, and so intoxicating. Her tongue slid past his lips, bold and delicious, and he played his along it, tasting her, kissing her back.

Chapter Four

*B*RIDGET HAD LOST her bleeding mind.

That was why she had thrown her arms about the neck of the Duke of Carlisle. Why she was kissing him as if he were the most delicious, decadent dessert she'd ever tasted. Why her entire body was a riot of sensation, why he had brought her to life, convincing her she should surrender all—her duties, her obligations, her beliefs—for one frantic beat of her heart, for one more kiss. One more sweep of his tongue over hers, one more deep, dark moan torn from his throat, one more press of his hard, powerful frame against hers.

This man was her enemy, she reminded herself.

He was dangerous to her.

Forbidden.

At dawn, she would be taking his nephew, leading him away from home, taking him to London. Bridget stilled in the act of kissing Carlisle back, wishing she knew what John wanted from the young Duke of Burghly. Why he had specifically asked for the boy. He had promised her the lad would not be harmed, but now she had spent time in the boy's presence and had developed a fondness for him, she wished she had never agreed to this untenable situation.

Perhaps sensing her sudden shift of mood, Carlisle broke the kiss, staring down at her. The moon's glow was bright and full tonight, casting a silver sheen over him, over the garden, so that she could almost convince herself they had landed in the midst of a fairy realm.

"Tell me, Miss Palliser," he said, his voice decadent and low, sending a sinful trill down her spine, "did you follow me into the gardens?"

Did he suspect her?

Bridget's breath caught in her throat as she studied the planes of his handsome face cast in shadow. How she wished she could see his eyes, read the emotions within.

She forced her galloping heart to slow to a trot. "I can assure you, Your Grace, that I would never follow a man like you anywhere."

"A man like me?" He canted his head, looking down at her, and she was uncomfortably aware the moon illuminated her for his perusal, whilst he remained an enigma. That his hands lingered upon her waist as if it was where they were meant to be moored. "Explain yourself, madam."

"A rogue," she forced herself to say, hating the breathlessness she could not hide. Hating the way her heart once more leaped when he slid a palm up her spine and she felt his heat through all the layers between them. "A gentleman with no greater concern than the whisky in his glass. A man born to privilege and power, who can take whatever he wants, who would importune a governess two evenings in a row."

"Rogue is an appellation I'll own."

Slowly, the hand at her back traveled, between her shoulder blades now. The caress made an ache settle low in her belly.

"But you know nothing of my concerns, Miss Palliser, or how they weigh upon me. Moreover, I fail to see how I have importuned you, when we have already established *you* kissed *me* first."

Had she the first night?

Yes, for she had been determined to use him in whatever fashion she could to further her cause.

Had she just now?

Shame made her cheeks go hot. Nay, of course she had not. She would not...

Lord in heaven, she had, hadn't she?

He had been the one to initiate their proximity, but the temptation of his lips had been her undoing.

"What are your concerns?" she asked him instead of arguing the point, for she knew a battle she would lose when she saw one. And perhaps she could learn something from him. Get him to reveal some information she might use against him. Convince him to reveal his vulnerable underbelly.

But he did not answer her. That wandering hand roamed to her neck, the touch of his bare skin upon hers a jolt to her already heightened senses.

"You ought not to be roaming in the dark alone, Miss Palliser. Return to where you belong and forget our paths ever crossed."

Two impossibilities, for she could no more return to her beloved homeland where she belonged than she could forget about him, a man who stood for everything she had vowed to fight against.

She did the only thing she could think of doing in that moment of raw, potent connection. Her own hand—also gloveless—raised, and she cupped his rigid jaw. Dared to stroke it. "Why are you roaming in the dark, Your Grace?"

She told herself she prolonged their intimacy to garner as many secrets about him as she could. To make him vulnerable to her. But the rough prickle of his whiskers into her tender flesh made her feel heavy and aching between her legs. Just one touch, so simple. So unnerving.

"Because the darkness is where I belong, my dear." His

long fingers tunneled into her hair, loosening the plaits of the simple braid she had tamed it into that morning.

She shivered, but it had nothing to do with the damp of the night, or the hint of chill in the air, and everything to do with him. With the man, rather than her enemy. *Diabhal.* "Perhaps the darkness is where we all belong."

He cradled the base of her skull then, holding her with such tenderness. She had never known a gentler touch, and how surreal—if not impossible—to think it had been delivered by her greatest nemesis, the most dangerous man in England. The last man she should ever allow to touch her. The same man who would see her jailed and hanged for her sins as others before her had been.

"What has the world done to you, Jane Palliser, to make you so cold?" he asked softly.

The manner in which he held her, the timbre of his voice, made her feel…cared for. How foolish, how truly weak of her. The Duke of Carlisle was not hers to keep. He was hers to destroy. And destroy him she must.

She answered him honestly. "The world has taken everything I hold dear from me."

"Then I shall not be the man who takes one more thing," he said softly, dipping his head to feather a tender kiss over her lips. "Go now, Miss Palliser, before you are missed, and before I am too far gone to let you leave."

He was right, for lingering here with him was a temptation she could not afford. Some weakness she had not realized she possessed within her was susceptible to his touch, to his mouth. To his kiss. It struck her then, bathed in the moonlight, surrounded by the Duke of Carlisle's strong arms, how easily the sins of the flesh could render boundaries and loyalties indistinct.

In another time, another place, perhaps they could have

met as lovers.

This was not that time, nor was it that place.

In this world, they were destined to be adversaries.

But first, one more kiss.

She tugged his head down to hers, and he allowed her to guide him, the massive, fearsome warrior in a duke's pretty clothes. This kiss was for her, all she would permit herself. Their mouths sealed, quick and furious, and this time she did bite him. She caught his lower lip between her teeth, nipping the succulent flesh until he groaned.

The Duke of Carlisle liked pain.

It was a revelation she tucked inside her mind, for later, when she could make sense of it. Bridget could not resist biting harder, until the slightest hint of his blood—a salty tang—was on her tongue. She swallowed it, wishing for a wild moment it was his seed instead, then tore her lips from his and her body from his arms.

The unlikely, moon-drunk union between them was at an end.

"Something to remember me by, Your Grace," she said.

And then she spun away from him, leaving the gardens the same way she had entered them. This time, his dark devil's eyes burned twin holes into her back with each step.

LEO WOKE WITH a bruised lower lip, a raging cock, an equally raging headache, and the memory of the governess's husky words: *Something to remember me by, Your Grace.*

He stared at the ceiling overhead, grateful he had found his way to a bed and had not spent the evening in the gardens, even if he did not recall how he had wound up in his present state, naked and flat on his back beneath the bedclothes.

It stood to reason Miss Palliser had not joined him. She had taken her leave after her parting gift, a hungry, hard kiss and a bite that had made him want to throw up her skirts, lay her down, and slam home inside her. Painful pleasure had ever been a weakness of his, and how this radiant creature in her prim dove-gray governess attire could somehow both sense that, and give him what he needed, had him closing his eyes on a groan and stroking his cock.

He did not know if she was experienced or an innocent. Experienced women knew how to give and receive pleasure, and they were goddesses, one and all. But he had never had a virgin before, and the thought of taking Miss Palliser's maidenhead—of being the first man to sink inside her tight, untried channel—made his cock even harder as he closed his fist over it, eyes closed to the early morning light, attempting to forget everything else.

Of course he could not do it. Would not do it. His code of standards refused to allow him to be anything but honorable, unless his actions were taken in the name of the Crown, in the name of protecting the lives entrusted in his care. It was why he had sent the beautiful governess on her way last night. Why he would take his leave this morning, returning to London in time for supper, and perhaps a visit to the intrepid Mrs. Giraud, who knew how to meet his particular needs whenever they arose within him and demanded to be answered.

But first, he would satisfy them with his hand and his imagination. Leo stroked his cock, thinking of how she had looked in the moonlight, her skin pale and ethereal, eyes glistening, her hair a dark contrast to the dreamlike silver cast of the rest of her. How she had tasted of wine and fiery, passionate woman. Of herself, Miss Palliser, the enigma.

He held his breath as he worked his hand over his shaft

faster. Already, moisture pooled on the tip of his cock, and he ran his thumb over it, wishing it was her cunny juices instead. And then his imagination took control of his mind, and he was back in the gardens with her. Back to the moment after she had drawn his blood.

Something to remember me by, Your Grace.

"I shall do the same," he would have told her, instead of sending her away. "Give you something to remember me by."

His wicked mind wondered how he would begin. Would he bind her wrists? Strip her naked and bite her nipples until she was writhing in passionate fury?

No, he decided as he increased the pressure and the pace once more. He would kiss her and kiss her, sink his tongue inside her lush mouth. Tug her to the ground and throw up her skirts. He would kiss along her stockings, his hands finding the luscious swells of her calves, and her stockings would be silken and smooth under his touch. Upward, he would go, until he was kissing her inner thighs, near enough to the wet, needy heart of her, where she was pink and swollen for him. He would spread her thighs, bury his face in her folds, and suck—

Fucking hell.

He came with more force than he could recall in recent memory, his seed jetting into the bedclothes. Sated pleasure washed over him for a beat, soon to be replaced by the sense that it wasn't enough. He wanted her in reality, though he could not have her. How mortifying to think the woman had him so at her mercy, he had spent to the mere thought of licking her cunny. Bleeding hell, he had not even sank his cock inside her.

But that would have to be another fantasy for another day.

The sun was already farther than he would have preferred

in its relentless trek across the sky, and having slept two nights in a row—thanks to Clay's limited, though blessedly good whisky cache—he felt more rested than he had in years.

Pity he could not touch the drink again this evening. Pity too he could not touch the governess.

His cock sprang back to life.

"Christ," he muttered, forcing himself from bed.

It would simply not do to continue lusting after his nephew's governess. The woman was untouchable. A temptation he could not afford to indulge in. Not to mention there remained something about Miss Palliser, for he refused to think of her as Jane on principle,—an indefinable quality, more a hunch of Leo's than a discernible trait—which made him suspicious of her.

Leo performed his ablutions, thinking he must warn Clay about his instinctive reaction to Miss Palliser. It could be nothing, but he knew his brother—newly reunited with his beloved son—would not want to take any risks where young Edward was concerned.

Washed and dressed, he rang for his valet. Though Leo, quite unlike most lords, preferred to dress himself, he nevertheless employed a man for the sole purpose of keeping himself and his belongings organized. Without Richland, he would be a hopeless, wretched soul. Or rather, even more of a hopeless, wretched soul than he already was.

"Your Grace," Richland greeted with his effortless aplomb. The elder man had been a solider in the Crimea, and in addition to being blessed with excellent organizational talent, he was also the sort of chap Leo would want on his side in a skirmish to the death. Richland could shoot and wield a blade, and he was no stranger to the theater of war. Despite the irrefutable fact that he was twice Leo's age, the man was as hale as any prize fighter and just as dangerous.

Richland had been assigned him by the Home Office, who had understood his need for a man he could trust. Leo was thankful for his aid and loyalty each day.

"Richland," he greeted, grateful for the sight of the man he trusted so implicitly, for it returned his mind to reality. To the dangers at hand, facing them from all directions, unseen and boiling beneath the surface of every quiet moment. "We will be leaving by noon. Please see everything is prepared for travel."

Richland, predictably, took the sudden change of plans in stride. He bowed. "Of course, Your Grace."

"Have you any correspondence for me?" he asked, almost as an afterthought. He had not been long in residence at Harlton Hall—a mere day—and it stood to reason he would not have received much information from the Home Office in that time. Still, with the rabid tenacity of the most vicious of the Fenian groups, one could never become too complacent.

"I do indeed have a telegram for you, sir," Richland said solemnly, reaching into his coat and extracting a sheet of paper. "It arrived not half an hour ago."

Damn it.

This did not bode well.

He took the missive from his valet. In its haste, the message had not been written in the standard code he and his operatives preferred. Just as well he would not need to tear open his waistcoat and extract the cipher wheel.

His waistcoat.

Damnation, the governess still had his waistcoat.

A fresh wave of suspicion blossomed inside him. She had promised to see it laundered, and though scarcely any time had passed between yesterday morning and this morning, it did seem odd she had yet to return it. Especially considering her almost unnatural eagerness to see it washed for him.

Unnatural.

The lone word sank into his psyche, plaguing him as he pored over the telegram.

Female sent stop Last of plotters stop Burghly House dead man stop Household infiltrated stop Leprechaun

Leo's blood went cold. Leprechaun was the code name of the highest level Fenian informant, Padraig McGuire, who had infiltrated the inner circle of the American Fenians. If he had dared to send Leo a telegram, unencrypted, the situation was dire, and chances were there was a hell of a lot more to the story than the succinct message expressed. He needed to find his brother Clay, and he needed to find him *now.*

"Thank you, Richland," he muttered, an automaton, his feet carrying him from his chamber.

He could only hope he wasn't too late.

And that the female plotter in question was not the governess he had kissed. The governess he had just…*hell.*

Of course she was.

The jagged shards fit together, forming a hideous picture. Miss Palliser was a Fenian. How could he not have seen it sooner? How could he have allowed himself to fall beneath her spell? She had played him like a bloody violin.

Her final words to him took on a newer, more terrifying meaning.

Something to remember me by, Your Grace.

In the corridor outside his chamber, he broke into a sprint.

Chapter Five

$\mathcal{B}$Y THE TIME Bridget reached the main road with the Young Duke of Burghly, her charge had grown noticeably worried. Though she had promised him they were going on a learning expedition, and even the head groom who had prepared their early morning gig for them had not raised any questions, the duke was a wise lad.

He recognized the scenery, knew which direction they were going. He fidgeted at her side, shifting in his seat, expression pinched. She knew he understood they were traveling back toward the train station.

"Mama did not say anything of a trip," the boy said, his tone fretful.

"It is a surprise," she returned, keeping her tone light as the horses thundered on, down the road, leading them both to an uncertain destiny. *For the good of the cause*, she reminded herself. *For Cullen. Anything to save his life.*

She was a soldier, performing the duty asked of her. She would deliver the boy because she had to, not because she wanted to. Cullen's future, or lack thereof, depended upon her every action, and she would do well to remind herself of that.

Oh, Cullen.

Thinking of him made her heart heavy, filled her with the sadness she kept at bay most days with zealous discipline. His boyish grin, sparkling blue eyes, dark hair marred by the cowlick she had so often attempted to tame, without success. How she loved him, loved him as she never had another.

Bridget closed her eyes for a scant moment as the gig they'd taken that morning rumbled toward the train station. And then she forced them open once more, for she alone was in charge of this nonsense. She was the driver, barreling toward mayhem.

And it was her fault. She was the one who had volunteered herself for this unwanted task, the most dangerous task John could have envisioned. Success was within her grasp, for she had done it, had she not? Here she was, Bridget O'Malley, the young Duke of Burghly at her side, having been pried from the bosom of his family with embarrassing ease that morning.

How easily a lamb could be led astray.

And not just lambs either, but the fiercest, most dangerous men could be as vulnerable. She had made the Duke of Carlisle a fool, had infiltrated his brother's household without an inkling of suspicion. She had kissed him. Flirted with him. Plotted against him beneath his nose, and he, the vaunted leader of the Special League, had been completely unaware. Bridget had faced him in battle, and she had won.

But you enjoyed his kisses, whispered that awful voice inside her.

You thrilled at his touch.

Yes, the Duke of Carlisle had been an Achilles heel. But she had also stayed her course, proving that not even her weaknesses could keep her from her duties and her loyalties.

Even so, she could not deny it was the stakes of this gamble that made her hands tremble on the reins, the knot of fear and guilt swelling inside her to ridiculous proportions. That made the bile rising in her throat continue to make its steadfast presence known.

"I want to go home, Miss Palliser."

The young duke's polite request, underscored with fear and worry, struck her in the vicinity of her already anxious heart.

Guilt, which had begun to drench her, turned into a deluge. He was but a child, and he wanted to return to his mother.

Stay the course, she reminded herself sternly when part of her wanted to continue her charade, instead of carrying through with the plan of abducting him. To return him safely to Harlton Hall after they drove about on their feigned expedition. To make it seem real. Return to her charmed chamber with the eastward-facing windows. Forget this had ever happened.

But that part of her needed to be stifled by the rest of her. Conscience and concern could have no place in this fight. It was all about gaining what the cause wanted, what they needed, by any means possible. Fair or foul. But more than that, it was about saving someone she loved. If she did as John ordered, she could help to free Cullen. She could not afford to lose sight of the goal of seeing him walk free and unencumbered on the streets of Dublin once more.

Kilmainham Gaol was a hell of a place for an eighteen-year-old young man to find himself on account of his poor decisions. She could only pray he would be the same young man she had known when he emerged.

Thoughts of prison made her grip on the reins tighten, her teeth grinding together with so much force, her jaw ached. She would not find herself in the same straits as Cullen, she vowed, for she was older. Wiser. More careful.

Surely she was.

"We shall return you to your home in a trice," she lied to the lad, struggling to keep her voice even and calm.

She knew she must say something comforting, though she

hated herself for deceiving him so thoroughly. For being the person who had been entrusted with his care, and yet also the same person who would betray him.

"But I wish to go home now, Miss Palliser," the young duke insisted again, a quaver creeping into his voice.

Of course he was frightened. He was a sweet, kind young boy who had just lost his father to murder. Whose mother had become the target of subsequent attacks. Who was himself at the mercy of a woman he had only known for mere days. A veritable stranger, and one he could not trust at that, though he did not know it.

Bridget thought of the lovely, kind, and welcoming Duchess of Burghly as the horse and cart plodded along. Her guilt grew, doubling and tripling within her, until it was all she knew, a sea of sickness.

"But we cannot go home now, Your Grace," she said softly. "Our adventure has only just begun."

"I do not like this adventure." The tremor in his voice lanced her. "I wish to return to my mother and father."

Doubts gripped her, tightening like manacles. "You will return soon enough," she lied.

"I do not think I would prefer a surprise this morning, Miss Palliser," the young duke pressed, concern in his voice.

Bridget felt as if she had swallowed a belly full of poison. She did not want to be responsible for separating the young man at her side from his family. It was wrong, and with each beat of the horses' hooves on the road, she was reminded.

It became a litany.

Wrong. Wrong. Wrong. Wrong.

Until she broke. There had to be another way. She could not do this. Bridget slowed the horses and guided the gig to the side of the country road. And that was when she heard the unmistakable thunder of approaching horses behind her.

Fear clawed at her throat, for she knew instinctively who

it was.

The Duke of Carlisle was coming for her.

And he would show her no mercy.

She extracted the pistol she had kept hidden within her pelisse, and though it was not loaded, pointing it at the wide-eyed lad and watching the color leach from his face filled her with the deepest brand of shame.

"Get down from the gig and do not move when your feet hit the ground," she ordered him. "Do as I say, and you will not get hurt. This I promise you."

"Please, Miss Palliser. I want my mama." A tear escaped the boy's eye, rolling down his cheek, but he did as she asked.

Bridget alighted after him and, the sound of her reckoning coming ever nearer, gripped the boy's arm. She led him into the dense wood with as much haste as she could manage, praying she had not made the biggest mistake of her life.

YEARS AGO, DURING the war in France, Leo and fellow League member the Duke of Trent had faced a group of bloodthirsty Prussian soldiers straggling from their army. Leo and Trent had been outnumbered, and he had slain three of the five soldiers himself, one with nothing more than his bare hands as he choked the life from the bastard.

That had not been the first, nor the last time Leo had faced down men intent upon his murder.

The hell of it was, he had not been fearful that day. He had never feared for his own mortality, for there were days when Leo did not give a damn if he were alive or dead. But he did fear for the lives of those he loved, and Edward, the young Duke of Burghly—Leo's bloody *nephew*—was among that small group of people.

As Leo stalked through the dense forest as silently as possible in an effort to surprise Miss Palliser from behind and rescue Edward, he was the most terrified he had ever been in his fucking life. The woman was mad. She had dared to abduct her charge, a peer of the realm, in broad daylight, and Padraig all but had named her as part of the ring of plotters responsible for the Duke of Burghly's assassination.

A dangerous, unpitying, hateful group of cowards—the sort who attacked unarmed men with surgical knives in the midst of a park. That was who she had thrown her lot in with. That was the caliber of woman who held innocent Edward in her grip.

Clay had just been reunited with his son. The anguish in his expression had slammed Leo in the gut like a fist. Even now, his broken words returned to Leo as he slowed, hearing the sounds of voices in the clearing ahead.

We have to find them, Leo. I cannot let anything happen to him. This is all my bloody fault, and I will not forgive myself if…

There would be no *if*, Leo decided. He gripped his pistol firmly, at the ready. He would gladly die before he allowed a hair to be harmed on the lad's head. He parted the brush, held his breath, and formed a plan as he watched.

Miss Palliser's back faced him, a weapon in her hand, the barrel pointing toward what he could only assume was Edward's head. She wore a bonnet over her dark tresses, her pelisse and dress the same unremarkable dove gray as the day before. To the uninformed observer, she would appear no different from any other governess. But he now knew what evil lurked in her heart. Knew she was not to be trusted.

Clay faced Leo and Miss Palliser, his weapon no longer in hand.

Damn it to hell.

Leo was Edward's only chance now. He aimed at her shoulder, calculating his ability to hit her with precision and avoid injuring the lad, as Clay spoke.

"Like hell I will allow you to take him from me," Clay called, taking a menacing step toward the woman.

She took two steps in retreat, hauling Edward with her, bringing them both nearer to Leo.

There's a girl, he coaxed silently. *Closer if you please.*

"Remain where you are, or I shall hurt him," Miss Palliser warned Clay, her voice like the crack of a whip.

Leo willed Clay to continue to distract her. It was their best hope. If she was close enough he could be confident of his shot, he would wound her, and Edward could run free.

"What do you hope to accomplish?" Clay asked, understanding his role all too well. This was not the first time they had worked together in this capacity. "Do you truly believe the harming of an innocent youth will make Home Rule possible?"

"What I hope to accomplish, and what I believe are two different beasts, sir," Miss Palliser said, taking another slow step and pulling Edward with her.

"Papa," Edward called out, his tone pleading. Hearing the fear in the lad's voice was akin to a spike in the heart for Leo. "I do not want to go with her. She said she will take me on an adventure, and then I can go home again. But I don't want to do that. I want to go home to you and Mama."

"Silence, Your Grace," Miss Palliser ordered Edward. "I must take the boy with me, but he will be returned."

Leo prepared his aim. His hands were steady. His heart was ready. He could do this. He could save his nephew. He bloody well had to, for if he did not, Leo could not bear it. His life had been lived, his mind was tainted, and he had already accomplished what he wished.

Why could the wench not have chosen him as her victim instead?

The undeniable rustling of someone racing through the

dense forest behind Clay broke the silence. Leo tensed, wondering if it was another Fenian, but then he saw the swirl of skirts and flaming hair, and knew it was his sister-in-law Ara instead. He took advantage of the commotion.

Held his breath.

Pulled the trigger.

His lone shot rang out.

The bullet struck its target, hitting Miss Palliser, cutting through her gray frock. A dark-red stain instantly spread as her body jerked forward. Her pistol fell from her slack hand. Blood ran down her arm in a rush.

Goddamn it!

He must have hit a vein, and while he had wished to injure her, he still needed the vile female alive so he could interrogate her. She crumpled to the ground.

Edward broke free of her and ran toward Clay and Ara, shouting. "Papa! Mama!"

Leo rushed forward, wasting no time in binding Miss Palliser's hands and ankles before withdrawing his knife and cutting a strip from her petticoat. He tied it above her wound tightly, fashioning a tourniquet to stay the blood pouring from her body. He retrieved her weapon and checked it, and that was when he made a most curious discovery: the gun bore no bullets.

She had been holding Edward hostage with nothing but an empty pistol and her own bravado. He pocketed her gun and stared down at her ashen face, wondering who in the hell she was.

He looked up at the happy reunion of Clay, Ara, and Edward—hugs, kisses, tears, proclamations of love—and vowed he would strip her, whoever she was, of every speck of information she possessed concerning the Fenians.

And when he had finished, he would destroy her.

Chapter Six

$\mathcal{B}$RIDGET WOKE TO aching arms, sore wrists, and a searing pain in her right upper arm and shoulder. She blinked, disoriented for a moment. Confused. Why was she not in her chamber? Where was the young duke?

This chamber, while nonetheless well appointed, was not her apartment with the three large windows, early morning sun, and charmed view of the verdant Harlton Hall park. The bed linens did not smell sweetly of lavender, but instead of stale sweat and the murk of sickness she recalled so well from her youth. She was bound to the bed, and she had been stripped down to her chemise.

That was when she remembered.

Someone had shot her. There had been the suddenness of the pain, tearing through her upper arm. The warm, wet trickle of blood—so much blood. It had been on her hand, red and dripping down her arm. And then the shock had set in, her teeth had rattled and her mouth had gone dry.

She recalled the leafy green trees overhead as she fell to her back, the shouts, the anxious voices of the young duke's mother and stepfather, sun piercing through the boughs, glinting like the promise of a far-off land. A land without suffering, pain, or fear. Then the dark abyss of nothingness had claimed her.

Now, she was a prisoner, being kept in a strange place,

attended to by a servant who refused to answer her questions aside from the necessary. She had been injured, the woman tending her—Annie—had said, and then had suffered an infection. Aside from those bare facts, she knew nothing.

For three days, she had been fed nothing but broth and gruel, wallowing in her own filth. No one heard her when she screamed. Or if they did, they were not inclined to answer.

She could recognize nothing. The window dressings had remained closed, with only thin strains of sunlight on the periphery to tell her whether it was night or day. Her female captor was pretty, but cruel. She seemed to take pleasure in Bridget's every discomfort. Two times a day, she appeared to aid Bridget in the use of the chamber pot and delivered her broth and gruel. In the evening, she brought her tea.

As lucidity slowly returned to her, and she had begun to regain her ability to comprehend, she had dared to ask questions.

Where am I?

Who is responsible for this?

Why am I being held here?

Each time, the woman remained silent. Each time, Bridget grew more frustrated. The tea the woman brought her was sweet. Laced with laudanum, she suspected, and she would have foregone it had she been given anything else to drink. When she slept, she returned to the darkness. She saw Cullen there, waiting for her. She forgot who she was, what she had done, and it was easier.

But this was the first time she had been bound.

A shudder racked her now as she searched the chamber frantically. In her state of half-wakeful confusion, she was desperate for the answers she had been seeking ever since she had regained consciousness.

Who had tied the knots on her wrists while she slept,

cradled in the arms of the opium her jailer fed her?

Whoever it was, Bridget knew one fact without question: she needed to escape.

Now.

Her first instinct—tugging at her bindings—only served to draw them tighter. A sudden, damning prescience settled over her then. When she had first come to, she had been caught up in her last lucid memories—of Mr. Ludlow imploring her, his wife racing through the forest. Of the lad trembling in her arms. She had imagined Mr. Ludlow had delivered her to the authorities, that he had secreted another weapon upon him somehow.

But an awful, niggling sensation within her told her she had been wrong. Horribly, foolishly wrong. She had no doubt who had brought her here, to wherever she now was. No doubt as to who had tied the devil's knots digging into her flesh. No doubt either as to whose bullet had burned through her body, leaving her weak and wounded and sick.

It could be none other than the Duke of Carlisle.

Though she knew it was futile, she tugged harder with her uninjured arm, an animalistic sound of desperation hatching from her throat. Of course it would have been him who had shot her. What else would he do to her now that she was completely at his mercy?

John's words pricked the edge of her memory. *The Duke of Carlisle is as black as they come. A heartless killer. One of the most dangerous men in the League. He is our greatest enemy, one that must be challenged with great caution.*

As if he had been conjured, the door to the chamber opened, and Carlisle himself stalked over the threshold. His dark gaze settled upon her with searing scorn. Long, elegant fingers slammed the portal at his back. He did not resemble a duke in the slightest. He was dressed in black trousers and white shirtsleeves, nary even a waistcoat.

"You are awake, madam?"

She said nothing, but his presence was enough to make her instinctively tug at her bindings once more, even as a raw and terrible pain ricocheted from her wound all over her body. Nausea swirled in her stomach at the sudden virulence of the agony.

"I would not do that were I you," he said calmly. "It will only make the binding tighter and more painful."

Fear blossomed inside her, for she recognized the face of a predator when she saw one. This was not the same man who had kissed her with passionate persuasion at Harlton Hall. The man before her wanted to tear her apart, piece by piece.

Despite his warning, and though she knew she should remain still, she pulled again savagely. A fresh, stinging pain cut through her, beginning at her wrists and surging up her arms. The wound reminded her with a vicious intensity that she was a fool. So too did it remind her of her abject failure. She had faltered when she could have bluffed. She had doubted when she should have stayed her course.

She had been bested by the man before her, and she did not like it. Bitter, futile anger coursing through her, she jerked again, with all the force she possessed. She bit her lip to stifle the cry of agony she would have otherwise emitted, not wanting to give him the pleasure of her pain.

He had crossed the room with calm, purposeful strides and stood at her bedside. "You would be wise to remain still. You suffered a great deal of blood loss with your wounding, and after that, infection set in. I should hate for you to tear open your stitches, forcing us to begin this process again. I'll be no one's nursemaid, and I am told by Annie she grows tired of being yours."

"I will not be still," she seethed, pulling at her restraints once more. "You shot me, you madman."

"Mm." He reached out, stroking one of her wrists over the cruel, cutting rope. Back and forth, his touch at once soothing, yet terrifying. "Says the madwoman who held a gun to an innocent child's head."

She would not have hurt the young duke. Never. But she would not defend herself. Not to *him*. Bridget maintained her silence, telling him with her eyes what she thought of him. He was the enemy. A ruthless, cunning man. A fearsome opponent. Here now, after all her days of recuperation, was the devil to collect his due.

"Do not touch me," she spat when his fingers curled around her wrist, his thumb rubbing tender circles over her pulse.

"Are your fingers burning?" he asked.

Yes.

"I feel nothing," she vowed.

"Do you know what I find odd, madam?" He continued rubbing her wrist, as if he sought to ameliorate her pain, which she knew could not be farther from the truth. "You attempted to spirit a young duke away from his family, and yet your pistol was empty."

"You disrobed me," she charged instead of responding.

"You were bleeding."

"Because of you."

"Because you absconded with an innocent boy," he returned coldly. "I shot you because you were holding a pistol to the lad's head, and I had no other recourse."

Yes, much to her shame, she had done that. The fearful breaths the boy had taken, the accusing brightness of his gaze, the trembling in his small form...all these remembrances added to her shame. She had never meant to involve the boy or cause him alarm in any way. If she had not been desperate, she would not have used him as she had done. She would never have done John's bidding in the first place.

"He would not have been hurt," she said.

"Your lack of ammunition is rather surprising, madam, even to me. I don't suppose the Fenians trust a cunny with a loaded pistol." The bite of his tone, so at odds with the tenderness of his touch, nettled her.

And though she had no doubt it was just as he had intended, she reacted all the same. "They trusted me with ammunition. It is merely that I refused to hold a loaded weapon to the head of a young boy."

Her soft heart had ever been her downfall. Bridget O'Malley was tougher than a wizened old tree, but when it came to children, even her jaded, cynical soul could weep. And though her days with the young duke had been limited, she had developed a fondness for the lad.

"You admit to your connections to the Fenians then." His tone was clipped. Scornful.

"I admit to nothing but the ability to carry ammunition," she said stoically, well aware she had said more than she should have. "I admit to knowing how to load and shoot a firearm."

"I do not give a damn what you do or do not know about a pistol, madam. You held a gun to the temple of an innocent child. You had no compunction about dragging him from his bed and luring him away from his home." His thumb pressed painfully into her wrist then, emphasizing the bitterness and rancor in his voice.

She clenched her teeth. "He was not hurt."

"You betrayed his trust. That will mark the boy forever." He pressed again. "What is your real name, madam?"

"Jane Palliser."

He was expressionless—calm, almost—but his touch was

anything but. He seized both her wrists in punishing grips which would have made her cry out with pain had she not bit her lip so hard she tasted the metallic tang of her own blood.

"Try again, damn you."

His face was near to hers now, his gaze boring, and she could see the delineation of each whisker on his jaw. He had not shaved in several days, she would wager.

"Jane Palliser," she repeated, goading him in part because she wanted to see how far he would go, and also, because she was no fool. If she revealed her identity, he would find a whole world of other means to hurt her.

He squeezed harder. "A warning, lady. You do not want to test me."

"A warning in return. I will not be broken." While her wrists were bound, her legs remained free, and she wasted no time in using her knee against him.

But her motions were slowed from the time she had spent in the sickbed, and she was still weak, in spite of the days she had spent recovering. He sensed her action before she could finish the follow-through, catching her knee beneath her chemise and stilling her in the act of smashing him in the groin.

"Do not fool yourself," he said with dangerous intent, his tone as smooth as silk, butter rich and deep. He gripped her bare skin, and she felt the contact like a brand. "You will be broken by me. I will crush you, madam. Before I deliver you to prison, I will know your every secret." His hand slid higher, jolting her as he made contact with her thigh, gripping her there as he joined her on the bed, his large body dominating hers with ease.

She hissed out a breath, grinding her jaw. Even weakened and in pain, she could not deny the pleasure Carlisle's rough touch sent through her.

How was it her body could so betray her with a man she loathed? How could the biting grip of her enemy upon her make her heart pound and the flesh between her legs tingle?

Being wounded had addled her. Likely, her mind had been afflicted by the fever. It was the only explanation she would accept.

She jammed her thighs together, keeping his hand from traveling higher. "More villainous men than you have tried to break me and failed, Duke. You do not scare me."

"Darling, there is no man more villainous than I." He smiled, but it was a hard smile, one laden with menace. "I ought to scare you. I ought to bloody well terrify you."

"Perhaps it is you who should fear me," she challenged, meeting his gaze. She was desperate. At his mercy. But she didn't give a damn. She had her pride, and she would go on fighting until she could fight no more.

"You?" His smile deepened, his gaze traveling over her in a manner intended to mock.

Instead, her entire body went flush with warmth.

Remnants of fever, no doubt.

"Aye, Duke," she responded, allowing the brogue she hid to emerge. "You ought to fear me. There's nothing more dangerous to a man than a woman he wants to bed. Especially when that woman is his enemy."

A muscle flexed in his jaw, but aside from that, he remained still, one hand clamped on her thigh, and the other on her wrist, the heat of his body radiating into hers. "If I had wanted to bed you, I would have already done so."

"Lie to yourself as you will, *Your Grace*." She did not believe him, nor could she resist the mocking jibe of his title. Though he burned with a banked fury, and his every touch was punishing and cruel, the attraction between them was as potent and undeniable as ever, simmering just beneath the surface of the moment.

"You're a bold thing, aren't you?" His voice was almost soft as he asked the question.

"I am whatever benefits me," she told him, and it was perhaps the most honest statement she had ever uttered. She had made her way through life on her wits, hard work, and determination, but she had also learned how to bluff. How to be a hundred different versions of herself to gain whatever suited her most.

"What would benefit you is telling me the truth," he countered. "Beginning with your name."

She did not hesitate in her response. "Jane Palliser."

"Jane Palliser is a fiction, and a poor one at that." He tightened his grip on her wrist once more. "I can make this easier for you. Grant me the information I want, and I will help you as best I can."

Did he think she was stupid enough to trust him?

His handsome face did nothing to distract her from his intention of sending her to prison.

"A tempting lure, but one I'll not accept."

"Do you want me to hurt you, madam?" he asked then, pinning her with his glare in much the same fashion as his massive body.

"Do you *want* to hurt me?" she asked. And perhaps there was something wrong with her—some part of her was broken—but she was breathless, awaiting his reply. She wanted the brute in him, it was true. Something in her relished challenging him. Pushing him beyond his limits.

Even now, exerting painful force against her, he remained calm. Ducal, almost. She wanted to see the animal beneath his gentleman's skin. Wanted to feel his bite, his fury. Wanted to bring him so low, he had no choice but to admit he was no different than she was.

"You do," she said into the silence, prodding him. Provoking him. "Hurt me, Duke. You like pain, do you not? Does it bring you pleasure?"

"Nothing about this is a pleasure." He released her, his lip curling, and rose to his full, impressive height. "Tell me what you know. I can force the words from you, or you can give them freely. Naturally, one will be better for you than the other. You seem the sort who wishes to save her own skin. I can give you that. I can make certain you are treated fairly in prison. All you need to do is give me the information I require."

Treated fairly in prison.

Did he hear himself?

Bridget vowed, then and there, she would escape him. Before he could take her to a dark cell and abandon her to her fate, she would do what she must to get away. She had been in prison once, could still recall the fetid scents, the anguished cries of the incarcerated, the dart of rats in the darkness.

No.

She would not be going back to a prison cell. No matter what it cost her. She would do anything—*anything*—else first.

"I have no information," she lied with ease. "I do not even know what information you desire. You seem to think me some sort of great criminal, when in truth, I am a governess who made a dreadful mistake."

"You are a Fenian who has been caught." His tone was deceptively smooth and calm.

Bridget knew a moment of remorse. She had pushed him to the brink, and she had been so certain she would spot a weakness in his armor. Something she could poke until it bled. He had given her nothing.

"Hurt me then," she demanded. "What do you prefer? Fists? An open hand? Perhaps more. Do you like to whip your prisoners? Would you like to lash me? Is that what interests you?"

"I do not mix pain and pleasure," he gritted. "Or I did not. Volunteer for the task, and we shall see which one of us is first to break."

Her nostrils flared. *Him. Without question.* "Yes, Duke. Let us."

"Tell. Me. Your. Name." He bit out every word as if each was its own sentence.

"Jane. Palliser," she said quietly. Calmly.

"Damn you, woman. You only hurt yourself in your stubborn persistence."

"I thought *you* wanted to hurt me, Your Grace. What's the matter? Am I robbing you of the pleasure?" She was pushing him again, and she knew it. Perhaps too far. But she didn't care. She was tethered to the bed no better than any criminal, and her body liked this raging beast of an Englishman far too much. "Be quick about it. I do not like to wait for my punishment."

Something flashed in his eyes, but his expression remained impenetrable. "Do not imagine I will give you warning, *Miss Palliser*. I already know you thieved my waistcoat and that you are guilty as sin. Your punishment will come when you least expect it. And have no doubt, my dear, that you will sing. Like a fucking bird."

His tone was vicious. So too his gaze as it raked over her.

She suppressed a shiver. It seemed they were at a stalemate, and her wrists and hands ached, as did her wound. Her body was in need of respite. "I require a bath. Do you allow your prisoners ablutions, or am I to be tied to this bed like an animal until you cast me into prison?"

He sniffed the air. "I will allow it on account of the fact that you stink, madam."

Her cheeks went hot, for her nose told her she did. Lord knew how many days she had been unconscious, sick with infection, and sweating. Her skin itched.

She would have told him to go to hell. Indeed, it was on her tongue, ready, but he spun on his heel and stalked from the chamber before she could manage a coherent sentence.

"English bastard," she muttered after him.

Her fingers felt as if they had been pricked with a thousand needles. Her wrists ached. And she was being held captive by the Duke of Carlisle. Fine turn of events this was.

FINE TURN OF events this was.

His captive was on her way to recovery, but she was as hardheaded and strong-willed as ever. He had not known, when he had left her here at his lesser Oxfordshire estate, Willoughby, if she would live.

But live she had.

And now he would need to bathe her, for he did not trust the woman who professed to be Jane Palliser—the woman who was decidedly *not* Jane Palliser—would not attempt to either slit his throat or escape the moment he loosened her bonds. How difficult it was even for Leo, who had seen untold evil in his years leading the Special League, to believe a small, beautiful woman like her could foster such an endless capacity for treachery. Her bravery knew no bounds. So too her foolishness.

The woman did not know when she was outgunned. Daring, fearless, and determined, she was a dangerous sort of female indeed. She was the kind of foe he could almost admire. Would have admired, except for her attempt to abduct his innocent nephew and her allegiance to the bloodthirsty Fenian menace.

Leo's jaw clenched as he stalked down the main hall. One of many in the vast entail, the house was staffed simply with a cook, butler, and a scant handful of maids and footmen. The structure was smaller and far less grand than he was accustomed to, yet had served its purpose well in this instance.

In the aftermath of rescuing his nephew from Miss Palliser's duplicitous clutches, he had flatly turned down Clay's suggestion he return to Harlton Hall whilst the Fenian virago recuperated. After the harrowing experience Edward had just faced, Leo had no wish to subject him to further fear.

He had taken his unconscious prisoner past the rail station to this house, knowing he could at least leave her here without causing any more harm to Clay and his growing little family. He and Ara had only just wed, for Christ's sake, and while Leo harbored no love for the grim institution of marriage, he was nevertheless glad to see his brother settled and happy, reunited with the woman he had always loved and the son they'd had together. He had earned his reputation for being cold and ruthless, but Leo loved his true family, and he would lay down his life for them.

His duties in London had forced him back to town, and he had left his prisoner in the care of the maid he felt he could trust most, and the region's best physician. To the Home Office, he had reported his captive officially dead for reasons all his own.

He found the servant, Annie, idly flirting with a footman. They broke apart when they saw Leo, but he understood all too well what they had been about. It was as old as the seas.

"Your Grace." Annie flushed, stepping away, righting her skirts, and dipping into an atrocious curtsy. She had been casting him longing eyes ever since his arrival with a wounded woman in tow, and he knew if he wished it, he could avail himself of her undeniable charms. Annie was a golden-haired beauty. Samuel, in comparison, was a large-footed oaf with a receding hairline.

Before his arrival here today, part of Leo had been tempt-ed to accept her unspoken offer. In the days following his prisoner's wounding, she had taken ill with fever and had been insensate for days. The physician had not been certain if she would survive the infection that had set in. He had spent many sleepless nights in London communicating with the Home Office and his agents, attempting to glean more information to assist him with his interrogations if his prisoner awoke.

Through it all, he had been plagued by an irritating abundance of suppressed lust which could only be quenched by sinking inside a warm, wet cunny and losing himself. But the trouble was, Annie was not the woman he wanted, and the woman he did want was not only his enemy, but on her sickbed, put there by him. Altogether an untenable situation.

Moreover, he was beginning to suspect from what he had viewed thus far—namely Miss Palliser in a bed which had not been stripped for days, wearing nothing but a chemise stained by her own perspiration—that Annie had not taken care of his prisoner at all as he had asked.

The sensitive nature of his missions meant none of his domestics were aware of his true position. He had fed his staff a story about Miss Palliser being a distant relative who was not only mad, but a danger to herself and others, and had left two of his own men behind to aid in guarding her. His sense of honor had required him to see a female tended to his prisoner while she was with fever. But he had seen at once Annie had not been the right choice for the task.

"The lady requires a bath," he said without preamble. "She is lying in her own filth as we speak, Annie. Tell me why her bedding has not been freshened and why she is wearing the same chemise I left her in a week ago."

Annie blinked, straightening her skirts. "She would not cooperate, Your Grace. As you said she was a danger who must be kept locked in her chamber at all times until you returned, I did not deem it wise to spend too much time in her presence."

Damn it to hell.

Or any time in her presence, which seemed far more apt. He despised Miss Palliser and her actions, along with everything she stood for, but that did not mean the sight—and smell, for that matter—of her had not affected him. He had noted it from the moment he had first gone to her chamber to find her sleeping the deep, calm slumber of a babe. And he had instantly sought to restrain her. Annie's message about their patient's recovery had reached him two days late since he had been hosting one of his infamous fêtes.

It had both begun and ended with a woman attempting to suck his cock. Different women. Both rebuffed. He had neither the time nor the inclination, though he had been tempted to accept not only both offers, but to drown himself in all the spirits and opium in Blayton House. He had not been this conflicted, this driven to the edge of the darkness dwelling within him, in some time, and he did not like it.

"The bath," he snapped. "See that it is readied. She will take her ablutions in my bathroom."

His order was partially self-serving. He had no wish for the domestics to witness the manner in which he had tied Miss Palliser to the bed. Also, he had placed her in a chamber ordinarily reserved for a governess. As such, it contained no private bath, unlike the ducal apartments, which had been renovated from their original, Jacobean splendor—or lack thereof—by his father the duke before him.

"Your chamber, sir?" Annie asked, frowning her disapproval.

He stared her down. She was not paid to disapprove. Nor was it her right, nor her place, especially given the state in which he had discovered Miss Palliser. "Yes, precisely as I said."

Samuel intervened. "I will see the bath prepared, Your Grace."

"Shall I attend her, sir?" Annie asked, her tone reluctant and more than just a trifle bitter.

He ought to allow the duty to fall to her, it was true. But he did not trust the banshee tied to the bedposts not to fillet poor Annie and eat her liver for dinner, leaving her to bleed out on the floor whilst she made good her escape. Nor did he particularly trust Annie, albeit in a different fashion. He suspected the two women possessed different shades of cruelty.

"I alone shall attend her."

Though he very much hated to accept the task, it must be him. She was cunning and crafty, *Jane Palliser*, and she knew how to fight. In a word, she was dangerous.

In two, damned dangerous. And since she had risen from the nearly dead, she was once more his albatross to bear.

"Very good, Your Grace." Samuel nodded.

Annie's expression soured. "I'm sure it wouldn't be proper."

Leo raised a brow and pinned her with the stare he used upon everyone who dared to oppose him. "The lady cannot be entrusted to anyone's care but mine. She is very treacherous and would think nothing of shooting you in the heart if it would suit her purposes." When Annie paled, he flashed her a taut smile. Occasionally, he forgot what it was like to be someone who did not expect lethal force, mayhem, and perfidy at every opportunity. "Never fear. I shall not allow her to harm you; that is merely why I must attend her myself."

"Yes." Annie swallowed, eyes wide. "Of course, Your Grace. We must and shall defer to your judgment."

"Indeed," he told her coolly. "You shall. Samuel, I expect the bath readied within the next half hour. Annie, have Cook prepare some clear broth and a light tea as a repast afterward. Perhaps some gruel. I expect she will be hungry as well. She looks too thin by half."

Though why he should give a damn about her appearance or whether or not she ate properly was beyond him. Indeed, he should not. But there it was again, something about *her*, that infernal woman. She dogged him, taunted him by her mere presence in his home. By her wide, blue eyes, the purple crescents beneath each. Her dirty shift, her dull, matted black hair. Even in her current state, she was more beautiful than any woman should be.

The footman nodded and left, hastening to his task, returning Leo to the responsibilities at hand. But the maid lingered.

She approached him after Samuel had gone, her blue eyes glittering with undisguised sensual intent. "Perhaps I could assist you later this evening?"

Perhaps she could warm his bed was what she meant to ask. The answer was no. Still no. Resounding.

"I fear I shall be otherwise occupied," he told her.

Her expression closed as she dipped into another curtsy. "Yes, Your Grace."

And then she was gone, leaving Leo once more alone. He closed his eyes and inhaled deeply. Hundreds of assignments over the years. He had dealt with villains, criminals, the most barbaric acts and men he had ever known. He had made decisions, led men to their deaths, to their adulations, to their ruin, to their triumph. And yet, in all those years, in all those deeds, he had never once hungered for the person at the center of his investigations.

Now, today, as all the days since he had first clapped his eyes upon her, he did.

He wanted his bloody prisoner. His body knew it. His cock understood it all too well. Regardless of her identity—who she was, where she had been, what she had done—he could not deny he remained attracted to her. Some wicked, deep-seated part of him whispered she was his.

The prisoner. Jane Palliser. The Irishwoman. The most beautiful woman he had ever seen. The one woman who managed, whenever he looked upon her face, to render him speechless. That was who he wanted. That was who he needed.

It was also who he could never, ever have. He banished all such unwanted thoughts from his mind and stalked back to where he had begun. His feet carried him back up the narrow staircase. Back to the door leading to *her*.

Miss Jane Palliser, or whoever the bloody hell she actually was. One thing was certain: she had lied to his sister-in-law about her qualifications. He vowed he would uncover the truth about her, beginning with her name. The more she longed to withhold it from him, the more he wanted it.

When he re-entered the chamber, he was not prepared for the sight that greeted him.

Miss Palliser's cheeks were wet. Her gaze met his and she sniffed, attempting to school her features into an expressionless mask. But it was of no use, for he had already glimpsed her. The real her. And he would now use it against her.

"A bath is being prepared for you in my chamber," he announced, closing the door at his back, before striding across the small chamber to her bedside. "You have been weeping, Miss Palliser. Why?"

She stiffened, tugging at her wrists as her eyes blazed into his. "Because I am in pain, Your Grace. I have been tied to this bed as if I am no better than an animal."

"You have earned your treatment with your own actions, madam," he reminded her.

"I have done nothing wrong," she denied, stubborn and beautiful to the last.

Even after having been ill with infection and fever, even bedridden for days and only just now on the brink of recovery, his prisoner was the loveliest woman he had ever seen. She took his breath and enraged him, intrigued him and confounded him, in equal measures.

"On the contrary," he countered swiftly, "you have done everything wrong. But you shall still have your bath, madam. You will have it in my chamber, as the bath is already laid out there, and I have no wish to cause extra duties in this household on account of you."

Perhaps he was being harsher than necessary. He did not give a good goddamn. The truth of the matter was—and he could acknowledge this in spite of his infernal weakness for the woman—she was wrong. Her cause was wrong. Everything about her was so very, horribly wrong.

Except for her lips.

He cursed himself for that rogue thought and turned his attention to the matter at hand, namely, getting Miss Palliser safely across the hall and bathing her, all whilst he kept her wrists bound. The best way, he deemed, was to free one wrist, bind them together, then free the other, leading her to the bath in that fashion.

He joined her on the bed and her eyes went wide.

He smiled at her without mirth, finding odd humor in the impossible situation. "You have no need to fear me. I have no wish to force myself upon any female, let alone a traitorous

Jezebel such as yourself."

"I am no traitor."

"You are an enemy of the Crown," he snapped, withdrawing his blade and slicing at the bonds on her wounded arm first. "And my prisoner. And most definitely a traitor."

She hissed as the blood surged back into her hand, and he knew it would be painful. He examined her wound, moving her arm with care, pleased with its progress. She was healing nicely now, and that fact, coupled with her moments of lucidity, had told him she would soon return to the world of the living. He had bound her accordingly, and he was grateful for his decision now. Perhaps some pain would encourage her to reveal her associates to him.

Pain along with the need to save her own hide.

"Where am I?" she asked.

"What is your name?" he returned, slicing the other rope, then hastily binding her wrists together before her.

She paled, crying out as he jostled her with more force than necessary. But, true to form, she remained stubborn. "Jane Palliser."

"Here is how this shall go, prisoner." He stood from the bed once more, gazing harshly down at her, unable to keep himself from noticing the dark circles of her nipples beneath her chemise. "You must give me information before I shall give you any. You may begin with your name. Until you offer me a truthful response, I will not reveal a damned thing to you. Don't, for a moment, think you can lie to me. I have my best men digging into your past."

Her eyes narrowed. "I want my bath."

Obstinate woman.

He took in her struggles to sit upright with her hands bound and the pallor of her skin. Perhaps he ought to assist her in her walk to his chamber, but he was not going to. Let the banshee suffer. Perhaps it would render her more amenable to making some revelations.

"Stand," he ordered. "You will walk to your bath, or you will have none."

Slowly, she moved her legs, sliding her feet gingerly to the floor, as if the effort required every bit of strength she possessed. And perhaps it did. Having been spoon-fed nothing more than broth by himself and Annie during her bouts of lucidity, and given water as she could swallow it, she was likely weak. Her small frame, hugged by her chemise, was noticeably less curvaceous.

He watched, impassive, as she attempted to stand and fell back to the bed on her rump. "Try again. If you cannot stand and cannot walk, you cannot go to your bath."

"Water," she said. "I need water."

"Demanding for a prisoner, aren't you?" He cocked his head at her, allowing all the anger and disdain building inside him to show. "If you cannot ask with manners, you shall not have it."

"Please," she gritted.

The gentleman within him—or what remained of it—knew he ought to feel at least a modicum of guilt at being so rigid and unfeeling toward a woman who had just been ill for so many days. But the agent for the Crown, who had dedicated half his life to service, refused to bend.

She is a Fenian, he reminded himself forcefully.

And not only a Fenian, but a woman who abducted his nephew and held a pistol to his head. That the pistol was empty was a matter of curiosity and not a reason to soften toward her in any way.

He fetched her the water, careful not to turn his back to her in case she was perpetuating an elaborate act, and returned to her side, holding the cup to her lips. She drank greedily, gulping. He watched her throat work, noting how creamy and pale it was in spite of himself.

"Enough," he snapped with more rancor than necessary, withdrawing the cup. "Any more and you shall be sick. You will stand now and walk to your bath, or you will forfeit the privilege."

Wordlessly, she stood on limbs as unsteady as a newborn foal. There was her daring, in full evidence. Silent and proud, she painstakingly walked toward him. Until her knees gave out, and her legs buckled beneath her, sending her to the floor.

With a muttered curse, he went to her, not thinking twice about scooping her into his arms. She bit her lip and closed her eyes as he held her, her body trembling.

Fucking hell.

The gentleman within him told the agent of the Crown he was being an arse, forcing her to walk when she was so obviously weak.

He told the gentleman to go to hell.

"No bath, then," he said sternly, moving to place her back upon the bed.

"Please," she said. "A bath, Your Grace. Please."

He weighed his options. She did need one. And perhaps if he helped her, had her fully at his mercy, he could garner the information from her he so desperately needed. His men had discovered as much about her as they were likely going to: she had rented rooms near a millinery shop where she worked for the months before she had been hired on as governess for Edward. Her references had been forged, but forged with an impeccable attention to detail.

Her landlady proclaimed her quiet and proper, with a brother who visited often. A small, slight, tow-headed man who was almost certainly not the brother of the raven-haired

Irish termagant in his arms.

A lover perhaps. A Fenian certainly. Mayhap a Fenian lover.

The thought made him scowl.

He wanted the *brother's* name.

He wanted all the information she had to give.

"I will carry you, but on one condition," he told her. "You must answer my questions."

Chapter Seven

*B*RIDGET HAD PROMISED to answer the Duke of Carlisle's questions. But she had not promised to answer them truthfully. As he carried her with ease down the long hall to another chamber—to *his* chamber—and the steaming bath awaiting her within, she reminded herself of that important distinction.

She did her best to ignore the broad, solid, muscled strength of Carlisle's arms engulfing her and the chest she was nestled against. No man had ever lifted her in his arms or held her so gently, as if she were fragile. That the duke was the man responsible was an improbability she would investigate later. When her mind was functioning properly. When her skin did not itch. When her body did not ache.

When she did not feel as if she had been run over by a carriage.

Inside the elegantly furnished bathroom adjoining his chamber, a male servant—the man, she guessed, who had drawn the heated water in the tub—bowed and left without saying a word. The bath looked like heaven, but when the door closed behind his back, they were alone. Carlisle's penetrating stare was upon her, drawing her attention from the paradise she wished to enter.

She could not look anywhere but into it. "Thank you. I believe I can stand on my own now. You may put me down and go."

"I will not be leaving you alone, prisoner." He raised a brow. "Do you think me a fool? Nay, do not answer. Clearly you do, else you would not have dared to flee with my own bloody nephew with the aid of the head groomsman. Tell me, how did you ever imagine you would be clever enough to escape me once I had realized what you'd done?"

Desperation had made her reckless. His proclamation of additional arrests at the wedding breakfast had told her just how limited her time was. At any moment, she could have been implicated by whomever had been captured. Often, the jailed were only too happy to reveal information concerning their confederates if it meant saving their own skins.

She swallowed, choosing to ignore what he had said, for she had neither the intellectual acuity nor the strength to battle him just now. "I do not require your assistance in the bath. Free my wrists, if you please, and I shall manage perfectly well on my own."

He laughed bitterly. "Regardless of whether or not you desire my assistance, you will have it. I do not trust you, madam, for reasons which must be painfully obvious to you."

Her heart thumped madly. Surely he did not mean to watch her while she bathed? Or—good, sweet *Dia*—to help her bathe?

"You cannot intend to remain here while I conduct my ablutions?" she asked.

"Of course not," he said, and relief swelled within her. "I intend to conduct your ablutions myself."

Any relief she had been experiencing dispelled instantly. She gaped at him. "But Your Grace, your presence within this chamber, alone with me, is improper in itself. To bathe me yourself...why, it is not only ludicrous, but impossible. I'll not countenance it."

Without missing a beat, he spun on his heel and strode for the door. "No bath then. Pity, for the water is warmed and prepared for you."

"No," she cried, for she had seen the bath. Had smelled it—it smelled of citrus and something else, something clean and wondrous. Her skin was fairly crawling with the need to be cleansed within its warm, welcoming depths. He could not take that from her. Not now.

Another thought occurred to her then. A sinful, vile one.

The Duke of Carlisle was attracted to her. He had kissed her. More than once. His tongue had been inside her mouth, his hands upon her body. Every action had shown her she was a woman he found desirable. A woman he wanted.

Perhaps she could use that against him. Maybe she could turn this situation about so that the advantage was hers. Maybe she could bring him to his knees after all. Not today, it was certain. But one day soon. Wherever they were, wherever he had brought her, it was not prison. Instead, it appeared to be a regular home attended by servants. Which meant all was not yet lost for her.

Escape remained possible.

"I give in," she conceded, knowing it was for her own cause. That was the sole reason why such a surrender was acceptable. It was either do what he wanted, or deny him, lose her bath, and continue on her way to prison when she was well enough. This was her best chance to regain her freedom. Her only chance. Cullen needed her. "Bathe me if you would like."

The words felt wrong as she said them, leaving her tongue like a leaden weight. But they also did strange things to the rest of her body. A fluttering began in her belly, and it had less to do with hunger than with the knowledge the Duke of Carlisle was going to attend to her in most intimate fashion.

His jaw tightened, the only sign he had even heard her words. Instead of answering her, he returned them to their initial position, by the bath, Bridget still in his arms. Slowly, he lowered her to her feet. "Steady now. Hold on to me if you lose your balance or feel weak."

He withdrew his wicked-looking shiny blade and brought it toward her. She flinched, uncertain of what to expect from this dangerous, enigmatic man. He plucked the sleeves of her chemise one at a time and laid the knife to them, cutting them with ease.

"This is my best chemise," she protested as it fell away in a silken rush of sound, dropping to the carpet at her feet.

"Not any longer," he said, but his voice had changed. Thickened.

She glanced up at him from beneath her lashes to find him examining her frankly, his eyes hot and consuming. Bridget remained still beneath his searing perusal. Even had she wanted to cover herself, she could not have done so given her bound wrists. Whether it was the strangeness of their situation or the lingering effects of her wounding, she could not say, but she stood before him boldly, not a hint of embarrassment.

She had been reduced to a body of demands and wants, stripped of her garments and her dignity both. And if she did not take care, she would suffer further depravations, not just at the hands of the Duke of Carlisle, but of her jailers when he delivered her to prison.

She shivered at the notion. "I am cold, Your Grace."

"Into the bath with you," he said gruffly, flicking his gaze away from her body at last. His expression remained as rigid and unreadable as ever. "The water will warm you."

Lifting her back in his arms, he hauled her up and lowered her gently, almost deferentially, into the bath. Hot water licked at her bare skin, and she could not quite squelch the moan of appreciation that rose in her throat. It emerged from her. His eyes darkened, fastening hungrily upon hers.

"You are warm now, yes?" he asked.

He had forgotten to mockingly call her prisoner, and for a beat, the intimacy of the moment pulsed between them, terrifying and tempting all at once. She was naked, and he towered over her, an enemy she could not dare trust. Bridget felt strange, her body soothed by the languid pull of relaxation, the sweet-scented water dredging her aches. Beneath it all, there simmered the remembrance that this was no ordinary encounter. He was her captor, and they stood on opposite lines in this unspoken war.

"Warm enough," she responded grudgingly. "Will you not free my hands whilst I am at my bath? You have my word I shall not cause a moment of trouble."

He raised an imperious brow. "Madam, you are nothing but trouble, and your word means less than nothing to me."

She supposed she had earned such a reaction. Very well. She would wash herself as best she could manage with her bound hands and painful arm. She winced as she extended her arms and fiery agony tore through her. "Soap, if you please."

But instead of handing her the bar as she supposed he might, he ran it over her skin himself. Beginning with her back and shoulders. Then her arms, carefully avoiding her bandaged wound, before swirling over her breasts. Bridget knew she ought to protest against his ministrations, but her wounding and subsequent illness had sucked all the fight from her. She had neither the strength of muscle nor the strength of will to defend herself.

And so, she sat still as the Duke of Carlisle washed her quickly and impersonally, as if she were a small child. He seemed to take great care in avoiding touching her directly.

He soaped her breasts beneath the water, and she could not quell the reaction it provoked in her, a desperate ache and the sudden puckering of her nipples in spite of her body's general weariness. Biting her lip, she averted her gaze away from him. Her response to him was the same as it had been the day she had first set eyes upon him at Harlton Hall, knowing full well who he was, and it remained every bit as unwanted.

He made quick work of her breasts, then withdrew the soap.

She flushed. "If you please, I would like to finish the rest myself."

"No." His tone was clipped. Abrupt.

This man had no mercy for her, and though she supposed she had earned none, her cheeks burned nonetheless. "Please."

She could not bear the thought of him cleaning her elsewhere. Her breasts had been intimate enough. But the rest of her…it was out of the question. Surely no gentleman would force such a thing upon her.

"Tell me what I want to know, and perhaps I shall," he relented.

Her gaze swung to his, and her flush deepened when she realized he had begun to roll up his sleeves, exposing his forearms. For a beat, her breath caught upon the sight, so masculine. Also intimate, laden with both his intent and the silent tension budding between them.

"What do you want to know?"

"How long have you been in London?" he asked calmly, his eyes never wavering from hers.

"I have not been in London at all," she forced herself to say. "I was lately at Edgware, in service to the Earl of Chalmsford."

His jaw tensed. "I warned you against lying to me, did I not?"

Yes, he had. She tipped up her chin, facing him defiantly, though it required all the strength she had left. "I am not lying."

A slow smile curved his beautiful lips. "You are lying, and we both know it. Time for the rest of your bath, prisoner."

He retrieved the soap, which smelled, it belatedly occurred to her, of him: warm, manly notes of ambergris and something earthy, yet clean. Now even her skin would remind her of him. Of this moment of ignominy that somehow seemed less humiliating as she watched his capable fingers wrap around the soap before disappearing beneath the water.

Keeping his strokes measured and quick, he worked the bar over her feet first, moving his way to her ankles and calves. She held her breath, heat rising once more in her cheeks. In her blood. Blossoming inside her. No one had ever performed such a personal ministration upon her, not since she had been a girl, and even then it had been nothing but a wash basin and a cloth by the kitchen stove for warmth. Her mother had not been able to afford the luxury of a deep tub such as this one.

When he reached her thighs, she clamped them together, denying him access to the most vulnerable part of her. Even if it was the part of her that cried out the most for his touch. He stilled, glancing up at her.

His face was granite hewn. Immovable. "Open."

Her skin was aflame. She stared into the impenetrable depths of his dark gaze. "No."

"Madam, I would prefer not to make you submit. I do not like this any more than you, but it is a necessity." As usual, his tone brooked no opposition.

"Cut my bonds."

"That is out of the question. You have already demonstrated you are dangerous and untrustworthy." His other hand disappeared beneath the water, gripping her knee. "I shall repeat. You can open and allow me to cleanse you properly, or I will make you. The choice is yours."

She closed her eyes against the sight of him, so strong and vital and handsome, his hands in her bath. But still she could feel his touch. He would not be shut out completely. The Duke of Carlisle was too great a force for that. She was tired and drained, and her arm ached. She was at his mercy, with no one she could trust and nowhere to go. What choice had she?

Once more, she gave in, allowing him to guide her legs apart. Allowing him to swiftly pass the soap over her nether regions. Even when he had finished and his touch was gone, she felt him. She felt him like a brand.

Attempting to maintain her composure, she remained still, eyes closed. His fingers were in her hair then, undoing the braid someone had plaited it into during her illness. Fingertips worked over her scalp. Again, he was more tender than she would have imagined, and she could not squelch the soft sigh that escaped her as he massaged her aching scalp, made her hair wet, and worked suds into it.

When he guided her head back to the inviting warmth of the water, she did not even protest. She lay limply, at his command, allowing him to do with her what he wished just as long as it meant his knowing fingers could continue their magic.

She would allow herself to be suspended from time and reality just this once.

It didn't matter who he was, not when he washed her hair with the gentle concern of a lover.

HE WAS A monster.

That was the only explanation for the painful cockstand he was currently sporting.

That was the only reason why the sight of his willful Fenian prisoner, wrists bound before her, body at his mercy, breasts on display as they rose above the water when he guided her head back, made him harder than he had ever been. Harder than a marble bust. That was why he could not stop devouring her with his sweeping gaze that took in all of her, as much of her as he could at once. Her nipples were the pink of a new rose. They jutted forward like offerings, begging for a tongue. He had no business looking at her or lusting after her.

She was his prisoner. His enemy. Strike that. Not just his enemy, but a dangerous one he would see clapped into prison when he was finished with her. One he would need to use every weapon in his admittedly vast arsenal against. Every mind trick, every manipulation, each show of force he had been taught—he would employ them all against her. Anything to get what he needed. To prove her guilt and the guilt of those conspiring along with her.

To send them all to jail where they so richly deserved to be.

And yet, when his instinct called upon him to be harsh with her, to use force, to push her to the brink however he must in order to gain the knowledge she withheld from him, he found himself being gentle instead. He worked soap into her scalp, rewarded by the breathy sighs from her lips.

Lips that were the same lush pink as her nipples.

Damn it, he was staring at her nipples again, washing her hair as if he were her servant. Or as if she were his mistress. It struck him then, like a lightning bolt, she was the only woman he had ever tended to so intimately. He wondered now why he never had, for the act of cleansing the Irish hellion in the tub filled him with a deep sense of gratification.

It was not the woman, he reminded himself, but the action. She was a desirable female. Her breasts were lush, full, and high, her waist narrow, her limbs curved and petite, her bottom full, her mouth kissable, her…

Fuck.

He was doing himself no favors.

"Time to rinse," he ordered in a gravelly tone, guiding her so that her hair was submerged in the tub, the only portion of her protruding from the water her lovely, pale face. Her eyes were still closed, and he ran his hand through the silken strands, using his fingers to comb out the tangles, until no trace of suds remained.

"Your true name, madam," he pressed, taking advantage of the moment.

Perhaps she would slip.

"Jane," she said on a hum of delight as he stroked the base of her skull, finding taut muscles there in her neck and kneading them. "Palliser."

Irritation surged. He had shown her more kindness than he had even supposed he possessed. He had carried her to her bath, washed her, and yet she still maintained the wall of misinformation she had erected. He removed his hands, allowing her to slip beneath the bath water.

She emerged a second later, sputtering and coughing.

Outraged.

She spun about in the large tub, facing him, her black hair sleek and flattened down her back. Her eyes were wide, incredulous. Burning with fury. "You villain! Do you mean to drown me?"

"I mean to make you honest," he drawled, not feeling a moment of guilt for sending her beneath the water. He had bent for her. Made exceptions for her. By God, he had not sent her directly to prison as he should have done—and true, that was for his benefit more than hers, but she did not know that—and yet she clung to her lies. She gave him not a crumb of truth.

It made violence burn within him. The need to punch something. To slam his fist into something. Anything.

She watched him with wide, defiant eyes. "I will never give you what you want, so you may as well resign yourself to it, Your Grace."

More anger seared him, and he welcomed it, for it was far better than desire. "Your bath is over, prisoner," he announced, then stood and hauled her unceremoniously from the water.

Carrying her like a babe, he deposited her on the nearest surface, which happened to be his bed. Also a grave error, for the sight of his prisoner, wrists bound before her—naked, wet, and utterly at his mercy—did strange things to his body. Uncontrollable things. Possession roared through him. Need. Desire. Want.

Closing his eyes against the vision of her nude on his bed, he toweled her dry before realizing there was no means by which he could wrangle her fresh, new chemise—a replacement for her stinking sickbed smock—over her body without first unbinding her wrists.

And this, he refused to do on principle. Instead, Leo brought her his dressing gown, fashioned of luxurious silk, and hung it over her shoulders, belting it over her bound hands. "Back to your chamber."

"What will you do with me?" she asked, her eyes burning into his.

"I do not know," he answered honestly. "That depends upon you, Miss Palliser."

Chapter Eight

SEVERAL MORE DAYS would pass before Bridget saw the Duke of Carlisle again. Six, to be precise. Not that she had been counting.

Very well.

She had been counting.

Trapped inside the chamber he had given her.

Six days at the mercy of Annie, who, as far as Bridget could see, possessed no mercy at all. Which meant Bridget had been forced to beg for future baths. She had not been treated to the delicious, full tub soak she had experienced in the duke's chamber. Instead, she was given a pitcher and bowl, a cake of soap, a cloth. The water had been cold. Old experience had guided her as she performed her ministrations all the same.

Her hands continued to be bound, but Annie's knots were not nearly as solid as the Duke of Carlisle's, which meant Bridget could sometimes escape her bonds and enjoy her freedom in the locked chamber she had been given before she heard footsteps on the stairway and hastened back into her bindings.

She had not been told where the duke had gone or why. One moment, he had been carrying her back to her chamber, wrapped in his dressing gown, and the next, the door had closed upon his back.

And so it was that the sixth morning of his absence saw her freed of her wrist bindings once more, thanks to Annie's ineptitude at knot tying, standing before a westward facing window, watching the birds fly about in the verdant summer grasses and leaves beyond. Wondering what would become of her.

Did Carlisle intend to keep her here, waiting, until she could not stand a moment more and confessed everything she knew to him? Or did he intend to instill a deep and abiding fear in her—the fear of the unknown, of him, of what he would do to her, prolonged by his absence?

She could not be certain.

All she did know this day, without doubt, was that by the time she heard the first creak in the hallway, it was too late to dive back into her bed and her bindings. And at that point, she was not even certain she cared. Her time in Purgatory needed to come to an end, one way or another.

And so she remained where she was, tensed but committed to her decision, as the door opened.

"You are free of your bonds, madam."

The voice, deep and low and velvety, a delicious rumble to her senses no matter how much she disliked the man, sent heat into her belly. Here he was at last, ready to face her. She turned to find him hovering on the threshold, tall, dark, and dangerous.

A menacing figure, formed of well-hewn muscle and jaded flesh.

The door snapped closed at his back.

"Yes," she agreed, returning his hard stare with one of her own. "I am free of my bonds. I am also healed of my wounds, and I grow weary of remaining in this place, Your Grace. Take me to wherever it is you intend. Deliver me to prison. See me hanged. I care not."

He moved then, striding inside the chamber, dwarfing it with his large, powerful presence. His hands were clasped behind his back. This morning, like the other day she had seen him here, he was stripped of his finery, wearing only solid black trousers and a white shirt. Not even a necktie or a waistcoat to provide him the trappings of his ducal authority.

"I have told you before, madam, and I shall tell you again: give me the information I need, and in turn, I will do my best to aid you."

How very tempting an offer that was, but doing so would mean betraying everyone close to her. Betraying Cullen. Leaving him to be sent to the gallows as he would certainly be sentenced. *Dear God*, but the mere thought of it—the noose tightening upon his young throat—made her ill. Made her cough into her hand, regaining what remained of her composure.

"I cannot."

"Who do you protect?" he demanded, as if he could read her thoughts, see straight through to the heart of her.

She wanted to look away from him, but she could not. His gaze trapped hers. "I protect myself," she lied.

For that wasn't true, was it?

Indeed, she was not the one who had started down this treacherous path, though she felt strongly and firmly in favor of Irish Home Rule. Her homeland's people, who knew it best, deserved to be responsible for creating and upholding its laws. Certainly not an English parliament that outnumbered the Irish and ensured they would remain at the mercy of England indefinitely. But it had been Cullen who had first involved the both of them with the Fenians.

Bridget had never imagined they would commit murder.

But they had.

Nor had she ever imagined Cullen would be in prison.

But he was.

And in the interim, the Duke of Carlisle was approaching her, his expression fierce. "Who is Cullen O'Malley to you?"

Just hearing the name on Carlisle's lips was akin to a blow to the gut. It meant he was close to unraveling the tangled webs of deceit she had been spinning for the last year. It meant he was as intelligent and formidable an opponent as she had been warned, for she had revealed nothing that would provide him a connection between herself and Cullen.

"I am sorry," she lied with a bravado she did not feel. At least this time, she was not clothed in only a thin chemise. Today, she wore a simple day gown offered her by Annie since her wound had healed well enough to enable her to dress herself. "I have never heard of such a name."

He stopped when he reached her, towering over her. His lip curled, and she knew an ill-timed memory of his kisses. His mouth moving over hers. His tongue sliding inside to taste her. To tempt her. His scent was intoxicating: the outdoors and his musky soap. She had never smelled anything better.

You must arm yourself, Bridget.

You must be strong.

You cannot afford to weaken for this man.

"More lies." His cold voice hit her like a lash.

She stared back at him, defiant, silent, vowing she would give him nothing.

"Is he your lover?" he asked silkily. "Your husband?"

Bridget ran her tongue deliberately over her lower lip, provoking him. "Are you jealous, Duke?"

His nostrils flared, the only sign he was affected. "As I said before, if I had wanted you, I would have already had you, darling."

Though he used the endearment in cutting fashion, Bridget could not stay the reaction it produced in her, a blossoming warmth. A frisson of that same, confounding desire he alone lit within her.

"It would have been force," she taunted, fighting against it, "for I would never willingly lie with you."

His eyes darkened, becoming almost obsidian. "Another lie. I wonder, madam, have you any truth in you?"

She stepped closer to him, drawn to his heat. His menace. The urge to shake him was strong. To prove he was not indomitable. "Here is a truth for you, Duke. You want me, and you cannot have me."

His jaw tensed. "I'll not fall for your wiles, banshee."

Banshee.

Yes, for him, she would wear that name. Bridget laid a hand on his chest, absorbing his warmth through her palm. His muscles flexed beneath her touch, reminding her of how strong he was, how capable of doing her harm. Oddly, she felt safe with him. He had shot her, but out of necessity, she knew. If he had wanted to do her harm, he'd had ample time and opportunity by now.

She stared at his mouth, remembering the possession of his kiss. Wanting more in spite of herself. "But you already have, Your Grace."

Those beautiful lips lifted into a smirk. "I have done nothing of the sort."

"Prove it," she dared.

Before she could blink or even take the next breath, his mouth was on hers, his hands cupping her face, his lips demanding her complete and utter surrender. She had no defense against his onslaught. Her arms went around his neck, undeterred by the dull pain in her wound, clutching him closer to her when she should have used the opportunity to take action. Strike him. Shove him away. Show him his touch and his kiss were both unbearable to her.

But she was his captive in more ways than one, and instead of taking a stand against him, she gave him everything he demanded of her and more. This—their physical connection, the undeniable attraction between them—was the only yielding she would grant.

It had been weeks since his mouth had last owned hers, and he did it again now with hungry skill, opening, forcing her response. She could not remain unmoving. Could not be invulnerable as she wanted to be. Because everything else fell away when his lips moved over hers, when his tongue slipped inside her mouth.

He tasted of the bitterness of coffee and his own indefinable, irresistible flavor. Any ability to think, to question the wisdom of her taunt, was vanquished by his kiss. She made a frantic sound born of greed and desperate need.

She wanted more of him. All of him. Nothing mattered. There was no future, no past. No boundaries, no opposing sides, no danger, no destruction, no fear or loss. There was only seduction and sin and this glorious man, and all her stuttering mind could think was that she never wanted it to end. Even if he was the Duke of Carlisle and her sworn enemy.

She must not forget who and what he was.

Be stern, she admonished herself. *Be strong, Bridget. You can find one hundred other men to kiss if you choose.*

Ah, but that was the problem. Her stubborn, ridiculous, wrong heart only wanted to kiss this one. The cold, hard, heartless duke. Her jailer. The author of her downfall. The man who would send her to prison.

Somehow, not even that last, jarring reminder stopped her. She was kissing him back, tongue inside his mouth now, fingers in his hair. The Duke of Carlisle's hair was smooth and thick. Some wildness within her prompted her to grab fistfuls and give it a gentle tug.

A growl emerged from him, and he kissed her harder, guiding her backward until she met the wall. He pinned her there, his mouth traveling down her throat. He found her wildly thrumming pulse with his tongue. And then, his fingers were upon the fastenings lining the bodice of her gown, plucking each button from its placket. Beneath it, she wore no corset, nothing but a fresh chemise. Her breasts spilled into his palms and he cupped them as her nipples stiffened into rigid peaks.

She could not stifle the moan that escaped her. His touch robbed her of the ability to think. Resistance was no longer an option if indeed it ever had been. Instead, she arched into him, her mound connecting with his thigh, separated by only three layers of fabric. The friction felt good. It felt freeing. But something within her also felt taut. Exquisitely tuned. She was an instrument ready to be played.

And without her needing to speak the words aloud, he somehow knew. He dragged her chemise down, exposing both her breasts to the air and his scorching admiration. His dark head bowed, and he sucked her nipple into his mouth. She had never before been touched so intimately. Indeed, it had never occurred to her that a man would do such a thing. In her world, a woman's breasts existed to suckle babes, and certainly not for pleasure but this...*sweet Lord and all the angels above*...this was...*oh.*

There did not exist a word for it in the English language. At least not one Bridget knew. *Faoi dhraíocht.* Spellbound. Her body was a spring, tightly coiled. She was hot and pulsing. Aching and needy and ready. Each ravenous drag of his mouth upon her nipple sent an answering undulation of something wicked and wonderful to her core.

She made the grave error of glancing down at him, of watching his handsome face nestled against her breast, his teeth gently nipping and tugging, his tongue swirling over the hungry pink flesh. It was the most erotic, exquisite scene she had ever beheld. His hand was beneath her skirts now, fingers tracing a path of sensation up her thigh. He found the slit in her drawers with unerring certainty.

A gasp tore from her. He skimmed her seam once, twice. Thrice. Parted her folds, dipped inside to find the bundle of flesh that ached most. Where she was desperate for him. For more. For release.

All the while, he continued to suck and tease her nipples, alternating between breasts. When he stroked her, she jerked, white-hot sensation rocketing through her. His forefinger moved, the pressure glorious, the rhythm intense, the friction everything she wanted. Wanton and desperate, needy and voracious, she lifted her leg, hooking it around his waist. He obliged her by making short work of the cumbersome fall of her skirts with one hand while continuing his torturous pleasure with the other.

It was too much.

Not enough.

It was everything she had never known she wanted and needed.

She bit her lip, stifled her cry, too proud to admit how much she wanted him. To concede she had been bluffing. That she longed for him. That she had to have him. Only him. It mattered not who he was, who she was. She was an animal, consumed by her base lust. By the sensations he evoked in her, by his finger on her slick, swollen flesh. Working her. Making her come undone. Winding her up. Building the pleasure until she could take no more.

She required him. This. He was air. He was life. He

was…

He rubbed her harder, increasing the pace and pressure. And just when she was about to lose herself completely, he tore his mouth from her breast and kissed her. It was a kiss that plundered. That ravaged. That took and transformed. That shook her to her very core, and she never wanted it to end.

A few more deft swirls of his fingers over her flesh, and she was lost entirely. She was his. At his mercy. Ready. Her eyes closed, head falling back to the plaster with a thump. But just when she was about to splinter into a thousand tiny shards of herself, he stilled.

"Look at me." His voice was rough, low. All command.

She obeyed, eyes open. He filled her vision: his high cheekbones, the blade of his nose, those beautifully sculpted lips. Whiskers stubbled his strong jaw, lending him an even more dangerous air than he already possessed.

"Tell me, banshee," he said softly, "is this force?"

She wanted to answer with the rebelliousness on fire in her soul. To lie to him, to tell him yes, that he was the last man she would ever want to touch her. But it wasn't true, and she could not make her tongue give voice to the words.

Bridget opened her mouth.

His fingers resumed their delicious movement. Slow circles at first, then faster. Harder. He was kissing her again, their breaths and lips and teeth clashing. They kissed violently, like two people at war. Her eyes closed once more.

"Answer me," he urged against her mouth. "Is this force, or do you want me?"

She tugged his hair and gave him a bruising kiss of her own in response, jerking against him, wanting his clever fingers to finish their torture. For a few moments, he allowed her to take the reins. She controlled the kiss, opened to him, slid her tongue between his lips. She demanded and he gave.

But then, the cord snapped.

He tore his lips from hers. "Open your eyes. Tell me now, have I fallen for your wiles?" His fingers quickened, knowing just what she wanted, needed, without asking or growing hesitant. He gave it to her, everything she wanted and more, and she fell apart in his arms, release ricocheting through her body with beautiful force. "Or have you fallen for mine?"

She opened her eyes, locking on his gaze. Pleasure seized her, took her breath. Took her ability to speak. She came in a thousand shards. Came with a thunderous force. Wetness leaked from her sex, running down her thigh. Shudders racked her body, and had he not held her pinned to the wall, she would have melted into a puddle at his ducal feet.

Bridget could not answer him. Dared not answer him. For he had just proven her a liar in the most visceral sense. She wanted him. Against logic. Against sense and reason. Against her inner sense of self-preservation. Strangely, it only heightened the moment for her. She wanted to be at his mercy.

To be his.

Whatever he wanted. Whatever he needed. In that moment, she would give it to him.

The last tremors of release washed over her, leaving her tingling and sated. Her eyes closed once more. This time, it was an effort to block him out. To forget her enemy was the man who had made her feel more just now than she had experienced in her entire lifetime.

"Always a liar, Miss Palliser," came the stinging scorn of his voice. He withdrew his hand, lowered her skirts, and stepped away from her. Cool air hit her bare breasts. "We are leaving for London fifteen minutes hence. I suggest you prepare yourself."

With that directive issued, he turned and stalked from the chamber, slamming the door at his back with enough force that the outdated, gloomy oil paintings on the wall danced. She watched them moving, allowing her knees to buckle. Allowing herself to slide down the wall until her rump landed on the carpet.

He had won this battle.

But not the war, she vowed.

Never the war.

LEO STOOD OUTSIDE the chamber door after he had slammed it and gave in to temptation. He raised his fingers, still glistening and slick with her juices, to his lips. And then he sucked.

Delicious.

She tasted better than any dessert he had ever consumed.

His eyes closed. He exhaled heavily. Inhaled. Exhaled again.

His heart was pounding. His cock was rigid. His confidence was burned to ash, set on fire by the conflagration that had occurred on the other side of the walls separating him from…he still did not even know what her true name was. It sure as hell was not Miss Palliser.

Miss O'Malley, perhaps?

Or worse, *Mrs.* O'Malley?

Damn it.

Damn him for his insufferable weakness where she was concerned, which rendered him incapable of staying away as he ought to. She was forbidden. His prisoner. His enemy. And yet here he stood, the sweet musk of her cunny on his tongue. Still thinking of the slick plumpness of her flesh, the husky sounds of surrender she emitted, the tremor of her body as she spent.

He would give anything to be the man inside her when she came like that.

Jesus.

Something was wrong with him. He was sick. A vile creature. The inclination toward the wicked and the wrong hovered on the edge of his every interaction with her. From the moment he had first seen her at Harlton Hall, he had wanted her. But then, she had been his nephew's governess, and his honor had not allowed him to dally with her as he had so desperately longed. Time had passed, yet he remained at the same untenable stalemate, albeit for vastly different reasons.

She was a woman he could never have.

A woman he must never touch again.

Leo made certain he had locked the door before he stalked down the hall. Each step he took mocked him.

Wrong, wrong, wrong.

It was a refrain inside his head. Everything he had just done to her within the chamber, every sensation rioting through him now, was wrong.

And yet he knew it without question. He would touch her again. He would kiss her again. As long as she was within his reach, he would bloody well do whatever she would allow him to do to her. Because he could not resist. Because she touched a part of him he had not known existed. A part that was weak and evil and vulnerable. That did not give a damn about her guilt or innocence. A part that was selfish and greedy and took what it wanted.

A better man than he would have made the woman who had abducted his nephew pay for her sins by now. A better man would have turned her over to the Home Office immediately so she could be imprisoned and sentenced as she deserved. A better man would not keep her within his control. Would not kiss or touch her. A better man would not want to sink home inside her.

Similarly, a better man would never have raised her skirts, found the opening in her drawers. He would not have bared her breasts and sucked her deliciously responsive nipples. He would never have heard her breathy, passionate intakes of breath.

But she was his weakness. His only weakness.

It was why he had stayed away. Why he had left a week ago after only returning for a scant few hours. He could not trust himself where she was concerned. But if he had hoped distance would have lessened the ache in his trousers that belonged solely to her, he had been mistaken. Because he wanted her more now than he ever had before.

And now, he wanted to lick her in truth. He wanted her spread beneath him on a bed, legs open. To suck her pearl into his mouth and sink his tongue deep inside her. Hell, if she was tied to the bed, even better, for he wanted nothing less than her complete submission.

It struck him then, with the force of a slap.

He didn't want to see her to prison.

Impossible, for doing so was his duty.

He could not shake the feeling. It was a hell of a thing. There he stood, in the same hall he had traversed hundreds of times before she had ever entered his world, and yet he was hopelessly changed. He had somehow formed an attachment to the woman who would sooner lie to him—the woman who would sooner open her goddamn legs to him—than be honest.

Wrong. Wrong. Wrong.

He traveled down the steps, making certain the domestics

were prepared to accommodate his imminent departure. When they reached London, he promised himself, he would notify the Home Office of her presence. He would see her commended to…

Holy hell.

He had forgotten to bind her wrists. He had been too caught up in thoughts of lifting the banshee's skirts and plowing into her. Leo spun on his heel and raced back in the direction from which he had just come, taking the steps two at a time. He reached the door and inserted his key into the lock. Misgiving churned inside him, for he wore no pistol, and neither did he have time to retrieve one.

Leo threw open the door, preparing for an attack.

Instead, he found her precisely where he had left her, back against the wall, bodice opened, chemise tugged back into place. She sat on the floor, drab skirts pooling about her, brilliant blue eyes still glazed as they met his.

He had expected to find a sword-wielding virago, a desperate woman about to make her attempt at escape. But she was such a small figure, almost childlike, and he knew another swift rush of shame at his callous treatment of her. The door clicked closed at his back, and he went to her, his strides eating up the distance between them.

"Miss Palliser," he said, lowering to his haunches before her, feeling like a cad. She was his prisoner, for Christ's sake. What had he been thinking to take advantage of her as he had? Though he had rushed back to attend to her bonds, the sole thing on his mind now was tending to her. "I beg your forgiveness for my actions. They were unpardonable. You have my word it shall not happen again."

"You returned to apologize?" she asked, her husky voice steeped in incredulity.

Another punishing lash of self-loathing unleashed itself.

"No. I returned to bind your wrists."

"Of course." Her lips, swollen and stained a darker berry hue from his kisses, compressed. "Perhaps you would be willing to wait until I restore my dress?"

He ought to retrieve her bindings and secure her now. His training and instincts told him as much. Yet he could not seem to move from this space now that he had once more found himself within reach of her. "I shall aid you."

"I am perfectly capable." Her fingers found the buttons, beginning to slide them through their neat moorings.

"Nevertheless, I am responsible." He began at the top, his touch grazing her throat as he started his work, and damn him if the mere glancing connection did not make him burn. What was it about this woman that he could not resist?

"You are responsible for a great deal worse." She gripped his hands, staying his motions. "I shall do this myself, Duke, if you please."

"I have apologized for my actions," he said stiffly. "You need not fear it shall happen again."

"You will not shoot and then ravish me a second time?" Her tone was arch.

He winced at her acid tongue. "I did not force you." He had not imagined her wild response, her wetness, or the power of her release.

"No." Her gaze lowered to her hands, which still held his. "You did not."

"Are you another man's wife, Miss Palliser?" He had not intended to ask the question, for it emerged from his own personal need rather than from the threads of his investigation he was attempting to tie together.

"If I say that I am?" Her eyes met his once more.

"It will change nothing." But even as he made the statement, he knew it for a lie.

"I am no man's wife." Her thumb stroked the top of his hand.

His cock twitched. He gritted his teeth, reminded himself why he was here. Who she was. Who they were to each other. It was necessity and duty, not want and desire. "Who is O'Malley?"

Her thumb continued its slow torture. "What do you know of him?"

Her interest was palpable. It occurred to him that she could still be lying to serve her own interests. Lord knew she had done it on every occasion they had spoken thus far. "I know he is one of the men responsible for plotting the attack on the Duke of Burghly," he bit out. "I know he is in prison awaiting his reckoning. What do you know of him, *Miss Palliser?*"

She pushed his hands away as if they were fashioned of flame and she feared her dress would catch fire. "I know that he is innocent of the charges against him. Cullen would not murder a bee. He has a good heart."

In her devotion to her cause, she forgot to tame her speech into the proper English elocution, and her brogue softened her speech. She spoke with the fiery passion of someone who loved him.

O'Malley… O'Malley… O'Malley…

Why was the surname so familiar, as if he had dreamt it before?

He stared at her, another forgotten name returning to him. It had been a year or more since he had last heard it.

"Bridget," he said suddenly, the name leaving his lips before he could contain it.

She blanched, confirming his suspicions.

She was not Jane Palliser. She was Bridget O'Malley, sometime shop girl, half sister to the Duchess of Trent, suspected Fenian sympathizer. Though she had caught the attention of his men a year before, she had disappeared, all evidence of her and her involvement in the Fenian cause both, had gone dormant.

What an interesting development, and now he knew who she was, he would have his answers from her. All of them. A smile stretched his lips, and he still tasted her on his tongue, mingling with the sweet tang of victory. "Miss Bridget O'Malley, we meet at last."

Chapter Nine

BRIDGET HAD TRADED one gilded prison for another.

She stood at a window in the chamber she had been given at the Duke of Carlisle's townhome and stared down into the bustling Belgravia street. It was a familiar pose. She had spent the weeks since her arrival at Harlton Hall observing the world beyond her window pane in one form or another, hopelessly trapped as any bird in a cage. And though she had vowed she would not sing, in the end, she had not needed to.

Carlisle had uncovered her identity on his own, connecting the trail of crumbs she had unwittingly left him. She had been so shocked from their encounter and his unexpected softness upon his return to her that when he had spoken her name aloud, she had given herself away. The duke was no fool. He was as wily as a fox. Though she had attempted to convince him he was wrong, the damage had been done.

He knew she was Bridget O'Malley. Half sister to Cullen O'Malley. Knew she was intertwined with the branch of the Fenians led by John that had been responsible for the Duke of Burghly's murder in Dublin.

She, on the other hand, still knew nothing of what Carlisle planned to do with her or why he continued to keep her his prisoner instead of delivering her to jail. During their journey to London, they had traveled in icy silence, her wrists once more bound. When they had arrived at his palatial residence, he had cut her bonds with a grim air.

Do not do anything rash, Miss O'Malley. You will not like the consequences.

Even now, a day later, his dark warning sent a chill over her. Here she was, trapped as neatly as a fly in the spider's web. About to become his dinner. Never mind the chamber in which he had installed her was the largest, most beautiful room she had ever laid eyes on, the sort of room she had not imagined existed. The bed and linens seemed dearer than gold, and everything smelled sweet and rich. The drapes were thick, the carpet plush, the pictures on the walls breathtaking. Whoever had decorated this room, from its polished, ornately carved headboard, writing table, and wardrobe, to its adjoining bathing chamber fitted with running water and a massive tub, had spared no expense.

One word summed it all: *álainn.* Beautiful.

Bridget wished she could say she was not impressed, but it would be a lie. She did, however, know a deep and abiding guilt at her surroundings when Cullen was clapped in gaol, enduring Lord knew what manner of conditions.

A gentle knock sounded on the door then, shaking her from her reverie. The duke never knocked, which meant she had a different guest altogether.

"Enter," she called, as if she were required to give permission as a prisoner, which she knew she was not.

The sound of a key being fitted into the lock reached her, one more reminder she was at the mercy of the Duke of Carlisle, a man who—if John was to be believed—possessed none. But the person on the other side of the door when it opened was the furthest one could reasonably get from the duke. A petite, golden-haired beauty came barreling over the threshold in a magnificent violet silk gown. Her face and her midsection appeared fuller than the last time Bridget had seen her.

Her American half sister, Daisy.

"Bridget!" Daisy's arms opened.

And though Bridget had never been the sort for shows of affection, having received so little of it herself all her life, she found herself in need of an embrace. She met Daisy halfway across the chamber, returning her embrace as best she could with her healing wound. It had been a year or more since they had last crossed paths in London, and that meeting had not been a pleasant one.

Daisy had come to inform her of her imminent wedding to the Duke of Trent. Bridget had panicked. She had returned to Ireland, only to regret her decision. For all too soon, Cullen had become implicated in the plots against the Chief Secretary for Ireland.

Much had happened to both Daisy and Bridget, it seemed, in that time. The reason for her sister's rounder cheeks and midsection made itself known to her as a full belly bumped against hers.

"Daisy." She jerked back, searching Daisy's gaze. "You are having a babe?"

Her sister smiled, tears glistening in her eyes. "Yes, and I will soon be as large as a milk cow. But that is neither here nor there. What does matter is you, Bridget. Where have you been? I was so very worried about you."

Bridget attempted a smile and failed. "I have been in Dublin and London and Oxfordshire and everywhere in between. But how did you know to find me here, and why have you come?"

"The Duke of Carlisle sent for me." Daisy's gaze scoured her face, as if hardly daring to believe she was real. "I thought it was a dream. You have no idea how hard we looked for you, how terrified I was that something ill had befallen you."

"I am sorry for worrying you," she said truthfully, shame filling her heart. Though she did not know her half sister very well, she wondered not for the first time if she had misjudged her.

Though they shared a father, they had precious little else in common. Daisy was the legitimate product of their father's marriage to an American woman, and had been raised accordingly in the home of one of the wealthiest men in America. A princess in her castle.

None of that wealth had been offered to aid Bridget, his illegitimate child. Bridget's mother had worked in a tavern, sometimes selling her body for bread, until she had found Sean O'Malley, a man who had used his fists far more than his brain or his heart. He had given Bridget his last name and more bruises than she cared to count over the years. But he had also given her Cullen, the brother she adored.

"I am *still* worried for you," Daisy said then, her tone serious. "Carlisle has been typically guarded with the information he would provide, but he was clear you have been abetting the Fenians. Tell me it isn't true, Bridget."

Bridget wanted to deny it, but she stared at her sister's big, bright eyes so like her own. And for the first time since she had last laid eyes on Cullen, she felt as if she were in the presence of someone who cared for her. Truly cared for her. Someone who cared was more rare and difficult to procure than gold.

So instead, she asked the question that had been eating her alive. "Did he say what is to become of me?"

"WHAT IS YOUR next move?"

Leo sat opposite Sebastian, the Duke of Trent, in his study.

"Hell if I know, Trent." And then he picked up the tumbler of whisky he had told himself he would not drink and drained it to the dregs in three burning gulps. With great effort, he controlled his features, keeping himself from coughing. *Damnation*, this bottle of spirits had more bite than he had recalled.

Trent had once been one of Leo's most trusted men. Until he had fallen in love with the American heiress he had been assigned to watch for Fenian connections and had withdrawn himself from service. That lady was currently on the floor above, entrusted with the keys to Miss Bridget O'Malley's chamber.

It had gone against the grain for Leo, particularly since he had at one time suspected the duchess of colluding with the Fenians herself. Her innocence had been proven, but Leo thrived on control, that which could be given and that which could be taken away. The dichotomy never failed to stir him, both in ways it should, and in ways it should not.

"You are keeping Miss O'Malley in the duchess's chamber," Trent pointed out unnecessarily, taking a slow, gentlemanly sip of his own whisky.

Yes. He was.

Was it wrong?

Yes.

Did he need to keep the troublesome banshee in a location near to him so he could monitor her?

Absolutely.

His decision had nothing to do with his inappropriate attraction to the woman. Not one single, bloody thing.

"The doors adjoining the chamber are locked." He frowned at Trent. "Where else am I to put her? In prison?"

The duke raised a brow. "There are half a dozen chambers that would be more suited. Tongues will wag, as you know."

His irritability, already heightened, exploded. "Which tongues? You and your wife are the only ones who are aware of her presence here. My domestics are accustomed to the depths of my depravity. If they do not blink at opium rooms, orgies, and nude women laid out as makeshift serving platters, they will not wonder why I have placed a strange woman in the duchess's chamber. If they do, I shall personally disabuse them of their curiosity."

"She is an unwed woman, and the sister to a duchess," Trent observed.

"She is a Fenian who masqueraded as a governess in an attempt to abduct my nephew," he returned heatedly. It was the same argument he made to himself every day, ad nauseam, when he reminded himself there was no reason for him to be attracted to her. No reason for him to want to touch or kiss her. No reason why his cock would get so goddamn rigid at the mere mentioning of her name or the thought of her.

"You said yourself the gun she used in the abduction was not loaded."

"Perhaps it was an oversight on her part," Leo said blackly. He had a cockstand. At half past ten in the morning. Whilst he was sitting in his study, facing one of his former agents. A man he considered a friend.

And it was all because he had thought about *her*.

"I think not." Trent frowned. "She went to Harlton Hall with one purpose, and her disguise was impeccable. It fooled even you. Do you truly believe she would have been too careless to load her pistol before taking the young duke?"

No, *damn it*, he did not.

And he did not like realization one bit, for it meant Bridget O'Malley had spoken the truth to him on at least one occasion, when she had said she refused to hold a loaded weapon to the head of an innocent child. It also meant he could not hold as much anger toward her as he wanted.

The anger kept the desire leashed.

As leashed as it could be, anyway, which—given the debacle of the day he had stroked her pussy until she came—was not terribly under control.

Hell, who was he fooling?

It was not under control at all. He wanted her. He also wanted to hate her. But the former was rendering the latter increasingly impossible, and here he was once more at a stalemate between control and duty, want and need.

"It makes no sense," he growled, because if he answered Trent's question truthfully, he would reveal himself and the unacceptable weakness he had for Miss Bridget O'Malley.

"Or it makes perfect sense."

He scowled. "Whose side are you on, Trent?"

"My wife's," he answered without hesitation, grinning like the fool he was. "When I left the League, I pledged my allegiance to her instead."

"Good God!" Leo was horrified. "Allegiances are to one's Crown and country, Trent. Not to one's *wife.*"

If the last word emerged like an epithet, he could not be blamed. The Duke of Trent's devotion to his duchess was unusual, irritating, and downright perplexing. Leo himself could not imagine being so consumed by a woman she overpowered his every thought, word, and deed.

Thank Christ all he felt for Bridget O'Malley was lust. Pure, unadulterated, sinful lust. Nothing else. Not one single hint of something else.

"You will understand when you have a wife of your own," Trent said, raising a brow.

"I'll not have one." His answer was succinct. Certain. He

neither wanted a wife nor imagined ever saddling himself with one. It would be an unnecessary encumbrance. A burden.

Much like Bridget O'Malley.

No. He would not think about her one more time.

Not about her mouth beneath his. Not about her nipples. Not about her cunny, how slick she had been, how perfectly she had tasted.

No, none of it. Blessedly, he was not so afflicted.

"I look forward to the day you do." Trent was smug. So smug Leo wanted to plant him a facer in that moment. "Then, I will have you repeat that sentiment and see whether or not you still regard it as true."

"Then we are fortunate indeed, because I will never wed."

The door to his study burst open in the next instant, before Trent could muster up a response. The Duchess of Trent appeared with his beautiful, raven-haired prisoner in tow.

"I know what must be done," the duchess announced to the room. "Carlisle, you must marry my sister."

WHAT IN THE name of all that was holy?

Bridget gaped at Daisy. At her *utterly mad* half sister.

What had she just said?

Surely Bridget had misheard her. For the words she thought Daisy had just uttered made no sense. They were a foreign language she did not speak.

Marry and *Carlisle* did not belong in the same sentence in relation to Bridget O'Malley. She was already at the mercy of the scoundrel far more than she would have preferred. She would sooner accept prison shackles than bind herself to her enemy.

"I'll not be marrying that banshee," Carlisle denied.

"Banshee?" Daisy demanded, sounding outraged on Bridget's behalf.

"It may be the answer," the Duke of Trent offered, the only calm voice amongst them.

"No," Bridget shouted over the din. Eyes swung to her, so she continued. "I do not even like him."

"You like me, banshee," he drawled, as arrogant as ever. His eyes glittered with frank remembrance.

And she would be lying if she said she did not instantly recall the wicked sensation of his long fingers stroking her flesh. But she was made of stern stuff, and though he knew his way beneath a lady's skirts, that did not mean he wasn't the epitome of English suppression of Ireland.

"Not in the sense a marriage requires," she parried, before she could think better of it.

His eyes blazed into hers, and she knew she had revealed far too much. She had also taunted him. Tempted him. The Duke of Carlisle was not the sort of man who would allow a challenge to go unanswered, and she supposed she ought to have learned that about him by now.

"I beg to differ, madam. Need I remind you why?"

"Carlisle," Daisy chastised, her tone aghast. "Tell me you have not compromised my sister."

That seething gaze descended upon her sister, and Bridget was glad of it. Relieved for the respite. Her heart still thumped madly, and the bothersome heat that rose within her each time she was in his presence refused to cool while he looked upon her.

"She is my prisoner," Carlisle said, rather than denying Daisy's request.

"He shot me," Bridget added.

His scrutiny returned to her, a lone brow raising to mock

her. "You were holding a pistol to my nephew's head at the time."

"The pistol was not loaded," the Duke of Trent said in a cheerful tone that almost suggested he was enjoying this.

"Bridget would never have hurt the boy," Daisy added with a confidence that could not help but touch Bridget's heart.

She had done nothing to warrant her sister's steadfast loyalty, but she could not deny it pleased her. "I would never have hurt him," she affirmed. "I was told to bring him back to London. It was what was asked of me."

Carlisle's stare was alert, intense. "Who asked it of you, Miss O'Malley? Give me a name."

"No." Daisy stepped before her, fashioning herself a living shield to momentarily block out all sight of Carlisle's determined glower. "She will tell you nothing until she is protected. I'll not allow it."

"Protected," Carlisle repeated, his tone grim. "And why should I wish to protect the woman I am about to see cast into prison for her crimes against the Crown and her efforts to incite outrages in England?"

"Because the information she possesses is worth far more to you than her imprisonment would be," Daisy responded calmly. "Bridget has been caught up in these dangerous plots through no fault of her own."

It was not entirely true, but Bridget kept that knowledge to herself. The truth was far murkier. She believed in Irish Home Rule, and she believed in forcing England to rectify the wrongs done to her homeland. But John had changed. He was not the man she once knew, and when the cause had grown more dangerous, the stakes climbing—when dynamite and death plots surfaced and her own brother had become imprisoned—it had been too late for her to extricate herself.

And now she could not, for Cullen's life depended upon her, and her alone.

"The information she possesses can be discovered by other means." The iciness of Carlisle's tone cutting through the chamber sent a shiver through Bridget.

She dared to steal a glance at him from around Daisy's protective shoulder. His gaze instantly caught hers, boring into her. His expression was rigid. Unyielding. Irate.

"She is a woman, Carlisle," the Duke of Trent objected. "You know as well as I do that none of those imprisoned thus far have been female. This is a delicate matter, and I suggest you tread with caution."

Bridget sidestepped her sister, for she would hide behind no one. Regardless of what it was, she would face her fate, head held high, without cowering. "I will be treated the same as any of my fellow countrymen. If the Duke of Carlisle wishes to imprison me, then imprison me he shall."

"No," Daisy said firmly, placing a staying hand on her arm, "he will not. After all the mayhem you created for Sebastian and I, Your Grace, aiding my sister is the least you can do to atone for your sins."

"I'll not fall on my sword by marrying a traitor," Carlisle growled. "Nor will I discuss this nonsense a moment more. I will not be marrying Miss O'Malley, and that is final."

"And just as well, for I would never marry you either," Bridget returned, stung in spite of herself by his vicious response.

It was precisely what she would have expected from him. After all, she was the enemy. She had attempted to abduct his nephew, a kind and innocent young lad, in an effort to help her brother's plight. She had lied to Carlisle at every turn, and the ring of men with whom she had become embroiled was dangerous and bloodthirsty. She was no good for anyone, including herself. But hearing Carlisle denounce her as a traitor, calling the notion of marrying her *nonsense*, hurt nonetheless.

Carlisle turned the full force of his frigid glare back upon her. "Marrying me would hardly be as horrible a fate as you would pretend, madam. You could do no better."

"That is not saying much for myself, is it?" she asked, unable to resist the jibe. "But then, I am a traitor and a criminal, am I not?"

"No, you most certainly are not." Daisy gave her arm a warning squeeze.

Bridget wondered again at her sister's game. They had discussed none of this—not one mad word of it—in the chamber earlier. She glanced back at Daisy, frowning. Daisy arched her golden brows, her expression clearly saying *trust me*. But Bridget had never completely trusted anyone. Not in the entirety of her wretched existence on this earth.

"I am afraid I must disagree with you, Carlisle," said the Duke of Trent then, drawing all attention back to him. "Marrying Miss O'Malley is in the best interest of the both of you. It will protect her in that you cannot be compelled to offer testimony against her. And it will protect you in that the Home Office will not question why you kept a prisoner in your various homes for a fortnight, rather than commending her instantly to prison."

Carlisle's nostrils flared, the only outward sign of his fury. "Trent, I called you here as a courtesy. Not so you could meddle in my affairs."

But the handsome Duke of Trent was unrelenting, and Bridget had to admit she was rather beginning to like Daisy's husband, Englishman or no.

"As you meddled in mine?" he asked.

"Is this your sick idea of retribution?" Carlisle's voice was grim. "I did you a favor, Trent. Look at you, a maudlin fool for your wife, so much so that you would stoop to threatening your superior in the name of abetting a traitor."

"My *former* superior." Trent appeared unmoved by the duke's angry accusation. "And no, this is not my idea of revenge, though I imagine there is a long line of poor sods who want nothing more than vengeance upon you. This is how I take care of my own. Miss O'Malley is my family now, and she is under my protection. Nor is it a threat, but rather a promise.

"You will procure a license, and you will marry her as hastily as possible, and if you do not, I will go to the Home Office with the information I have in regard to your secreting of Miss O'Malley. Arden has been hungry for your position for years, and he will have no qualms replacing you. When she is no longer in danger, you may annul the marriage as you wish. For now, our first priority is making certain she cannot be dragged off to prison by you or anyone else."

Yes, Bridget liked the Duke of Trent indeed. Except for his awfully, severely misguided notion she must marry the Duke of Carlisle, everything he had just said was lovely.

"I will not marry him," she protested again to the room at large.

Daisy took her hands, her expression softened with sympathy. "I am so sorry, Bridget dearest, but you must. It is the only way to keep you safe."

Something inside her shifted. It was not slow and meandering, not a gradual change, but fierce and sudden. It was a bolt of lightning in a summer sky. A deluge of rain pouring unexpectedly from the clouds rather than a fine mist which turned into a steady torrent.

She stared at Daisy, and the awful realization hit her.

Marrying the Duke of Carlisle could be the best—perhaps

even the *only*—way she could save Cullen. If she was cast into gaol herself, she had no chance of aiding him at all. But if she remained free, she could still see him freed as well.

For her brother, she would do anything.

Even if it meant wedding the devil himself.

Chapter Ten

$\mathscr{L}$EO HAD NEVER been less inclined to celebrate an occasion in his life. Indeed, he had been at funerals which held a more joyful air. And for all that, he may as well be attending his own for the implications of what he had just done.

The wedding breakfast consisted of ten courses, and only because Brodeur, his French chef, had lost his head upon being informed of his employer's imminent nuptials. Leo did not touch courses one through seven—all that had been served thus far—for he had no appetite.

The woman at his side, Jane Palliser-turned-Bridget O'Malley-turned-the Duchess of Carlisle, did not seem any more eager to eat. She had been wringing her hands in her lap for the past hour, and for the time before that in the carriage ride following their hasty wedding, and for the time before that as she had faced him and spoken her vows.

Her expression continued to be that of a woman who had just witnessed a death. He knew the feeling well. He had witnessed deaths, after all. Had caused them in the name of the Crown and his own self-defense. Every action he had taken in the years since he had been at the helm of the Special League had been without regret, without remorse. It had been done knowing he had no choice, that what he did was in the best interest of his queen and his country.

What he had done today had been selfish.

And stupid.

He had married Miss Bridget O'Malley, a Fenian collud-er, a liar, and God knew what else, and he had done so to save his own skin. Because Trent, a man he had previously counted a friend, had been correct. The Duke of Arden wanted the League for his own, so badly the man would leap at the chance to supplant Leo should word of his misconduct with Miss O'Malley be revealed. And the League had been everything to him for so long it was like a part of him, as inseparable as a limb.

He would do anything to continue leading it, including sacrificing his honor.

His own weakness where Miss O'Malley was concerned had done him a favor. His deceptions with the Home Office concerning her death had left him free to do as he wished. Even when he had returned to London to conduct his investigations, he had not revealed the reason for his inquiries. Which meant keeping his misconduct a secret would be terrifyingly easy. All he needed to ensure was the silence of the Duke of Trent, which he already had, and his brother Clay.

Leo winced at the thought and reached for his wine gob-let. It wasn't whisky, but it would do. He dreaded informing Clay of what he had done. Even now, he felt as if a dagger had been slammed between his ribs. He had betrayed his best friend to protect himself. What manner of man was he?

Another course was removed.

Words reached him, dimly at first, as if arriving from another chamber, so consumed had he been in his own burning thoughts.

"…and of course, you shall come and stay with us," the Duchess of Trent was telling Miss O'Malley.

Christ. Strike that

She was his wife now, was she not?

And despite the bile rising in his throat, he could not stay the swift surge of lust such a thought inevitably brought. His body did not know what a traitorous banshee Bridget O'Malley was, and it had plans all its own. Plans he would not deign to acknowledge.

"No," Leo bit out, slamming his wine back onto the table with so much force it sloshed onto the pristine linens.

Three sets of eyes swung to him. The Duke and Duchess of Trent had been the only others present to witness his ignominy. His mother Lily would have his hide when she learned of what he had done, and that she had not been invited. The haste—and the awful deception and nefarious choice of bride—had precluded him from extending such an invitation.

"No?" The duchess's eyes narrowed upon him, and he was once again revisited by the distinct impression the lady did not hold him in high regard. "But my sister and I have been separated for so long. Surely you can part with her for a bit to allow us to make up for our lost time."

"No," he repeated succinctly. And when the eighth course was laid before him—*les salades à la Parisienne*: a confection of lobster, vegetables, and truffles—he stabbed it viciously with his fork despite never having truly developed a taste for lobster.

"Your Grace," the duchess persisted, "surely you can see reason. Sisters ought not to be without each other for as long as we have."

The lobster in his mouth was cold, oily, and tasted of the murk of the sea. He swallowed it whole to remove it from his tongue. "She will remain here with me," he said tightly. And then he found his wine goblet, gulping the remainder of it down.

"But I am sure you would be more at ease with me elsewhere," said his wife.

His. Fucking. Wife.

Damn if his cock didn't twitch at the reminder.

More wine was what he required. An efficient footman dancing attendance recognized his plight and refilled his glass. "I would not, my darling. I cannot have you far from my side or my sight."

He infused his words with meaning, though he spared all of them from further elaboration on account of the servants at hand. To his household, this was a real marriage. Miss O'Malley—*Christ, the duchess*—had received her official introduction to the staff. If anyone had wondered why she had already been installed in the duchess's chamber under lock and key for the last few days, they were wise enough not to question it.

Indeed, the domestics at Blayton House were accustomed to his eccentricities, and they were well paid to turn a blind eye to his myriad indiscretions. Wild parties, drunken revelers, any manner of depravity—nothing surprised them. To the public, he was a careless rakehell, a notorious voluptuary with a wicked reputation. It was how he hid so well behind what he truly did working for the League.

"I suppose that is settled then," said his wife with a notably tart inflection in her lilting voice. "I am to remain here as His Grace's prisoner."

Devil take the woman.

She possessed an instinctive knack for pushing him to the very brink. For taunting and tempting and running him ragged. He had never met another female like her.

Leo stabbed at his salad once more, taking care to choose a vegetable this time. "How fanciful an imagination you do have, wife. Such a wit."

Her brilliant blue gaze narrowed on him. "No more a wit

than you, *husband.*"

"I never thought to see the day, Carlisle," Trent said then, choosing that moment to gloat. His grin could not be hidden. The bastard was enjoying this.

"I hope you know what you have unleashed," he said, raising his glass in a mock toast. "For it will all fall upon your shoulders."

It was true he had orchestrated the marriage between Trent and his duchess during the course of an investigation into her Fenian connections. As it had turned out, the true villain had been the duchess's father and not her at all, but in the end, Trent had already fallen in love with his duchess, and nothing else had mattered.

Leo had no doubt he would not prove so fortunate. Where the Duchess of Trent had been proven innocent, Bridget O'Malley had already been proven guilty. He had ample proof of her Fenian ties. No realm existed in which he could forgive her for those sins.

Trent raised his own glass. "I have broad shoulders, Carlisle."

"You will need them," he gritted.

You will also need a goddamn phalanx of soldiers guarding you, he promised inwardly, *for vengeance will be mine.*

This egregious interference and betrayal would not go unpunished.

By that point, the wedding breakfast had become as volatile as a Fenian bomb itself. At any moment, it would explode, sending shrapnel tearing into everyone in attendance.

He signaled to his butler. "I do believe we have enjoyed enough of this course, and we may proceed to the next."

His butler appeared aggrieved for a brief moment, until he schooled his features into their familiar, expressionless mask. "Yes, of course, Your Grace."

The servants scurried into action, removed the course. Silence descended, heavy as a boulder, punctuated only by the sounds of the domestics at work. The slight clink of cutlery, the clean sweep of china from the table dressings. The door closing behind the last of the servants, leaving the company of four alone once more as the next course was fetched.

The Duchess of Trent scowled at him. "If you think to abuse my sister, you had best think again, Carlisle. You are meant to be protecting her. The only place for her to be is with me. I shall vouch for her and look after her."

"You forced me to marry her, and now she is mine," he said, hating how much he liked the pronouncement. Loathing the effect those words had upon him. The vile creature dwelling within him enjoyed having Bridget O'Malley at his mercy.

He wanted her there forever, at his side. In his bed. His willing captive.

But those were fantasies, and his duties were firmly grounded in reality. In truth, he needed her. He needed her words, her admissions, the names she would provide. Any information she could give, and he could not lose sight of that important fact.

"Carlisle," cautioned Trent. "Surely there is no need to upset the ladies on a day meant for celebration. What would the harm be in allowing her to stay with us? You made it clear you do not want a wife."

"I need to interrogate her," he reminded the duke. "Or have you so swiftly forgotten her information was a part of this bargain with the devil?"

"I have not," Trent acknowledged, solemn and cool. "I will have your promise you will treat her with the deference she deserves. She will answer your questions, but you must be a gentleman."

Leo flashed him an evil smile. "I am always a gentleman."

He felt Miss O'Malley's eyes on him. *Christ.* He could not continue to think of her as Miss O'Malley, for if he slipped and referred to her thusly to the domestics, questions would abound. More importantly, he did not want the connection of her surname with her brother's, incarcerated in Dublin as a Fenian sympathizer.

He considered this marriage one more extension of supporting his cause. Lord knew he had played a great many roles already in his work for the Crown. What was one more?

"I will remain here as the duke wishes," said his wife then, her smile forced.

He was seated near enough to her to feel the tension radiating from her, and he suspected it matched his own. She had made it clear she did not wish this union any more than he did.

Before anyone could speak, the ninth course arrived.

BRIDGET WASN'T PREPARED for the knock at her chamber door.

When it sounded less than a quarter hour after she had returned there following the interminable wedding breakfast, she nearly let out a squeal of alarm. Any hope she maintained that it was a servant on the other side of the door died when she bid her visitor to enter and the Duke of Carlisle stepped over the threshold.

Today, unlike most other days she had been in his presence, he wore his ducal authority as regal as any prince. He was dressed in the same elegant black coat, waistcoat, and trousers he had worn to their wedding ceremony, the stark white shirt beneath setting off his dark hair and eyes to perfection.

She found herself wishing he was less handsome. That his features were harsher, his nose longer, his chin weaker. Anything to lessen the unwanted effect he had upon her. How difficult it was to see him now with that equally unwelcome word springing into her mind like the report of a pistol.

Husband.

Dear God, she had bound herself to this man.

As he stalked toward her, his expression as formidable and unreadable as ever, she took an instinctive step in retreat.

Certainly, he was not expecting to consummate their union, was he?

Their marriage would be ended as soon as it was feasible to procure an annulment. He had promised.

He stopped short of her, a mocking smile quirking his well-molded lips. "You need not fear I have come to exercise my husbandly rights, banshee. I have merely come here to have a frank discussion with you regarding the nature of this union. And do cease wringing your bloody hands, or I shall have to bind your wrists once more."

She clasped her hands at her waist. "I was not wringing my hands."

"You have been at it all day, madam."

Perhaps she had, unwittingly. She was not ordinarily so easily worried or vexed. But then, neither was she ordinarily forced to marry her enemy. And she must not forget nemesis was what the Duke of Carlisle was to her, regardless of any other title he wore, and despite the vows she had spoken that morning. She did not dare trust him.

"Forgive me if it would seem I have reason for my disquiet."

His lips flattened. "If anyone ought to be experiencing disquiet, it is the man who has just somehow shackled himself to a lying, manipulative Fenian conspirator who attempted to abduct his own nephew."

She suppressed a flinch at the viciousness of his words. "I am not a monster, Your Grace."

"You are far too beautiful to be a monster, my dear." His smile faded, and the smoldering quality of his gaze intensified. "More like a siren, luring men to their demise."

Was it possible the almighty Duke of Carlisle feared her? That he feared how much he wanted her? Or did he refer to her connection to the ring of plotters responsible for the death of the Duke of Burghly?

In truth, she hated what they had done. Their violence had been despicable. Cowardly.

But she would not think of that now.

"I never lured you or any other man," she denied softly.

"It matters not. What does matter, however, is the information you can provide me." His unyielding tone was a bitter reminder of why he had married her. Likewise, why she had married him.

And what she must now do.

She inhaled slowly, keeping her face as devoid of expression as possible. "What do you wish to know?"

"Who sent you to Harlton Hall?"

If she told him the truth, John would be arrested, and any chance she had of freeing Cullen would be over. If she lied, she betrayed her sister. The decision, even now, when she'd had days to consider it and weigh the good against the bad, was not an easy one. Daisy had saved her when she had not needed to, and Bridget would forever be grateful for the reprieve. But she had known Cullen since he was a babe wrapped in swaddling, red-faced and wrinkly with a crop of inky hair. She had helped their mother to raise him. She would sooner betray Daisy than see Cullen swing from the gallows.

"Who sent you to take the Duke of Burghly?" he demanded again.

"Thomas O'Shea." It was the name she had devised, the one she had practiced in the three days she spent waiting for her dreaded nuptials.

She knew no one by that name, but the time it would take for Carlisle and his men to investigate would be all the time she required to escape him. It was Cullen's only chance.

"Look me in the eye when you speak," Carlisle demanded roughly.

Drat.

She had not realized her gaze had strayed. It snapped back to him now with unerring precision, and she wondered what he saw when he looked upon her.

"What else would you like to know, Duke?"

"Why you are lying to me again." His voice was guttural, his stare intense.

That had not been the request she had envisioned.

Her heart thumped. Her hands, still laced together at her waist, went damp. But she refused to look away, bracing herself.

This is what you must do, Bridget. For Cullen's sake.

"I am not lying."

He gave her a grim smile. "Did you know, darling wife, when someone tells a lie, there is a sign? A symptom, if you will, of the disease of their dishonesty. I've studied you long enough to know yours. Do you know what it is?"

"I told you the truth," she insisted.

"Ah, and there it is again." He cocked his head, studying her as if she both fascinated and repelled him simultaneously. "Very well. Since you don't wish to play my game, I shall tell you what it is. When you lie, your pretty little nostrils flare."

She swallowed hard, wondering if this was a test, or if he was truly that talented at uncovering a deception. Either way, her only choice was to stay the course. "The man told me his name was Thomas O'Shea," she repeated.

"I am certain he did." His tone made it plain he did not believe a word she said. "What was this Mr. O'Shea's address?"

"He did not give it." That much was true.

Carlisle said nothing, his inscrutable gaze plumbing hers for so long, she felt as if they were engaged in a duel. "Where were you to take the boy?"

"London." This too was accurate.

"Where in London?"

"I do not know." A lie.

"Your nostrils, my dear." He sneered. "Perhaps I shall have to gain the information I need from you in a different fashion. Is that what you would have me do, Miss O'Malley?"

"Have you forgotten I am the Duchess of Carlisle now?" she asked, unable to resist needling him even though she knew quite well how foolhardy it would be to prod the angry lion within his own cage.

"In name only." He came closer. "Perhaps I should rectify that."

"I would never stoop so low." The taunt, more reckless than the first, fled her lips before she could stop it.

A sinful smile curved his mouth. "I can prove you wrong with ease, *wife*."

"You say it as though it is an epithet," she pointed out, irritatingly breathless at his proximity.

What ailed her?

She was Bridget O'Malley, fierce and strong. He was the Duke of Carlisle, and they fought on different sides of the same war.

She did not want him. Could not afford to desire him.

Yet, she could not deny the thrum of her pulse, the flood of heat between her thighs, the pulsing ache in her core. The need for more of the sweet release he had given her. Her body was the true traitor, it would seem.

"You *are* a curse to me, banshee," he said bitterly, but then his touch was upon her, and it was just the opposite. His long fingers stroked her jaw with slow and tender deliberation.

The decadent scent of him enshrouded her. His eyes shone like jet beads as they fell to her lips. She ran her tongue over them, recalling the ferocity of his mouth on hers. His kisses had been as intense and beautiful as the man himself.

"You are equally my curse," she returned.

Complete truth.

"Not dissembling this time, my dear?" His smile turned wolfish. "How intriguing."

Her cheeks prickled with embarrassed heat.

How could this man read her so well? Was she so affected by him she had lost her ability to gird herself?

The pad of his thumb brushed over her lower lip then, and she could not stop her reaction. She inhaled swiftly, swaying toward him against her will. One step forward, and her skirts were crushed between them, her hands no longer laced together, but on his chest. She did not even mind the twinge of pain in her healing arm as she moved, for he was solid, muscled heat, and she was helpless to do anything but absorb him.

One of them moved. Perhaps it was him. Perhaps it was her.

She could not be certain, and her mind could not be bothered to decide, for the Duke of Carlisle had sealed his lips over hers. She forgot why she should extricate herself and run in the opposite direction. Some faint voice of alarm within her cautioned this too could be a tactic. A means to seduce her and make her vulnerable to him, to lower her guard so he could gain the answers he wanted.

But she told the faint voice to go to the devil, because the Duke of Carlisle had not kissed her in days, and now that she had his lips, she was going to revel in them. She kissed him back, ravenous. Enemies they may be, but here was the one manner in which they came together in utter perfection.

He nipped her lip. She bit him back. His hands were in her hair, undoing every intricately woven strand of her braid, each loop and pin wrought by the lady's maid she had been given that morning to prepare herself for her wedding day. She shoved at his coat, sending it to the floor. Her fingers found the cold buttons of his waistcoat, and these too she undid while running her tongue against his.

She had no notion of what she was doing. All she did know was she could not stop. Did not want to stop. The waistcoat fell, and she felt the kiss of cool air at her back as her bodice gaped. He dragged his lips to her ear, down her throat. One by one, her buttons opened. Her bodice inched lower and lower. It was only when she shifted to aid him in removing her arms from the sleeves of her gown that a reminder tore through her.

Pain, radiating from the place where he had shot her.

She cried out, stiffening.

Recalling.

His mouth was on her throat, hot as a brand, but he had stilled. "Where in London?" he asked again. His fingers brushed over the skin he had bared between her shoulder blades, playing over her spine.

She shivered, wrenched herself away from him before she succumbed to any further folly, and forced herself to look him in the eye once more. "I do not know."

His lips were darkened from the effects of their bruising kisses, and Lord have mercy on her, but she liked the evidence of their frenzied connection. "Shame on you, Duchess. You give yourself away again."

Duchess.

Lord have mercy on her all over again, for she also liked the sound of that title on his tongue. The realization threw her. She was not meant to enjoy his kisses or his touch. She certainly was not meant to grow accustomed to the notion of being his wife. Or to be tempted to share his bed.

And then something else occurred to her. Perhaps he had only kissed her to gain the answers he wanted. "Do not dare to kiss me again," she told him coolly. "Ours is not a true marriage, and you have no right to take liberties."

"Your recollection of which one of us is the aggressor continues to be misguided."

Had she kissed him first once more?

Mortification sent a fresh wave of heat to her cheeks, but she refused to acknowledge it. "I think not, Your Grace."

A smile teased his lips. "There is the flare once more."

She glared at him. "Take your flare to the devil."

"But if I do, I must bring you with me. Would you care to begin again, banshee? Where in London were you meant to take the lad, and what was the name of the man who assigned you the villainous task of abducting an innocent child?"

"I already told you his name was Thomas O'Shea. I was meant to meet him at the rail station with the boy, and he was going to gather him from there." Half lie, half truth.

Carlisle rubbed his hand over his jaw, watching her intently. "Damn you, Bridget O'Malley, I will have the answers I require from you, or you will suffer for it. Until you answer me truthfully, you will remain locked within this chamber. You will only leave when I come to collect you. If you attempt to escape or cozen a servant into allowing you egress, I will not hesitate to deliver your troublesome hide to prison, where I should have taken you immediately upon our return to London. Is that understood?"

"Perfectly." She was to remain his prisoner, and it did not surprise her. She would use her time alone to study the weaknesses of those around her. She had, by her best guess, little more than a fortnight until Cullen was tried. The newspapers she had last read had been clear in the timeline of the trials of the conspirators. She had already lost far too many weeks in her failed attempt at absconding with the young Duke of Burghly.

"Excellent. I have important matters requiring my attention. I shall leave you alone to reflect upon the wisdom of cooperating with me." He paused, giving her a sinister look. "And cooperate with me you shall, madam, or I promise you that you will not like the consequences."

Chapter Eleven

$\mathcal{T}$HE DUKE OF Carlisle had forgotten her existence.
Bridget was certain of it.

Days had passed. Precious, dwindling days. Yet, she had not seen him since the day of their ill-fated nuptials. Her last view of him had been his departing back, insufferably broad, the fine white fabric of his shirt stretched indecently taut over his shoulders. He had not even bothered to reclaim his coat and waistcoat.

She had snatched them up, folding them and hiding them neatly amongst her meager possessions. Though she was ashamed to admit it, she had withdrawn them at various interludes, stroking her fingers over the well-constructed garments. Once, she had—to her eternal chagrin—buried her nose in them for a hint of his scent.

Her meals had been delivered to her by her lady's maid, the click of the lock in the door the only heralding of an arrival. Each time, Bridget held her breath, hoping it would be him. Each time, she was disappointed.

She stared down at the London street below, watching a bevy of carriages pull up to Blayton House. Watching as a parade of lords and ladies in their evening finery flocked up the front stairs, descending upon the home like wealthy, distinguished butterflies. When the click of the lock sounded this time, she spun, prepared to pounce.

Once again, it was not the duke, but his emissary, Wilton, bearing a dinner tray and wearing her customary expression of one part pity, one part guilt. "Good evening, Your Grace."

"Good evening, Wilton," she returned the greeting with a sigh. If the woman thought it odd her employer was keeping his new duchess behind a locked door and pretending as if she did not exist, Wilton never revealed it.

She was loyal to a fault. Each occasion upon which Bridget had attempted to glean some information from the domestic, she had held her tongue and excused herself from the chamber. With every turn of the lock in the door, Bridget became increasingly convinced she would have to take action. Her chamber had no means of climbing safely to the street below, and she could not simply leap, for she was on the third floor.

There was no hope for it. She was going to have to cudgel Wilton over the head and steal her keys. She did not want to do it, especially since she had grown rather fond of the woman over the last few days. She dressed Bridget's hair beautifully, and she always brought her extra hothouse pineapples for breakfast. But it was either leave Wilton untouched on account of the pineapples, or escape, and Bridget knew what her answer must be.

"What has Monsieur Brodeur prepared for dinner this evening?" she asked, her stomach growling at the rich scents wafting to her from the delicacies prepared by Carlisle's talented French chef. She had never eaten so well in her life, and she had no doubt she never would again.

"*Filets de Boeuf Piqué à la Talleyrand.* Cocoa tartelettes for dessert with *fraises.*"

Bridget wandered closer to the delectable food. Her stomach approved, but first, she required some answers. "Tell me, Wilton, what manner of event is happening this evening?"

Wilton averted her gaze, occupying herself by fussing with a serviette. "One of His Grace's fêtes, I am afraid. We did think they may end, but…"

She trailed off, apparently realizing she had said too much.

Bridget frowned. The Duke of Carlisle did not seem a man given to hosting balls or soirées. And that was the precise moment she noticed Wilton had neglected to replace her key upon the ring at her waist and instead had left it atop the table, calling to Bridget like an abandoned cache of diamonds to a thief.

Perhaps if she was clever enough, she would not need to bludgeon poor Wilton after all. She edged closer to the key and offered the domestic some distraction. "What manner of fête is it? His Grace neglected to mention it to me."

Wilton's lips thinned, her countenance going pale. "I am certain it is not in my place to say."

Bridget was within reach of the key now. "Perhaps you might tell me anyway. There does seem a rather large number of guests arriving."

"It is not…" Wilton's words trailed away and she turned her attention back to the idle straightening of Bridget's plate and utensils.

As she fussed, Bridget slowly covered the key with her hand. "What is it, Wilton? Why do you seem so troubled?"

"No reason at all, Your Grace." In her agitation, Wilton folded the serviette, then unfolded it.

Bridget palmed the key and slid it down her sleeve. Here was her chance. "I do believe I shall have a bath before sitting down to my dinner, Wilton."

Wilton turned back to her with a pensive frown, and for a moment Bridget feared she had been caught. "As you wish, Your Grace."

Bridget waited until the elder woman was out of sight in the bathroom. Waited for the familiar creak of the pipes as hot water was called for. Heard the splash of water in the tub. And then she grabbed her skirts in one hand and raced to the door as quickly as she could. By the time she reached the hall and spun around to close the door, Wilton was rounding the corner. When she saw Bridget, her eyes went wide.

"Your Grace, you cannot—"

With nary a hint of guilt, Bridget snapped the portal shut, withdrew the key, and locked it. After all, Wilton had been acting as her jailer, and at least she hadn't had to suffer an aching head this way.

Smiling, Bridget made use of the décolletage of her gown by tugging at the ribbon trim and dropping the key down her chemise. The cool metal landed between her breasts, trapped by the tightness of her corset and unable to move. Her time was running thin. She had no doubt Wilton would make excessive use of the bell pull until someone came to her aid. Which meant if she wanted her freedom to last, she was going to have to make herself disappear.

LEO STOOD ON the periphery of the libidinous gathering he held every week without fail, a whisky he had not bothered to taste in hand. He had spent the last three days living on coffee and the briefings he received from his agents and the men he had planted in the Fenian ranks in England and abroad, trying to make sense of the mystery that was Bridget O'Malley.

His wife.

There was the mocking reminder, never far from his thoughts.

He had married the woman.

But unraveling her secrets was proving as futile as the night was dark.

He shifted, thinking better of leaving his whisky untouched, for his head was thumping, and his skin felt as if it were on fire. The pressure behind his eyes threatened to explode. Even his throat was raw and sore. He gulped down the whisky, stifling a wince at its bite. The room around him seemed to swirl for a moment, until he forced himself to concentrate.

Sleep. He needed it. Ordinarily, when his moods struck him, they did not last more than a day, perhaps two. But there was no time to sleep, and waiting for him on the other side of the door connecting his chamber to hers, lay the woman who had consumed him from the moment he had first seen the inky cloud of her hair and the snapping fire of her eyes.

Ever since he had tasted her lips.

And her cunny. Though not in the way he would like.

Perhaps his true problem was he needed to bed someone. Anyone. Anyone but her. He cast his glance about the chamber, watching his guests laughing, talking, and disappearing into chambers. Music played faintly over the din, but no one came to Blayton House to dance the cursed minuet. They came here for sin.

Leo had not joined in the depravity since he had gone to Harlton Hall—since he had kissed the banshee—and what better night to reclaim his wicked streak? If only his face was not so hot, his body not so aching. He was tired, but despite his need of a warm bed and half a day's worth of rest to restore himself to an ordinary state, the cockstand in his trousers would not be relieved.

And he had tried.

Thrice daily.

To his shame, he could not spend without thinking of

sinking his prick into either her sweet cunny or her pink mouth. Especially her mouth. Releasing his seed down her throat and watching her swallow.

Ah, fuck.

This was not good.

He tipped back his glass of whisky once more to find he had already drained the contents. A lone drop landed on his tongue, a symbol of the futility of his attempts at escapism, it would seem.

The sea of lords and ladies and scoundrels and mistresses shifted. For a moment, his eyes lit upon a familiar figure. Golden hair, swept into a knot, curls framing the sweet, angelic face. Recognition gripped his gut.

Eyes he had gazed into many times before met his.

Jane was here.

His Jane.

No. Ashelford's Jane. For she had never been Leo's, re-gardless of how much he had once loved her, and she had proven so with her defection. She was the Duchess of Ashelford now, walking toward him with contrition making her beautiful face solemn.

Christ, she was just as beautiful as she had always been. But what the devil was she doing here, at one of his notorious fêtes?

She was happily in love with her husband. And Leo had begun these sordid parties initially because of her, but later, as a means of concealing the true nature of his covert work with the League. Appearing the dissolute rakehell tended to keep one from being suspected of running the most elite, clandes-tine group of men in England.

He was burning up now. His skin prickling with goose-flesh. Part of him was hot as the flames of hell, and part of him was beginning to take chill. He gritted his teeth, looked away from her, and motioned for a servant to refill his whisky. He needed more. If Jane intended to speak to him—if she had dared to enter his territory in such fashion—he needed to numb himself.

And then she stood before him, ethereal in an evening dress of pink silk, smelling of rose petals, just as she always had. "Leo."

"Your Grace," he bit out, reminding her they were no longer betrothed. No longer on familiar terms.

Hell, he was not well enough for this unexpected meeting, whatever it was, between them.

"I hope you do not mind my trespass," she said softly.

For a moment, he did not know if she referred to the fact she had been carrying the Duke of Ashelford's child whilst promised to him, or if she referred to her presence at Blayton House this evening.

"Of course I mind," he told her unkindly, for as far as he was concerned, he owed her no benevolence at all. She had betrayed him with another and thrown him over, and all these years later, he still had not forgotten what she had done to him. Though he had moved forward, his anger and hurt had not entirely dissipated. Perhaps they never would. "What the hell are you doing here?"

She flinched as if he had struck her. "I arrived with Lady Edgemont. I had hoped to speak with you."

The Countess of Edgemont was as lusty as they came. She had six children by, it was rumored, six different lovers, and she was a regular in attendance at Blayton House. He had not realized Jane was now running with such a fast crowd, and he had to admit the knowledge gave him pause.

Still, he was so tired his eyeballs ached, and he was so spent the room seemed to be swaying about him. Refusing to cancel the evening's festivities had been a grave mistake, and he was beginning to see that now.

"We have nothing more to say to each other," he told her icily, his voice hoarse from the pain in his throat.

What was the matter with him?

He had grown accustomed to his dark moods. They had been a part of him for as long as he could remember. As were the nights without sleep. It was what made him so good at leading the League. He could throw himself into the work, and it gave him purpose. Meaning. When he could not sleep, he pored over documents, information, intercepted communications, anything he could get his hands on. But this, the feverish burn of his skin, the ache in his head, the pounding inside his skull...*Jane*...were complications he did not need. Did not want.

"I am sorry, Leo."

Her gentle contrition nettled him. The chamber about them swirled like the pictures he had seen from France, splotches of color, dreamy swirls that somehow turned flecks of pigment into hushed landscapes and portraits. He had imagined this moment since she had thrown him over for Ashelford. He had fancied her abject repentance would move him.

But it did not.

"I am not sorry," he returned truthfully. She had shown him who she truly was that day.

Nothing she could do or say all these years later would induce him to ever trust or care for her again. That particular ship had long since sailed, been attacked by a hurricane in the Atlantic, and dragged down to the depths of the sea, never to be seen again.

Strange. Perhaps he was finally freed of Jane's ghost. Freed as she stood before him. But he was not freed of the confounded illness. The servant had replenished his whisky, and he poured it down his gullet now. Not because he could not face Jane, but because he wanted to stay the throbbing in his skull and drown out the heat threatening to consume him.

It did none of those things.

Instead, it heightened his exhaustion. He was a man who had driven himself beyond his earthly limits, and he knew it. Three days without sleep—or perhaps even four, he could no longer be certain, for after a time they all cobbled together into one loop of infinity—was too many.

"Please, Leo." Jane placed a hand on his arm. She moved nearer. So did the scent of roses.

Instead of finding familiarity and comfort in it, he felt ill. His gut clenched. He wanted to extricate himself from her, to walk away, but his body had turned into an anchor. It was heavy. *He* was heavy. And tired. And burning.

Suddenly, in the crowd, as if conjured by his wildest imaginings, appeared one ethereally beautiful face framed by black hair. A pale face with a slight, retroussé nose, a lush pink mouth, bright eyes and thick, long lashes. Her beauty robbed him of breath, hit him in the chest like a blow. Though Jane still stood directly before him, he stared past her, meeting the gaze of the banshee he had wed.

Surely her appearance was a result of the illness that seemed to be assaulting him. For there was no way she could be here, in this chamber, her eyes filled with daunting Irish fury.

"Leo?"

He wanted to remind the Duchess of bloody Ashelford she could not call him by his Christian name. But his mouth did not function, and his tongue seemed dead. He swayed. A grip of tremors assaulted him. Cold through the heat. Such an odd sensation: though his skin was on fire, his body felt as if it had been encased in an ice block. And with his head pounding, his eyes burning, body tired and drained from all the nights he had spent in his study, drinking coffee and poring over documents...

The room swirled. Voices seemed to echo in his head. Bridget was approaching, moving closer in a swirl of angry skirts.

How?

There was Jane again, blinking, beautiful. "Leo?"

Two of her.

Damnation, he was seeing double now. It was what happened only when he reached his limit. When his body had become so drained there was nothing left remaining to give. This had happened before. He could handle it. He could take control of himself.

"Duke?"

Oh, Christ.

There was the second face. The one that haunted him in his waking dreams. The banshee he could not resist. His midnight-haired siren, with the luscious mouth and the sparkling eyes standing before him. Only this time, the eyes shimmered with anger. With malice.

What in the hell was she doing down here? How had she escaped, and what manner of mayhem did she intend to inflict?

He was sure he ought to be concerned enough to collect her and return her to her chamber, but the whisky and the fever—which he was now certain he possessed—had imbued him with an eerie sense of calm.

"Jane," he said, gesturing, "allow me to introduce you to Her Grace, the Duchess of Carlisle. Darling, this is the Duchess of Ashelford, an old friend."

Bridget O'Malley's eyes widened, searching his.

She was his wife, he reminded himself.

He ought to stop thinking of her as anything else. Another shiver shuddered through his body. Cold. He was so bloody frigid now.

But how did that make sense when his skin remained on fire?

Hot and burning. His body heavy. So heavy. Heavy as his eyes, weighed down by all the nights he had eschewed sleep in favor of combating his dark mood.

"Carlisle?" came his wife's sweet, husky voice. "Are you well?"

"No." He was not certain if he said it, but he thought he did. The chamber spun about him once more. And then he could no longer stand.

He dropped to his knees.

The room faded to black.

THE DUKE OF Carlisle was seriously ill.

Bridget knew it before the doctor had even been sent for. She knew it as she waited in the drawing room with the lovely blonde duchess who had been at his side when he had collapsed. A lovely blonde duchess she very much wanted to ask to leave. Or forcibly shove out the front door.

The revelers had disbanded in the wake of Carlisle's illness. A man passing out rather seemed to have a dampening effect even upon the truly licentious. And there was no other way to describe the men and women who had gathered at Blayton House that night. Bridget had wandered in and out of chambers, witnessing all manner of shocking acts, before she had finally found the cipher of a man she had married.

Union in name only or no, the Duke of Carlisle was her husband.

Not the interloper duchess's husband.

Even if she acted far too familiarly toward him, clutching his sleeve as he fell, weeping prettily over his slumped form, referring to him by his Christian name. Entwining her fingers lovingly through his.

In the upheaval following the moment Carlisle had fallen to the floor as if he had been shot, Bridget's first instinct had been to remain by his side. She ought to have fled as she had originally intended, until she'd caught a glimpse of him in the ballroom as she'd passed. One look, and she had known something was amiss. It was rather troubling now when she revisited it in her mind. She had fallen to her knees at his side, frantically searching for some sign he had been attacked, convinced he had been stabbed or poisoned, for no shots had been fired.

Why had she been concerned for his wellbeing? Why had she not escaped when she'd had her chance?

With Carlisle passed out, Wilton locked in her chamber, and a crowded ballroom of drunken revelers, her disappearance would have gone unnoticed long enough for her to have escaped.

And yet, her only thoughts had been for him.

Now, seated in the sitting room adjoining the ducal apartments awaiting word from the physician, Bridget frowned at the duchess as much as she frowned at herself. It was far easier, however, to inflict her displeasure upon the other woman, who was wan and golden and infallibly beautiful, like a Venus come to life.

Bridget did not like the woman. Not one bit. "You may go, Your Grace. I shall tend to my husband from this moment forward."

The duchess's lips pinched. "I was not aware Leo had married."

There it was again. *Leo.*

It occurred to Bridget she had never referred to Carlisle in such intimate terms. His given name was Leopold. She had not known he preferred a sobriquet. Had certainly never wrapped her tongue around it.

But apparently, this woman had. An insidious voice inside Bridget wondered just what else of Carlisle's the duchess had wrapped her tongue around. A sour bolt of something she refused to believe was jealousy hit her. Ruthlessly, she tamped it down.

"And why are you a person who ought to receive the announcement?" she asked, not caring if she was rude. The woman was intruding, and Bridget did not like the notion Carlisle had once been on intimate terms with her.

"We are old acquaintances," the duchess said quietly. "I care for Leo very much."

Bridget forgot she was not Carlisle's wife in truth in that moment. Forgot she had no claim upon him, forgot their union had not been—and never would be—consummated. All she could think about, all she could summon, was the righteous outrage that had sparked to life inside her from the moment she had seen another woman interacting so intimately with the duke.

"I care for him as well," she snapped, only to realize what nonsense she had just said in an effort to match the duchess, verbal thrust for verbal thrust.

Her union to Carlisle was in name only.

It was a marriage of convenience.

She had no right to be jealous. To want to keep him for herself.

And yet everything within her was flaming, territorial. The Duke of Carlisle, right or wrong, belonged to Bridget more than to this pallid waif.

What fire had she to offer him? What stubborn resistance? What daring?

A man like Carlisle deserved a woman who was his match.

A woman very much like herself.

Lord have mercy on her.

She was not meant to think such things.

And with the ashen pallor to Carlisle's skin, along with the ferocious fever terrorizing his body, she could not even be certain he would survive whatever ailment had seized him. To see a large, strong man felled with such ease, his body trembling and skin on fire, had been worrisome indeed.

Nay, she could not care for him. He was her enemy.

The duchess offered her a small smile, but it did not reach her chocolate-brown eyes. "I am certain you do care for him. How can you not? He is your husband, and he is a noble and honorable man."

Noble?

Yes.

Honorable?

Bridget was not so certain.

Before she could respond, the door to Carlisle's bedchamber opened, revealing His Grace's personal physician. Bridget shot to her feet and went to him, not liking the grim cast to the man's features. "How is His Grace, Dr. Cabot?"

The doctor clutched his black bag of medical instruments, looking grim. "Unwell, I am afraid. I have done what I can to make him comfortable. If this is a fever that will pass, he should improve in the next two days. However, if it is something worse, he will not."

Bridget's stomach knotted. "Something worse, Doctor?"

"Has His Grace been coughing?" he asked.

Surely he did not think Carlisle had consumption, did he?

Bridget swayed on her feet before collecting herself. "No."

He had not, had he? Not on the day they had wed, anyway. But how was she to admit before this stranger and the woman who most certainly still harbored tender feelings for Carlisle that she had not seen her own husband in days? That he had been keeping her locked in her chamber because she was not, in fact, his true wife but a prisoner?

It was a miracle the servants had not already seized her and attempted to seal her back up within the duchess's apartments.

"Excellent," the doctor said, nodding. "His lungs sound healthy, but that could change. I am concerned by the fever, Your Grace. He will require someone to attend him, bathing his brow with cool compresses, or submerging him in a cold bath if he awakens, to keep his temperature from remaining too high."

If he awakens.

Bridget did not like the sound of that. "What else must be done for him?" she asked.

"I have left some quinine, which may also help to reduce the fever and make him more comfortable, along with instructions. I have administered an initial dose, which will enable him to rest and has already lowered the fever."

Bridget swallowed down a sudden wave of fear he would not get well, brought on by past experiences. In her world, when someone took ill, help for them was rare if not impossible.

She had tended to many invalids in her life. She had nursed her mother before her death. She knew what to do. No servant would be relied upon for this task. She trusted no one better than she trusted herself. Perhaps for the Duke of Carlisle, that would be a frightening thought indeed, but though he remained her enemy in this war they fought, the need to tend him beset her.

"Thank you, Dr. Cabot."

The physician nodded. "Send for me, Your Grace, at the slightest change for the worst, should it happen."

She swallowed again at the notion of Carlisle growing more ill than he had already appeared. "Yes, of course. Thank you, Doctor."

If the servants attempted to wrest her back to her chamber and lock her within now, they would have a fight on their hands. She would blacken the eye of any man—or woman for that matter—who tried to take her from Carlisle's side. Later, perhaps, she would investigate the reason for her need to take care of him. For her reluctance to leave his side when fleeing him would be in her best interest.

Dr. Cabot took his leave, then a presence appeared at her side, unwanted and unwelcome.

How had she forgotten the duchess remained within the chamber, a trespasser? Moreover, why was the woman still here, and what was her connection to Carlisle?

"May I see him before I leave, Your Grace?" the duchess asked. "Forgive me this intrusion, but I am worried for him."

Bridget searched her gaze, torn. She could deny the woman with ease. Certainly, she ought to. "Why did you come to Blayton House this evening?" she could not resist asking.

She wanted answers. She wanted the Duke of Carlisle's secrets.

A sad smile flitted over the other woman's lips before disappearing. A shadow clouded her gaze, a glimmer of something undistinguishable.

Regret, perhaps? Longing?

"Leo and I were betrothed once. I do not suppose he told you, as it is old news indeed." The smile returned, just as sad. "In the end, I chose another over him. I thought I chose wisely, but I was wrong. You need not fear me, Your Grace. I have no designs upon your husband, being wed myself, but I did want to tell Leo how sorry I was for the hurt I caused him. I still wish to do so, even if he cannot hear me."

This ethereal beauty had once been Carlisle's fiancée.

It made horrible sense.

And she had jilted him. Had hurt him. It was knowledge Bridget could use in her favor, though the knowledge felt intrusive. One more small sin against her soul. Strangely, the notion of the powerful, omnipotent Duke of Carlisle having been in love with the delicate creature before her, only to have his heart dashed, did not give her a drop of pleasure. Instead, it filled her with bitterness.

And jealousy.

And a strange, territorial urge to refuse the woman entrance.

But who was she to deny the duchess?

Bridget was Carlisle's opponent, someone he dared not trust. Someone he reviled. She was the woman he had only married out of necessity, because the Duke of Trent had forced his hand. Because he had wanted to save his own skin.

"Very well," she allowed grudgingly.

Rather than offer the woman any obligatory words of reassurance that she was not intruding or trampling upon Bridget's good graces, she turned on her heel and led the way into Carlisle's bedchamber.

The gas lamps were turned low, but the chamber was so indicative of the man, it almost stopped her on the threshold. The carpet was rich, thick, and dark. The wall covering was gray damask, interrupted by shelves lined with books and paintings. The pictures on the wall were striking, desolate landscapes. And there, in the midst of the immense solid oak bed dominating an entire wall, lay an unusually still and helpless Duke of Carlisle.

Her heart clenched.

Her feet moved, flying over the carpet, closing the distance between them, until she was at his bedside. There he was, pale and slumbering beneath the bedclothes. A sheen of perspiration slicked his brow. His breathing seemed normal. She planted her hand upon his forehead, testing the heat of it.

Still scalding.

She ought to be celebrating her good fortune and slipping out the door, into the night. Disappearing from his life forever. And she would, if only the mere thought of leaving him did not fill her with a hollow ache she did not dare comprehend.

He needed her. She would not leave him now. She should. Her every instinct for self-preservation told her to go. To run. To hire a hack. Take a train. Flee! Be gone!

Yet, there he lay, at the mercy of whatever sickness had chosen to menace him. Just a man, after all.

Her man.

No!

Not her man, and who better to remind her of it than his spritely goddess? As if on cue, the duchess appeared on the opposite side of his bed like an apparition. It nettled Bridget to face someone who had known him for longer. Who had shared a past with him. Who had once—and perhaps still— owned his heart.

"I have never seen him ill," the duchess whispered, reaching out as if to touch him, then apparently thinking better of it and withdrawing.

"Nor have I." But then, she scarcely knew him, though he was her husband.

Her gaze roamed back over his handsome face. How different he looked in repose. How vulnerable. All the starch had fled him, all the rigidity, and she could not quite stay the accompanying pang in her heart.

"You love him," the duchess said, startling her from her reverie.

Bridget nearly swooned. She blinked. Cleared her throat. Skewered the woman with a glare. Of course she did not love the Duke of Carlisle. She did not even like the man. He was fine of face and form. He was strong. He knew how to kiss. How to bring her pleasure, much to her shame.

But he was the Duke of Carlisle.

Bridget did not love him.

She had never loved anyone other than her brother Cullen, and yes, even her sister Daisy. Reluctantly at first, it was true, but Daisy had more than proven herself to Bridget. She was loyal, trustworthy, caring. Yes, Bridget loved her family.

Not Carlisle. Never him.

She began to deny it. Opened her mouth to form the word *no*.

Her mind suddenly traveled back to Harlton Hall. Their connection there had been undeniable, intense, and instant. Her attempt to meet John's demands at the expense of Carlisle's nephew had failed.

Yet instead of sending her directly to prison, he had taken her to his home. He had tended to her himself when she had been weak. Though he could be cruel and cutting, he was also a man who had the capacity for kindness.

Perhaps that was part of the reason why she was still here at Blayton House, ensnared in her conflicting emotions, facing a ghost from Carlisle's past and the specter of his illness, all at once. That and the guilt which threatened to consume her whenever she thought of the fright she had caused the young Duke of Burghly. The need to do penance burned inside her, undeniable.

"You need not answer me," the duchess interrupted her

thoughts. "I can see it plainly on your face. I am sorry for my intrusion. Pray believe me when I say had I known Leo had married, I would never have... I had assumed, given the nature of the party... But it matters not. I merely wish him well, and I wanted him to know I am sorry. So very, very sorry for what I did to him. Will you convey that to him for me, please?"

Her dislike for the woman did not decrease after such an odd apology, half insinuation, half regret. One sentence more than all the others she had uttered combined struck Bridget like a blow.

I can see it plainly on your face.

She thought Bridget looked like a woman in love. A woman in love with the Duke of Carlisle.

How ridiculously, utterly foolish. He was her jailer, her enemy, the man who thought her despicable. The man who kissed with more passion than she had ever known possible in the mere fusing of two mouths together.

No, she must not think such errant thoughts now.

She found her voice at last. "I will most assuredly convey your apology to the duke, Your Grace."

"Thank you." The duchess's voice was brittle. So too, her expression, as if the slightest movement would fracture her. As if she took great care to keep her emotion from betraying her. "Take care of him. He is not as heartless as he would have the world believe."

Heartless was precisely what the Duke of Carlisle was. John had warned her. His reputation preceded him, and Bridget had been the recipient of his wintry gaze and biting scorn more times than she cared to count. But then she thought once more of the man she had seen at Harlton Hall, teasing his nephew, a man who loved his brother and Mrs. Ludlow very much.

"I bid you good evening, Duchess," she said, confused by the jumble of feelings within her.

The duchess swallowed. "Good evening, madam." For a moment, she extended her hand, as if to trace it lovingly over Carlisle's brow before apparently thinking better of it. Without another word, she left.

Bridget turned her full attention to Carlisle, who had begun mumbling something incoherent and thrashing about on the bed. She rang the bell pull without hesitation. Though she had no inkling of what her reception would be from the domestics, particularly those who knew she had been essentially a prisoner locked in her chamber, she had no time to spare.

The Duke of Carlisle needed her, and like it or not, she was all he had at the moment. She brushed a sweaty hank of dark hair from his forehead. He shifted again, muttering something.

"Hush now, Duke," she whispered, "I shall see you through this."

This time, one word emerged with perfect, concise clarity.

"Bridget."

Her name.

"I am here, *mo chroí*." The endearment left her without thought. Too late to call it back. It hovered in the air like a beam of sun, radiant. Illuminating. Warming.

My heart, she had called him, and the most frightening thing of all was it sounded just as it felt.

Right.

Chapter Twelve

$\mathcal{L}$EO WOKE TO late-afternoon light filtering over his bed and the soft curves of a woman pressed against his side. Lemon and bergamot teased his senses because he had been stupid enough to see that a servant procured her favorite fragrance. Slow, even breaths interrupted the silence of the chamber, accompanied by the distant din of the street below and the rhythmic ticking of a mantle clock.

Either the illness which had gripped him had sent him to hell, where he likely so richly belonged, or the foggy memories of Bridget O'Malley at his bedside and the sweet traces of her perfume in the air meant she had been tending to him. And not only had she been tending to him, but she was still in his bed, sleeping alongside him as if it were where she belonged.

It most assuredly was *not* where she belonged.

But that did not mean he didn't enjoy having her there. It also didn't mean he did not turn his head slowly to the side, all the better to bury his nose in the silken skeins of her midnight hair. *Christ*, even her hair smelled delicious.

If he had been dragged behind a runaway carriage, he could not have felt in worse condition than he did now. Even so, damn it if his cock didn't twitch to attention. He took the opportunity to study her as she slept. How innocent she seemed. As serene as an angel.

Hell.

His illness must have rotted his brain. Where was such maudlin tripe emerging from? An angel and Bridget O'Malley did not belong in the same thought. The fiery banshee was as far as one could stray from the beatific.

She had tended to him though, had she not?

As the fever claiming him had ravaged his body, his rare moments of lucidity had been marked by her presence. Her husky voice singing lilting ditties, her fine-boned hands pressing a cool cloth to his brow, her arms helping him to lift his head so he could drink water.

He recalled asking, surly as a bear, why she was in his chamber.

Her response had been simple. Baffling. *Because you need me, Duke.*

He had not needed her. He was a man who needed no one. He was the Duke of Bloody Carlisle. He did not even require sleep.

The daring of the woman. She wore her hair confined in a heavy coil of braids pinned to her crown, but a few tendrils had come free. One curled over her cheek, and he could not resist brushing it away. As he did, his touch grazed her face. Her skin was a smooth temptation beneath his fingertips. Suddenly, he found it impossible stop his tender exploration.

Over her cheekbone, down her nose, pausing at the perfect pout of her rosebud lips. Just the whisper of a touch, one swipe of his thumb, but it was enough to jostle her from her dreams. Thickly lashed eyes fluttered open, and he found himself ensnared in the brilliant gaze of the last woman in the world he could trust and the only woman in the world he wanted.

She smiled sleepily at him, and it struck him that it was the first genuine smile he had seen gracing her luscious lips.

"You're awake." Then she blinked, jolting into a seated

position. "You're awake!"

His own lips curved, but it well could have been a grimace. "Am I awake?"

Her hand went to his brow, checking to see if he was feverish. Her palm on his skin was a soothing balm and a deep ache, all at once. Suddenly, he was starving for her touch, for any point of contact between them.

"I must be dreaming," she said, her brogue in strong evidence. "Surely this cannot be the Duke of Carlisle making a sally?"

"Yes." He grinned more. Though his body was weak and weary, he was simultaneously imbued with the simmering rush of wakefulness, his body humming with gratitude to be free of the fever and in such proximity to her as well. "It can be and it is. I fear the illness rotted my mind."

"You do not feel feverish," she announced, her touch lingering as if she too was reluctant to sever the connection. The air was thick and smoldering with something. His illness and her determination to see him back to health had momentarily removed the barriers keeping them from each other.

He did not want them back, though he knew they were necessary. "I believe the fever has mercifully broken. How long was I ill?"

Gradually, the strains of reality were returning to him, intruding.

"Two days. You were very ill, Carlisle." Her smile faded. "The entire household was quite worried for you."

He noted she had said the household and not her. Why it irked him, he could not say. Or perhaps he could, but he wished not to. And then something else belatedly occurred to him, even more troubling. "Why are you not in your chamber? And how did you come to be in mine?"

"Wilton inadvertently locked herself inside my chamber."

When she said it, her nostrils gave a small, adorable flare. He instantly admonished himself for such an observation. This woman was trouble. And she was lying to him. Again.

He stared her down calmly. "You are giving yourself away once more, my dear."

"Perhaps Wilton had some assistance in locking herself in my chamber."

"Indeed." *Trouble* was far too tame a word to describe her. "But that does not explain your presence here. Why would my staff allow you to tend me on your own?"

She flushed, removing herself from his bed with stiff grace, spending an inordinate amount of time fussing with her skirts before deigning to offer a response. "You are not the easiest patient, Your Grace. You gave poor Wilton such a fright with your caterwauling, and the incident involving the broth meant the domestics were only too happy to allow me to take on the onerous burden of looking after you."

He vaguely recalled hollering and throwing a bowl of broth against the wall when he had been gripped in the throes of the fever. He had been certain someone was poisoning him. It was simply the suspicious nature of his mind, coupled with the illness. No poisoning caused the symptoms he had suffered, and he knew that now with a clear, lucid mind. He had simply taken ill, much as the knowledge aggrieved him. He preferred to think of himself as invincible, but the world occasionally liked to remind him of just how wrong he was.

"Christ," he muttered. "I did not frighten you?"

"You seemed calmest in my presence," she said.

This time, her nostrils did not flare. Not even a tiny twitch.

Damn it.

She was telling the truth.

More fragments returned to him. Her husky voice, lilting and soothing. She had spoken to him in the language of her homeland. Had soothed him, comforted him. When he had been cold, she had layered him in blankets and wrapped her warmth around him. When he had been hot, she had traced cool cloths over his heated skin, bathing him.

Why would a Fenian rebel tend to her captor with such tender dedication?

It made no more sense than the leader of the Special League assigned with eradicating Fenians marrying one and finding himself falling under her spell.

Against his will.

Very much against his will.

Not that it mattered. Either way, the burgeoning emotions he felt for her, swelling like the rising tide in his heart, were a betrayal of his duty, his family, and his men. Bridget O'Malley was not meant to be his wife. And neither was he meant to want her to remain that way.

"Thank you for your diligence," he forced himself to say, discomfort making his tone abrupt. Leo prided himself on the inability to feel a goddamn thing. But whether it was the sickness or his own bloody weakness, his cold, dead insides had been hit by a spring thaw. "You need not have done what you did."

"I know." Her gaze did not stray from his. "I wanted to do it. I have a great deal of experience tending to invalids. Consider yourself fortunate I did not bind your wrists while you slept as you did to me. Or leave you beneath the dubious care of Annie."

He deserved those barbs. "You know as well as I that you could not be trusted."

Abruptly, she turned in a swirl of skirts, moving to a table across the chamber. "What of now?" she asked, her back to him.

If only he knew the answer to that question. "Logic tells me no."

Bridget faced him and closed the distance between them, seating herself once more on his bed. She offered him water, and he had not realized how parched he had been until that very moment. "What does the rest of you say?"

His cock said it didn't give a damn whether or not he could trust her.

And his heart…his heart said yes she could be trusted. Yes he could trust her. He already had.

But he admitted none of that aloud. Instead, he accepted the water from her and gulped it down in large, greedy swallows. It occurred to him that with her back to him, her body obscuring his view of what she had been about, she could have adulterated his water somehow. The truth was, however, she could have done anything she wished to him while he had been ill, and yet, she had not. Instead, she had taken care of him until she was so exhausted she laid down at his side and fell asleep.

No woman had ever shown him such care, aside from Lily.

"Enough," she cautioned sternly, plucking the cup from his weakened grasp. "If you drink too much at once, you shall be ill, and I'll not be mopping up your mess."

His stomach clenched as if on cue, then offered up a loud, angry growl. "I think I require sustenance, if you would be so kind."

"I will see that some broth is sent up."

"Broth can go to the devil." He gave her his most ferocious frown. "I require something fortifying. Beef. Chicken. Ham. Even some bloody boiled potatoes would suffice."

The banshee actually clucked her tongue at him. "The

doctor was clear you are to have liquids only when you first wake. You need to follow his orders or risk sacrificing your health. I have already had reports from the domestics that you spend entire days without sleeping. Little wonder you took ill. Moreover, you know as well as I your French chef would never serve boiled potatoes."

Grim disbelief swept through him. The woman had been consulting his physician concerning his illness and recovery? And she had interrogated his servants about his lack of slumber? That was to say nothing of the comment concerning Monsieur Brodeur, which was utterly accurate.

He could not like this. It was as if she had settled in. Made herself at home.

It was as if she were his wife in truth rather than in name only.

"I do not want broth, madam," he bit out, aware he sounded stubborn. Perhaps even childish. Not caring a whit. He wanted something fortifying. He was already mending. He had neither the time nor the inclination to be an invalid.

Her eyes glinted as they bored into his, and he swore the wench was enjoying this moment of role reversal between them.

"You will have broth or nothing. And afterward, you shall bathe. You stink, Duke."

Here too were words he had spoken to her before. But she was also not incorrect in her assessment, and he was willing to sip broth like a consumption patient and bathe if he could have what he wanted most in return. "Very well. I shall have the broth and the bath, but I must insist upon one condition."

She raised a brow. "Name your condition."

If she wanted to truly play at a reversal of roles, he was more than willing, regardless of how much he knew he should not. He met her stare with an unflinching one of his own. "I want you to bathe me."

THE BATH IN the bathing chamber adjoining the ducal apartments had been prepared. It was warm and sweetly orange-scented, humid air clinging to her lungs as Bridget inhaled. The massive tub was empty, but that was a problem which would be remedied soon enough when she helped the duke into it.

The thought should not fill her with such trepidation, but it did. It plagued her with the repetitive tenacity of a small child asking his mother an endless barrage of questions. Cullen had been no different with her as a lad. She could still hear his little voice now.

Why is the sky blue, Bridget? What is the sky made of?

She loved her brother. Needed to help him to escape from Kilmainham by whatever means she could, and she must not forget that.

Where do clouds go when the moon is out, Bridget? Why do our feet stop growing when we get old?

"Why indeed," she grumbled to herself, her eyes stuck upon the steaming tub, knowing what it represented.

She was going to see the Duke of Carlisle.

Naked.

She was going to lay her hands upon his bare flesh. Stroke his corded shoulders and strong arms with a soap-laden cloth. Trail suds over his chest. Dip her hand beneath the slick warmth of the water. Run the cloth...elsewhere.

Another why plagued her then: why had she agreed to such madness? Why had she remained at Blayton House, tending to the Duke of Carlisle for two days, when she could have fled and been long gone from his reach?

She tried to tell herself it was in Cullen's best interest if she stayed, gleaned as much information as she could, and used her evidence as a means to bargain with John and gain her brother's freedom. But the truth of it was, Bridget had stayed on because she had wanted to.

There it was. Shameful and wicked and wrong. A betrayal of her own flesh and blood. Of everything she stood for. She could admit it to herself, own her ignominy.

"I am ready, wife."

She gave a start at the resonant voice, rumbling with heat and mystery and power, even though he was scarcely recovered from the illness he'd suffered. Bridget turned to find he had walked to the bathing chamber unassisted.

He wore a dressing gown belted loosely at his waist, a vee of beautiful chest bared to her wandering gaze. Beneath its hem, his calves were strong, his feet large, yet surprisingly elegant for a man of his immense size. He was pale, his dark hair in need of a sound washing, his jaw shadowed by the potent masculinity of his whiskers. Although he had been ill for two whole days, not even the sickness that had ravaged him could detract from his appearance.

She strove to keep her countenance an expressionless mask. "You should have called for me, Duke. I would have assisted you."

"You would have assisted me with one hand, and a sharpened knife clutched in the other behind your back, yes?" he asked.

She flinched at the question. "If I had wanted you dead, English, I would have had ample time to accomplish it. Instead, I nursed you through your illness."

"Fair enough, banshee," he returned, his eyes assessing. "Forgive my attempts at being droll. It requires an old, unpracticed muscle. But I am not so weak that I cannot reach the tub on my own strength, though I thank you for the offer."

He came toward her then. Not in the stalking, thunderous manner he often possessed, but slowly, taking each step with care. He came near enough to touch, and then his long fingers were upon the loose knot keeping his dressing gown in place.

She knew she ought to look away, to grant him privacy. Or perhaps to exercise her own sense of modesty. But she feared, where he was concerned, she had none. And she could not wrest her gaze from him as the knot opened. He turned, presenting her with his back, and then the dressing gown gaped. The twain ends of the belt dangled at his sides. One shrug of his broad shoulders, and the entire garment slipped away from him.

It pooled on the floor, forgotten.

A gasp tore from her before she could quell it. *Lord in heaven*, the man was a masterpiece. No sculptor could have carved a more perfect work of art from marble. His legs were long and strong, his bottom high and taut. She had never imagined that particular part of a man could be a thing of beauty, but on him it was. His back too was magnificent, muscled and lean at his waist, leading to broad shoulders. He moved his arms, stretching, and the thick cords in his shoulders and arms flexed. Here was the evidence of his well-honed power.

She could not speak a word. Her mouth went dry.

Slowly, he stepped over the rim of the tub and lowered his body into the water, letting out a guttural groan of pleasure as the warmth washed over him. That gorgeous, masculine sound echoed between her thighs where she felt aching and heavy and wet. Even her nipples hardened beneath her corset.

Bridget had just seen the Duke of Carlisle naked.

She had seen his arse.

Beneath the water, he remained utterly, deliciously nude. And now she would have to touch him. To bathe him.

How would she manage it?

She felt as if she were about to swoon, and Bridget O'Malley did not swoon. Not ever. Perhaps it was the consequence of witnessing her first entirely nude man.

The back of him, anyway. He had kept his front to himself, and she had to admit a stab of disappointment at the denial, along with a flush of curiosity. Though she was a virgin, a lass who grew up in the stews of Dublin, then went on to become a shop girl in London, she had known her fair share of amorous-minded gents. She was no stranger to the ways of the world.

She had been kissed and wooed and groped. Her skirts had been raised. When she had been sixteen, she had allowed Thomas Muldoon to stroke her in her nether regions, and when her mother had discovered what she'd done, her ears had received a sound boxing.

Other boys and men, both before and after Thomas, had made attempts. She had rebuffed most, allowed kisses from a scant few. No one—not one single man—had ever had the same undeniable pull as the Duke of Carlisle. He robbed her of the desire to want anyone other than him.

"Plotting my murder, banshee?" he asked, draping his arms over the lip of the tub, sending fat water droplets dripping to the tiled floor. His dark head leaned back. He sounded as weary as he must be, after having taken so ill over the past two days.

The intimacy of the scene—him in his bath, his skin bare and glistening with the kiss of warm water, steam swirling around them, the decadent scent of citrus and musk perfuming the air—conspired against her. Made her forget why she must never allow herself to feel even a hint of feelings for him.

Too late, crowed her heart.

"Not your murder," she forced herself to say, taking up the soap and cloth left by his manservant when he had readied the bath. "But perhaps revenge." She had not forgotten he had allowed her to dip beneath the water when he had been helping her to bathe.

"It is in poor taste to exact revenge upon a man who has just been ill," he protested.

She rounded the tub and realized his eyes were closed.

Did he trust her that implicitly already, or had the sickness sapped him of all caution?

She could not be certain, but either way, warmth unfurled within her as she stared at him. His brow was smooth, lips slightly parted, and even his jaw, ordinarily tense and sharp, appeared relaxed. She liked this side of him. He seemed more…human somehow. Less a god of war and more a simple man.

But she must not allow herself to get caught up in such confounding thoughts. "Surely it is not in any more poor taste than attempting to drown a woman you have already shot," she said drily, seating herself on a small chair alongside the tub left there for just such a purpose.

"There was good reason for both of those actions," he said, eyes still remaining closed. "Though you may rest assured that when I shot you, I only intended to disarm you, and when I dunked you in the tub, I only wanted you to answer my questions."

She rolled back her sleeves one by one, knowing the water would eventually grow cold, and she could only delay the inevitable for so long. The soap and cloth sat in her lap, mocking her. "I *was* answering your questions, as I recall."

"Ah, banshee. I am too tired to argue with you. Tomorrow, we shall return to daggers drawn, but for today do you think we might call a temporary truce?"

Something inside her had become hopelessly addled, for she liked that sobriquet on his tongue, referring to her. *Banshee.* She admired the strong column of his throat, the delineation of his Adam's apple, the sulky pout of his mouth.

How could she ever call a truce with this man?

How could she not?

Just one day, whispered her heart. *What could be the harm?*

Tomorrow, she could worry about vengeance and Cullen and the unseen war being waged all around them. Tomorrow, she could recall an illegitimate Irish shop girl, with a brother in gaol and more ties to the most dangerous ring of Fenian plotters than she cared to count, must never, ever allow herself to soften for the enemy.

"For today," she agreed softly, dipping the cloth in the water before trailing it over the arm nearest her.

A companionable silence fell, interrupted only by the gentle slosh of the water. She took to her task with more pleasure than she would have admitted. Over his skin she traveled, in motions meant to soothe as much as cleanse. She lathered his arms and chest in soap. His neck, his shoulders. With each pass of the cloth over him, an answering lick of fire burned in her belly. He was so beautiful. So vulnerable to her. The combination was heady. The ridiculous urge to press her lips to his throat would not leave her.

"You sang to me." The sudden timbre of his voice gave her a start. "When I was with fever."

She glanced up to find him watching her with a heavy-lidded stare. Her cheeks went hot with the combined shame of being caught ogling him and being caught warbling when she had supposed he could not hear.

She cleared her throat, turning her attention back to soaping his shoulder. "Forgive me for subjecting you to the torture of my lamentable singing."

"Your voice…it's beautiful."

Bridget met his gaze once more. It was certainly not what she had expected him to say. She enjoyed singing to herself, but she had never sung for anyone else. Not even Cullen. Not her mother. No one.

Except for the Duke of Carlisle.

But her voice was not beautiful, and she knew it. "You need not say so out of a sense of obligation." She returned her attention to his chest, wishing it were not quite so magnificent.

"Nonsense," his voice was gruff velvet to her senses. "I would not say so unless it were true. Your singing is lovely. I was hoping, in the interest of our truce, I could convince you to sing for me again now."

Her stomach clenched at the notion. "I am afraid I cannot, Duke."

"Leo," he corrected, his tone warm. Almost flirtatious. It reminded her of the first night they had met, before he had realized they were bitter enemies. "Also on account of the truce."

She swallowed a sudden lump in her throat. She was thawing toward him. Softening and weakening. Feeling emotions she had no right to feel. And yet, she was helpless to stop it.

"Very well," she allowed, in spite of herself. "Tonight, you shall be Leo, and I shall be Bridget. Tomorrow, we can return to the opposite sides of the battlefield."

"Bridget."

She liked the way his lips moved when he said her name. Liked the sound of it in his crisp accent and deep baritone.

Liked it far, far too much. She bit her lip to keep from smiling and turned her attention back to her task. "Leo."

"Yes." His eyes had closed once more. "I like the sound of that. Sing for me now, Bridget. Please."

Somehow, singing for him whilst his lids were lowered and he was not pinning her to her chair with that dark, consuming gaze of his, seemed easier. Possible. She soaped his right shoulder and biceps, and then the lyrics were flowing, the melody humming around them. The song she sang was one of her favorites, a haunting tune from the days of Napoleon, *The Bonny Light Horseman*.

She washed him as the ballad filled the air around them, soaping and rinsing, rinsing and soaping, admiring his firm flesh, all the ways his body was so different from hers, singing as she went. " 'And the dove she laments for her mate as she flies. 'Oh, where, tell me where is my true love?' she sighs. 'And where in this wide world is there one to compare with my bonny light horseman who was killed in the war?' "

When she reached the haunting final verse, the chamber was filled with such stillness, she flushed all over again. She rinsed the last of the suds from his chest and arms. "There you are. All clean."

His eyes opened, burning with warmth. "That was stunning, Bridget."

Bridget, he had said. Not banshee. Not madam. Not Miss O'Malley.

But *Bridget*.

Before she could say anything, his hand caught hers, the grip firm and strong. "*You're* stunning."

An indescribable sensation rocketed through her, exploding like a blossom of fireworks against the ink of an evening sky. For a beat, she could not move. Could not look away from him. Her heart thudded with such tenacity she swore she could hear it. Perhaps he could as well. Their wet fingers tangled, a simple connection, and yet, the lone gesture signified so much.

She had never felt the need to hold on to another person's hand more.

She didn't want to let go.

Ever.

As soon as the thought entered her mind, she chased it away, reminding herself she would let go. She had to. She hadn't a choice. Cullen could only be extricated from prison by foul means, and even if she trusted the duke enough to unburden herself to him, the only means he would offer by way of assistance—indeed, if he could offer any at all—would be fair. Fair would not work for an Irish lad with a mountain of false evidence against him. Only foul would, and for foul, she required John.

A tremor passed over her. She withdrew her hand, then fussed with the pitcher she would use to pour over his hair to wet it so she could work the shampoo through the thick, dark strands.

"Something is troubling you," he observed.

"Nothing is troubling me. Your water shall cool if we tarry any longer." She dunked the pitcher into the tub, allowing it to fill. "I'll need to wet your hair so I can wash it."

He allowed her to move him, positioning his body more toward the middle of the tub, then guiding his head back so his handsome face was upside down before her. Even from such a silly angle, he was broodingly beautiful. Those knowing eyes of his sought hers.

"What is everything you hold dear?" he asked suddenly.

Their positions meant she could not help but stare at the fullness of his lower lip, the lip she had once bitten hard enough to draw blood. But his question took her aback despite her preoccupation. Or perhaps because of it.

"My family," she answered truthfully. "Why do you ask?"

"You once told me the world has taken everything you hold dear from you." He paused to sigh in delight when she began working the shampoo into his hair, massaging his scalp as she did so. "I have not forgotten."

And so she had, a lifetime ago, it seemed, when she had been Jane Palliser, and she had kissed him with wild abandon. How strange to think she was now his wife. Washing his hair as if it were a commonplace occurrence, tending to him on his sickbed as if he were a loved one in truth rather than the man she'd been forced to marry to save herself.

She said nothing, focusing all her attention on washing his hair. Bridget was starting to discover she liked taking care of him in this fashion. She enjoyed having the big, strapping Duke of Carlisle, so powerful and dangerous, at her mercy. She liked touching him. Washing him. Looking after him. It struck her then that he was a man who had no one. He spent his days and his nights so engrossed in his work he did not sleep. He had an army of servants, but no one else here in London with the rest of his family in the country.

"Have you no family left other than the Duchess of Trent and O'Malley?" he asked as she began rinsing his hair.

Suspicion pricked her. Was he using this truce and their temporary détente as a means of extracting more information from her?

It was entirely possible. He was quite cunning.

"None. What of you? Is your only family Mr. Ludlow, his wife and the young duke, and Mrs. Ludlow?"

His full lips compressed into a grim line. "The only family I care for, yes. The woman who birthed me is on the Continent, and she can bloody well remain there."

There was bitterness in his tone and shadows in his eyes,

and both pricked at her heart, though she knew they should not. "You do not love your mother?"

Although hers had not been perfect, she had tried her best for Bridget and Cullen, and Bridget had mourned her when she had died far too young. Years had passed, and she missed her still. The absence of a life did not lessen one's longing for it, but time served to dull the anguish it caused.

"The dowager Duchess of Carlisle? No." He said it with finality.

She filled the pitcher once more to give his hair a second rinsing, and the wide chocolate-brown eyes of the golden duchess returned to her, along with a jab of something unpleasant. "Do you have someone else in London? A lady you love, perhaps?"

"I have a wife I cannot trust." His tone was wry.

"You are trusting me now," she reminded him as she gently worked her fingers through his hair with one hand while pouring water from the pitcher with the other.

"On account of our truce and my gratitude to you for nursing me back to health."

She was not sure she liked his answer. "There was a very concerned duchess here on the day you took ill. A beautiful woman. The Duchess of Ashelford, I believe it was."

He stiffened, the tenseness returning to his jaw. "I have no inkling why she would come here."

"Haven't you?" Bridget was not convinced.

"No." Again, he was cool. Concise.

"She wanted me to convey her sincere apologies to you," she pressed, though she knew it was wrong. Carlisle's past was none of her concern. Nor, truly, was his present or future. He had just reminded her of the fragility of their union. Of how it would necessarily end. And did she not remind herself of the selfsame truth often?

His lips curved, but since he remained upside down, she could not discern the sort of smile it was. "What else did she say?"

Intriguing response. She was not certain she liked it. In fact, she was more certain she did not. Was he interested in the Duchess of Ashelford?

Of course he would be.

The woman was a veritable goddess.

She gave his hair one final rinse. "There you are. I am afraid I do not recall what else she said, though she was adamant about reaching your bedside."

He said nothing, merely returned to a sitting position in the tub.

Well, then. Bridget had bathed him, agreed to his truce, and her duties were at an end. She alone had nursed him through his illness. Not the golden, sainted, beautiful Duchess of Ashelford. A woman who was a true duchess rather than a pretender. A woman who had spoken of Carlisle as *Leo*, who had shared a past with him, who had meant enough to him that his jaw had hardened at the mentioning of her.

She stood, drying her hands on the silk of her skirts without a care for if it stained them. "I do realize ours is a marriage in name only, and you were forced to wed me. But would it be too much to ask your lovers to refrain from visiting your home while I am in residence?"

"Bridget."

She was already halfway to the door when he called her name. She paused, refusing to turn back to him, for he had an uncanny ability to read her thoughts and mood by examining her expression and searching her gaze. "Yes?"

"Face me." It was not a command, yet neither was it a plea, issued in his deep voice, enough to send a shiver through her.

But that did not mean she would heed him. She was Bridget O'Malley, by God, and she bowed and scraped for no man. "No."

"Please, Bridget."

After a slow, deep inhale and exhale to calm her turbulent emotions, she turned back to him. His hair was wet. His chest glistening. His expression concerned. "The duchess is not my lover. She was my betrothed once, but she chose another man over me. I cannot fathom why she was here, nor why she importuned you, and for that I am wholeheartedly sorry."

Bridget studied him cautiously. He seemed sincere. Contrite. But there was also the matter of the social gathering he had hosted. "Perhaps you would be kind enough to explain the nature of the soiree I intruded upon after I escaped from my imprisonment."

He closed his eyes for a moment, leaning his head back. "Ah, Christ. I thought we had established a truce for today."

"Good evening, Your Grace."

"It is Leo," he growled, "and despite your forcing me to consume nothing more than tepid broth for my dinner, I am well enough to stop you should the situation merit it."

"What shall you do?" she challenged. "Throw me over your shoulder? I think not. If you wish our truce to continue, and if you want me to remain in this chamber, then you owe me an answer, *Leo*."

Chapter Thirteen

*T*HROWING HER OVER his shoulder was a tempting invitation.

She was right. He did owe her an explanation. By God, he owed her more than one. And the hell of it was, it would seem he owed her far more than mere explanations. He also owed her his life. He had been seriously ill. He had not realized how ill until consciousness had returned to him in stages. Until he had attempted to stand and walk on his own for the first time.

It had required every bit of strength and determination he had possessed to force himself to the bathing chamber. Now, he was relaxed and warm after her tender ministrations, and damn it to hell if he hadn't enjoyed her hands upon him far too much. The sensation of her washing his hair had been pure heaven, and though she had studiously avoided soaping him below the water line, he could only imagine how decadent it would feel to have her hand upon the rest of him.

His cock twitched to life at the thought. Good to know that, while being with fever had made him maudlin, it had not affected the most important part of him whatsoever. But the time for dwelling upon his desire for her was not now. Not when she faced him defiantly, eyes blazing.

"I am sorry for hosting the fête. In truth, I had forgotten about it, as the arrangement is rather a longstanding one." He paused, for disclosure was foreign to him. Leo had spent half his life hiding his work for the League out of necessity. But Bridget already knew who and what he was, and making an admission to her would not signify. "The parties are a part of my efforts to conceal who I truly am. If all London thinks me a wastrel rakehell, they will not be inclined to hold the candle to me and question further."

Her posture lost some of its starch, her countenance softening. "It is rather an ingenious method of hiding in plain sight."

He had always described it thus. Despite their obvious differences, he considered her a worthy opponent, and he admired her cunning and intelligence both. Her compliment filled Leo's chest with a burst of warmth.

"Thank you." He allowed his gaze to rake her form. "Is our truce still intact?"

Damnation, but the dresses the Duchess of Trent had sent over for her hugged his wife's figure with a commendable tenacity. Today's gown was ice blue, nipped at the waist, and she had unbuttoned and rolled back her sleeves to reveal her forearms. He had seen her naked before, and the sliver of ivory flesh on display should not make him feel so voracious, but as he looked at her now, he felt a sudden kinship with the starving man who had been given a feast.

A pink flush tinged her high cheekbones, no doubt the result of his thorough perusal. He liked ruffling this woman's feathers. Getting beneath her skin. And Christ, but he loved knowing he affected her. That try as she might to remain true to her godforsaken cause, in his arms she was as sweet and malleable as summer honey.

"There remains the matter of your imprisonment of me," she reminded him, the starch that had left her bearing finding its way into her voice instead. "You disappeared for three whole days, keeping me locked in my chamber. It required an act of forgetfulness on the part of Wilton for me to even escape, and just in time too, for you needed me."

You needed me.

The words wrapped around his heart like a briar, tightening. Painful. He prided himself on never needing anyone. On never being weak or dependent. He was the Duke of Carlisle, the leader of the League, and he was as hard and as cruel as the world had made him.

He was going to tell her as much.

"Yes, I did."

But his tongue betrayed him.

She appeared as shocked as he felt by the confession. Her dudgeon sagged before him like an ascension balloon on its way back down to earth. "I am amazed you admit it."

Her opinion of him remained low, it would seem. Perhaps his decision to keep her locked in the duchess's apartments had not served to enhance it. "Do I seem an unreasonable man to you?"

"You seem a proud man." She tilted her head, considering him with that bright gaze. "A stubborn man. A man who still has not offered an explanation for locking me in my chamber, as it happens."

"Because I did not dare trust you," he bit out, brutal in his honesty.

She flinched, and the sight should not have cut through him with the precision of a blade, but it nevertheless did. "Do you trust me now, Leo?"

His name in her soft, sweet voice did things to him. Already he was feeling more alive than a man who had been laid low by fever likely ought to. He knew all too well he could not give in to the temptation she presented. His body was not strong enough for that yet.

Not to mention that it was a horrible, awful idea. An

impossibility. He could engage in fantasy where she was concerned. He could employ his hand. But he must not allow it to progress any further.

"I shall consider your silence a resounding no," she said, and the disappointment in her tone was undeniable.

Did he trust her?

She had tirelessly nursed him back to health. His own manservant Richland had attested to that fact when he had arrived to ready the bath, and Bridget had briefly returned to her own chamber to freshen up. She could have fled. Or even smothered him with his own pillow.

"You may consider it a reluctant yes." If he sounded unwilling, as though the words had been torn from him, it was because he was and they had.

Also because he could scarcely believe it himself. But it was undeniable. Try though he might to ignore it, to suppress it, to avoid it, something had shifted. What he felt inside was akin to the same burst of surprise he'd had as a lad when he had risen in the morning to find the landscape newly covered in a fresh skin of white snow. The same brief moment of breathtaking appreciation filled him now as he held her eyes.

Her face, so lovely, so often guarded and closed off, changed. Smoothed and softened. Her smile reached the glittering depths of her gaze. "I am glad of it, Leo."

Damn it all to hell.

The strangest thing about it was, he was too. As wrong as he knew it was, the deep, abiding bloom of rightness in his chest refused to be denied. He trusted Bridget O'Malley.

May the Lord have mercy upon his soul.

THE DUKE OF Carlisle trusted her.

Bridget ought to be filled with smug eagerness. Plotting the ways in which she would dupe him. How easy he had made it for her. How simple it would be to use his words and the knowledge against him. And yet, doing so was not even on her horizon.

Something unspoken and undefined existed between them. She felt it as he completed his ablutions while she watched, because he had told her he wanted her company. She felt it as his strong body rose from the tub, rivulets of water licking down his lean back and his buttocks. It simmered beneath their companionable silence as she helped to towel him dry and handed him a nightshirt to don. It hummed through her as she guided him back to his bed, their arms linked, his tall, broad form leaning into hers, searing her with heat.

It burned a path straight to her heart when she settled the bedclothes around him and glanced up from her task to find him watching her with a molten look. She stilled, palms frozen in the act of smoothing the counterpane over his chest. That gaze undid her. Confused her. Set off a fresh flurry of warmth inside her.

"I should return to my chamber now," she told him, though in truth she hated to leave his side. Leaving meant their truce would be over, and she would meet him again in the morning with all their demons and ghosts keeping them apart. "You need to rest to regain your strength."

He startled her by taking both her wrists in a gentle grip. "Don't go."

Her heart thudded. "I should."

"I should let you go," he agreed.

She licked her lips, willing away the ache deep inside her. A most troubling ache, because for the first time it was not just the burn of her desperate attraction for him but something far more true and deep. "Yes, you must."

"I cannot." His thumbs rubbed in slow, maddening circles over her inner wrists, tempting her with his words every bit as much as with his touch. "I am loath for our truce to end so soon. Stay with me?"

It was the most exposed she had ever seen him, including when she had seen his naked arse earlier. Bridget could not shake the feeling this was a time of reckoning for them. She could refuse him and leave, erect the necessary barriers once more. Or she could give in to what they both so clearly wanted. Perhaps even what they needed.

For tonight.

Just one night.

What could be the harm?

In the morning, she would wake, return to her side of the demarcation line. Fortify herself for what she must do. Prepare to leave him, betray him, and save her brother.

The reminder gave her pause.

Since when had carrying out her original plan become *betraying* the Duke of Carlisle?

She was wading into treacherous flood waters, and she knew it. At any moment, they were likely to sweep her to her doom, and yet here she stood, lingering, hating to leave him. "I ought to return to my chamber. Do you not wish to lock me in there once more?"

He shook his head slowly. "I told you, Bridget, that I trust you. I'll not be your jailer again."

The statement was a stunning one, particularly coming from him. If only he knew how little he should trust her. The knowledge was acid, churning in her stomach. "Thank you, but all the same, I cannot stay. It would not be wise. We are not husband and wife in truth, and no good can come of my remaining in your chamber, now you are mending."

But he did not release her wrists, nor did his thumbs stop their tender travels, and neither did his gaze allow her to look away. "I am too tired to be anything less than a gentleman. You have nothing to fear in staying here."

"In your bed?" She was more tempted by the invitation than she cared to admit. She had eaten a hasty dinner in her chamber while his manservant had attended him, and though the hour was early, she too was weary from the grueling days of tending him and fretting over him. There was nothing to stop her from settling into bed alongside him and surrendering herself to the bliss of slumber.

Nothing except for ration, reason, and all the instincts within her screaming she could not afford to get too close to this man. She must guard her heart. Remain impervious.

Too late for that, mocked her heart.

"My bed is large." His voice was husky, a decadent rumble that made her ache and long for that which she must not want. "You are small. There is ample room. Please, Bridget. Your presence calms me."

She could not believe it was so. "How can I calm you? You loathe me."

"No." His hands explored higher, moving over her forearms, which remained exposed from assisting him with his bath. It was too much. She wanted to tear away from him. She never wanted him to stop touching her.

"I tried, wife. Believe me, I tried. You are the one vice I cannot seem to deny. Everything else, I can control. You are the only lure that dogs me, and I am too weary to fight you now."

She wondered at his comment about vices, recalling he had been thoroughly soused the first evening she had met him at Harlton Hall. Yet, he had not smelled of spirits, nor seemed as if he tippled in all the subsequent weeks she had spent in his presence. Something told her he had hidden facets she had yet to see.

Something else told her she wanted to see them.

And not to find weaknesses she could use against him, but because she…why, she cared.

There it was, the realization as jarring as it was unwanted.

She, Bridget O'Malley, *cared* about the Duke of Carlisle.

Which was precisely why she needed to deny him his request, extricate herself from his gentle grasp, and put some much-needed distance between them.

"I too am weary," she conceded. It was perhaps the most honest she had ever allowed herself to be with him, emerging from some place deep inside herself that refused to be stifled. It was the part of her that had been lonely and fearful, desperate and hungry, the part of her that had belonged to no land, to no man. Wild and restless, the rawest recesses of her spirit.

It was her heart.

"Stay with me," he said again. "Just for the night."

"Very well," she found herself relenting against everything she possessed—aside from that willful weakness that called itself a heart, that was. "For the night. But you must give me your word that nothing untoward will occur."

"I give you my word," he said easily.

Too easily. But she could hardly argue the matter. "And only on account of our temporary truce. I do not want you to think I am getting soft for you, Duke."

The ghost of a smile flirted with his lips. "Only one thing about you is soft, banshee, and we both know what that is."

The wicked man. Somehow, in the ease that had fallen between them, the casual intimacy, *banshee* lost its bite. Instead, it sounded rather like an endearment. Heaven help her, but she liked it more each time he spoke it. "You are a difficult man to deny."

A full smile curved his lips, and though he appeared ex-hausted—purple crescents bruised the tender flesh beneath his eyes to attest to how much his body had recently endured—he was so handsome her breath caught and a familiar pulse flared to life between her thighs.

"I would not have it any other way."

Nor would she. But before they engaged in any more banter, and before he caressed her arms with any more maddening finesse and she lost her ability to resist him entirely, she knew she must change the subject. "You are certain you want me here?"

His expression sobered, dark eyes burning into hers. "I have never been more certain of anything."

"Then you must assist me in removing my garments," she blurted through lips that had gone dry.

Excellent change of subject, Bridget, she chastised herself. It seemed as if the connection between her rational mind and her mouth had been completely, hopelessly severed. How was requiring his assistance in disrobing a safer choice?

His eyes gleamed. "With pleasure. Turn 'round, if you please."

He released her wrists at last, and she spun about as he asked, her full skirts whirling around her like a bell. She steeled herself against temptation, took a deep, calming breath and held it as she felt him go to work on the line of buttons concealed on the back of her gown.

One by one, they slid from their moorings, starting at her lower back and traveling all the way to the last button at the top. She was short enough he could reach it without difficulty. Still questioning the wisdom of her decision, she nevertheless shrugged her shoulders, allowing the gown to fall to the floor in a murmur of silk. She removed her corset cover and petticoat before allowing him to pluck the laces of her corset free. They loosened, and she removed it too.

Clad in nothing more than her chemise, stockings, and drawers, she hastily gathered up her garments and laid them upon a chair in tidy fashion. When she turned back to him, he was watching her with a strange expression.

She felt suddenly awkward. Though it was certain there was nothing inappropriate about a wife sharing a bed with her husband, the undeniable truth remained that they would inevitably annul their union and go their separate ways. All of this—each moment of tenderness, all the emotions, every word, glance, and touch—would eventually be erased.

Why did that thought bother her so much?

Leo seemed to sense her conflicting emotions. "You need not be shy with me, Bridget. Come to bed where you belong."

Did she belong there? Lying at his side? Breathing in his scent, absorbing his heat?

Nay. She could never. She could not change who she was any more than she could change who he was. They were two people who had never been meant to be together. Two people who had been brought together by extraordinary circumstances. And those same circumstances would also tear them apart.

But despite all that, her feet were moving. She was crossing the chamber, going back to him. She turned down the gas lamps, bathing the chamber in darkness. Knowing her way by rote, she found the side of the bed opposite him, and she made hasty work of removing her stockings and drawers, and plucking the pins from her hair, allowing it to fall heavily down her back.

"I hear rather a lot of fabric rustling, wife. Could it be that you are getting naked in spite of all your protestations toward maidenly modesty?" he teased through the heavy silence that had descended.

"Removing my stockings." Her face went hot even in the darkness. She did not dare to refer to her drawers aloud. Too many cumbersome fabrics beneath the bedclothes rendered it impossible for her to sleep. But she was attempting to avoid falling deeper into ruin than she already had, so surely there was no reason to mention any of that.

"Christ," he muttered. "You should not have said that. I thought it was the bedclothes, but now I am cursed with imagining what I dearly long to see."

"I am finished now," she said, throwing back the blankets and settling in. She rolled onto her side, facing away from him. All the better for her to resist him, she reasoned.

But in the next breath, a large, warm body was pressed against her, radiating heat into her. An arm went around her waist. He pressed a kiss to her nape. "Good night, wife." His lips grazed her ear as he spoke.

She should have felt more trapped than she had in the duchess's apartments when she had been locked within. But instead, she felt...at home.

There was no other way to describe it. Something about Leo at her back, his large body curling against hers like a shield, his arm over her as if she were his in truth, flooded her with the sense of absolute, undeniable rightness.

There was nowhere else she belonged in this world, in this moment. She was certain of it.

"Good night, husband," she returned to him softly, staring into the velvet darkness of the night.

All that met her was his slow, even breathing. He had already fallen asleep.

She bit her lip against the sudden sting of tears. How safe and comforted he must feel with her in his arms. How very wrong he was. Hating herself for what she must do, she reached for the hand that rested lightly over her belly. She laced her fingers through his.

"I am sorry," she whispered into the night, knowing this was all they could ever have. Wishing there could somehow be more. Knowing there could not.

Unburdened as best as she could be, she fell into a deep, comfortable sleep, wrapped in the arms of the man who was meant to be her enemy, but who was fast turning into her savior.

Chapter Fourteen

IN THE SEDUCTIVE glow of morning sunshine spilling in behind the window dressings, Leo was beautiful. Rest, sustenance, and his bath had restored the color to his skin. Bridget told herself she was dreaming as he devoured her with his intense stare and stroked her unbound hair with a gentle hand.

"Good morning," she said as a test. For surely, if she were still sleeping, he would not answer. Or she would wake herself from this false world of promise and tenderness and sweet, blossoming need.

"Morning, banshee." His voice sent a trill of pure pleasure through her, down her spine, settling between her thighs as a pulse of want. His hand continued to stroke her hair slowly, maddeningly.

She loved the way it felt, passing over her scalp, down her cheek and throat, to rest above her breast, then moving to start the journey all over again. Bridget felt like a cat. Part of her wanted to purr her contentment.

He seemed pensive by morning light. Different somehow, as if something within him had changed unalterably. How she wished she could remain here, in this charmed moment forever, warm beneath the cocoon of his blankets, her body nestled against his, his face relaxed of its ordinary tension, his touch that of a lover's.

Dear God, she was in dreadful danger of losing her heart to this man.

She knew it the same way she knew her name was Bridget Mary O'Malley.

"Why do you frown?" His fingertips grazed the furrow between her brows in a gentle touch.

"No reason," she lied.

"Your tell is giving you away, banshee."

Drat.

She expelled a breath, bit her lip, weighing the wisdom of confessing.

Did she dare?

In one exhalation, she did it. "I am afraid I like you too much."

There.

Done.

Except, his hand stilled. Then he moved to cup her cheek instead. That touch, so simple and innocent, burned her with the force of a brand. She tingled. Came to life. Part of her could not resist nestling her cheek more fully into his palm. It was so hot and reassuring. His touch, when freely given in tenderness, was her panacea.

His thumb stroked over her lower lip once. Twice. His expression turned pensive. "The first day I saw you at Harlton Hall, I thought you were the most beautiful woman I had ever seen."

She smiled sadly, all too aware of their disparities. "And then you realized who I was, and everything changed."

"No."

His thumb was back upon her lower lip. Pressing gently. No longer stroking. And it was maddening, for part of her wanted to open her lips and suck that thumb into her mouth and part of her wanted to nip it with her teeth.

"What then?" Her question emerged as a breathless whisper.

Here, in the early morning stillness, the rest of London—and everything that would conspire to keep them in their separate worlds—fell away. How easy it was to pretend they were husband and wife, two people who had fallen in love. Two people who belonged in each other's arms rather than at each other's throats.

"I realized you are also the most dangerous woman I have ever known," he said then, his tone as solemn as his expression. Those fathomless eyes burned into hers. "Because you make me forget everything but wanting you. When I look at you, I see a woman who can strip me of loyalty and duty, of everything and anything but you. When I look at you, you are all I need, all I hunger for. You make me weak. So damn weak."

His confession stole the breath from her lungs. To think she could hold such power over the Duke of Carlisle was both thrilling and terrifying. Thrilling, because knowing she affected him so deeply pleased her on a feminine level which had nothing to do with their clashing ideologies.

Her hands framed his face, and his whiskers prodded her palms like reminders. A pointed *aide-mémoire* that she had no right to be here with him, to be touching him so freely, to allow herself to feel such tenderness toward him. To want to kiss him as desperately as she did now.

"You make me weak too," she confessed, going against her every instinct. Certainly against reason. Flouting her promises to John, the loyalty she owed Cullen and the cause, her promises to herself. This was a mistake, and she knew it. She was selfish and she was greedy, and she was weak.

She had spent all her life tending everyone else. She had borne the responsibility, shouldered the duties from her mother, from Cullen.

How many decisions had she made beneath the crushing weight of all her responsibilities? How many times had she done something she had not wanted to do because she thought it was her duty, what she needed to do for everyone else who relied upon her?

Bridget had never realized it until this moment, but now she saw how easily and completely she had trapped herself. How she had fashioned herself a prison from which there was no escape.

Here, now, was her chance. This moment, this man, were hers for the taking.

They seemed to move as one. Or perhaps she moved first. Perhaps he did. All Bridget knew was that in the next breath, their lips met in a kiss. It was slow at first, a sweet meeting of mouths, his lips fitting to hers, his lower lip between the seam of hers. The kiss was languorous. Decadent. They took their time, devouring each other long and slow. Savoring.

Their tongues had not even touched, and she had never experienced a more intimate kiss in her life.

He made a low sound of need, and she felt it in her core. The kiss deepened, their mouths opening, hands wandering over each other's bodies in worshipful caresses. He wore nothing but a nightshirt and she her chemise, leaving two thin fabric barriers between them. Their tongues tangled. One of his hands found the hem of her chemise and dragged it upward, his warmth trailing up her calf, over her knee, all the way to her thigh.

His caresses traveled higher still, until his fingers brushed over her sex. The breath hissed from her lungs, her body jerking into his touch. Just one glancing caress, and she was ready to come undone. He had touched her before. Had pleasured her before. But something about this time, this enchanted morning, with the walls separating them briefly torn down, heightened her excitement into a brilliant, blinding crescendo.

He kissed her hard and deep before tearing his mouth from hers, his breathing harsh. His gaze was almost black as he met hers. "I want you, Bridget."

Four simple words.

Wicked.

Words she ought to ignore.

Words she felt between her thighs as a rush of wetness, a hungering for more. He had promised to be a gentleman, and he had kept his word last night. But by the tempting morning light, she did not want a gentleman. She wanted a man, unrepentant and wild, dangerous and delicious. She wanted him. *Dear God*, how she wanted him, her heartless duke, the enigma she had married, the answer to every question rioting inside her.

Bridget kissed him again, kissed him hard and deep. Kissed him until her lips were bruised, and their breaths mingled in heavy pants. Kissed him as his fingers found her aching flesh with ease, parting her folds, discovering the knot at her center. He touched her there, a stroke, a swirl, and she felt as if she were lit up from within, as if she were glowing, a house on fire, burning with her own, destructive need.

"I want you too," she whispered back.

He tore his nightshirt over his head, then he hauled her chemise away as well. As one, they moved until Bridget was on her back with Leo atop her. Naked flesh came into contact with naked flesh. Something firm and hard and hot prodded her lower belly. New kisses began where the old kisses ended.

They were voracious, equally matched in their passion. Her hands were on his shoulders, his back. In a sudden burst of daring, she found his buttocks, and his flesh was as firm and tempting as it had appeared the evening before when she had shamelessly watched him get into his bath.

His tongue was inside her mouth, and she sucked. Moaned. Her hips moved in their own rhythm as his questing fingers continued to play with the bundle of flesh that was so receptive to his touch. She jerked against him, wanting more. Wanting harder, faster, more, more, *more*.

Olc. Wrong. This was so wrong.

She knew it, and yet, she could not stop…

Ceart. Right.

It was also so right. So very, hopelessly, unbelievably, deliciously right.

He broke the kiss, dragging his mouth over her throat like a brand. Open and hungry. Licking. Sucking. Biting. And she could not get enough. Beneath him, she bucked and writhed.

"Bridget," he whispered her name, half prayer, half epithet, as he kissed the curve of her breast, palmed and cupped it. His tongue swirled around her nipple, making it stand erect, causing her breath to quicken.

A pulsing ache pulled in her belly, almost as if a cord within her had been drawn into a triple knot. "Leo."

Her fingers found his hair, smooth and silky and thick. She tugged, earning a groan from him, and then she recalled that he liked pain. Did it make him feel alive? Make his blood rush through his body? Make him weak? Guided by instinct, she raked her nails down his back, then dug them in, scoring a path back up to his shoulders once more.

He sucked her nipple into his mouth, the hot, wet tug almost undoing her. He stroked her with increasing swiftness and pressure. She moved against him, arching, thrusting, overwhelmed by sensation. She wanted more. She wanted everything.

As if he heard her unspoken request, the tentative teasing

of his caresses changed. He slicked his forefinger over the swollen bud of her sex, flicking over it in rapid, strong motions, finding the sensitive place beneath the plump nub. He worked her there, applying firm strokes with an increased pace that made her wild. Bridget jerked against him, thighs spread. The tip of his middle finger found her entrance, dipping against her channel with delicious pressure only to withdraw. Every instinct inside her told her to move her hips, bring that finger inside her. But when she tried, he had already removed his touch.

It was maddening. She wanted him. All of him.

And she wanted him now. Inside her. Claiming her. Bringing her to the edge before she shattered in delicious release. He sucked her nipple once more before kissing a path of fire down her body. His hands found her inner thighs, spreading them wide. His gaze was hot upon her, the most private part of her. A part no one had ever seen.

She knew she ought to feel some semblance of shame for allowing herself to be so revealed before him, but she could not summon anything more than a raw, unadulterated wave of desire. Not even a protest. Not a sound. All she could feel was how badly she wanted that sinful mouth. All she could do was revel in the possessive way he looked at her, as if she were his, as if he wanted to devour her.

"More beautiful than I imagined," he murmured, and she was not certain if he spoke the words to himself or to her.

He had thought about her, then? Had he lain alone in his bed at night as she had, thinking of this passion between them, longing to give in? She lost the ability to wonder any more when he kissed the curve of her belly, then trailed a scorching path to the apex of her thighs. Then lower still, not stopping until his beautiful head was framed by her pale, spread legs.

He glanced up at her, and his eyes were obsidian, holding her in their thrall. "I'm going to taste your perfect, pink cunny now. I'm going to lick you and suck you until you spend, and I want you to watch."

A trickle of wetness seeped from her core. His hot breath fanned over her in a tantalizing caress as he spoke. His mouth was so close, his wicked words bringing her ever closer to the edge. She felt swollen and needy and greedy, every part of her body tensed, ready and willing for whatever pleasure he would visit upon her.

She moaned and attempted to rock toward him, but his hands on her thighs kept her from making contact with him.

"I'll give you everything you want, but you have to obey me." His thumb stroked over her engorged flesh, making her entire body twitch. "If you stop watching, I stop. I want there to be no doubt who is bringing you pleasure. Understood?" He gave her another slow, maddening swipe with his thumb.

Bridget ought to object to his demand she obey him, but there was something about the deep, delicious sound of that word in his voice which heightened her desire. She cried out, half whimper, half plea for more, even though she didn't know what more was. All she knew was she wanted it. Wanted anything he had to give. He blew over her flesh.

"Say *yes, husband*, Bridget."

He was pushing her, and she wanted him, but even made desperate by the sensations he brought to life within her, she balked at his demand. She was aching, needing something she did not understand. Her breasts and nipples felt full and needy, so she cupped them, and it felt so good she rolled her hips.

His thumb rubbed her in a circular motion, then up and down. The friction was delicious, but then he stopped just when she felt the slow buildup tightening within her.

"Say *yes husband*, darling, and play with your nipples while you watch me."

Oh God.

She couldn't say it.

Couldn't do it.

Couldn't *not* do it.

"Yes husband," she said at last, pinching both her nipples between her thumbs and forefingers as he watched.

The words and the action heightened everything. More wetness dripped from her center. Leo made a growl of approval in his throat. "Now I'm going to give you what you want. Don't stop watching, and don't stop touching yourself."

His authoritative tone did nothing to diminish the fires burning through her blood. She wanted him so much he could say anything, do anything, and she would watch and she would tell him whatever he wanted to hear. Bridget was merely that desperate for this man, that drawn to him, that owned by him.

His tongue flicked over her then, over the sensitive bud hidden between her folds. It was shocking. Beautiful. It felt as if she had been catapulted into heaven for a brief, incendiary moment.

And then she fell down, landing in iniquity and sin, and there was no greater joy. Nothing she could ever experience again in her life would be better than the Duke of Carlisle's tongue upon her there, in that secret place. It was a revelation. The wet slide, the skilled play...*oh*. Too good. Far too good. She was lost. Close to breaking. Her body had tightened, and she knew she would fly apart at the slightest provocation.

He moaned against her, as if he were as lost to desire as she was, and the sound heightened her every sense. All the while, he never broke eye contact. Nor did she, watching him as he pleasured her, torturing her breasts as he had asked. She had never imagined her own touch could feel so good, but with their gazes connected and his tongue lapping over her, she felt almost as if the touch were his instead.

His mouth closed over the taut bud that longed for him the most. He sucked and sucked. Used his teeth until she was crying out, squeezing her nipples into hard pink buds that longed for his tongue. And still he continued, undeterred. The guttural sounds he emitted made her wild. It was as if he relished every lick, every suck. As if he could not get enough of her.

And she knew the feeling well, for she was certain she could never get enough of him either. Not enough of his kiss, his mouth, his tongue, his beautiful body, those long fingers, the full, massive length of him, hard and ready. She wanted to suck it. To take him in her mouth and pleasure him the same as he was doing to her. She wanted him to lose himself in the same way, and she wanted to be the one responsible, and...

Oh dear heavens, oh dear heavens...

She was going to spend. The spring was coiled, tightened. He had worked her into a fine frenzy, and he had done it so well. She lost control. The dam inside her burst, and she cried out, shuddering as a great rush of pleasure washed over her. She came hard and fast, the sweet, liquid rush of her release leaving her losing herself in the oblivion of his dark, possessive gaze. He licked her seam, lapping up every last drop that emerged from her.

"I could lick your pretty little cunny like this forever."

Dear God.

She wanted to respond, but he had robbed her of the capacity for speech. She was boneless, weightless, mindless. And his words... They left her without words of her own. They left her with an answering, delicious ache inside her. If he wanted to use his tongue upon her in such a delightful way forever, he would not find her an objector.

He kissed her sex, making another deep sound of satisfaction in his throat that she felt all the way to her toes. And then he and his wicked mouth and hands moved back up her body in slow, sweet torture. Kisses on her belly. A tongue in her navel. Kisses higher. He gently removed her hands from her breasts and sucked one nipple into his mouth, before biting the other. And then his mouth went higher still, finding her throat, his lips pressing over the place where her heartbeat hammered against her skin. He kissed it. Sucked.

"I want inside you," he said against her skin. "You are mine now, Bridget O'Malley. I mean to keep you."

She was not meant to feel an exquisite rush of something tender and bright and beautiful inside her at his declaration. Something warm and unexpected, piercing her heart. Something that felt a lot like love.

Love. Grá.

She loved him.

As the realization fell upon her, she clutched him in a tight embrace, holding him to her as if she could keep him here forever. Atop her, believing in her, being the man she needed him to be.

It was not too late. She could tell him no. She could leave his bed, his chamber, his house, before she did irreparable damage to him. To them both. But the weakness in her would not allow her to make any decision save one.

"I am yours, Leo."

He groaned. His fingers came between them, sliding through her folds. She was so slick, the sounds of him toying with her were wet and luscious in the chamber. The sweet perfume of her was redolent in the air. Her hip hooked around his waist naturally, bringing them closer. He kissed her cheek, her jaw, reaching her lips at last. Their mouths fused, open and hungry. She tasted herself on his tongue.

Round and round circled his fingers, the pressure and the pace enough to make her explode in no time. She reached her pinnacle, jerking against his knowing caresses. Tremors shook through her, the passion white-hot. Her eyes closed, and she moaned into his mouth, never having broken the kiss. More moisture dripped from her, coating his fingers, and this time, he did not stop playing with her as he had before. This time, he continued, finding her channel. He stroked her there, running his knowing touch over the dip where he was made to seat himself.

He broke the kiss, gazing down at her, breathing harshly. "I need you."

She stared into his gaze. "Yes."

And then, his fingers were replaced by the head of his cock. It was larger, warmer, smoother than she had expected. Firm and bold, brushing over her entrance. Her hips undulated, seeking what only he could give her. Seeking him. He gave her what she wanted, easing in slowly. Just the tip of him, and she was stretched wide. The sensation was strange yet good. He pressed deeper, sliding inside, and she felt tight, hot, as if she might burst.

He stilled. "Have I hurt you?" His voice was as strained as his expression.

"No." She caught his beloved face in her hands. "You could never hurt me."

But I *could hurt* you. *I* will *hurt you.*

Nay. She would not think of that now. Not in this moment of divine connection. She had never felt closer to another.

His hips rocked, and he drove himself inside her farther. "Christ, banshee. You feel like heaven. So tight and wet and...*fuck.*"

She liked his vulgar word. Liked the way he was losing his rigid grip upon his control. She wanted him to lose it entirely. Guided by instinct, she moved beneath him, her inner muscles clenching, bringing him inside. "All the way, Leo. I want you inside me so deep."

It was the only prompt he needed.

With a cry, he thrust. The barrier of her maidenhead was rent, and she knew a sting of pain as it gave way. But then, his fingers were right there on her flesh, flicking over her swollen bud, chasing away the hurt. All she felt was full, so full of him.

"Did it hurt, love?" He kissed her. "Tell me if I should stop."

She kissed him back. "Don't stop. Don't ever stop."

He began moving inside her, and everything changed. In and out, slow and steady and deep he drove. As one, they arched and flexed, gave and took. Her body was ready, and when the next climax claimed her, it was violent and potent. She clenched on his cock, and he thrust deeper as she exploded around him, her flesh pulsing with the force of her release.

He rode her with long, slow strokes, kissing her, loving her with his body and his lips at once. And then, he stiffened, and inside her she felt the warm, hot rush of his seed, filling her, marking her as his.

She held him to her as the last waves of his release subsided, wondering how she could ever bear to leave him now.

Cinniúint. Fate.

He was hers.

Chapter Fifteen

$\mathcal{L}$EO SLEPT THE slumber of the dead.

When he woke again, it was with no notion of how much time had passed. For a beat, he did not even possess a recollection of where he was or how he had found himself there. His sleep, ordinarily plagued by nightmares, had been oddly dreamless, and it took him a beat to recall he was at Blayton House in London. In his own chamber. That earlier that morning, he had made a decision which would either prove his gravest mistake or his ultimate redemption.

Sunlight splashed around the edges of the window dressings. The time of day could be late morning or afternoon, as the curtains were layered for the times when he needed to fall into bed during daylight hours and sleep, following days without it.

His body was replete with the deep sense of bliss that always visited him after a thorough fucking. And this morning had been nothing if not thorough. It had also been life-changing, in more than one sense. He had consummated his marriage. Had experienced the most decadent, soul-searing rush of physical release he had ever known. Both of these things would be cause for celebration in ordinary circumstances.

These were not, however, ordinary circumstances.

Stretching languorously beneath the bedclothes, he

reached for her, only to find her side of the bed empty and cool to the touch, bereft of all signs of her, save the lingering scent of bergamot and citrus. He threw back the counterpane to make certain he had not imagined losing himself inside Bridget's body. The rusty splotches of her virgin blood were there, as much proof as he required.

Thank Christ.

It was real, and he had made his choice.

She was his, and he was not letting her go. There would be no annulment. There would be no turning her over to the Home Office. She was his wife, and he had planted his cock and his seed inside her to solidify that claim.

His actions ought to fill him with a deep sense of shame, for he loved his brother and he loved the League, and his duty to the Crown had always come first, without a single regret on Leo's part. And the shame was there, undeniable, salt poured into a festering wound. But it also filled him with an equally deep sense of satisfaction, for he cared about Bridget O'Malley in ways that terrified him more than facing a hundred Fenian bombs about to detonate did.

For the first time in all his years in service to the Crown, Leo faced a conundrum.

A rather unusual and troubling conundrum.

He wanted Bridget in his life, at his side, as his wife, more than he wanted to run the League. If he could not have her and the League both—and his formidable sense of honor said he could not—then he would need to give up the League. His mouth went dry at the thought.

But then the door to the bathing chamber opened, and the soft sound of bare feet padding toward him on carpet reached his ears the moment before Bridget appeared, black hair wet and trailing down her back, clad once more in her chemise. Even in the dim light, the dampness of her skin rendered her chemise transparent. He could clearly see the fullness of her breasts, the dark-pink peaks of her nipples, the mound between her legs.

Her eyes went wide as a furious blush stained her cheeks. "Oh! Leo. I... You are awake."

He thought of how responsive she had been, how she had given him exactly what he needed—a combination of stubborn defiance and delicious submission—and how she had been wild and unashamed in her sensuality. The image of her cupping her breasts and pinching her nipples as he licked her pearl made him hard all over again. He stifled a groan, shifting beneath the blankets to alleviate his discomfort.

"I am very much awake," he said wryly. This woman was made for him, and she was his Achilles' heel. They had much to discuss, for he knew she remained distrustful toward him, and she had not divulged everything she knew to him. He would need to change that.

"I had a bath," she said softly. "You needed your rest, and I didn't wish to wake you."

He noted how she hovered awkwardly on the periphery of the chamber. "Come here, Bridget."

He had not been certain, knowing her as he did, if she would accept his command or if she would show him her stubborn side. To his surprise, she listened, crossing the chamber and not stopping until she reached his bedside. She smelled of his soap and shampoo, and his scent upon her made his cockstand even harder.

"We can still have the marriage annulled," she said on a rush.

He caught her hand and tugged her gently, forcing her to join him on the bed. With his free hand, he swept a few stray wet tendrils of hair from her face. "I meant what I said. You are mine now. There will be no annulment."

Her gaze searched his, her expression troubled. He leaned forward and kissed the furrow between her brows to make it smooth. A raw, unprecedented surge of tenderness hit him as he looked at her. With her hair wet, her face pale, clad in only a thin scrap of linen, she was more vulnerable than he had ever seen her before. Not even when she had been injured had she been so open to him.

But she was still troubled. "It was a moment of weakness for both of us, I suspect. You need not fear I will expect you to bind yourself to me forever because of one mistake."

"It was not a mistake." He caressed her silken cheek, the contact of her skin beneath his sending a fresh tug of desire to his groin. For this woman, he was weak. From the moment he had first laid eyes on her, it had been that way, and nothing—not discovering the truth, not her mad antics on behalf of her cause—nothing changed that. "I want you as my wife. Our situation is a complicated one, I will grant you, but if you are honest with me, I can formulate a plan of battle. I can see we both make it through this unscathed."

It was not precisely what he meant to say, and as soon as the words left him and she stiffened beneath his touch, he knew it had been the wrong choice. "Did you bed me so I would tell you everything you want to know?"

"No." *Damn it*, was that all she thought of him? Why would she give her body to a man she did not trust? He caught her chin in a gentle yet demanding grip when she would have looked away. "I bedded you because I have been half mad with wanting you from the first time I saw you. I want to help you, Bridget. I *can* help you. But you need to trust me."

"Trust you," she repeated. "How can I? You are the man who threatened to take me to jail, who told me he would break me. *Namhaid*, you are my enemy."

Bridget O'Malley was like a wild creature, ready to take flight or claw her way to the death if she must. He wanted to protect her. To soothe and console her. To wrap her in his arms and let her know she would never need to fight alone again, that he would fight for her now. That they could fight together, for each other.

He did the only thing he could think of doing then, lowering his mouth to claim hers. The kiss began chastely, but she opened beneath him, moaning, and his tongue sank inside to tangle with hers. Chaste was not a word that existed between Bridget and Leo. She was his, and the sooner she admitted it, the sooner she resigned herself to that fact, the better for the both of them. Thus far, they had been attacking their mutual problem as opposites. But if they worked together, they would be stronger, the outcome far better.

And he needed that outcome the same way he needed her. He had not experienced such an overwhelming need for a woman before her, aside from Jane, and even that had been a mere flickering candle compared to the raging inferno he felt for Bridget. She had changed him.

He tore his mouth from hers when everything in him screamed to deepen the kiss. "I am not your enemy, Bridget. I am your husband. I mean those words more than I have meant any others I have ever spoken."

She stared at him, her lips swollen with his kisses, bright eyes solemn. "You are a duke, Leo. I am the illegitimate daughter of a Dublin tavern wench. I believe in Irish Home Rule, and you are determined to do everything in your power to stop it. Even if I were to trust you, I do not see how we can overlook such vast differences."

She was not wrong about the obstacles facing them, but being himself, he had already begun weighing all their options in the days before he had taken ill. It was what he did—he planned, studied, strategized, researched, worked to get to the heart of a problem and pluck it out by its root. None of the barriers were insurmountable. There was a way around everything if one was daring and creative enough to do it.

"Look at me, Bridget O'Malley Carlisle," he commanded, refusing to allow her eyes to stray from his. "I am a duke, but you are my duchess. I do not care who or what you were before we wed. And even if I did, I am the son of a woman who has never cared for another person in her entire life. How is it my right to judge anyone else? She bore me out of duty, and when I was a child, she hurt me in spite and with a selfish need to garner attention for herself. I come from a poisoned union. I too believe in Irish Home Rule, and the only thing I am attempting to stop is the subversive campaign of violence being waged by those who mistakenly think killing innocents is the means by which they will obtain their goals."

The furrow between her brows had returned, but this time it was deeper. "Your mother hurt you?"

He had not intended to mention his mother's sins. Indeed, it had happened so long ago, and unlike the dark moods that continued to plague him, he had become adept at keeping that awful part of his past from his mind. "Yes."

This time, her touch was on him, gentle and comforting. Her fingers on his jaw. "Tell me, Leo."

He closed his eyes, a wave of nausea returning to him along with remembrance. Purging it from his mind, forgetting it had ever happened, had been the means by which he had carried on with his life ever since his father had banished her to the Continent after the last time. He did not realize he was trembling until he felt Bridget's arms close around him. Until she urged his head to rest above her solidly thumping heart. Until her hand stroked lovingly over his hair, again and again.

He would not embarrass himself by weeping.

He would not.

"Leo," she whispered. "Tell me, please."

"When I was a lad, I suffered from violent illnesses," he began, hating to revisit the hideousness of his past and yet feeling somehow soothed by unburdening himself to her. "I would be healthy one day, and the next, I was violently ill, vomiting, unable to hold down any food, covered in a rash. It went on for years. Sometimes, I was healthy for a year at a time. When I was away at Eton, I was hale as a horse. And then I would return home, only to grow ill again. My—Mrs. Ludlow, my brother Clay's mother, she suspected my mother after a time and had her watched.

"My mother was soaking fly papers to obtain the arsenic in them and poisoning my food. The doses were always small enough to make me ill and never kill me, but...she was not kind to me, and I always knew she had no love for me. The day her treachery was revealed was the day I realized my own mother loathed me."

"Oh, *leannán*." Her arms tightened around him. "I am so very sorry. I have heard of such a thing, mothers poisoning their own babes, but I never could have imagined..."

He pulled back, made uncomfortable by his revelations. Aside from Clay, their father, Lily, and the dowager Duchess of Carlisle, no one else had ever known the truth. His father had forced his mother to leave for the Continent in exchange for not sending her to jail for her crimes, fearing the scandal and the harm it would cause his family.

"I do not want you to pity me," he said hoarsely. "It was a long time ago. I only told you so you would see that I may have been born to become the Duke of Carlisle, but I too have my demons. I am no better than you. No different."

"I do not pity you." Her gaze searched his, her hand cupping his jaw once more to stroke it gently. "I ache for you.

I ache knowing the one woman who should have loved you and protected you most was the one who was doing you harm. How dare she do such a thing to you? If she were here now, I would claw her eyes out for hurting you. I would take my knife and—"

He silenced his fierce warrior wife with his mouth, kissing the rest of her words away. Kissing her and kissing her, with gratitude and tenderness and raw, pure need. He kissed her as if this was their first and their last, putting all of himself into it, trying to show her how much her compassion meant to him.

How much *she* meant to him.

He pulled his lips away and pressed his forehead to hers. "Thank you."

"No, thank you for sharing that part of you with me." She kissed him slowly, tenderly. "Thank you for reliving your pain to tell me the truth. I am so very sorry, *mo chroí.*"

My heart, she had called him. He knew enough of the language of her homeland thanks to intercepted dispatches and various communications he had received, both ciphered and raw.

Leo pulled back to take her in, her midnight hair drying in luscious skeins of curls around her face, her retroussé nose and blue eyes and pink lips utter perfection. "What does that mean, those words you said just now?"

She did not hesitate. "My parsnip." Her nostrils flared, almost imperceptibly.

His lips twitched. The woman would never learn her lesson. He kissed her again. "Mayhap one day soon, you will trust me enough to tell me the truth. Until then, I am, as ever, your faithfully devoted parsnip."

Bridget stared at him, eyes wide like a doe caught in the wilderness. For a moment, he thought she would turn and flee. But then her lush mouth rippled with mirth. The smile she gave him was roguish. "I trust you, my faithfully devoted parsnip, else I would not be here. But this is difficult for me. I have been alone for so long, and you are the embodiment of everything I have always believed was wrong."

Her confession should not have felt like a blade between his ribs, but it somehow did. Despite what she said, she was not ready or willing to trust him entirely. Not in the way he would need her to if they were to both make it through his plan unscathed. And in Leo's mind, anything less was unacceptable.

She would not make this easy, but then, she had never made anything easy between them. Not from the day they had first crossed paths. And he had wanted her all the more for it.

"You are not alone any longer," he told her, and he had never meant words more. "I am your husband, and I will do everything in my power to keep you safe."

A shadow of something—worry, or perhaps fear— darkened her countenance before flitting away once more. Her lips compressed for a moment to a fine line, almost as if she struggled with herself. "My heart," she said on a rush. "*Mo chroí* means *my heart*."

"I already knew that," he confessed. The feeling they had crossed boundaries, that they had made definitive, real progress, could not be subdued. Hope rose within him, hope they could make their union work. That she would open to him. Trust him. And hope that one day, if he were so fortunate, she would love him as he loved her.

He stilled. His heart stilled. Everything in him stopped. Froze.

He did not love Bridget.

No.

He lusted after her. He liked her. He admired her, yes. He

respected her mind and her cunning and stubborn determination. He enjoyed her naked beneath him in bed. Her cunny was a thing of devious, devilish magic, and he could not wait to sink inside it once more. She had been so tight and wet, and she had milked him dry of every last drop.

His cock surged beneath the bedclothes, demanding attention.

All those things were true. But love? Love was a fantasy, a fiction, an implausibility. It was a chimera latched on to by few who truly experienced it, and millions more who never had a chance of finding it. Rarer than a diamond. More dear than gold. Love was impossible.

"What else do you know?" she asked him, dashing his thoughts with her honeyed voice.

And that was the precise moment he knew for certain. As he sat there in bed, wrapped in her embrace, their lips a breath away from the next soul-searing kiss, nothing between them but her chemise and her determination to cling to her homeland loyalties, the most stunning, staggering, horribly awful realization struck him. It happened in much the same manner he imagined a man about to be run down by an omnibus experienced. One moment, he was on his feet, alive, going about his day, and the next, he was staring down his own demise, unable to move in time.

Boom, he was struck. The force of the blow sent him reeling. He flew through the air figuratively, landing on his metaphorical arse in a pile of allegorical horse dung.

Fuck, fuck, fuck.

He loved her.

He loved Bridget O'Malley, the Duchess of Carlisle, and there was no turning back now.

"I know that I want you." It was the most honesty he could give her for now.

Until he determined where they stood—and where he would stand with the League, given his marriage to a known Fenian sympathizer, who had a brother in jail for plotting the death of the Chief Secretary for Ireland—he did not dare offer more. He could not hide the facts from the Home Office and his agents forever.

Everything had changed for him now their marriage had been consummated. The truth would have to be faced, and when it was, he had no doubt he would pay a substantial price.

But that day had not yet come, and Bridget was all soft, warm, womanly curves in his arms. Her lips were only a scant inch from his, awaiting his possession. Repercussions could wait. For now, he had her, and while he had once considered her a burden, he now saw her for the gift she was, the light to his darkness. So he kissed her again.

She made a sweet sound of surrender, her mouth moving with a frenzy to match his own, her arms twining around his neck. The weight of his responsibilities and duties fell away, replaced by her silken skin, her lush lips, her tongue moving against his. They would find a way, he vowed. He would save them both.

Their kisses deepened, hands rediscovering each other's bodies as though they had not just made love mere hours before. She was on his lap, her chemise riding high around her creamy thighs, legs splayed. Through the bedclothes, his straining cock pressed into the moist heat of her core, and he could not resist thrusting into that delicious friction. Wanting more, needing more.

He swallowed down her moan, coasted his palms up her hips, skin on skin as she rocked against him. Her body had been awakened, and though he had been no innocent, in a sense, his had as well. Never before had he experienced such a deep, abiding need. A hunger so fierce it threatened to shatter him into a thousand jagged pieces of himself. Desire so potent it made him forget everything and everyone but her.

His hands were on her waist now, guiding her as she ground against his cock like she was riding him. Oh how he wished she were, her tight, drenched cunny clenching him like a fist. But she was likely sore, he reminded himself, and he had no wish to bruise the tender flesh which had only been breached for the first time that morning. There would be more mornings, more nights—a lifetime of them—to satiate the desire roaring through him.

This was about Bridget. About giving her pleasure. About watching her come undone. He kissed down her throat, licked her ear, tongued the smooth dip behind it until she gasped, writhing against him. Then lower, a starving man attempting to consume the feast laid before him. Through the fine barrier of her chemise, he latched on to a nipple and sucked.

She caught fistfuls of it and yanked it over her head until she was naked. He allowed himself the glorious pleasure of looking upon her for a moment. Her midnight hair was a wild tumble down her back, her eyes were wide, pupils dilated, mouth swollen from kisses. She had not stopped moving over his cock, and with each aching pass, her breasts, full and tipped with hard pink nipples, swayed like offerings. Her cunny was spread over him, glistening with the evidence of her renewed desire, the sweet jewel hidden in her folds visible with her every undulation, then hidden again.

"Christ, you're beautiful, banshee." The words were torn from him. Breathless. Half prayer.

She was every brilliant sunrise he'd ever seen, each awestruck breath he'd taken, the sum of every little miracle bestowed upon him; all these things and more, so much more. She was a goddess and he wanted to worship her as she deserved. How had he lived his entire life without knowing her, without touching her? It was impossible to imagine, for he could not go a day without her now.

He had never believed in fate until a governess in a gray gown had upended his world. But the governess had turned out to be an Irish rebel with a soft heart. A heart he would make his.

She continued working herself over him, finding the rhythm and pace she liked, head thrown back, hair cascading like a curtain of ink. She had never been more beautiful, and he was a sinner. A horrible, imperfect sinner, because he did not give a damn about his duty in this moment.

Leo lowered his mouth to a breast, sucking, biting. His fingers dipped into her sex, finding her pearl. She was so slick, so engorged, and he could not resist giving that responsive bud a stroke. Then another.

"Leo." His name on her lips was one-half moan, one-half beg. "I want to touch you."

Fucking hell.

He wanted it too. So badly, he caught her around the waist with one arm, lifting her while his free hand whisked away the bedclothes. Cool air licked over his heated skin, and then the wet kiss of her cunny was on his bare thigh as he settled her back down.

"Oh," was all she said as her tender flesh connected with his. Her gaze lowered to his cock, rising against his stomach, rigid, thick, and full, seed already seeping from the crown. "May I?"

"You never need to ask, darling. My body is yours." He took her hand, guided it to his painfully hard prick, and wrapped their fingers around the shaft as one. Slowly, he showed her how to touch him. How fast to slide her fist, how much pressure. Together, they worked him into a frenzy, until his hips were twitchy with the need to thrust and the pleasure pulsed in his ballocks, a sign he would soon spend. All the while, she continued to restlessly move against his thigh, seeking relief.

"I want you inside me, Leo."

Sweeter words had never been spoken in the history of man.

Yes, cried everything within him. *Take her. Fuck her. Pin her to the bed with your cock.*

But he could not. She was a novice, and it was his turn to be the one to take care of her. To tend to her as he should have done when the fever had claimed her after he had wounded her, rather than relegating her to the questionable auspices of Annie.

"You will be sore, love," he warned. "It is too soon. But there are other ways we can give each other pleasure."

"Show me," she whispered.

Another surge of need made his cock even harder. He rolled them as one until she was on her back once more beneath him. He settled between her thighs, his cock glancing her soaked folds. Her beauty struck him. She looked so innocent. So unencumbered by whatever secrets and demons she carried about on her small shoulders. Demons he would slay. Secrets he would learn. He kissed her, unable to resist, catching her succulent lower lip between his teeth.

He took control. In the bedchamber, as in every other aspect of his life, Leo needed authority. Dominance. He thrived on it. Craved it, and he wanted it from Bridget more than he wanted his next breath. "Touch your cunny."

Her eyes widened, the inky lashes fluttering. He had shocked her, and for a moment, he feared she would not play his games. But then she surprised him with one word. "How?"

He took her fingers, guiding them to her clitoris. He

moved with her, using her own hand as if it were his, showing her how he intended for her to pleasure herself. Quick strokes, side to side, pressure beneath the hood. Her breathing went ragged, her hips already started to jerk up from the bed. She was so responsive, so passionate, filled with fire. Perfect for him.

Leo swallowed, unable to wrest his gaze from the delicious sight of their fingers pleasuring her in unison. "Just like this, banshee. Pet your pretty pussy for me, won't you? I want to watch."

He released her, bringing his hand to his cock. He was on his knees between her spread legs, and he felt like a god. Her fingers stilled as he worked his shaft, root to tip. He looked away from the erotic sight of her core, drenched and on display for him, her fingers on her pearl, touching herself because he had asked it of her. The same sweet pink of her nipples infused her cheeks.

"Give yourself pleasure," he urged. "Show me."

Her gaze met his and clung. "It is wicked."

"Be brazen for me." He stroked his cock, ran his thumb over the head. Damn, he was close. So close. Just from watching her. From the way she—the wildest, fiercest woman he had ever known—submitted to him in the bedchamber. He had played games with other lovers, some who had been more depraved than even he had been. But he had never been so hopelessly, deliriously in the thrall of another woman. Never about to spend in his own palm from watching a woman touch her own cunny.

Her fingers moved. Once. Twice. Her hips undulated. Thrice. And he knew he had won this particular battle.

"Yes. That's the way, love." He pumped his raging hardness. Breath hissed from his lungs. "Pretend it is my fingers fucking you. Do whatever feels good. Hard and fast, soft and slow. Whatever you want."

Her fingers moved in time with his hand, stroking, rhythmic, heightening their mutual pleasure. The chamber went quiet, the only sounds the wetness of her folds, the friction of his hand, their labored breaths, soft sounds of surrender.

"Leo," she whispered. "Touch me."

Damn.

Her plea was too much. He could not resist running a finger over her seam with his free hand as he continued to work himself into oblivion with the other.

"Spread your legs wider." He wanted to see all of her, wanted to see what he had claimed. What was now his.

God help him, she did exactly as he asked, without hesitation. Her legs moved farther apart, and she was open, continuing to pleasure herself. She was so beautiful, so perfect. All that sleek flesh, those swollen folds, plump and ready. He could not resist. His hand had a will of its own. His finger sank deeper, finding the heart of her. The place he had so fully owned mere hours before. And then he was inside, the hot, slick walls of her gripping him, sucking him in, telling him this was where he belonged.

Too much.

Not enough.

Everything.

He was going to explode. He met her gaze. "Come for me, love. Come with me."

Her lips parted, her fingers flying furiously over herself, her cunny constricting around his finger, the only invasion he dared allow himself this soon. "I'm falling in love with you, Leo."

Whether it was her confession, or the fact he was so close, her pussy gripping his finger deliciously, the air perfumed with the sweet scent of her desire, he would never know. Her submission, lying open and bare and at his mercy. Her eyes wide on his. Whatever the cause, he lost control. Pleasure catapulted through him. His ballocks tightened. He grasped his cock with one last, hard stroke.

The dam burst. He lost control. Aiming his cock at her cunny, he surrendered. His climax tore through him violently, and he spent. Thick white spurts of his seed shot all over her glistening mound, on her fingers, on her pearl. She moved with jerky motions, her body tensing, twisting, and then the tremors rocked through her too.

A moan left her lips. Her channel tightened around his finger, sucking him deeper. He absorbed the spasms, milking his cock of the last drop of his climax. And then he collapsed to the bed alongside her, utterly sated, exhausted, completely in her thrall.

His seed had been in her. Was painted all over her now. He had marked her. Claimed her.

"You are mine forever now, Bridget Carlisle," he told her when he could at last force his mind to function, his lips to form words. From this day forward, she would never again be Bridget O'Malley. She was his duchess, his wife.

Simply his.

"Aye," she agreed softly, as breathless as he was. But then she startled him by framing his face in her hands and yanking him to her for a long, slow kiss. Her way of marking him. "And you are mine, Leo. I'll be keeping you as well."

Christ, her brogue. He kissed her nose.

Smitten, that was what he was.

Chapter Sixteen

"*Y*OU ARE SMITTEN with the Duke of Carlisle," Daisy pronounced, the second time in the past sennight someone had accused Bridget of having amorous feelings for Leo.

Apparently, she was not as adept at hiding her emotions as she had fancied.

Her cheeks went hot. They had just withdrawn from the Duke of Trent and Leo at the dinner table, leaving the men to their port. Her bottom had not even yet grazed the gilded settee she had chosen for herself. As it was, she jerked and almost missed her seat.

She caught herself in time, passed her hands over her skirts as she settled in, attempting to force the telling flush on her skin to abate. "Nonsense. I do not even like him."

"So you have protested before." Daisy's tone was smug.

Bridget studiously avoided her half sister's gaze, looking instead at the carpet. Then at a picture hanging on the wall. Then at the hands primly folded in her lap. "I do not know what you are talking about."

"I cannot credit it. When Sebastian first suggested the notion of you and Carlisle entering a marriage of convenience, I was convinced the two of you would eat each other alive," Daisy continued, utterly unrepentant. "He is a cold fish, and you are the proudest woman I know. Two more opposite creatures could not be found. You are full of passion and convictions, while he is cool and methodical. Passionless as a cucumber."

That description rather nettled. And though she did not wish to make herself the object of further scrutiny, her feelings for Leo had altered everything. She could not allow him to be maligned. Besides, she had firsthand proof there was nothing passionless or cold about the man. Good God, the wickedness he had visited upon her...the mere thought of it was enough to nearly send her up in flames right here.

Over the precious past few days, they had been lost in each other, closing off the outside world, existing in a charmed honeymoon, as if their problems and differences could forever be ignored. She had surrendered herself to that pleasure. To him. But she knew their time was limited. That it would end.

It was an inevitability.

"There is far more to him than the face he shows the world," she defended him, continuing before she could think better of it. "And there is nothing cold or passionless about him."

"I knew it!" Daisy crowed, clapping her hands together. "The way the two of you glanced at each other over dinner when you thought no one else was watching...I nearly caught flame myself just from observing."

Bridget studied her nails. Examined the perplexity of her knuckles, those strange little whorls interrupting a finger's otherwise faultless perfection. "I do not like him."

It was a lie. Of course it was a lie. But even now, she was not ready to examine her feelings and what they meant. They existed. She loved him, and that love was an uncontrollable, untamable thing, as much a part of her as a limb. But it terrified her.

Because they came from different worlds, disparate beliefs.

Because her brother needed her, and because to a certain extent, she and Leo would forever be two people existing on different sides of a very clear line. But when he touched her, when he kissed her, and Lord in Heaven, when he made such wicked demands of her in the bedchamber—when he told her she was his—she could forget.

Still, beneath it all simmered one ugly, horrible truth: she would have to betray Leo. She would have to leave him, regardless of how much she did not wish to do it. In spite of how deeply she longed to stay here with him forever and forget everyone and everything else.

The truth could only be avoided for so long. It lurked like an ugly, pulsing shadow waiting to claim its victims and return them to the ether.

"Bridget, look at me," her half sister demanded.

Bridget pursed her lips, looking everywhere else. She could not shake the feeling Daisy would read everything she was so desperate to keep from her and more if she met her gaze.

"Bridget."

Stubborn woman. She supposed it made sense. They did share blood, after all, and Bridget knew her own faults all too well. She flicked a glance to her sister, her face going hot all over again. "What would you have me say? He and I are enemies by definition."

Daisy's shrewd gaze plumbed hers. "No longer, I suspect. My dearest sister, no one knows better than I the conundrum in which you find yourself. Sebastian thought I was guilty of aiding the Fenian cause because of our father, when in truth, I was innocent. I thought he had betrayed me. When our misunderstandings were solved, and we allowed ourselves to love each other, everything changed."

"But I am guilty," Bridget blurted before she could still

her foolish tongue.

She loved her half sister, and she was grateful to her for her steadfast intervention on her behalf, but she was not certain she could trust her. Indeed, Bridget's life experiences had taught her to trust no one, and that was what she did. Even with Leo, though she loved him and had given her body to him, there remained a part of her she reserved only for herself. It was the part of her that would go into action should he ever betray her.

Why, then, would she do something as foolish as confessing her sins to anyone, even if it was Daisy?

"I know you are guilty, dearest," said her half sister, shocking her with her calm acceptance. "It is why Sebastian and I felt it was best for Carlisle to marry you. It was the only way we could be ensured you would remain safe."

Bridget's brows snapped together as she attempted to make sense of the revelation. "You know?"

"Of course I know, Bridget. You disappeared without warning and could not be reached. I had word that you had become embroiled in a particularly cutthroat band of Fenians. You attempted to abduct the Duke of Burghly, and though I know you had no intention of doing him harm, I am afraid your past leaves one with a rather clear picture."

Her frown deepened, for this made no sense. None whatsoever. "You knew I was guilty, and yet you wished to help me anyway?"

"Of course." Daisy smiled at her, and though there was a tinge of sadness in that smile, it was undeniably genuine. "I know your heart is good, Bridget, and you would not take the actions you have unless you felt as if you had no choice in the matter. You are my sister, and I will always do everything in my power to help you."

Tears stung Bridget's eyes. Tears of gratitude. Of love. For so long, she had been an island, her shores battered by violent seas on all sides. Alone. But she was beginning to realize she need not remain that way. That there could be strength in admitting others into her heart. If only she could keep them there. If only she could pause this moment, and never move forward into the maelstrom inevitably awaiting her.

"Thank you, Daisy," she said softly. "I will always remember how good you have been to me, when I have least deserved it."

"You deserve it, Bridget. It is only you who has convinced yourself you do not."

Bridget did not bother to argue the point. She alone knew the truth. She was not worthy of anyone's kindness, compassion, or love. She was betraying her brother with each day that passed, allowing him to rot in Kilmainham while she fell more in love with the enemy. And when the time came, she would have no choice but to betray Daisy and Leo too.

The only thing she deserved was scorn.

LEO WAITED FOR the Duke of Trent to cease choking on his port. This was decidedly not the reaction to his declaration he had anticipated. Very well, he supposed he ought not to be surprised, but still.

He fixed Trent with a narrow glare. "Will you recover, do you think, or are you passing on to your reward?"

The duke gave another exaggerated cough. "Forgive me. Will you repeat what you just said to me? I believe I must have misheard."

Leo knew what the blighter was after, but he decided to be deliberately obtuse. "Will you recover, do you think—"

"Not that bit," Trent interrupted with a dismissive wave

of his hand. "The sentence wherein you claimed to possess the capacity for emotion. I confess, I thought you were dead inside."

Leo gritted his teeth. "I thought I was as well. It would seem we were both in err, and moreover, that fate and fortune harbor the devil's own sense of humor."

"You do realize you just confessed to being in love with a Fenian conspirator?" Trent asked, raising a brow. "The very same woman who abducted your nephew and held a pistol to his head?"

"The pistol was empty." The words left him before he could hold them back or attempt to examine them.

But Christ, once they had emerged, he wished he could recall them, for he had unwittingly taken up the cudgels for Bridget in the exact same fashion Trent had not long ago. He was acutely aware of just how much had altered in the intervening time since that day.

Trent grinned. "The mighty Duke of Carlisle, felled by one Irish lass. I never thought to see the day."

Leo barely resisted the urge to smash the duke in his teeth. "Have you finished gloating now, or do you require more time?"

"Another minute more, if you please." Trent's smile widened. "You must admit, this is highly irregular."

"Thoroughly unwanted," he growled. "Entirely foolish. I am aware I have taken leave of my senses, thank you. As they do not seem likely to restore themselves to me any time soon, perhaps we might move our dialogue forward, before I deliver you the sound trouncing you deserve."

"It would be no trouncing, and you know it." Trent raised his glass in a mock salute, still making no effort to disguise his delight.

The duke was a formidable opponent. But at the moment, he was not inclined to acknowledge Trent's pugilistic prowess. At the moment, all he wanted to do was pound the man's face in until he stopped grinning like a child who had just been given a pony for Christmas.

"It would be the trouncing of the century," he declared, his tone as grim as he felt. "Indeed, it *will be* if you do not cease exulting in my misery. I require your aid."

Trent took a sip of his port. "My aid? Wonders shall never cease."

He skewered the duke with a look he hoped conveyed his severe displeasure and impatience both. "I would hate to have to strangle you with your necktie before we rejoin the ladies. Murder just after dinner seems so terribly uncouth."

"You need not issue warnings, Carlisle." Trent sobered at last, frowning. "What do you need of me?"

He sighed, a weight settling upon his chest, constricting him, threatening to swallow him whole. "Your promise you will see my wife is taken care of should anything happen to me. I need to know she will always be safe and looked after."

Trent's frown deepened. "Jesus, Carlisle. Of course I shall see her protected. She is my wife's sister. But why would you need such a promise from me?"

The dread grew, tainting all the bittersweet tenderness and hope that blossomed inside him whenever he and Bridget were naked in each other's arms. It grew and it grew.

He steeled himself, somehow meeting the duke's gaze without flinching. "I have a plan."

WHEN THEIR GUESTS had taken their leave, Leo dropped a kiss on Bridget's brow and laced his fingers through hers. Shaken from her conversation with Daisy, and the knowledge she would soon have to leave this idyll and the man she loved behind—possibly forever—she allowed him to guide her to the ducal apartments. They traveled in silence, neither of them seeming to need words.

The door had scarcely closed on their backs when he took her in his arms and kissed her. His mouth on hers was a beautiful gift, one she could not help welcoming. How she wished she could kiss him like this every night, that he would always be hers. Her arms locked around his neck, her tongue ready for his. There was something different in his kiss tonight. A sadness.

Or mayhap that was merely a projection of her own confused feelings. She kissed him back with more ferocity than necessary, their teeth knocking together as she inhaled deeply of his familiar scent. Spurred on by a growl in his throat, she bit his lower lip, wanting to somehow mark him forever. He groaned and nipped her in return, deepening the kiss until she sagged against his broad chest.

When at last their mouths parted, he gazed down at her, his breathing harsh, expression chiseled from stone. His stare was the pitch of midnight bereft of stars or moonglow.

"I trust you, Bridget, but I need to know if you trust me."

Did she trust him? Strange how she had not even bothered to question it these last few days. Their union had become something stronger than she had ever imagined it could be. Something real and true and deep. She trusted this man with her body—to touch her and take her and give her pleasure, to lead her to the edge of comfort, and challenge her to go one step further. She wanted to believe him when he said he would protect her, when he said she was his and he meant to keep her as his wife in truth.

She swallowed, settling for partial truth. "Yes, I trust you."

He nodded once, his expression as intense as ever, jaw a rigid plane carved from marble. "Good. You can trust me, banshee, and I vow it upon my life. Upon my mother's life."

Despite herself, she frowned, for the latter avowal was not entirely reassuring.

"My true mother," he amended. "Lily Ludlow, the only mother I have ever known. I vow it upon her life."

Bridget nodded, for in one of their late-night dialogues, he had revealed to her how deep his love for Mrs. Ludlow ran. With good reason, it would seem, for the woman had shown him as much love as she had shown her own son. "I believe you, Leo."

He took her hand, his large, warm one dominating hers. A jolt of energy rocketed through her at the contact, just as it always did, landing between her thighs in a delicious tug of want.

How was it the mere touch of his hand could make her so desperate for him?

It made no sense, and yet, it did. Despite all the reasons why they should never be together, there was something elemental about them that was so very right. She would never be able to stay away from him.

"Come with me," he ordered, and before she could protest, he led her to the massive bookshelves dominating one of the walls of his chamber. Stopping just before it, his free hand shot out, fingers reaching beneath a shelf, almost as if testing its texture.

But then a mechanical click snapped through the silence between them, and he pushed on the shelves. They gave way under his pressure, revealing a dark passageway within. The light from his chamber illuminated several feet, and cool air, along with the undeniable scent of a room that had been kept closed for too long—must and dust—a century or more of walls that had been lived and loved in.

But this dark, desolate passageway seemed rather eerie. She could not help but to feel as if he intended to lead her to her prison cell at last. Her trepidation must have shown on her features, for he squeezed her fingers with his in a gesture of reassurance and lowered his head to drop a kiss on her cheek.

"You are safe with me, Bridget," he whispered against her ear. "Always."

She believed him when he uttered those words, so she allowed him to lead her into the passage, bringing a handheld lamp along with him which illuminated only a mere scant foot before them. Once they were inside the passageway, he released her hand and found the mechanism within the wall that slid the door closed once more.

They were closed off from the outside world entirely.

Hidden from everyone and everything.

Bridget should have been frightened of the notion. Once, before she had come to know Leo, she would have been terrified to follow him blindly into the darkness. But he was the man she loved. And so, when his fingers found hers once more, she laced them tightly to his, allowing him to lead her where he would.

They traveled through the darkness, making two turns and going down a set of steps, before they reached a small chamber. One by one, he lit the gas lamps within, and with them all burning at once, the room seemed rather like any other, aside from its distinctive oblong shape and its lack of windows.

She cast curious glances around her, noting a solid but beautifully carved desk, chairs, a handsome sideboard with decanters and tumblers, and pictures hanging on the wall. Oils, all of them, done in dark and somber tones, mostly landscapes. One in particular captured her attention—the silhouette of a female form, a raging deluge of rain pounding down around her.

She turned to him, feeling awkward, as though he had just shown her a glimpse of what it looked like inside himself. He watched her with an expression she could not decipher. "What is this place?"

"It is my haven." His lips quirked into a self-deprecating half-smile. "Less than five others know of its existence, and you can now count yourself among them."

"Thank you for trusting me enough with its secret," she said, understanding how much this meant for him.

For Leopold Travers, Duke of Carlisle, this was as close to an admission of his feelings for her as he could reasonably get. She understood it for what it was, and she appreciated it all the same. Leo was no ordinary man, and neither was she an ordinary woman. Together, they might have had a chance at being extraordinary, were there not other forces conspiring to tear them apart.

"I brought you here to show you how much I trust you," he said. "But I also brought you here so we could have a private conversation. This is the one chamber in the entire household where I am ensured nothing that is said shall be overheard."

His dark gaze on hers gave her pause.

And then, suddenly, epiphany.

"You brought me here so I would confess." If bitterness tinged her voice, it could not be helped. What had seemed a beautiful gesture, indicative of the way he felt for her, suddenly seemed tawdry. A cruel joke he had decided to perpetrate against her. Here, it seemed, was the heart of the difference she had sensed in his kiss. Perhaps that kiss had been their last. A goodbye.

"I brought you here so we could be honest with each

other."

"No." Feeling suddenly like a caged animal, she spun on her heel and ran for the door, only to realize it had been sealed once more. Frustrated, she ran her hands along its carved wood surface, her fingers probing for release mechanisms, even the slightest hint of abnormality.

"You'll not find it."

The soft warning at her shoulder had her turning her ire toward him.

How dare he be so handsome? So unfairly beautiful? How dare he make her feel special by bringing her here before revealing the reason why?

Gritting her teeth, she cast him a sidelong glance. The sharp, sculpted planes of his face, those dark eyes, that sensual mouth and the beautifully hewn features made her catch her breath, despite the anger rising within her. "What was your intention in bringing me here?"

"Truth."

"Your truth or mine?" she could not help asking.

"Ours." He cupped her face. "No one will hear us here. I'm going to help you, Bridget. But I cannot help you unless you tell me everything. I need to know how deep your involvement with the Fenians runs. I need names. Specifics. Truths. Your truths are our truths, and with the answers you give me, I can extricate you from this godawful mess. I can extricate the both of us."

She wanted to tell him everything. Oh, how she wanted to confess all, to believe he would help Cullen. That he would help her.

But she was also terrified.

"I've told you everything I know."

His lips flattened, his eyes going cold. "Have you forgotten I know when you are lying to me?"

She closed her eyes for a moment, shutting out the sight of him. "What I have not forgotten is you and I are on opposite sides of a war. This armistice will not endure. You and I both know that."

"You are correct, Bridget. It will not." His voice held a razor's edge of anger as he paused, appearing to consider his next words. "That is precisely why I have brought you here. Open your eyes and look at me, damn you. See me."

She shook her head, eyes still tightly closed. If she could not meet his gaze, she could remain firm in the decisions she must make. He was her Gorgon. She could not look. Would not look. She needed to be strong. Her reckoning had reached her sooner than she had imagined it would, and in an entirely different manner, but there was no denying it any longer.

It was here.

"I cannot," she said resolutely. "You must resign yourself to knowing I will go, Leo. I will leave you, because the man tasked with apprehending Fenians cannot also be the man who is bedding one."

"You are not a Fenian, damn it. You are my wife." Though his tone was harsh, his touch remained tender, his thumbs tracing her cheekbones in slow, tender strokes.

Those strokes made her weak. Weak as she must not be.

"Am I not?" With a cry, she opened her eyes at last, seeing his beloved visage through the sheen of her tears. "I am a proud Irishwoman, and I shall be until the day I die. I am not of your kind, nor would I wish to be. I have hosted the men you seek to imprison in my parlor. I count them trusted friends. I have kept their secrets and done as they wished of me. Does that not make me guilty?"

"What crimes have you committed, damn you?" he demanded.

"Coercion," she said solemnly. "Arrest me. Take me to

prison now. Make it swift."

"Damn you, Bridget. I am not taking you to prison. I am trying to help you."

She shook free of him, seeking to put some necessary distance between them. She could not think when his skin was upon hers, when he stroked her with the soft seduction of a lover. When the anguish in his expression pierced her heart like the blade of a sword.

She stalked to the opposite end of the narrow chamber, arms wrapped protectively around herself, before turning back to face him. "Perhaps I do not want your help, Leo. Has that occurred to you?"

It was not true, for she would love his help. But she feared he would not give it, and if she revealed everything to him, he could use it against her. As it stood, all she had to protect herself with was the answers he wanted. If she gave them to him, she would be defenseless.

He remained where she had left him, his bearing stiff, his mien grim. "Tell me one thing, if you please. Why do you keep their secrets for them?"

Because she did not dare to trust him entirely. Because he was her ruin, her downfall, her only weakness, and her every sin. Because she owed her brother loyalty and love. Because she could not turn her back on him.

But she said none of those things. Her heart hammered away, her palms damp, her mouth dry. "Because I must. I swore an oath to them, and I keep my word."

Even from across the room, his anger was as palpable as a lash. "I am your husband. What of the vows you made to me? Will you not keep your word to me?"

She swallowed, unable to answer. He stalked toward her, a storm of a man, tall and broad and powerful, and enraged. There was nowhere for her to run, no means of escape, so she remained where she was, chin high.

"You said you were falling in love with me," he reminded her. "You claim to trust me. Are you a liar, Bridget Carlisle?"

"O'Malley," she corrected miserably.

"Carlisle," he gritted back, his lip curling. "Do you not realize you are more mine than theirs? Do you not realize I am the man who has saved you from prison, perhaps even from the gallows? That I would do anything to keep you safe from harm?"

She wanted to be Bridget Carlisle. How she wished she could be. How she wanted to fall into him. To make him hers always, rather than for the handful of enchanted days she had been fortunate enough to know.

"My brother is in Kilmainham Gaol," she said suddenly, startling even herself by broaching the topic of Cullen.

"I am aware." His gaze turned assessing. "He is being held along with the other Phoenix Park plotters who assassinated the Duke of Burghly. Are you telling me you had something to do with the plotting?"

She shook her head slowly. "No. I had no notion of what was about to happen. Nor did my brother. Cullen feels strongly for the cause, but he is a lad. Practically a babe. He would never conspire to hurt anyone, let alone to kill so viciously."

She suppressed a shudder at the newspaper reports she had seen concerning the murders. The assassins had used surgical knives to slash the Chief Secretary of Ireland and his undersecretary to death in Phoenix Park when the men had been innocently walking along. A handful of men had been arrested for the crimes, and she had known them all. One was her own brother.

"The evidence against him is undeniable," Leo said calmly, his countenance softening.

"Nothing is undeniable," she argued staunchly. She believed in Cullen's innocence.

The other men, also men she had known, were harder sorts. They were older, harsher, more touched by life's bitterness than her brother. Two of them were battle-hardened Americans who had fought in that country's civil war. They were men who had already killed hundreds of times before.

Cullen was different. He was sweet and kind and good. His only guilt was in loving his country far too much, and in falling into the company of the wrong sort of men. From the moment of his arrest, she had never faltered in her belief he was innocent.

"I know you want to believe the best of him because he is your brother, but he has been inextricably linked to the plotters. There is nothing you can do for him now, Bridget."

The tiny bud of hope inside her shriveled into a desiccated husk. This was precisely the response she had expected from him. The response she had feared. "What if there was something you could do for him, Leo? Could you help him? Would you be willing to do so for me?"

"I wish I could, but I am a mere man, and I have precious little influence in Dublin where he is incarcerated. Even were I inclined to offer him aid, I do not think it would make a difference. I am familiar with the case against both him and the other conspirators. You must prepare yourself for the worst, I am afraid."

She nearly doubled over at Leo's words. They were not hard or cutting, not cold or biting. Instead, they were soothing. Sympathetic. As if he truly hated denying her. As if he truly cared. And she could not bear that. Because he was also telling her she had no other choice, that the last path left to her was the selfsame path that had brought her to Leo in the first place. The path that had made her his wife. The path that had made her lose her heart.

He would have her heart forever.

But she would not have him.

Bridget swallowed down the bile. Loss was a terrible monster, and she had not been prepared to lose Leo yet. In truth, she would not be ready to lose him ever. He was a fine man, an honorable man, who shouldered duty and responsibility with equal aplomb. Who never faltered. She would miss him. God, how she would miss him.

"You…are certain?" she asked, struggling to gather her emotions and her words. "Cullen, he is a lad of eighteen. Our mother died when he was a wee one, and I have been mother to him for so many years. He depends upon me. He needs me."

"I am sorry, darling. Justice must be had for the men whose blood was spilled that day. I know you do not want to believe it, but the facts are incontrovertible. He was one of the conspirators." Leo folded her in his arms then, and although everything between them had just changed forever, she held him back as if he were the only anchor keeping her from being swept away by a raging tide. In a way, he was. He had become necessary to her. He was beloved. He was the husband of her heart.

The husband she could not keep, for how could she be so selfish as to leave her brother to die at the end of a hangman's noose?

She pressed her ear to his chest, listening for the rhythmic pulse of his heart. It should have given her comfort. Solace. Hours ago, it would have. Yesterday, it was a blessed thump she absorbed with her bare palm. Today, it filled her with dread.

"You did not bring me to this chamber to betray me?" she asked when she found her tongue at last.

He kissed her head again, his large hands never pausing in their calm, fluid motion over her back. Soothing. Loving. "No, banshee. I did not. I meant what I said when I told you that your truth is our truth. I may not be able to aid your brother, but I can and will help you. But I cannot help you if you are keeping secrets from me. I need you to tell me everything. Can you do that? Will you do that?"

No.

How she wished she could. But he was still the enemy, and Cullen remained in Kilmainham, and the only hope she had of rescuing him lay with John.

Her face was still tucked against his chest. He could not see her expression, and nor did he force her to face him. Her tells were a secret between herself and the supple fabric of his coat, the hard heat of his chest radiating beneath.

"Yes," she whispered, hating herself for lying to him yet again.

Knowing she had no choice.

Chapter Seventeen

$\mathcal{L}$EO HELD BRIDGET'S hand in his as they returned to his chamber and the secret panel snapped back into place. He sensed her desire to flee him, the need for escape evident in the way she caught her lower lip between her teeth and the tenseness she exuded.

But he was not ready to allow her to flee him.

No, instead he wanted something else entirely.

He wanted to tie Bridget to his bed.

Not as punishment. But for pleasure. Tonight, in his secret chamber, she had told him the truth. Or her version of it. Leo was no fool. He sensed the holes, the snags in her story, bold as imperfections on fine silk. She was withholding information from him. He could not be certain why just yet. Or what it meant for him. For her.

For them.

All he did know was, by the time he had finished questioning her, he had been all too aware part one of his plan would prove an utter, abject failure. He would need to proceed with the second, much riskier part.

But tonight was not about plans.

It was not about the differences and secrets keeping him from his wife. It was about making her his so thoroughly and deeply neither one of them would ever be the same. So she would never forget where she belonged. They were bound inextricably now, regardless of what happened between them. Regardless of what decisions she ultimately made.

That was the thing about the woman he loved: he likened her to a butterfly. She was too quick, too beautiful, too fragile, getting close enough, then inevitably flitting away before he could catch her. And he did not doubt she was poised for flight yet again. Her posture was stiff and awkward, her gaze shuttered.

"I ought to return to my chamber," she announced into the thick silence. "My lady's maid will be awaiting me, and I am already tardy."

"You do not need a lady's maid." Slowly, careful to allow her to deny him at any moment, he tugged her nearer with their entwined hands and caressed the delicate protrusion of her collarbone with the other. Her skin was warm, smooth, luxurious as velvet. He stayed his touch above the hollow at the base of her throat where her pulse fluttered. She wore no necklace, and he realized he needed to rectify the omission. Her elegant throat deserved sapphires and diamonds. He would buy them for her. Drape her in them.

"I do need my lady's maid to prepare for the evening," she protested, but this time, her voice was breathless. She made no effort to shy away from him.

"Sleep in my bed again tonight." He did not want there to be distance between them. "I shall assist you, should you require any aid."

She inhaled swiftly as his touch glided up the column of her throat, stopping to curl around her in a gentle hold. His fingers threaded through the silken cloud of hair at the nape of her neck. His thumb traced the lobe of her ear, one more part of her body he would have to worship.

"Leo." His name seemed torn from her. Those brilliant blue orbs glittered into his. "What do you want from me?"

The answer was simple.

And also complicated as fuck.

He wanted her body, her heart, her love, her trust. He wanted her to surrender the final piece of herself she continued to withhold from him. Yes, *surrender*. That was what he wanted: her complete and utter surrender, full stop. He wanted her to be his without shame or hindrance, without guilt, without barriers, without the differences she clung to as if they were a shield.

But he would begin with the physical, for it was where they always meshed best. He would begin with simple, basic touch. With human need. With the desire that always burned into a raging maelstrom whenever they were alone. Together, they were molten.

"Just you, darling." He lifted their linked hands to his lips, kissing the top of hers. He would pleasure her so thoroughly she would never be the same. "Just you."

A husky sound emerged from her, half want, half aching need. "You already have me. Here I am. Yours."

But there remained part of her she kept for herself alone. He had pushed her far enough for one evening, however. Though he had once vowed he would break her, it was the last thing he wished to do now.

He kissed a path to her wrist, wanting to devour her whole. "Are you mine, banshee?"

"You know I am."

Higher still he went, all the way to the lush skin of her inner elbow, so incredibly supple, so delicious. Her skin smelled faintly of lemon there, fresh and bright. He licked her, his tongue finding a new place to gauge her heart's frantic beats. She gasped. He smiled into the flesh he teased.

And then he raised his head, meeting her sultry stare. "Show me."

Her lips parted, the pupils of her eyes going round. "What do you want me to do, Leo?"

Her bold question made his cock—already straining against the placket of his trousers—go completely erect. He released her hand at last, dragging her mouth to his for a long, thorough kiss rather than answering her with words. She made another soft whimper, and the raw need in her voice nearly brought him to his knees. Already she was desperate for him in the same way he was for her, and he knew if he lifted her skirts, parted the slit in her drawers, he would find her folds wet, the plump bud hidden within eager to be stroked.

She was a welcome conflagration.

But he wanted to prolong this. To take her so thoroughly, by morning light, there would be no question in her mind she was his in every way. So he broke the kiss and forced himself to maintain a solid grip on his control. "I want you to give me *carte blanche* to do whatever I wish to you."

Her eyes went wide, her tongue flicking over her kiss-swollen lips. "Whatever you wish?"

He did not miss the note of trepidation in her tone, and though the unknown often heightened the pleasure for him, it was not his intent for her to fear him. "Whatever I wish as long as it gives you pleasure," he elaborated.

Her gaze plumbed his, searching for something. Reassurance? An inkling as to his depravity? He could not be certain. This too was an exercise in trust, so he held his tongue, allowing her to mull it over in her mind.

Just when he was convinced she would deny him, she gave a swift, jerky nod. "Very well."

Lust, pure and raw, surged through him. But along with it came the swift current of something else, something even more potent and primitive and powerful: love. He loved this woman so damn much it was a physical ache.

"You are certain?" he forced himself to ask.

"Yes." Nothing more than a sibilant sigh, her acquiescence.

But it sent him over the edge. "Good. I want you naked."

Her eyes never leaving his, she reached for the top button on the long line marching down her bodice, the line that had been driving him bloody mad ever since she had first descended for dinner earlier. It slipped from its mooring with ease. Her small, nimble fingers moved to the next. Then the next. All the way down she went, until she reached the last and her bodice gaped open, revealing the lush mounds of her breasts pushed high beneath her corset.

So much beautiful skin on display. Such temptation. All his, all for him.

His mouth went dry.

"Do you like it, Leo?" Her query was a seductive murmur, and it sent heat down his spine.

"Do I like what?" he rasped.

He watched, riveted, as she opened another hidden fastening and shrugged free of first the sleeves of her gown, then the full tiered skirts, until they fell in a single rush of silk to the carpet. She stood before him in a corset cover embroidered with roses, a fine chemise, creamy silk stockings, and lacy white drawers. With her black hair, vivid eyes, and lush pink lips, she was a siren, just as he had once said.

She took off the corset cover next. "When I obey you. Do you like it when I obey you?"

He gritted his jaw to keep from touching her. "Yes."

Though they had only spent a handful of nights learning each other's bodies, it did not surprise him she had already discovered what pleased him most, which actions garnered the greatest reactions from him. It was a matter of course she would know how to undo him. How to make him even weaker for her than he already was.

"What shall I remove next, Duke?" She lowered her lashes, watching him with a sultry stare.

Damn it to hell, but he even loved the way she called him by his title in that sinful brogue of hers. "Your chemise."

She gripped two handfuls and with one elegant motion, had it over her head and tossed to the floor. From the waist up, she was bared to his hungry gaze. He drank in the sight of her full breasts, the rosy tips already hardened into stiff peaks.

"What now? Do you want me to touch myself again?"

Ah, hell.

She was outmaneuvering him, flanking him like an invading cavalry storming around a defenseless phalanx of infantrymen. "Yes. Cup your breasts."

Once more, she did as he requested, her small hands holding each breast from beneath so her nipples jutted forward like offerings. He could not wait to suck them. But first, he wanted her desperate. He wanted them both desperate.

"Have I done well?" she asked, and he could discern from the smoky undertone of her voice that her desire had been heightened every bit as much as his.

"Pinch your nipples," he ordered her instead of answering her question. The saucy minx would not get his praise just yet. She needed to wait. To learn the art of patience.

She took each nipple between her thumbs and forefingers and pinched, rolling and tugging until they were even harder, ruddy color rushing into the peaks. The sight of her standing before him, submitting to his every whim, clad in nothing more than stockings and drawers, skin flushed with the pleasure of touching herself, was enough to send another stab of need to his already engorged prick.

Their wicked games were having an effect upon her as

well, for her mouth was slack, her breathing growing choppier. She did not instantly parry his demand with a question of her own.

"How does it feel?" he asked her, watching her fingers pluck and pull.

"Not as good as your mouth," she dared to say.

His cock twitched against his trousers once more. If he did not speed up this process, he would spend before he even touched her.

"Your drawers," he said darkly, bemused by his own lack of control where she was concerned. "Remove them."

Gaze burning into his, she released her breasts and reached for the waistband of her drawers. One by one, she slid more buttons from their temporary homes. With a hand on either side of her full hips, she pushed at the fabric until it too vanished. Wearing only her stockings and garters, she faced him, and no woman had ever been as glorious as she was in that moment.

"Am I naked enough for you?" She was part defiant, part seductress. Like some wicked goddess come to earth to make him hers.

Leo slid a finger beneath his necktie, loosening it, before he tugged on the ends and whipped it away from his throat. Next came his jacket and waistcoat. But he ignored her question all the same, because there did not exist a world or a life within which Bridget would ever be naked enough for him. He wanted her stripped bare, physically and metaphorically, on display for him alone. Weak for him the same way he was for her.

In love. He wanted her so in love she would confess the last vestiges of her truth to him. So in love with him she would entrust him with anything: her crimes, her heart, her life. God knew he trusted her with his, even when he had no good reason to do so. Even now, when she loved him with her body, yet kept him at bay.

"On the bed," he told her. "Now."

She turned her back to him, and he watched her backside sway as she walked to his massive bed, using the small stool he had procured specifically for her to climb atop it. He was instantly reminded of the first night they had met, when she had led him to the library and he had trailed behind, admiring the flutter of her dove gray skirts.

Everything inside him screamed with the urge to strip the remainder of his clothes and simply join her there. To spread her pale thighs and settle himself between them, fucking them both into a sated delirium.

Control, he reminded himself. *Maintain your control.*

He took a deep breath and one step toward the bed. She lay reclined upon it, watching him, all those lush curves on display. He unbuttoned his shirt and tore it over his head. His breeches were next, and he did not stop until he too was divested of every stitch.

He joined her on the bed, and she reached for him.

"No." They were playing this game by his rules. "You do not touch me unless I give you permission."

The brilliant hue of her eyes deepened. Her tongue flitted over her full lower lip. "I want to touch you, Leo."

"Do you trust me?" It was the second time that evening he had posed the question. But this time, it held a world of other meaning.

She hesitated, her pupils dilating. "Should I?"

"Yes. Always." He skimmed a hand down her thigh, trailing over her calf, finding her elegant ankle bone and rubbing gentle circles over it with his thumb. "I would never hurt you, Bridget."

"I know."

He wasn't certain if he believed her, but for now it was enough. It had to be enough, for it was the only admission she would give him.

Slowly, he removed each silk stocking from her legs. He kissed his way up her gorgeous body, intent upon his goal. She sighed and shifted restlessly against him, seeking, he knew, to assuage the ache blossoming between her thighs. He was rigid too, both from the dominance she had allowed him to exert over her, and the lush press of her body against his, the sweet scent of her—lemon, bergamot, *his*—the knowledge of what he was about to do…

Control, he cautioned himself again.

"Give me your wrists," he told her then.

LEO'S DEMAND TOOK Bridget by surprise. She had expected something else. More kisses on her mouth and throat. More wicked teasing. But she sensed something else in him tonight, a wildness, the veneer of his civility worn thin. A savagery that somehow had its root in the emotions and desires burning between them. It was something she didn't entirely understand, but she was not afraid of it, nor of him.

Wordlessly, she did as he bid, offering them to him, palms upturned, arms outstretched. He looped first one stocking around her right wrist, tightening the knot, and then the other around her left. Wordlessly, he guided her wrists over her head, fastening each stocking to the carved spindles in the headboard.

She made no effort to stop him or object. The position she was now in was reminiscent of waking up after the catastrophe at Harlton Hall, when she had been wounded and at his mercy. Her wound had healed, and how odd to realize she was more at his mercy now than she had been on that day.

This time, he held her heart in his hands.

He caressed her arms, lingering at the puckered flesh where the bullet had marred her forever. Lowering his head, he pressed a reverent kiss over the evidence of their tumultuous beginnings. "I am sorry for shooting you that day."

His apology startled her. "I would have done the same, had I been in your position. But I would have aimed differently."

He kissed his way to her shoulder. "Ah, but then I would not have my beautiful wife tied up beneath me now, would I?"

No, he would not. He had spared her, and when he should have seen her clapped into prison, he had saved her by marrying her. Then he had gone and made her fall in love with him. He had made her want things she did not deserve and could never have. An ache burned through her, underscoring the heavy desire pulsing in waves from her core, a reminder this too was fleeting. That her time with him was limited.

"Are your bindings too tight?" he asked, tracing her lips with his fingers, just a ghost of a touch, but one that nevertheless made a spark simmer to life within her.

"No." She caught him in her teeth, delivered a playful nip to the fleshy pad of his forefinger. "Am I your prisoner again, Leo?"

He flashed her a wicked smile, melting something inside her. "I'm tempted to keep you tied to my bed all night, but you are no prisoner, darling. This is purely for pleasure. I want you at my mercy."

"I already am."

His head dipped, his lips claiming hers in a kiss that was fierce and hungry. "Desperate for me."

"That too," she admitted without shame, breathless.

Their gazes met and held. "Good."

His lips moved over hers. They kissed and kissed. Somehow, being unable to touch him heightened her pleasure. His tongue was in her mouth, his hands coasting over her body until a great, swelling pang of need radiated from her cunny to her breasts. She writhed against him, making her nipples graze the muscled wall of his chest, grinding her wet sex against his hardness. The head of him glanced over her pearl, making sparks of fire lick up her spine.

"More," she begged.

He bit her lower lip. "Ask nicely, Duchess."

She undulated her hips again, seeking more of him, more connection, more friction, more anything. More everything. Her body had taken control of her mind, and it existed only to be pleasured by this man. To be beneath him. To be touched by him. Loved by him. "Please."

His fingers dipped into her folds, giving her the pressure she wanted, rubbing over her in fast, delicious whorls. He kissed his way to her ear, licking, biting. "You are mine forever, banshee." Down her throat next, sucking, raking his teeth along her sensitive skin. He reached her breasts, suckling one peak into his mouth.

"Yes," she cried out, the hot suction sending a surge of wetness to her core. She felt it seep from her, and then his finger was there, slicking the moisture over her channel, delving inside her. His thumb found her pearl as he stroked, bringing her to the precipice with such ease.

"Say it," he urged, quickening his pace, a second finger joining the first. He sucked her other nipple. Nipped it.

"Oh, Leo." She clenched on him, the first spasm beginning to unfurl. Bliss, white-hot and uncontrollable, tore through her as she gave in, riding his fingers, watching him suckle her breast. "I am yours. Forever." Her voice cracked.

Her body cracked—perhaps even her soul cracked—as the rush slammed into her. Pure, molten release.

And then his fingers were gone, replaced by the thick head of him. Her legs opened wider, hips tipping to welcome him. He slid home in one quick, deep thrust. They sighed as one at the beauty of it.

He was inside her, and she was stretched wide, filled. The last strains of her climax ebbed. But then he kissed her again, and he moved, withdrawing almost entirely so only the tip of him remained inside her. For a moment, her flesh was hungry, bereft, longing. He slammed into her again.

"Forever," he whispered into her mouth, withdrawing his cock.

In his low, delicious baritone, it was a promise, a prayer, and a benediction all in one. "Yes."

"Always." He thrust once more.

It was slow, steady torture of the most depraved and divine sort. She could do nothing but meet him halfway, with her words as well as with her body. "Always."

He pulled back until he slid from her body entirely, his pulsing cock against her slick entry. "Promise me you trust me enough to always seek me out first. If you are in danger, if you are in trouble, come to me Bridget."

She closed her eyes, unable to meet his gaze when she made a promise she was bound to break. "I promise."

His clever fingers found her pearl once more, working the swollen nub as his cock stroked over where she wanted him most, denying her and torturing her at once. "Look me in the eye when you make me your promise, Bridget Carlisle."

Her eyes opened at his command, at the intensity of his voice. His handsome face was harsh, jaw a grim, tense angle. His eyes seemed to see straight through her. For a moment, she was convinced he knew she would leave him. That he knew no matter how much she loved him, no matter how well he pleasured her, she would always be a Fenian, and he would always be the man bound by his honor, duty, and loyalty to a Crown that sought to keep her homeland beneath its thumb.

"Bridget." Something in his expression shifted then. Some of the severity faded. He seemed softer somehow. More vulnerable. "I love you."

His words stole her breath. She stared at him, stricken, feeling as if she had just been hit by a locomotive. But then he moved, flexed his hips, and he was inside her once more, deep, so deep. And she was helpless, so helpless.

"I love you too, Leo," she confessed.

He stilled for a beat. It was as if time stopped. There was only the two of them, ensnared in each other's gazes, reveling in the enormity of their shared emotions. He loved her. She loved him. They loved each other.

His mouth was on hers. She kissed him back with the desperation clawing up from within her. He moved again, thrusting in and out, faster, harder, his fingers working their magic. She came apart violently, her body tightening on his, shaking beneath his onslaught, and it was even more beautiful than before. One more surge of his cock inside her, and he stiffened, crying out his release as a burst of warmth rushed inside her.

In the aftermath of their wild joining, he untied her, kissed her wrists, and carried her to the bath. They bathed in the massive tub, Leo at one end and Bridget at the other. He washed her as if she were a child, incapable of taking care of herself. And she let him, trying to erase from her mind all memory of the promise she could never keep. They had each other for now, these stolen, precious moments.

It would have to be enough.

Chapter Eighteen

*L*EO ARRIVED AT the residence of the Duke of Strathmore obscenely early the next morning. A bleary-eyed butler greeted him and led him to Strathmore's billiards room. He had not sent word ahead of his visit, but it did not matter. Griffin, a fellow League member and one of Leo's most trusted men, suffered from a familiar problem—an aversion to sleep. Regardless of the time of day or night Leo called upon him, Griffin was always awake.

With night came the demons lingering in a mind's darkened shadows.

Leo knew it all too well.

So it was no surprise when he entered the billiards room to find Griffin wearing rumpled white shirtsleeves and black trousers from the night before. He was sprawled in an overstuffed chair, cup of coffee in hand.

"Carlisle," he greeted, shifting as if to rise.

Leo held up a staying hand as he crossed the threshold. "Do not stand on my account." He settled into a chair opposite him and waited for the butler to disappear, leaving them alone, before continuing. "Rough evening, Strathmore?"

Griffin's lip curled. "Rough year would perhaps be more apt. I have not slept in three days, and I am thinking if I go a fourth, I'll be sticking my spoon in the wall at last."

"Not as soon as that, I hope," he said mildly, accustomed

to the duke's grim moods, for they so often mirrored his own. Trauma had a way of tearing a man apart from the inside out. "You are one of the best men the League has."

"The ranks of your soldiers are declining." Strathmore raised a brow. "First Trent and Leeds. Now your own brother. Who will be next to go? You?"

It was not out of the question. He held Griffin's stare, unflinching.

Griffin sat up straighter, sloshing hot coffee over his hand in the process. "Goddamn," he howled, reaching for a napkin and frantically dabbing at his reddened skin. "A fine morning this is. I've burned myself, and you are sitting before me, telling me you are leaving the bloody League."

There it was, the vocalization of the realizations that had been swirling through him ever since he had married Bridget. Realizations he had been reluctant to acknowledge, for the way they would necessarily rearrange his life as he knew it.

He expected to feel a tremor of uncertainty hearing those words aloud for the first time. Certainly, he had anticipated he would feel the lash of fear, the bitter sting of regret. Some trepidation at the gaping maws of change facing him. The League had been his life for over fifteen years. It had been his albatross and his momentum, his saving grace and his dogged duty.

Instead, where the heaviness in his heart ought to lay, he felt only lightness. He was not the same man he had been when his sense of duty had led him into the League. If he needed to leave now, he was prepared. There had been a time when he had clung to it as if it were his life source because he had been terrified of who and what he would be without its comforting force.

But comfort could so easily turn into a cage. Comfort had a limiting effect on what and who a person could be. And he found he no longer wanted to be Carlisle, the leader of the Special League, the man who was owned by his duty and his toils, the man who had no time for a wife or a family of his own. For little Bridgets and tiny Leos. He wanted those babes, goddamn it. With her.

He just needed to be able to trust her first. To convince her she could trust him.

"Are you going to deign to answer me, Carlisle, or are you going to remain silent and brooding, interrupting my morning coffee?" Strathmore asked insolently.

He sighed. "My departure from the League may be a necessity."

"Sodding hell." The duke made a wild gesticulation with his cup, resulting in another shower of scalding liquid, this time raining on his lap. "Fuck."

"Always a man of scintillating conversation." Leo could not resist the jibe. Even so, he was concerned. Strathmore was a decided ruin this morning, more so than he had been of late. "Are the nightmares growing worse?"

Once, heavily influenced by whisky, Strathmore had confessed he still suffered nightmares from his time in captivity in Paris more than a decade before.

"To Hades with the nightmares, Carlisle. Tell me you are not leaving the League."

He pondered the notion of his departure yet again, turning it around in his mind, and any angle from which he approached it, he only felt surprisingly free. Content. At peace.

"I cannot tell you that, and I will explain why directly." He paused. "First, I must have your promise everything I am about to share will remain between the two of us alone. I am keeping the Home Office and the rest of the League in the dark. If you find issue with that, advise me now, and I will take my leave."

"I am loyal to you," Strathmore assured him darkly. "Though only Christ knows why. Tell me what the hell is going on, if you please."

He took a deep breath. "I married a Fenian."

Strathmore, who had the misfortune to have just taken a sip of coffee, spat the dark liquid into the air and all over his already besmirched trousers. "Tell me you are jesting! I beg you."

"Capital thing that your trousers are black," he observed, perhaps unkindly. "And no, I am not jesting. Nor would I about a matter so grave."

"Why? How? Jesus, I had not even realized you'd wedded anyone. Did she hold a pistol to your head? Threaten to slit your throat? Cudgel you over the head and give you amnesia?"

He was not surprised Griffin was unaware of his matrimonial state. He had not bandied it about. In general, aside from his libidinous parties, he kept to himself. He showed a façade to London and threw himself into his work for the League. Few people, aside from those who had attended his ill-fated fête and the Duke and Duchess of Trent, knew he had a wife at all.

"I married her to save her," he said then, realized as he said the words aloud it was the truth. He had not married her because the Duke of Trent had forced his hand. He had married her because he had seen in her the other half of his heart, and he had been selfish and greedy, and he'd allowed his avarice to triumph over even his duty to the League. "But first, I shot her. I had received information she was involved with the ring of Fenians responsible for planning and carrying out the Phoenix Park murders."

"Holy God, Carlisle." Griffin gaped at him as if seeing him for the first time. "You are truly the madman everyone says you are."

"Yes," he agreed, inclining his head, "I am. And you, my friend, ought to seek out church this Sunday. I cannot help but feel you and the Lord have some grievances to work out. Your language certainly suggests it."

"You married a bloodthirsty Fenian, and you are suddenly concerned about the state of my soul?" Strathmore chuckled. "I shall worry about my eternal damnation and leave you to fret over yours. I cannot help but think wedding and protecting a murderess is a far greater sin."

"Take care. You are speaking of my duchess." Those his tone was calm, beneath his skin raged a seething, protective inferno. He would allow no man to disparage his woman before him. Not even if it was a man whose aid he needed to recruit. "And she has never murdered anyone."

At least, not that he was aware of. *Good God*, what a thought. He ought to be troubled this omission did not concern him more than it did. But the heart was a strange and fickle organ, and it loved who it loved. And he loved Bridget. Christ, how he loved her.

"You said she has ties to the ring responsible for the Phoenix Park assassinations," Griffin reminded him, outrage underscoring his tone. "How can you defend such a creature?"

It was a question that had plagued him initially, driving him mad as he sought the answer, so he did not hold the asking of it against the duke. "I believe the ties are forced. Her brother is Cullen O'Malley, one of the ring of suspects imprisoned for the plots. I believe her connection to the ring extends from him."

"You *believe*." No fool, even though he looked like hell and had just passed several sleepless nights, Griffin hit upon the fact Leo most wanted to bury beneath other information. "Are you telling me you do not know for certain what her ties are? Have you not asked? Have you not investigated on your own?"

"I have asked," he admitted grimly, his mind flitting to all the times he had attempted to extract information from his reluctant, stubborn, rebellious, maddening, beautiful bride. "She has not been forthcoming. And of course I have investigated. I've been making discreet inquiries with my sources from the moment I realized who her brother was. I've turned up nothing thus far, save a mountain of evidence against him."

"I beg your pardon." Strathmore's tone was incredulous now. "The omnipotent Duke of Carlisle has married a Fenian, who refuses to disclose the nature of her relationship to the barbarous murderers who slayed the Chief Secretary of Ireland and his undersecretary? And you are simply accepting her lack of cooperation?"

He swallowed. When phrased in such bold, confronting fashion, he could not deny the answers to Strathmore's queries. "Yes to both of your questions."

"Have you taken complete leave of your senses?"

Yes. It was painfully apparent he had. Falling in love made a man lose his wits faster and more thoroughly than any other condition.

He ground his jaw. "No. I merely know my wife. Better, even, than she supposes I do. I know she is involved, but I also know there is a good reason for it. A reason she refuses to divulge to me. That is why I need you."

"Me?"

"You." Here was his second plan, about to be sprung into motion. "I need you to reach all the men we have planted within the Fenian ranks. Let them know Bridget O'Malley has married me, and make certain they spread the knowledge with their Fenian contacts. I would do this myself if I was certain we could trust them, but it is imperative no one know I am the source of the information, and I do not dare put my faith in anyone but you."

"Why me?"

"Because you are the best we have in our ranks," he said honestly. Strathmore had been through hell on earth, and he had survived. He was damaged, but he had survived. And he was honest, loyal, and brave. There was no other man he would entrust with this all-important task, aside from Clay.

"Why not Arden?"

Leo stiffened at the mentioning of the Duke of Arden, who had been determined to take Leo's place for the last two years at least. "He and I have no love lost. I do not trust him, Strathmore. I do not have any intention of losing my wife. We need to flush the Fenians from their nest and put this to rest."

Griffin was oddly alert for a man deprived of slumber. "What if she is guilty?"

"She is not guilty," he gritted. Every action he was taking was predicated on that truth. He wanted her to be free to love him. Wanted to be free to love her as well. "But regardless, when this mission is completed, I am relinquishing my position. The actions I have taken in recent weeks have not been in the best interest of the League, and I know it. I also know the time has come for me to take a step back."

"For your sake, I hope she is not guilty, Carlisle."

"She is not," he repeated. And he believed it. He believed it to his marrow. He knew Bridget O'Malley, and not just every delectable inch of her body, but her heart as well. She was stubborn and fierce and fiery, independent, strong, and sometimes foolish. Brave and inspiring and beautiful and his. She was not a murderess. She believed in Home Rule, but as for the rest of it, he could find no evidence she had ever had a hand in the atrocities that had happened in Dublin. She was not guilty. And he was going to set her free of the burdens of her past and prove her innocence, even if it cost him the League.

She meant more to him than that. More to him than anything. Than anyone. And here was a realization that should take his breath. Make fear grip him. Yet again, all he felt inside was peace. Rightness.

Strathmore nodded. "I am more than happy to give you the aid you need. The information will be spread by the end of the day. But Carlisle, you need to have armed guards in place, on the chance these villains do not approve of her marrying an Englishman."

"I have men in place as we speak."

"Of course you do." The duke paused, his gaze sharpening. "Did it occur to you these fiends may come after you specifically for taking one of their own?"

He was not untouchable. They had come after the Duke of Burghly, had they not? Yes, the thought had occurred to him, but he didn't give a damn. He would do anything for Bridget. To protect her. To keep her. To make her his forever. "Let them come for me if they dare. I will be ready."

Strathmore stared at him in silence for so long, Leo fought the urge to twitch. And then he finally broke the silence. "Why did you shoot her?"

"She was attempting to abduct Clay's son." He admitted this only out of necessity.

"Jesus." Griffin shook his head. "I realize I have not slept in three full days, but this is lunacy, even by my standards. Please tell me Clay knows you married the woman."

Leo wished he could answer in the affirmative. "He does not." And it was something he needed to rectify. He loved his brother, cherished him, and as far as he knew, Clay, his new wife, their son, and his mother were still in Oxfordshire, in a state of bliss he hated like hell to interrupt. But it was inevitable, a reckoning he would face as stoically as all the rest of what was to come.

"Oh, hell."

"Precisely." Leo's tone was grim. He wished suddenly for a coffee. Or a whisky, even if it was unseemly early for such an indulgence.

"You love her, don't you?" Griffin asked softly.

"Yes." More than anything. More than anyone. Hopelessly. Helplessly. "I do."

"You're a bigger fool than I thought you were, Carlisle."

"Yes," Leo agreed again, unrepentant, without hesitation. "I am. I have one more request for you. I also need you to use your Dublin contacts to find out everything you can about Cullen O'Malley."

Specifically, just how guilty he was. Or how innocent.

One way or another, the truth would emerge.

And Leo would be waiting.

THE DAY HAD come.

For at least the hundredth time since its arrival the day before, Bridget scanned the terse contents of the missive from one Mrs. Eudora Templeton.

> *My dear Duchess,*
> *I would like to offer you my sincere felicitations on your recent nuptials. I hope you might join me for tea tomorrow afternoon at half past two. I trust you are familiar with the address.*
> *Kind regards,*
> *Mrs. Eudora Templeton*

The three simple sentences were innocuous enough. Anyone else who read them would have assumed an acquaintance desired her presence for some harmless afternoon tea. The only trouble was, Mrs. Eudora Templeton did not exist.

Like Jane Palliser, she was a fiction. One invented by John for just such a purpose; to contact her without anyone else being made the wiser. An icy cold noose of doom seemed to tighten upon her throat. Her hands trembled as she carefully refolded the letter, hiding its bold scrawl. John had returned to London, and he had somehow discovered her shameful secret.

He knew she had become the Duchess of Carlisle.

She steeled herself against a sudden clench of her gut, a rush of bile in her throat. Her past had just been resurrected like a specter from the grave to remind her who she was and where she truly belonged.

She could not remain Leo's wife.

She did not deserve him, and she never had. She was not worthy of a man as honorable and good as he. She was a thief disguised as a guest, lurking through his home, counting the candlesticks whilst he fed her dinner. She was a bad woman, a criminal. Bridget O'Malley did not belong in the splendor of the duchess's apartments in Blayton House.

The damask wallpaper, thick carpets, polished and gilded furniture, and the handsome paintings on the wall all reminded her of it. Even her gown, borrowed from Daisy, fine navy silk more sumptuous and beautiful than she had ever dreamed of wearing, seemed to mock her.

It was a shell, a disguise. Fine trappings to cover the ugliness that lay beneath, a woman with an inconstant heart, who could not be true to anyone she loved. Not her brother, not her half sister, not her husband, not her homeland. What a pathetic impostor she was, pretending to be everything she was not. Torn in a hundred different directions. Nothing left of her to give anyone.

She had been selfish since marrying Leo. These last few days had been the best of her life, spent in his arms, in his bed, learning the joys of each other's passion. Simple moments too, such as eating breakfast together. Just that morning, he had forked up a bite of his egg and offered it for her to taste. Reading poetry to him while he laid his head in her lap. Watching him sleep.

He was a beautiful man, and for the charmed span of their brief union, he had been hers, and she had felt like a queen, as if all things were possible. As if there would be a solution she could find that did not involve betraying the man she loved.

But there was none to be had, and she knew it now with the grim evidence of her abject failure folded in her hand, those few words burning into her skin like the devil's brand. The mantle clock told her she was running out of time. She had an hour to spare until she needed to meet John, and she had yet to contrive a suitable means of explaining her desire to depart Blayton House, which she had not done once during the course of their marriage, and to do so alone.

Leo would be suspicious.

He was not a fool, and though he had proclaimed his love for her, sometimes she caught him watching her when he thought she was not looking, and he wore the expression of a man who had brought a wild creature into his home and remained uncertain of whether or not it was truly tame. Whether or not it—*she*—could be trusted.

She could not be.

Her decision to heed John's call proved that. Bridget told herself she owed Cullen her allegiance more than Leo. That she must choose her love for her flesh and blood over her love for the man she had only known a scant few weeks. It was only fair. Only sensible. And besides, John could well have news concerning Cullen. Surely his trial would soon be set, and they would need to take action to free him from prison before his sentencing could occur.

She could only pray John's price would not be too steep. In preparation of this day, she had sewn a small, hidden pocket into the skirt of the dress she wore. Inside it, she kept the cipher key she had removed from Leo's waistcoat at Harlton Hall. She had originally sewn it within the lining of her corset, a fortuitous decision, because it meant no one had discovered it on her person and taken possession of it during her wounding and illness.

All this time, she had kept the cipher key. There had been many instances when she had been tempted, oh so very tempted, to reveal her theft of it to Leo. To return it to him. But something, some warning voice in the back of her mind which recalled all too well the sting of poverty and the bitterness of working for a pittance in shops, had not allowed it. That voice had promised her she must keep such a valuable treasure for the day when she would need it most.

And the day had come. She hoped surrendering it to John would keep him content. That it would serve her well enough to at least see Cullen spared from the hangman's noose. Bridget tucked the summons from Mrs. Eudora Templeton into the hidden pocket along with her other contraband.

How she wished she could reveal all to Leo. But it would be futile, and she knew it well. Even if she confessed to him now, why should he believe or aid her? He had made his opinion of Cullen's incarceration abundantly clear. He would not help her brother.

Justice must be had for the men whose blood was spilled that day.

She could still hear his quiet assertion. She pressed a hand to her lips to choke back a sob. The worst of it was, she could not argue with him. Those who had plotted and committed the savage murders in Phoenix Park had been wrong. But Cullen was not among their numbers. She knew it with all her heart.

Her husband, however, did not. He had made it abundantly clear to her precisely where he stood on the matter of her brother's innocence.

I know you want to believe the best of him because he is your brother, but the evidence against him is significant. Even were I inclined to offer him aid, I do not think it would make a difference.

Now, just as it had days ago during their heated conversation, Leo's words scored her like a dagger delivering painful pricks to her flesh, again and again. Leo did not believe in Cullen because he did not know him as she did. Because he did not love him as she did.

How could she forgive herself if she allowed her brother to go to the gallows? How could she bear to choose between the two men she loved?

She inhaled. Exhaled. Told herself she could do this. She had to do this.

Because she had no choice.

Five steps, six, seven, twelve to her chamber door. She lifted the latch and stepped into the hall. Centuries of Carlisle ancestors gazed at her with censure in their eyes as she swept past their portraits. More silent, damning reminders she did not belong here within these walls.

Impostor, they said.

Liar, those paintings whispered.

Thief, they charged after her.

Yes, she was all of those things, and she could not deny it

as she descended the magnificent stairway. Each step brought her closer to her reckoning.

Why was it she felt as if she were the one facing a grim death on the gallows?

Hargrove, the butler, approached her as she alighted from the last stair. He was dignified and stiff in bearing at all times, but with his grandfatherly shock of white hair and his propensity for kind smiles when she least expected them of him, he had fast become a favorite.

"Your Grace," he greeted her. "His Grace wished me to convey to you he had an unexpected matter to attend to this afternoon. He will join you for dinner."

Relief washed over her.

She would not have to lie to Leo. Not yet. "Very good, Hargrove, and quite timely, as I have a need to go shopping this afternoon. Would you please see to it that a carriage is readied for my use?"

"Of course, Your Grace. Would you like to review the dinner menu for this evening?"

How she wished she belonged to a world in which such a triviality was commonplace. Where she hailed from, one was merely content for sustenance. Far too many had starved during famine, losing their lives at the hands of Englishmen like Leo. It had never occurred to her to ask if he was a landowner, and the realization filled her with shame.

She clung to that shame now, needing it, needing the reminder of all the empty bellies and dead tenant farmers left behind by English landlords in times of scarcity. "I am certain it will be lovely, Hargrove. The carriage is all I require, if you please."

Chapter Nineteen

$\mathcal{L}$EO WATCHED FROM the window of an unmarked carriage as Bridget emerged from Blayton House. The sight of her, dressed as elegantly as a duchess ought to be, regal in her jaunty hat and blue afternoon gown, wearing only a wrap loosely hooked over each elbow, was enough to make nausea churn inside him.

He had spent the days since enlisting Griffin's aid in his plan alternately doing everything in his power to show his wife how deep his feelings for her ran, and waiting for some form of communication to arrive for her, sent by one of her Fenian connections. It arrived within mere days, an innocent enough missive from Mrs. Eudora Templeton. An invitation to tea at half past two.

And he had waited some more for Bridget to bring him the missive. To confess to him. To tell him she trusted him enough to give him the truth at last. To ask him for his aid.

He was still bloody waiting.

Her defection was akin to a kick to the gut, or a cudgel to the head. This was not the outcome he had envisioned when he had developed his plan, when he had involved Strathmore. He had imagined Bridget would believe in him and love him enough to trust him. That she would unburden herself and ask for his help.

He had been wrong.

Deadly, stupidly, *horrifically* wrong.

Oh, he had realized as much when she had not mentioned her unusual correspondence to him at dinner the previous evening. When he had gone to her bedchamber and kissed her and fucked her senseless, she had not spoken a word of the supposed invitation to tea she had received. When he had joined her for breakfast this morning, he had remained stupidly hopeful she would unburden herself.

But she had not.

And instead of taking her in his arms and promising her they would solve this problem together, he was watching her from afar as she climbed into his carriage. She was meeting a Fenian, alone, in secret. There was only one reason why she would be doing such a thing, and it made him want to retch.

She had chosen the Fenians over Leo. Of course she had, and he had been the biggest fool for believing in her. For listening to her when those deep blue eyes met his and she told him she loved him. For falling in love with her himself. For thinking his love could ever be enough.

The carriage containing his faithless wife jostled into motion, and he knocked on the wall of his carriage three times in sharp succession, the sign to begin following. He had chased her down before, and it would seem he would need to do so once more.

BRIDGET STOPPED THE carriage at the millinery where she had once worked. It was near enough to the rooms John kept she felt comfortable finding her way from there. She gave the driver instructions to return for her in an hour's time and pretended to enter the millinery until the conveyance lumbered out of sight. Then she walked as hastily as she could to her true destination.

Taking care to make certain she was not being watched, she skirted the building—an apothecary's shop—to the rear where she could find the entrance to the simple lodgings John had been renting for the last year using the alias Reginald Palliser. Jane Palliser was a shop girl who could come and go without notice, visiting her brother.

Everything had been carefully plotted and planned, and how easy it was now to return to the life she had lived before going to Harlton Hall. Up one narrow flight of stairs, past a door with a faulty latch, her fist raised to rap on the last door five times in quick succession. It was as if no time had ever passed. As if she had never become the Duchess of Carlisle. As if she had not lost her heart to Leo.

Except for the pain in her heart and the aching bitterness in her soul.

The door opened. John stood there, silhouetted by bright afternoon light pouring in the window at his back. He caught her to him suddenly in a tight embrace, and startled, she hugged him back. It should have felt familiar. Comforting. Instead, it felt like a betrayal.

Because it was.

"Come inside, sister," he invited, playing their roles though it seemed unlikely anyone was within earshot.

Don't do it, cried her heart.

You must for Cullen's sake, cried the rest of her.

Bridget did as she was bid, stepping over the threshold. John closed the door behind her. They were alone, facing each other. He had grown a beard in the time since she had last seen him, and his hair was in need of a trim. His frame seemed more gaunt than before, the plum shadows beneath his eyes more pronounced.

"How is Cullen?" she asked into the silence that had

descended between them, for it was all she could care about. All that mattered. It was the sole reason she stood here before him. "Have you seen him? Do you know when his trial shall be?"

"He is weakening," John said grimly. "It is to be expected. The conditions he faces are harsh, and the trial is set for a fortnight from now. We are running out of time where he is concerned, I am afraid."

Her heart clenched painfully. "That is what I feared."

"You did not take the young duke as I asked of you," John observed coolly, his expression impenetrable.

"I attempted to, but I was caught and shot," she said truthfully. "I did the best I could, John."

"We were depending upon you, Bridget. Cullen was depending upon you."

His censure hit her like a lash. She stiffened. "I am aware. As I said, I was wounded and fell ill. I did as much as I could to bring the young duke to you as you had asked of me. In the end, I could not manage it."

"And yet you had time to wed yourself to the Duke of Carlisle." John made a low whistle, his tone mocking. He was a short man, not much taller than she was herself, but she wondered for the first time if she should fear him. If he would attempt to do her physical harm. "Tell me, Bridget, how did that come to be?"

It occurred to her she could either be honest with him or she could feed him the version of the truth he would find the most useful. If she exaggerated her loyalties, made it seem as if she had married Leo to aid the cause, perhaps John would be more inclined to help Cullen even without the Duke of Burghly in his grasp.

"I married him for the cause," she lied. "When the plot fell through and I was wounded, I created a new plan. I decided if I could entrap him, convince him I loved him, he would be ours. Think of it, John, what could be better than having access to the leader of the men charged with arresting those who would aid and abet our cause?"

His lips compressed into a firm, grim line. "Why did you not contact me? Why did you not send me a message? Explain to me why I needed to learn of this from someone else, why I needed to be the one who made contact."

"I had not the means of contacting you that would not be discovered by Carlisle," she said. "He may have married me, but he is hardly in the palm of my hand, and he is too intelligent, too wary not to be suspicious of me. He already knew I was a Fenian because of my disastrous attempt at spiriting the young duke away."

She wondered for a brief, dizzying moment if her words were true. Since their feelings for each other had changed, Leo had been unrelenting in his declarations of love. He had given her pleasure. Had changed her forever. But what if he remained suspicious of her, even after all they had shared? The question made her frown.

She wished she knew the answer.

But part of her was beginning to suspect she did, and furthermore, it was an answer she could not like.

To her relief, John nodded, some of the strain seeming to dissipate before her eyes. "I feared as much. Your marriage to him is rather fortuitous, as I have formulated a new plan, one that will far surpass any others in the past."

Wariness hit her. "I gathered some information from him, John." She reached into her hidden pocket and extracted the cipher key, holding it out for him to take. "I believe this to be the diagram used to translate ciphered messages the League sends amongst its ranks."

He took it from her, unfolded it, his eyes scanning the

contents. "Well done, Bridget, but I am afraid this is not exactly what I had in mind."

"What *did* you have in mind?" she asked, the wariness turning into dread, sinking through her like a stone.

He tilted his head, considering her. "Would you kill for your brother, Bridget? Would you kill to save Cullen?"

Her blood went cold, everything inside her withering like the flowers beneath winter's ice. "I did as you asked, John."

"You did not bring me the boy." His voice was hard now, edged with steel. "It would have been the perfect plot, exchanging his life for those of our men in Kilmainham. Not only did you fail me, and fail Cullen, but you got yourself shot and captured in the process. I am afraid your marriage—fortuitous though it may be—and your discovery of this cipher key are simply not enough. We need action and destruction, complete and full war, if we aim to truly accomplish what we want."

Fear closed around her heart, tighter than a fist. "I did the best I could. Tell me, what would you have done with the young duke had I been able to bring him to you?"

He had told her the young duke would not be harmed. But doubt weighed upon her, along with dread. Had she been foolish to trust this man? She was beginning to wonder if she had ever truly known him.

He canted his head, smirking at her. "Whatever would have aided our cause the most. This is war, Bridget, and war begets casualties. It's only a natural state of things."

The breath rushed from her, bile rising in her throat. Thank God Leo had stopped her that day. She would have unwittingly led the goodhearted young lad to his murder.

"He is an innocent," she said, tears stinging her eyes.

His eyes burned darker, anger stiffening his expression. "And how many innocents do you think the damned English have killed? How many lads died with hunger gnawing their bellies, because greedy English landlords demanded their rent during famine? Do you think any of the rich lords gave a damn about all the Irish they sent to their deaths?"

She flinched, for they were arguments she too had raised. She had always believed in Home Rule, and she had not been averse to tactics that would frighten the English into righting the wrongs done to the people of her native land. The brilliance of fighting against a wealthy, powerful nation with nothing more than civilian foot soldiers had appealed to her. Independence had seemed necessary.

Fighting against authority, she could approve. Death, however, was taking the cause too far. Murdering the Chief Secretary in cold blood in the midst of a park had been too far. Attacking the man's innocent young son was the devil's own work.

And she had been complicit. The realization made her ill.

"He is an innocent, John," she repeated. "I believe in Home Rule, but I do not believe in killing to obtain it."

"That's a pity, Bridget." He raked her with a scornful gaze. "Because I'm afraid you'll be the one doing the killing."

She felt as if she had somehow gotten trapped inside a nightmare. "No, John."

"Do you want Cullen out of Kilmainham?" he pressed, his voice toneless.

The thought of her brother trapped inside the gaol made her shudder. "You know I do."

"Then you will do as I ask."

"How can you be certain he will be released?" she demanded, not wanting to hear the price for Cullen's freedom for fear it was the cost of her own soul.

"I told you, I have eyes and ears within the prison. Freeing him will not be an easy or a simple task. But in return for your show of loyalty, I will see it done."

"That is what you said before," she pointed out, delaying the inevitable sentence he would deliver. "I did what you asked of me, and yet my brother remains a prisoner."

"You failed miserably, as we have already established." He drew nearer, and the scents of pipe smoke and hair oil assailed her. "There will be great danger in liberating Cullen from Kilmainham. In return, there must be great reward. The Duke of Carlisle took a liking to you, else you would not be here now."

"He does not like me at all," she denied.

"Untrue, or you would have been clapped in irons immediately, bullet wound or no. Yet he tended to you, married you." John's smirk turned nasty. "Why do you think that is, Bridget?"

She pressed her lips together, staring at him, not wanting to answer.

"I'll tell you why it is." He took another step closer. "You lifted your skirts for him. There is no other reason. But I don't care about your treachery. All I care about is ending him. He's too dangerous, and he knows too much."

She almost retched, then and there. "I will not kill him, if that is what you are asking."

John's smile faded. "I'm not asking, Bridget. I'm telling you it's what you must do if you want Cullen freed from gaol."

Good, sweet God.

Bridget clenched her fists in her skirts. "You should aid Cullen without a price."

John shook his head. "Everything in this life has a price. Your brother, in exchange for the Duke of Carlisle. You shall be the Delilah to his Samson."

Denial shot through her, making her stomach clench. "I

cannot do it, John. Do not ask it of me. I will do anything else, anything but this, if it means Cullen can be freed."

"This is the price." John was solemn as a holy man presiding over a funeral. "Your brother's trial looms, my dear. He will be sentenced to hang, and you know it. Your brother's life, in exchange for the duke's."

"Never." The word emerged from her before she could think better of its utterance.

But as it happened, it ceased to matter, for one moment she stood alone with John, listening to the vitriol pouring from him, and the next, the door broke open. It slammed against the opposing wall with such violent force, plaster rained to the floor.

And on the threshold, there he stood. Leo. Her husband. The man she loved.

Only this man was different. He was cold. Aloof. Pistol in hand, the barrel pointing at John. He did not even spare Bridget a glance.

Dear God.

Leo had followed her here. He had known.

Of course he had.

He had not been looking after other matters this afternoon. He had been waiting for her to leave. Spying upon her. Watching her.

"Carlisle. Good of you to arrive," John spat, and it was in that precise moment Bridget realized he too had a pistol in hand. His pistol, however, was trained upon Bridget.

Her heart thudded.

"You would train your weapon upon a defenseless woman, rather than the man you seek to murder?" Leo asked John, his tone biting. Colder than she had ever heard it.

"Is she precious to you?" John asked, the barrel of his pistol never wavering from Bridget's head.

"She means nothing to me." Again, Leo did not even look in her direction. His dark gaze was fixed upon John instead.

His words may well have been an act. Bridget could not tell. But they stung just the same.

"Perhaps I will kill her while you watch," John suggested.

Her gaze flew back to the man she had once counted a friend. The barrel of his pistol remained pointed at her. "John."

"Shut up," he barked at her before turning his attention back to Leo. "What shall it be, Carlisle? Do you want me to put a bullet in her pretty head, or are you going to lower your weapon?"

"John, please," she intervened, terrified. Terrified for Leo. Not even for herself. She did not believe John would shoot her, but if he did, well...she had been wounded before. But *Leo*. If something happened to Leo, *because of her*, she would not be able to carry on. "This is madness. Lower your weapon."

"Here is your chance, Bridget," John surprised her by saying. "You can kill him now."

Bile churned, working its way up her throat, threatening to choke her. "Yes," she agreed, determined to agree with him regardless of what he said. He was a madman. All she wanted was Leo safe from harm. "I will do anything you ask, John. Only give me a weapon, and I will do it."

She swallowed again, arm outstretched. John reached inside his coat and extracted a second weapon, all while keeping the first upon her. Her fingers grasped the pistol. He relinquished it.

"I will give you to the count of five to pull the trigger, Bridget. If you don't do it, I will shoot you instead," John told her, colder than Wenham Lake ice.

"John," she objected.

"Leave the lady out of this," Leo protested simultaneously. "This is between the two of us, as men."

"No." John shook his head, eyes flitting wildly between Bridget and Leo, jaw rigid, clenched with determination. "Until the count of five, Bridget. One. Two."

Bridget knew what she had to do. She had fired guns before. She would wait until five and make her move.

"Three. Four. Five."

Bridget pointed the pistol at John and pulled the trigger.

It clicked.

Nothing happened.

Her heart dropped.

John sneered at her. "I knew I couldn't trust you, you stupid whore. Spreading your legs for the enemy and then—"

The violent report of a pistol tore through the small chamber. A perfect blossom of red spread on John's forehead. His eyes rolled. The pistol fell from his fingers, and in the next moment, he too fell to the floor in one loud thump.

It was over.

And Leo was unharmed, thank the Lord.

Stifling a sob, she looked to her husband, relief bursting inside her, thinking to throw herself into his arms. But what she saw kept her rooted to the spot. In his place stood a stranger. He stared at her, an implacable expression chiseled upon his handsome face.

"Gather yourself, madam. There is much awaiting us this day, and you will need to be strong."

"Leo," she began, starting toward him.

"No." He held up a staying hand, his voice hard, punishing. "Do not insult my intelligence. Do not dare to offer me more of your lies."

"Please." She was not above begging. The terror of the moment, the fear that had coiled within her like a serpent, was making her weak. She needed him. Craved his embrace, his reassurance.

But she had forfeited her right to those. She realized that now. She had betrayed him in coming here, and he would never forgive her for her terrible mistake.

"It is over, madam. Collect yourself, and then the men must come in to take the body. He will not receive the justice he so richly deserved, but perhaps our maker will rectify that. You, on the other hand, must wait to receive your sentence."

"Leo," she said again, needing him to hear her. To understand. "I only came here because of Cullen. I would never have betrayed you. I pray you know that."

"You could have come to me with your concerns. I would have helped you, Bridget. I pray *you* know that." He paused, grimmer than she had ever seen him. "But you did not seek me out, did you? You did not trust me enough for that. No, instead, you trusted a villain who would point a pistol at your head to gain what he wanted most. A man who would just as soon kill you as use you to abduct an innocent child for his own nefarious purposes."

"It is not what you think, Leo," she said. "He promised me he would aid my brother. That he would help him to escape from Kilmainham."

"He was lying to you," Leo snapped. "Using you to force you into doing what he wanted. And you allowed it."

Yes. She closed her eyes for a brief, steadying moment, before forcing them open once more. He was right. She had been so very foolish and naïve. Torn between right and wrong, husband and brother, love and duty, want and need. But she could see the difference now. Too late.

"I love you, Leo. Please believe me." It was pathetic, and she knew it, even as she said the words.

But he remained unmoved. "Only a mindless fool would

believe anything you say, madam. You have betrayed me and fooled me, used me and lied to me, far too many times for me to give a damn about a single thing you say ever again."

She flinched from the sting of his verbal assault, but in the end, there was nothing she could say, and nothing she could do, to erase what had already happened between them. He was right. She was wrong. John was dead.

A handful of men appeared on the threshold then, bursting forth, pouring into the chamber.

"Escort the duchess to Blayton House," Leo told one of them. "Do not let her out of your sight."

"Leo," she tried.

"Not now, madam," he snapped. "I want you gone."

Chapter Twenty

*Y*EARS AGO, WHEN she had thrown him over for a duke with an older title and a more prestigious lineage than he could boast, Lady Jane Reeves had taught Leo a lesson: *only a fool trusts blindly.* Somehow, he had forgotten that old knowledge when he had fallen into the eyes of a raven-haired Irish siren.

But he remembered it now, a fortnight after he had put a bullet between the eyes of the last member of the vicious Fenian ring who had plotted the death of the Duke of Burghly. Fourteen days after he had last looked into those brilliant blue eyes, shining with tears, when he had turned his back on her and left her behind at Harlton Hall. Fourteen nights since he had last slept with her at his side, since he had last kissed and touched and sank inside her.

Fourteen was a small number in comparison to all the rest of his days. Paltry. Smaller than a dust mote.

Why then, did it feel like an eternity? Why was she all he could think of just minutes after he had finalized stepping down as leader of the Special League?

His carriage rocked over the streets of London, putting distance between his past and his present, hurtling him forward into a new era. One that filled him with trepidation. He stared out the window, numb. It wasn't the familiar buildings or the crush of other carriages and pedestrians he saw. Rather, it was her.

Bridget, his wife, his duchess, his love.

Her cloud of dark hair, her bright eyes, the mouth he loved to kiss. She was a ghost who haunted his every waking and sleeping hour. She was everywhere, and yet she was nowhere within reach.

He missed her. He loved her. But loving her wasn't enough. Needing her wasn't enough. When he had followed her to the dingy rooms above an apothecary where she had gone to meet John Mahoney, he had been terrified for her. Terrified he would lose her.

But in the aftermath of what had happened that day, a cold realization had struck him. She had betrayed him by seeking out Mahoney, had even given the man a cipher key she'd thieved from Leo's own waistcoat, and he could not trust her.

Not now. Perhaps not ever again. He had been wrong about her, and nothing had illustrated that painful fact more than the sight of her standing in those rooms, colluding with a Fenian plotter, instead of trusting Leo. He had not known what to do with her, and his initial fury had been so great, the only solution he could settle upon was sending her to Harlton Hall. Away from him.

He had taken her there, left her with his mother and his brother. Turned his back on her. But she had remained with him even as his carriage had rumbled away that day. Even as he had boarded the train bound for London. Even as he had thrown himself into his work for the League with an unprecedented, grim abandon.

For the first three days of her absence, he did not sleep. He had killed a man, and though it was not the first time he had done so in the name of duty, there had been something different about this man. It was not enough the man was dead. Leo wanted to know all there was to know about him, and he had given himself over to the instinct to dig deeper, to unearth the buried secrets of Mahoney before it was too late.

He had scoured London. Interviewed everyone he could find who had a connection to John Mahoney, or Reginald Palliser, the alias he was known by. Using his and Griffin's sources, he had gleaned a great deal of information. The picture Leo had begun to place together had been stunning.

In Mahoney's rooms above the apothecary, a treasure trove of evidence against him and a dozen others had been discovered: false beards, revolvers, addresses of fellow plotters, telegrams, a map of London, and packages of lignine dynamite. With the new information they had gathered, he went to the Home Office, and a fresh wave of arrests occurred.

Interviews with the newly incarcerated men had added the final details in proving Mahoney had been the ring leader who had plotted the Phoenix Park murders. And further, that he had been actively plotting to lay bombs at railway stations in London at the time of his death.

In the wake of the arrests, another undeniable truth had emerged. Cullen O'Malley had not been an active conspirator in the plot to kill the Duke of Burghly. He had been a pawn, manipulated by John Mahoney. The conspirator who had turned Queen's evidence and implicated Bridget's brother had also been acting under the influence of Mahoney. The charges against Cullen O'Malley in relation to the murder of Burghly had been dismissed, and just yesterday, he had been released from Kilmainham gaol.

Leo's carriage stopped outside Blayton House.

Like an automaton, he alighted and walked up the front walk. Ordinarily, today would be a cause for celebration. He and Griffin had managed to see another dozen dangerous men stopped before they could do harm to civilians. An innocent man had been released. A villain was cold and dead, moldering in the ground.

But these victories were bittersweet, because the one resolution he wanted more than all others would forever elude him.

The door opened, and there stood Hargrove, waiting for him as always, ready to take his hat, gloves, and coat. "You have a visitor, Your Grace."

For a moment, his heart thudded into a gallop, daring to believe it could be her.

"Mr. Ludlow is awaiting you in your study," Hargrove continued, dispelling the notion in the next breath.

His brother Clay had come to London. If he had left his new wife and son behind in Oxfordshire…

Leo's heart beat even faster.

Bridget.

Was something wrong? Had she taken ill? Left him?

"Christ," he muttered.

He did not even recall handing off his garments to Hargrove. One moment, he was standing in the entryway, and the next he was stalking into his study. Clay stood at his entrance, his expression unreadable. Like their shared father, and like Leo, Clay was tall and broad. The scar on his cheek gave him a menacing air, but beneath his harsh mien, he had the heart of a kitten.

Under ordinary circumstances, Leo would be thrilled for his brother's company. But these were no ordinary circumstances. "Clay. What the devil are you doing here? Is it Bridget? Is she well?"

"It is good to see you too, brother," Clay said grimly, lifting a brow. "I was beginning to think you had forgotten you had a wife. How heartening to realize I was mistaken."

He deserved that jibe, and he knew it, but that didn't

mean he liked it. Leo raked his fingers through his hair. "Damn it, don't play games with me, Clay. Answer the question."

But his brother did not seem at all inclined to take pity upon him. "Which question?"

"You know which bloody question," he growled. "My duchess. Is she well?"

"Well enough," Clay said mildly. "She has been experiencing some illness recently. Mother is quite pleased by it. You might be also, but I cannot be certain. That is also the reason I have come."

Bridget was ill. Fear squeezed his heart.

"What ails her, and why would Mother or I be pleased she has fallen ill?" He longed to smash his fist into something. The wall, perhaps. He could send crumbles of plaster raining down. Make a hole so large it would require patching.

Yes, perhaps some damage and destruction would be just the thing to cure the darkness inside him.

"My wife is suffering from the same ailment."

Leo stared at his brother, trying to comprehend. "Goddamn it, Clay, cease talking in riddles and tell me what is wrong."

"You are going to be a father. Your wife is with child."

Air fled his lungs. He could not breathe. Or speak. Joy rushed through him, chased quickly by fear. Bridget was going to have his babe. It defied logic. He could not wrap his numbed mind around such a possibility. That together they could have made a child. That he would be a father.

"Sit down," Clay advised him, clapping him on the shoulder and leading him to a chair. "Before you fall down."

Leo surrendered to gravity. His legs gave out, and his arse planted itself in the chair. Still, he could not seem to breathe or form coherent words. He had never been so shocked. So filled with the tender riot of happiness and awe.

"Take a deep breath, old man."

He did at last, gasping it in, feeling like a drowning man whose head had just broken the surface of the water long enough for him to breathe. Gradually, sanity returned to him. "I am younger than you are," he reminded his brother in a voice that sounded rusty. Thick with emotion.

"And far less wise," Clay observed unkindly.

He frowned. "I would argue that point."

"Yes, you would. But I would still be correct. Evidence: here you sit in London, while your lovely wife has been abandoned in Oxfordshire for the past fortnight."

"My lovely wife betrayed me," he bit out, "and she was hardly abandoned. She had the company of all the rest of my family."

"She feared for her brother," Clay said softly. "She made mistakes, but she has owned them and apologized for them all. We have forgiven her for what she did to us and to Edward. She and Ara are getting on like sisters, and they are already plotting up a Ladies Home Rule society."

Of course they were. He was not surprised to learn his family had already fallen in love with Bridget and forgiven her. She had stolen the heart he no longer thought he possessed. She was special and she was rare, the sort of woman a man longed to unburden his secrets to, even those he had never previously fathomed saying aloud.

But she had also hurt him. She had done the one thing he did not think he could find it within him to absolve: she had lied to him and colluded with the enemy. Had told him she loved him, spent every night in his bed, welcomed him into her body, and yet she had kept the summons she'd received from John Mahoney a secret. She had gone to meet the man.

"I am grateful you forgave her," he said honestly, staring

into the carpet as if it would provide him some much-needed answers. "I am merely not certain I can do the same. This is deep, Clay. It goes not just to the bone, but to the very marrow."

"Clearly you must have harbored some tender feelings for her at some point, else she would not be carrying your babe," Clay observed.

Correctly, damn him.

"I love her," he admitted, and it was also true. Her betrayal had left him angry and disillusioned, but it was not the same as Jane's betrayal so long ago. Because he loved Bridget, and he had never loved Jane. He knew that now.

"Hell, Leo. What are you doing here in London?"

"My duty." And he had. Finalizing the investigation into John Mahoney had been his driving force. The man had manipulated his wife and landed her brother in Kilmainham. He had also intended to abduct Edward, and he had orchestrated the slayings in Phoenix Park. He was a dangerous, murderous coward. Leo had wanted to be certain any lingering connections to him were in prison where they belonged before anyone else could be hurt.

"The League can wait, brother." Clay rested a hand on Leo's shoulder. "You have greater responsibilities now."

"The League will wait forever." He looked up from his meditation upon the carpet at last, meeting Clay's gaze. "I resigned from my post today."

Shock flitted over his brother's ordinarily stoic mien. "You resigned?"

He inclined his head. "Yes."

"*You?*"

A wry smile quirked his lips at Clay's disbelief. "None other."

"Sodding hell, Leo. The League is your life. Why did you

not tell me sooner?"

It had been his life, yes. But the strange thing was, when he looked back upon the years he had devoted to service, he realized the League had been his only life. There had not been time or energy for anyone or anything else. The League had been his duty, and he had loved being at its helm. But in other ways, it had also been his anchor.

Today, he had sliced that rope, leaving the anchor on the bottom of the sea, and he did not regret it. If only the decision to move forward with Bridget could be as easy and clean.

"The League was my life," he agreed, "but now I am ready for another life. A new one."

"Make that life with your wife and your babe," Clay said.

"I want to," Leo said with raw honesty. "But I am not certain if I can."

BRIDGET SAT AT the small escritoire in her chamber at Harlton Hall and frowned down at the letter she had been attempting to write as another wave of nausea made her gut clench. Mornings filled her with dread. They were spent gagging at the slightest hint of a scent—almost any scent, even lovely ones like flowers seemed to punish her unmercifully—or casting up her accounts into a chamber pot.

By lunch, she was able to take weak tea, and by afternoon, she was functional and human once more. It was an irony of the richest order that Ara, her new sister-in-law, who was also increasing, suffered no such ill-effects of her condition. Bridget supposed if anyone ought to suffer richly for her sins, it was her.

But even through the misery that had become her days in the last week, one thought kept her happy.

She was going to have Leo's babe.

It was enough to make facing each day worthwhile. Over a fortnight had passed since Leo had unceremoniously delivered her to Harlton Hall, not staying long enough for the dust to even settle on the drive, before he had swung back into the carriage and headed back to the train station and his life in London. The life she was suddenly no longer a part of.

The letter mocked her, a quarter written, two sentences struck through, another not even finished. She had accepted her exile as best she could. She understood Leo's anger and hurt and that he needed time. She knew she had wronged him most grievously. Knew too she had been misguided, that she had made the wrong decision, a decision which had placed the both of them—and, unwittingly, their babe—in unnecessary danger.

She regretted what she had done every day.

But she could not return to the awful moment when she had decided to heed John's call. She could not change her mind. The dye had been cast. Her choice, however foolish and reckless and hurtful, had been made. Her only defense was she had been desperate to help her brother, and she had believed she had made the choice which would enable her to do that.

With a sigh, she reread her letter as composed.

My ~~Darling~~ Dearest ~~Husband~~ Leo,

I write you this letter to inform you I am with child. ~~The child is, of course, yours.~~ If you still wish to pursue the annulment, I recommend you do so with haste, as it will become impossible when my condition becomes apparent. ~~It is my most sincere hope you will not do so.~~ I am so very sorry for everything.

"Damnation," she muttered aloud, crumpling the latest

attempt in her fist. Perhaps she was being too conciliatory, too apologetic. The blame was not solely upon her shoulders, was it? Her movement sent a fresh wave of sickness through her, and she had to swallow in quick succession, fighting back against the by-now-familiar bile.

A tap at her door interrupted her self-loathing.

"You may enter," she called, reasoning it was either Ara or Lily Ludlow.

The kindness and compassion Leo's family had shown her—a stranger dropped into their midst, and one who had previously caused them a great deal of anguish at that—never failed to humble her. She had not known people with such giving hearts existed in this bitter world, and she was grateful she, undeserving though she may be, had found them.

Lily swept inside, followed by a servant bearing a tea service tray. Wearing an emerald-green morning gown trimmed with lace, ribbon, and intricate beading, her dark hair shot with silver strands swept into an elaborate coiffure, she was stunning.

She beamed at Bridget. "How are you feeling this morning, my darling daughter?"

She mustered up a smile for Lily's benefit. Her cheer was infectious, and as a motherless daughter, Bridget could not deny the notion of having this lovely, giving, kindhearted woman as a mother figure was incredibly alluring. "I am feeling as well as can be expected."

Learning she was carrying Leo's babe had been a shock. She was wise to the world, but for some reason, she had naively imagined they would need to be married longer for such a circumstance to occur. She pressed a loving hand over her flat abdomen, marveling at the life growing within her, such a fragile miracle.

Lily instructed the domestic to deposit the tea tray on a

low table, then dismissed her, waiting until the maid had gone to turn back to Bridget. "Have I interrupted your correspondence? If so, you need only say the word and I shall go."

"No." Bridget rose, walking with minced steps to join Lily in the small seating area where they ordinarily shared a late-morning tea. "I was attempting to write a letter to Leo and failing miserably, I am afraid."

"Ah. That explains your expression when I first entered." Lily came to her, casting a comforting arm about her waist and guiding her into a chair as if she were an invalid. "There you are, my dear girl. I brought my ginger tea once more, the blend that seemed to settle your stomach yesterday."

In addition to possessing one of the most giving hearts Bridget had ever known, Lily also excelled at gardening. She cultivated her own herbs and blended the flowers, leaves, and stalks into teas and tonics. The spicy, delicious tea she had brought to their impromptu morning visit yesterday had indeed soothed the roiling upset of Bridget's stomach.

"Thank you," she said, with genuine appreciation as Lily handed her a steaming cup and saucer, and the familiar, soothing notes of the tea hit her nose.

Bliss.

For the second day in a row, her stomach did not object to the delicious scent. It was nothing short of miraculous.

"It is my pleasure." Lily seated herself on the chair opposite Bridget. "I know all too well how unpleasant your condition can be."

Bridget sipped her tea, hoping it would combat the fresh wave of nausea that had assailed her just then. "It is a happy condition. I can only hope Leo will find it the same."

Lily's lips compressed, her eyes growing sad. "Leo has a soft heart. He has been wronged in the past. Do not give up on him, my dear. He needs you. The past has made him slow to trust, and even slower to forgive, but he will come back to you. My Leo is different than Clay. Both of my sons have been wounded and wronged, but one by the woman who should have loved and protected him the most."

"He told me about the duchess," Bridget said softly, hating to revisit such evil even by the mere mentioning of the woman. "What she did to Leo, poisoning him…" she shuddered with revulsion. How a mother could deliberately harm her own son was beyond Bridget's comprehension. "I am so grateful he has you."

"I am proud to call him my son. Others would frown upon me, would never recognize me. Not Leo." Lily's smile softened, her eyes glistening with tears. "He has been unhappy for so long, Bridget. He deserves happiness. He deserves to be loved. You love him. I know you do, and I know he loves you as well. From the moment you first came here to Harlton Hall, I sensed something different about you. I saw the way he watched you then, and I knew you would be the one for him. A mother can sense these things."

Guilt struck her anew for the way she had initially met this wonderful woman, for all the deceptions she had perpetrated and the pain she had left in her wake. "I am so very sorry for what I have done. When I came here, I thought it would be simple. An assignment to carry out, and I would save my brother's life. But it became far more."

Lily took a sip of her own tea. "Love always becomes more than we bargain for. When I first met Leo and Clay's father, I was a singer. I lived my life on the stage. I traveled the Continent and even went as far as New York City before coming back to London. It was my largest show. And there was a mountain of a man waiting for me afterward, a duke, the handsomest man I had ever seen. He wanted to make me his mistress, and I had no intention of being any man's kept woman."

"What did you tell him?" Bridget asked, eager to hear Lily's story, this untold piece of Leo's past.

Lily chuckled. "I told him to go to the devil. He was newly married, though unhappily so, an arranged marriage he had been forced to accept. I had no wish to be any man's mistress. But he was persistent. He returned, night after night. Followed me to different cities. Once, he turned up in Paris. It was the night I gave in. That man had loved me enough to chase me, even when he had no reason to. A hundred other women, all more easily obtained than I, could have been his instead. But he chose me.

"He pursued me. And he loved me. It took me some time to realize that. To accept I would always be his mistress and never his wife. But in the end, the love we shared and the life we lived was worth any sacrifice I ever made. I realized the most important decision you can ever make in your life is to love someone. Loving is not easy. It is raw and messy and hard-won. But it is also worth every struggle made to gain it."

Lily's story warmed her heart. It gave her hope. And courage too. Maybe all was not lost. "How do I make Leo follow me to Paris?"

Lily grinned. "Oh my darling girl, you won't have to go as far as Paris. I have it on good authority he is already on his way here as we speak." She paused. "And if he isn't, I shall hunt him down and box his ears."

Bridget had no doubt she would.

Chapter Twenty-One

$\mathcal{L}$EO LANDED BACK at Harlton Hall much as he had what seemed to be a lifetime ago, with a small cadre of servants and one armed guard, dusty, travel-worn, and weary. This time, there was no impending wedding, and he had not spent the previous night surrounded by the most depraved and licentious acts imaginable. Instead, he had spent it stroking his cock and wishing his hand had been his wife's delectable cunny.

He was also accompanied by two additional people. One was Clay, who had convinced him to flee London. The other was a surprise for Bridget.

Here he was, prepared to do his duty.

Duty was still everything to him, but it held a different, deeper meaning now: *family*. His family was in the process of expanding. Exponentially so, it would seem.

Clay was having a babe.

Leo was having a babe.

And he had another brother.

An *Irish* brother.

He glanced at Cullen O'Malley as the carriage slowed to a halt before Harlton Hall. Freshly arrived from Dublin, he was slight of figure, gaunt-cheeked from his imprisonment, and young, so very young. But he had Bridget's black hair and blue eyes. That they were siblings was undeniable. He was mild mannered, a friendly lad, grateful to no longer be imprisoned, and the second statement he had made to Leo after thanking him for his freedom had been a threat.

If you ever cause my sister any grief at all, Carlisle, you will have me to answer to.

Yes, Leo rather suspected Cullen would fit right in with this protective, eccentric, thoroughly odd clan he loved.

"Your sister will be most pleased to see you," he told Cullen. "She worked tirelessly to have you freed."

"She put herself in danger for me, and I know it." Cullen bowed his head. "I cannot thank you enough for your persistence on my behalf. I am sorry to have mixed her up in the circles I found. I...thought they were my friends."

"We are your friends now, lad," Clay told him, offering him his hand.

"Your *brothers*," Leo added, putting his hand forward as well. "Our family is small, but fierce, and you will always have a home with us."

"Always," Clay reaffirmed.

Cullen nodded jerkily, seemingly too overwhelmed to speak. He shook both their hands, and then the carriage door opened.

They descended, one by one, soles finding the solid gravel of the Harlton Hall drive. Leo clapped Clay on the back. "I expect you are eager to revisit your bride."

Clay gave him a meaningful look. "You as well, brother. Do not be a fool."

He was about to say he would not be, that he was going to attempt to speak to Bridget, to solve their differences, when the door of the hall opened. A trio of females burst forth, skirts flurrying down the front stairs, one dark-haired lad following in their wake. Ara, Lily, Bridget, and Edward met them halfway.

Leo did not miss the astonished joy on Bridget's lovely face as she took in the sight of her brother. "Cullen! My God, Cullen, is it truly you?"

O'Malley stalked forward, arms open, and a sleek blur of skirts launched herself at him. Leo was dimly aware it was his wife, elated to greet her brother after so long. Cullen's arms tightened around her, and he rocked backward, lifting her feet from the ground. As one, they twirled, laughing, clutching each other delightedly. Leo watched their unabashed joy, and for the moment, the sweet panacea of contentment washed over him.

Ara too had flung herself at Clay. Edward had come next, attaching himself to Clay's leg. Lily swept Leo into a sweet-scented embrace, pressing a kiss to his cheek. "You have come back, my darling son. Where you belong."

He hoped she was right, that he was where he belonged at last. That his love for Bridget would be enough to heal the distance between them.

"Yes," he agreed, his throat going tight with emotion, the back of his neck itching.

"Find your way back to her, Leopold," Lily whispered in his ear.

Only she could call him by his full name with impunity.

He smiled, releasing the fierce mother hen in his arms so she could greet Clay and Cullen. Bridget extracted herself from her brother's embrace and turned to Leo, tears of happiness shining on her cheeks. Her elation faded before him, her expression growing guarded. Solemn. Her arms were not open.

"Thank you for bringing my brother home," she said, as formally as she would to any casual acquaintance.

He wondered if he had waited too long, pushed her too far. Her stiff greeting was a barb to his heart. "You are welcome, wife. I trust you are well?"

She looked no different than she had when he had last set eyes upon her, except perhaps a trifle more pale. It was almost impossible to believe she carried a life within her womb. A life they had created together, in love, although they met again as detached as strangers.

"I am as well as can be expected," she answered, a world of meaning simmering beneath her words.

They walked into Harlton Hall, their divides intact.

But it felt wrong. So horribly wrong.

His mother was right. Bridget was his other half. He had to find a way back to her. A way back to *them*.

BRIDGET STOPPED JUST short of Leo's chamber door that evening, her hand outstretched. The closed door was symbolic of their marriage. How fitting it was he stood on the other side, just out of reach, this barrier between them as if it had been erected of her own making, a product of her sins against him.

She did not deserve the man on the other side of the door. That much she knew. But she wanted to deserve him, and he had met her halfway by coming here. Or at least, she wanted to fight for the chance. To fight for him. For them. For what they could be together.

Lily's words returned to her.

The most important decision you can ever make in your life is to love someone. Loving is not easy. It is raw and messy and hard-won. But it is also worth every struggle made to gain it.

Love was worth swallowing her pride, and so was Leo. She owed it to him—owed it to herself, to the tiny heart beating within her—to take this chance. To try to make him see she was still the same woman he had fallen in love with. That she was not perfect, but she loved him. She loved him fiercely and fully and deeply, and there was not one single thing in this world she would not do for him if it was within her power.

A short, deep breath for courage.

And then she tried the latch. *Unlocked.* The door opened, as if willed by a magic hand, swinging inward. There he was. Her eyes lit on him, hungry for any sight of him she could garner. She had not realized how desperate she was for him until she had seen him striding up the drive alongside her brother and Clay, tall and impossibly handsome.

He stood now in the center of the chamber, clad in a dressing gown and nothing more, his bare feet and calves peeping out from beneath the hem. She crossed the threshold without invitation, closing the door at her back.

His bearing went rigid, gaze burning into her. "Duchess. What do you require?"

So icy and formal. He treated her as if they had never shared such wild and wicked moments in each other's arms. As if they had not been as close as two people could be. Her courage faltered for a moment, wilting beneath the ice of his indifference.

Again, Lily's words recalled themselves to her, venturing back into the recesses of her mind when she most needed them.

Leo has a soft heart.

He has been wronged in the past.

Do not give up on him, my dear. He needs you.

Yes, he did. Bridget knew it just as surely as she knew she needed him in return.

"I require you," she announced boldly.

Something flared in his eyes, but she could not be certain of what it was. Interest? Irritation? Anger? Oh, how she wanted to believe it was the former rather than either of the latter.

"I beg your pardon, madam?" He raised a brow, his face a study in cold, dismissive hauteur.

He may be the duke, but she was the duchess.

She tipped up her chin, warming to her cause. It occurred to her there may be another way back into his heart. Or at least back into his bed. From there, she could make the rest work. All she needed was a path. A glimmer of light.

"I want you naked."

It was a mimicry of the words he had spoken to her not long ago. A daring move on her part, but this was her battle plan. She needed to be bold or risk losing everything that was important to her. Risk losing Leo.

And she would never lose him, she vowed.

They stared at each other. She did not flinch.

"Naked," she repeated in a voice that lashed through the room, echoing off the walls. "Now."

Molten-brown eyes seethed into hers. His entire bearing was rigid, from his broad shoulders to his tight, chiseled jaw. He could have been a statue. But she would not retreat. Would not back down. "Now, Duke."

A small flicker of movement caught her attention. His fingers, long and tapered and strong, fingers she loved on her skin, inside her, shifted. Found the knot on his dressing gown. Pulled. The knot came undone. The belt went slack, twin ends falling apart to dangle at his sides. His robe gaped.

One shrug of his shoulders, and it was on the floor.

He stood before her, magnificent. Nude. Oh, how she had missed the mouthwatering sight of that well-defined chest, the slabs of muscle on his abdomen, the quiet strength of his upper arms, those broad shoulders, capable of holding so much upon them. And then her gaze tracked downward, lingering on his lean waist, the grooves at his hipbones, his firm horseman's thighs, long legs, his cock, which was impossibly large, hard and thick. Yes, she had missed that too.

But most of all, she had simply missed *him*. Her beloved, enigmatic, harsh and dominating, yet tenderly soft Leo. Had missed being able to be near to him. Had missed his dark eyes, his full lips, his wit, his kindness, his embrace, his kiss. Every little part of him. She had missed it all.

Do not get maudlin now, Bridget, she admonished herself. *Stay the course.*

"Here I am," he said roughly. "Naked before you, madam."

How she loved him. Would always love him, even if he could not find forgiveness in his heart for her. But she had to believe he could. That he would.

"On the bed," she ordered.

Over the course of the time she had known him, she had learned him well. She knew his past helplessness with his mother had shaped him into the man he was. From governing the League, to the manner in which he ruled his life and everyone in it with ordered precision—even within the bedchamber—he craved control. He relinquished it for nothing and no one. And so, she understood she was taking a risk, not only in trespassing in his chamber, but in attempting to shake him in such a fundamental way.

He would either tell her to go to the devil, or it would work.

She held her breath and waited.

"Has no one ever taught you the virtue of good manners, wife?" he asked silkily. "If there is something you want, you must ask prettily. You must say please. Or get on your knees."

She recognized his attempt to regain control of the situation, but she was not going to allow it. They were doing this her way or no way. Ever since the rift between them had turned into a yawning chasm, she had been attempting to do things his way. To remain at Harlton Hall and do penance, to give him his space, his distance from her, time. Whatever he needed.

She had wronged him, and she knew it.

But she was growing impatient. She loved him, and she wanted a true marriage with him. Not only did she deserve it, but their babe did as well. She wanted all of him. His heart. His soul. His body. His absolution.

"On the bed," she prompted him again, maintaining her determination and her strength. She could do this. She *would* do this.

At long last, he moved, turning on his heel and stalking across the chamber to his bed. She watched the muscles in his bottom flex, admired his strong thighs and calves. His body was beautiful, and she was going to worship it. She was going to do penance her way.

In her own dressing gown, she had her stockings carefully tucked within a pocket. He watched her warily as she approached the bed, eyeing her as he might a wild animal.

She was not inclined to reassure him. "Give me your wrists, Duke."

"Do you mean to slit them, banshee?"

His expression was serious. So too his tone. She hated him for asking the question. And yet she understood it all too well. "I suppose you will have to trust me."

"The last time I trusted you, you nearly got us both killed." His observation was as unyielding as his tone.

Her heart ached. "I am sorry for that day, Leo. Sorrier than I can possibly convey. I know I should have come to you the moment I received his summons, but I was afraid. Time was running out for Cullen, and John was the only one who had given me hope of rescuing him. Had I any inkling of how mad he was, I would never have gone to him. And I would never willingly put you in danger. I love you far too much to lose you, *mo chroí*, though I fear I already have with my foolishness."

So much for her determination to be strong. She had already revealed her every vulnerability. He watched her now, eyes searching, seeking, and she could not help but to feel although he was the naked one, she had been stripped down far more intimately than he.

"You haven't lost me, Bridget. I am your husband." He held out his hand. "Come."

She hesitated, for this was not part of her plan. She was meant to be seducing him. Convincing him. "Let me finish, if you please. I have more to say."

His hand remained outstretched. "Say it while you're lying here with me. I've been missing you for all the days we have been apart, and I find I cannot bear another moment without you in my arms."

It was all she needed to hear. All the broken pieces inside her seemed to suddenly fuse together. He had come for her, had he not? And he had just admitted to missing her. He had seen her brother freed from prison. With trembling fingers, she untied the belt on her own dressing gown. A shrug of her shoulders, and it slipped to the floor, forgotten.

She placed her hand in his. His warmth reassured her, his gentle grip melting the icy fear around her heart. One tug, and she was on the bed, falling into his arms. He caught her to him, anchoring her there, Bridget atop his powerful body, looking down into his beloved face.

"I once thought my only allegiance was to my country, to the land where I was born," she told him. "And then I met you, Leo. You changed everything for me, like a storm that sweeps along a shore and changes the coast forever. I will never be the same. You made me whole, and I cannot be complete without you."

His hands were on her back, caressing, leaving a trail of fire in their wake. "I am furious with you for being stubborn and headstrong and not coming to me that day, but I understand how deep your love for your brother runs. I see now how torn you must have been. You broke your promise to me, and seeing you in danger, that bastard pointing his pistol at you…"

His body shuddered beneath hers.

"It is over now. He cannot hurt anyone ever again." She framed his face in her hands, the prickle of his whiskers against her flesh a welcome abrasion. How beloved he was to her. How necessary. "I will never break another promise to you so long as I live. You are all I want. All I need, *mo chroí*. If you cannot forgive me, I understand. I only ask that you let me love you."

Tears blurred her vision. She blinked them away, sending a droplet to splash on his lips. He drew her head down to his for a kiss that was slow and tender, and she tasted the salt of her sorrow on her tongue as it melded with his.

Gently, he rolled them as one until she was on her back and he was atop her, his body cradled between her thighs. He broke the kiss, staring down at her, his expression for once open and unguarded.

"You are already forgiven, my darling. But I must ask for your pardon as well. Can you forgive me for not heeding your concerns about your brother's innocence until it was almost too late? And for being such a stubborn, hardheaded fool that I stayed away from you for so long, when the only place I should have been is here by your side?"

"Yes." Happiness and relief and love, so fierce and strong

and consuming, burst within her. "Of course I forgive you, my darling man. I love you."

"I love you, Bridget Carlisle," he said tenderly, his hand coming between them to cup her belly. "And I love our babe as well. I stepped down from my position with the League before leaving London, and all I want to do is make a home and a family with you, to love you, to laugh with you, to journey through life with you. Forever."

He had given up his position? "Oh, Leo, they did not make you do it because of me, did they?"

"No. It was my choice. The time had come, and I am glad for it now that I know we will have a little banshee soon."

She smiled up at him, her heart full. "Or a stubborn little duke."

"Perhaps one of each." He grinned as his lips met hers once more.

And then, the time for talking was decidedly done.

Epilogue

*L*EO STARED DOWN in awe at the small pink face wrapped in blankets in his arms. Rose had Bridget's nose and ten tiny fingers and ten tiny toes, along with a shock of raven hair atop her head. She screwed open her small mouth and let loose a wail to rival any banshee.

"She has her mother's temperament," he announced, grinning as he tore his gaze from his daughter and settled it instead upon her mother.

Bridget was propped up in a sea of pillows in her chamber at Blayton House, another equally beloved bundle in her arms to match the one in his. She looked exhausted, but happy, her brilliant eyes glistening with her contentment. "The Duke of Carlisle and his clever sallies. You wished this upon us, you know."

Becoming a mother suited her. She was more beautiful now than ever. And so strong. So bloody strong it took his breath.

"I did nothing of the sort, darling."

"You most certainly did." There was no heat in her voice as she lovingly stroked their son's thatch of dark, silky hair. James resembled his sister in every way, save his nose, which was almost definitely Leo's. "One of each, you said, and look at us now."

Patting Rose's bottom and rocking her in his arms to

313

soothe her, he thought back on the day of their reconciliation at Harlton Hall. How fitting it was that the place where they had first met had also been the place where they rediscovered their love. He was so damned glad he had come to his senses. The last few months with Bridget had rushed by in a blur of blissful happiness. He loved her more with each day that passed.

Having twins had come as a shock. A pleasant shock, and indeed a terrifying one, but pleasant all the same. As Bridget's time had neared, her petite frame had scarcely been able to support her belly. It all made sense when the doctor had announced, immediately following the birth of Rose, that another Travers was about to make his way into the world.

And so, here they were one week later, the proud parents of two demanding, miniature people. His mother was overjoyed. Ara had given birth to a daughter not long before the arrival of the twins, which meant Lily now had four children to dote over.

"I have never been fond of doing anything in half-measures, you know." He rocked the hungry infant in his arms, cooing to her. "There now, my little love. Mama will be ready for you soon."

Bridget removed their sated, sleepy son from her breast and readjusted her gown before she held him to her shoulder, patting his back. "Do you ever miss it, Leo?"

He traced a finger down Rose's nose, marveling for at least the hundredth time at how small and perfect she was. "Hmm? Do I ever miss what, my love?"

"The League," Bridget prodded.

He went to her, gently laying Rose in her left arm and taking James from her right arm. "Not for a moment," he said truthfully. "Everything I want and need in this life is right here within these four walls. All I had to do was fall in love with the enemy."

Bridget situated Rose at her breast. She had insisted she would not use a wet nurse, despite having two babes to feed, and thus far, his fierce wife had been able to manage the incredible feat on her own.

She glanced up at him, flashing him that saucy, secret smile he loved best. "After you shot her, of course."

She would never let him forget the unconventional start to their love. He grinned right back at her. "It was the only way I could catch her."

"I am so very glad you caught her, my darling man," she said softly. "I love you."

"I love you too, banshee. Now and forever."

His son snuggled against his chest, slumbering the deep, innocent sleep of babes. Everything was right in Leo's world.

Dear Reader,

Thank you for reading *Heartless Duke*! I hope you enjoyed this second book in the League of Dukes series and that you fell in love with Leo and Bridget's story the same way I did when I wrote it. If you've read my books before, you already know I'm a fan of the antihero and I'm a sucker for bad boys gone good, and Leo is the embodiment of both. Bridget is my favorite kind of heroine to write—a badass with just a little hint of punk rock circa 1882. Bringing these two together for their happily ever after was great fun.

As always, please consider leaving an honest review of *Heartless Duke*. Reviews are greatly appreciated! If you'd like to keep up to date with my latest releases and series news, sign up for my newsletter here (scarlettscottauthor.com/contact) or follow me on Amazon or BookBub. Join my reader's group on Facebook for bonus content, early excerpts, giveaways, and more.

If you'd like a preview of my upcoming standalone *Dangerous Duke*, Book Three in the League of Dukes series featuring Griffin, Duke of Strathmore, do read on.

Until next time,

Scarlett

Dangerous Duke
League of Dukes Book Three

BY
SCARLETT SCOTT

He's lethal and ruthless.

Suspended from his work as an agent for the Crown, Griffin, Duke of Strathmore, exists under a dark cloud of suspicion for crimes he didn't commit. He's on a desperate race to clear his name by any means, until a grave error lands him under house arrest with the last sort of distraction he needs.

She's the sister of his nemesis.

Lady Violet West is about to be married to the most boring man in England. When the disgraced Duke of Strathmore lands in her lap—literally—she decides he is the answer to her longing for adventure. Though her brother is convinced of Strathmore's guilt, Violet isn't as certain.

Falling in love is out of the question.

Griffin doesn't want her interference. Violet won't take no for an answer. So begins a secret partnership between the fallen duke and the determined lady. Their quest to uncover the truth leads to danger and desire. But the most perilous risk of all is losing their hearts.

Chapter One

1882

*V*IOLET HAD NOT intended to trip the Duke of Strathmore.

Nor had she meant for him to land in her lap.

But as his large body pitched forward into her silken skirts, hands finding purchase on her bosom, she could not deny it was the most interesting thing to have happened to her since...*well,* ever.

Far more exciting than listening to Charles drone on about horticulture. Unless she could eat it, she had no desire to know the name of a plant. And even then, the name truly did not signify, unless she was required to ask her brother's chef to prepare it for dinner.

Yes indeed, Strathmore tumbling into her lap was infinitely better than spending the afternoon reading a book, while Great Aunt Hortense snored into her needlework. Or a bleary morning with only herself for company, because Lucien was far too busy with whatever nonsense recently interested him at the Home Office.

Bemused, she stared down at the giant she had inadvertently felled with her crocheting. His left hand had landed upon her right breast, and his right was buried in her skirts.

Was it her imagination, or did his fingers deliberately tighten upon her, as if he were testing the size and weight of the bosom he had unintentionally discovered?

She ought to be horrified. Shocked.

His shoulders were shaking, she realized, vibrating beneath his coat.

Oh dear.

Was he injured? Weeping?

Violet laid a hand gingerly upon his biceps, startled to feel its flexed strength beneath her touch. "Duke? Are you hurt?"

His head raised.

Her heart did something odd. It stumbled, then galloped. Her breath caught. Here was her first sighting of their infamous house guest, in proximity. His dark hair was too long, his eyes astoundingly blue, his lips far too full for a man's mouth, his jaw covered in a neatly trimmed beard.

When he had first entered the salon, she had been struck by how handsome he was. But he was not just handsome. He was striking. His face had character. It was intriguing, from the bump in the bridge of his nose, to the lines bracketing his vivid eyes. The air of tarnished elegance he exuded somehow magnified his masculine beauty. She had never seen a duke— or any gentleman for that matter—like him.

"I am relatively unscathed," he said at last, removing his hand from her breast.

That was when she realized belatedly he had not been weeping or in pain at all. Rather, he had been laughing.

And a smile on that mouth was something to behold.

She blinked. Tried to summon up thoughts of Charles. Her betrothed too was undeniably handsome. Well-titled. The Earl of Almsley, Viscount Nattingworth, Baron Erstwhile.

Or was it Viscount Nattingwhile and Baron Erstworth?

She could not seem to recall. Mayhap it was the overly large duke who was still all but in her lap addling her wits.

Perchance it was the unseasonably warm weather. Late spring, and hotter than July. Where was a fan when she needed it? Why would the duke not stop trapping her in that brilliant gaze? What would the bristle of his whiskers feel like beneath her fingertips?

No.

That is wicked, Violet. You must not think such thoughts.

What would those lips feel like pressed to hers?

She was willing to wager they would not be arid and cool like Charles's. Instead, they would be warm and supple, coaxing and perhaps even demanding...

Drat it, Violet. Cease this at once.

"I am sorry about the crocheting," she said, needing to say something so her whirling thoughts would quiet. "I did not mean to catch you with it."

She did not even like crocheting but Aunt Hortense deemed it a suitable activity for a lady because the queen herself enjoyed the practice. Admittedly, Violet's appreciation for the skill was hindered by being dreadful at it.

"I should have watched where I was walking." A rueful grin flirted at the corners of his lips now. "I did not expect anyone to be within, and I am afraid I was rather preoccupied with my own thoughts. I did not notice your string until it had felled me."

His hand was still in her skirts, and he remained on his knees before her. She resisted the urge to reach for his left hand and place it back upon her breast. Why had the weight of him, that forbidden touch, felt so irresistible?

She wetted her suddenly dry lips. "It is a bad habit, leaving the ball of wool halfway across the chamber, in the midst of the floor. If I had not pulled it toward me with the intention of sparing you from falling over it, you likely would not have tripped in the first place. The fault is all mine."

"Nonsense, Lady Violet." He rose at last, towering over her with his broad, strong frame. "I am the interloper here."

"Yes," she agreed, before thinking better of it. Her cheeks went hot. "That is to say, you are a guest, Your Grace."

Should she stand?

Craning her neck at him was dratted uncomfortable, but he remained near enough to her that if she stood, she would brush against him. And if she touched this man, she felt certain she may swoon.

Where was a fan when she needed one?

His smile faded, his jaw going rigid, expression hardening. "A forced guest is hardly a guest, Lady Violet. It would be more apt, perhaps, to say I am a prisoner."

"But Lark House is not a jail," she felt compelled to protest. In truth, it had been hers for four-and-twenty years, and it would remain so until she left it for the next one. The thought of having to share a home with Charles's mother was enough to make her eyes twitch.

"We shall agree to disagree, my lady." His gaze traveled down to her lap, leaving a path of fire in its wake. "What are you making?"

Her flush increased, and she swore she felt it to the roots of her hair. "It is meant to be a seed pouch for my fiancé. He is a horticulturist."

Strathmore frowned. "That sounds deadly dull."

Her sentiments exactly, but that didn't mean his dismissive tone did not nettle her, for it did. "On the contrary, sir. It is horribly interesting."

His lips quirked. "You have the 'horrible' of it right, I would reckon."

"To think I was feeling guilty for tripping you," she snapped. Charles was as interesting as a pile of sawdust, but having this breathtakingly handsome, arrogant duke point out the shortcomings which already grieved her was irksome indeed. "There is no need to be cruel."

"Honesty and cruelty are two distinct beasts." His stare worked its leisurely way back to hers, so intense, a shock of giddiness rippled straight through her.

Ruthlessly, she banished it and stood, tired of him looming over her, the judgmental beast. But she miscalculated her haste, and his nearness, which meant that once she rose, she had nowhere to go but into his chest.

So she did.

Her palms flattened over the muscled heat of him. Even through the layers of civility, he was hot. Smoldering like a flame. And she was drawn to him.

Why could she not stop staring at his lips? Why did she insist upon wondering what they would feel like upon hers?

"Lady Violet?" His tone was darkly amused.

Blinking, she raised her gaze back to his. "Yes?"

"I would like to beg your fiancé's pardon," he surprised her by saying.

There.

That was better, was it not?

The man had simply needed a reminder of how to conduct himself in a gentlemanly fashion. Suspected of treason though he may be, he was still a peer of the realm. A duke.

"For insulting his love of horticulture?" she asked, telling herself she ought to remove her hands from Strathmore's person. It was unseemly, the way she was touching him.

"No." He traced her jaw with a lone, long finger, stopping at her chin, tipping it gently up. "For kissing his fiancée."

Before she could say a word of protest, that sinful mouth was upon hers.

Want more? Get *Dangerous Duke*!

Don't miss Scarlett's other romances!

(Listed by Series)

Complete Book List
scarlettscottauthor.com/books

HISTORICAL ROMANCE

Heart's Temptation
A Mad Passion (Book One)
Rebel Love (Book Two)
Reckless Need (Book Three)
Sweet Scandal (Book Four)
Restless Rake (Book Five)
Darling Duke (Book Six)
The Night Before Scandal (Book Seven)

Wicked Husbands
Her Errant Earl (Book One)
Her Lovestruck Lord (Book Two)
Her Reformed Rake (Book Three)
Her Deceptive Duke (Book Four)

League of Dukes
Nobody's Duke (Book One)
Heartless Duke (Book Two)
Dangerous Duke (Book Three)

Sins and Scoundrels
Duke of Depravity (Book One)
Prince of Persuasion (Book Two)

Stand-alone Novella
Lord of Pirates

CONTEMPORARY ROMANCE

Love's Second Chance
Reprieve (Book One)
Perfect Persuasion (Book Two)
Win My Love (Book Three)

Coastal Heat
Loved Up (Book One)

About the Author

Amazon bestselling author Scarlett Scott writes steamy Victorian and Regency romance with strong, intelligent heroines and sexy alpha heroes. She lives in Pennsylvania with her Canadian husband, adorable identical twins, and one TV-loving dog.

A self-professed literary junkie and nerd, she loves reading anything, but especially romance novels, poetry, and Middle English verse. Catch up with her on her website www.scarlettscottauthor.com. Hearing from readers never fails to make her day.

Scarlett's complete book list and information about upcoming releases can be found at www.scarlettscottauthor.com.

Connect with Scarlett! You can find her here:
Join Scarlett Scott's reader's group on Facebook for early excerpts, giveaways, and a whole lot of fun!
Sign up for her newsletter here.
scarlettscottauthor.com/contact
Follow Scarlett on Amazon
Follow Scarlett on BookBub
www.instagram.com/scarlettscottauthor
www.twitter.com/scarscoromance
www.pinterest.com/scarlettscott
www.facebook.com/AuthorScarlettScott
Join the Historical Harlots on Facebook

Made in the USA
Columbia, SC
29 November 2019

84049190R00200